PRAISE FOR
I READ WHAT YOU WROTE

"*I Read What You Wrote* is a beautifully written and powerful story about family and friendship, how random lives can become intertwined, and how love can cause both incredible joy and unbearable pain. Based on her mom's own memoirs, author Jill Hales reminds us that life is complicated and sometimes cruel. Systems meant to help us may fail and allow loved ones to suffer. Yet, unexpected bonds that develop in our lives can provide respect, support, and ultimately peace."

- Jami Smith, MSN, RN-BC, ONC
Owner, JLS Clinical Writing & Consulting, LLC

"Jill Hales has crafted a poignant and inspirational fictionalized memoir of her family's gut-wrenching experience of being unable to help a loved one as they experienced neglectful abuse at the end of their life. Through this journey, Hales gives us a way to make sense of the unthinkable while restoring our faith in others whose methods may be unconventional but full of love."

- Shirley Amitrano
Author, Screenwriter

I Read What You Wrote

Copyright @2024 by Jill Hales

Available online at:

www.jillhales.com

Library of Congress Cataloging Data

I Read What You Wrote / Jill Hales

ISBN: 978-0-464-36425-2

All rights reserved. This book or parts thereof may not be reproduced in any form, stored in any retrieval system, or transmitted in any form by any means—electronic, mechanical, photocopy, recording, or otherwise—without prior written permission of the publisher, except as provided by United States of America copyright law. For permission requests, write to the publisher, at at the address below.

Forest City Publications
PO Box 9220
Tucson, AZ 85738
www.forestcitypublications.com

This is a work of fiction. Names, characters, businesses, places, events, locales, and incidents are either the products of the author's imagination or used in a fictitious manner. Any resemblance to actual persons, living or dead, or actual events is purely coincidental.

For my mother

I READ WHAT YOU WROTE

JILL HALES

CONTENTS

Acknowledgements	i
Chapter 1	12
Chapter 2	14
Chapter 3	17
Chapter 4	19
Chapter 5	22
Chapter 6	27
Chapter 7	31
Chapter 8	33
Chapter 9	38
Chapter 10	42
Chapter 11	52
Chapter 12	55
Chapter 13	59
Chapter 14	65
Chapter 15	69
Chapter 16	76

Chapter 17	79
Chapter 18	83
Chapter 19	85
Chapter 20	90
Chapter 21	94
Chapter 22	98
Chapter 23	102
Chapter 24	105
Chapter 25	110
Chapter 26	118
Chapter 27	121
Chapter 28	125
Chapter 29	129
Chapter 30	136
Chapter 31	138
Chapter 32	140
Chapter 33	145
Chapter 34	159
Chapter 35	163
Afterward	167
About the Author	177

ACKNOWLEDGEMENTS

This has been an incredibly long journey. I never thought I would get to this point with a book. I am so excited. I am truly grateful to many people who were instrumental in me completing this adventure. I wouldn't have even begun if it wasn't for my wonderful husband, John, who gave me the idea in the beginning. He has given me the encouragement and time to complete this book, and I will be forever grateful.

I need to thank my children, Emily, Elizabeth, and Jack for their support as they rallied around me during this whole process. Emily and Elizabeth for lending me your ears countless times and helping me with your recommendations.

I am so incredibly grateful for my siblings (thank you Mom and Dad for giving us each other and the knowledge of the importance of family); God has blessed me with the love and support from them my whole life. I'd like to especially mention Kelly for allowing me to come to your beautiful home and work through the direction of the book, multiple times and Kay for your incredible knowledge, support, and numerous phone calls. Thank you both for the countless 'backlash' gatherings and too many bottles of wine to count. Tim, Jeff, and Greg, thank you so much for being the rocks of our family.

Dad would be so proud.

To my Aunt Jan, thank you for always being there for me and my siblings (your other children), we couldn't have made it through everything without you. And needless to say, thank you mother for sharing your memoirs; because of your hard work and dedication we have a special piece of you, you have left a legacy.

My editor, Lara Helmling, you have helped me bring this story to life. I have learned so much from you and appreciate the countless hours helping me become a better writer. To my friend, Jami, my soul-sister in loving books, thank you for previewing my book, giving me advice and always being there for me. Shirley, what can I say, your input was pivotal, and I am humbled by the time and support you have given. To Olivia Nugent, you managed to capture exactly what I had envisioned for my book cover, you are truly an artist.

And finally, thank you to all the healthcare professionals, including all of the dedicated hospice workers that help families day in and day out. Though you may not realize it, your efforts make a world of difference to us.

CHAPTER 1

CAROL 1941

My school day nemesis was the street I had to cross in front of Fire Station Number 4. It could be dangerous for there were no such persons as "crossing guards" when I was a young student. But with practice and a good deal more experience, the challenge became easier. These continual crossings gave me at least some confidence in my ability to judge speed and distance.

Standing on the corner one day, I looked both ways, then back again, as I had been taught. I quickly calculated the speed of an oncoming pickup truck against the speed of my short chubby legs (just like my mother's I once proudly announced to my kindergarten teacher). But I had miscalculated. By the time I neared the other side of the street, the truck hit me. Its right front bumper knocked me to the curb, and I lost consciousness for a few seconds. As I began regaining some of my senses, I heard people running toward me.

The truck driver and a few firemen came closer, but I kept my eyes closed. Both curious and scared about what might happen, I was afraid to let them know I was awake. My rescuers carried me into the heretofore forbidden sanctuary of Fire Station Number 4. Ever so gently I was laid on a cot, then cool compresses were placed on my forehead where a sizable lump had formed.

JILL HALES

The accident plus my enchantment at being the center of attention inside these normally tabooed walls made me feel a bit heady. With eyes still closed, I savored the attentiveness of the rescuers who anxiously surrounded me, asking questions. "Can you hear me, little girl?" someone asked. "Are you all right?" asked another. And still another asked, "What's your name?" I had my own set of questions going like, 'what will Mother say when she finds out? And Marilyn?' Another question was, 'Will Daddy give me a spanking?' My anxious reverie was interrupted when I heard the word "hospital." Instantly, I decided to wake up. "Where...am...I?" I drawled in a slow measured tone, like some fainting romantic heroine I'd seen in a movie. I saw the truck driver's face change immediately from white to pink as he smiled with relief.

My feelings in that moment were pure jubilation. Escorted home by these Galahads in navy blue uniforms, I experienced the same exuberance as the pan-pounding people who filled the streets after the papers announced the end of World War II. But my triumphant mood was short-lived. Mother and Dad seemed a bit blasé about the whole thing and cautioned me to be more careful in the future. 'Oh well,' I thought, 'I have new friends at the fire station.'

From that day on, they never failed to say "hello" every time I passed by.

CHAPTER 2

AMELIA 2017

The smell of antibacterial cleanser was not helping my queasy stomach one bit. I moved through the maze of cubicles to my spot.

I thought about my nursing friends who had warned me against taking a hospice nursing position. They told me flat-out I was crazy. "It's too difficult, Amelia," they'd said. They had regaled me with all the reasons I shouldn't do it. Somehow, I knew this was the right thing for me. I knew I could help my patients and their families.

Now I had to prove that I was right.

The first thing I did was organize my desk. I was hoping I had everything I needed. I had my training manual, my medical instruments, and the files on each of the patients that I had been assigned. Around my neck was the stethoscope, given to me by my dad for graduation, and by my right hand was a big cup of coffee. Looking around the small space, my gaze fell on the picture on my desk of my sweet JJ and Olivia and my husband Jake. Beside it, my nameplate: Amelia Bowden. I wanted my kids and Jake to be proud of me, but even more importantly, I was proud of myself for finally getting here. After weeks of initial training then several more weeks shadowing Karen, I was ready.

At least, I hoped I was ready.

I had done everything I could do to prepare. I had watched how Karen managed patients and their families. I had taken notes on how she organized her day and completed her daily notes and reports.

I felt as prepared as possible for my first day on my own, but still my heart beat a little faster than usual and my breath was a bit more shallow.

"Hi, Amelia. Are you excited for your first day on your own?"

I looked up to see my boss leaning on the upper edge of the cubicle. "Hi, Diane. Yes, but I am nervous too. I hope that nothing comes up that I don't know how to handle."

"You'll do great!"

My stomach lurched again. Somehow, Diane's unrelenting positivity was no help today. "Thanks, I sure hope so. At least I know all my patients already."

"Not quite all of them."

My eyes widened.

"I need you to take on a new patient. I wanted to go over the details with you before you see her this afternoon. Here's the file." She handed me a brown folder.

A new patient. My mind raced with all the things I would need to do. Dutifully, I took it from her and opened it.

"You can read it later. I'll give you a brief on the situation, and then I have to go. I've got a team meeting in ten minutes."

I closed the file. "Okay."

"Her name is Carol Schultz. Dr. Houser saw her yesterday

and approved her for hospice. You'll see as you read through her file that she has multiple diagnoses, including congestive heart failure, dementia, and metastasized cancer stemming from a small tumor on the duct of her pancreas. She requires daily pain medication and one of our most important tasks is to make sure her pain is managed and that her medication is going where it should go."

"Going where it should go? What does that mean?"

"Apparently, she would run out of her prescription a few days prior to her refill date. From what Dr. Houser gathered, this happened practically every month. The distribution of narcotics is highly regulated, as you know. The pain doctor was concerned about how the medication was being administered so he stopped writing her prescriptions."

Trying to understand, I asked, "Do you think she was overmedicating herself?"

"We don't know," Diane explained. "Her husband said that he would give it to her correctly, but we honestly don't know. It will be imperative that you educate him on recording the amount and time of every dosage. I would like you to provide him with an easy form for him to use to record the drug administration. We can review this form weekly."

"I will make sure to do that. I will also make sure I get a handle on her pain level between doses."

Diane shrugged.

She seemed doubtful. My heart raced a bit more. "Maybe that's why she was taking too much. Maybe the effects of the medication were wearing off too soon." I tried to sound confident.

"Great idea. See, I know you can handle this. But I do want

to caution you about one other thing. Apparently it was her children that pushed for us to be taking care of her. Earl, her husband, is not too happy about us being there so you will have to get him to trust us."

I gulped. That little piece of information scared me even more. I could set him off without even knowing why or how, and then, worse, I would disappoint Diane or Karen who had spent the last month training me. I began to sweat. With as much confidence as possible, I said, "I will do my best."

"I know you will. Have a great first day."

With that she walked away from my cubicle, and I was alone with my thoughts. I stared blankly at the name on the folder she'd just handed me: Carol Schultz. I sighed. "There's no turning back now, Amelia," I told myself aloud. My voice had that tremor in it that it always got when I was in over my head. Except I wasn't this time, I told myself. I wasn't in over my head. I could handle this.

I stood up. The best thing I could do was get started.

I visited my first two patients with good results. They had both been in hospice care for about 6 months. They were rapidly declining. It tore my heart in two to see them at the end of life, but I had to focus on helping them be comfortable and guiding their families to make good decisions.

With a successful morning under my belt, I decided to treat myself to my favorite fast food. I hummed to myself happily in the drive-thru lane. Even grumpy George hadn't been as difficult as I had feared. Maybe it was because I was by myself for the first time and he decided to go easy on me. Maybe it was the larger dose of morphine the doctor had prescribed. Whatever the case, it had been a good visit.

I pulled into a parking spot for a few quiet minutes. I could have gone into the restaurant, but I wanted some time to myself, and the car seemed to be the best place. I bit into my burger, complete with all my favorite toppings, and sipped the sweet taste of carbonation to wash it down. The perfect combination. I dug in with a second bite.

My mind wandered to what I would do this afternoon.

Carol Schultz: 9314 Chestnut Lane.

I stopped chewing for a second. The taste in my mouth turned rancid. I hurried up and swallowed, pushing away the unbidden worries. There would be time enough for them after lunch.

CHAPTER 3

AMELIA

I pulled into the driveway of 9314 Chestnut Lane. It was a pale yellow house with faded white trim. The short path beside the two-car garage led to a small porch. It looked similar to the others in the retirement community. All of the homes were the same pale yellow or white and each had one palm tree in the middle of the front yard. The white rocker and tall wooden welcome sign made it at least a bit unique. I rang the bell at Carol's house and waited, my heart pounding in my chest once again. I checked my phone for the time, making sure I gave them an opportunity to get to the door. Elderly people walked slowly, and it was important to take that into account. After two full minutes, no one had answered. I rang it again, leaning in to see if I could hear the doorbell ring. I heard the chime.

I wondered what to do. They should be here. I had called to confirm an hour ago. Earl had answered and said they would be home. I could hear the reluctance in his voice, and there was something else. It sounded like animosity.

The waiting was not helping my state of mind. It was nerve-wracking enough to enter a perfect stranger's private home, much less when I wasn't welcome.

Everyone had secrets. I knew that well from Jake's work stories as a firefighter. When people acted like Earl did, it usually meant that their secrets were dark and closer to the surface. I thought of how often Jake had to enter situations like this, going into someone's home. The difference was he was never alone.

I waited another minute. I raised my arm to knock on the door instead, but just as I did, an elderly woman with a cute blond bob opened the door. She was dressed smartly in a pair of khaki slacks and a shirt printed with a bouquet of flowers. She was thin, frail, and yet she smiled at me. Our eyes met. I saw something there. A connection. I smiled at her, realizing in that moment it was the first time I had smiled all day. "Hi, I'm Amelia, I'm from hospice. I'm here to see Carol. Are you Carol?" I enquired.

"Yes, please come in."

Her voice was sweet and gentle. I began to think it would work out fine to have her as a patient. Still, I dreaded meeting Earl.

I stepped into the house, following Carol as she shuffled through the entryway. Immediately, a pungent smell assailed my senses. I breathed through my mouth to reduce its impact. The foyer was small and dark. I swung the front door closed behind me. A framed collage of old photos hung on the wall. They were all smiling, as in most people's family photos. I knew from experience there was always a darker truth lurking behind those smiles.

Turning to catch up with Carol, I bumped a little green side table. "Whoops," I said. I struggled to steady the three objects on the table: two small framed photos and a brushed gold statue of a pine cone. I glanced up. Carol hadn't noticed. My gaze fell on the two open doors flanking the table I had just plowed into. I peeked around the corner of the first door. It contained a bed, but that's where its similarity to most bedrooms ended. Piles of unfolded clothes covered the bed and the floor was littered with stacks of books. It looked more like a storage room than a bedroom.

My encounter with the table had also put me in view of a faux ficus tree. I noted with a chuckle that someone had accidentally watered it at some point. The dried puddle of water left crusty white edges on the pale pink tiled floor.

I felt a twinge of guilt rise in me. My mother's voice, "Don't be nosey," echoed in my mind. I reminded myself that it was my job to make sure Carol was living in a safe environment. The condition of the home was part of my purpose. I moved my attention to the second door which revealed a full bathroom decorated with typical Florida colors of pinks and greens.

Continuing along Carol's path into the living room, I did a quick scan. It was a decent-sized room. The first thing that caught my attention was a huge TV on top of a cabinet of cluttered shelves. The blaring voices of news pundits filled the room, their images solemn and fixed on the screen. There was also the couch, which was facing the entrance to the room, a coffee table and two chairs. The chairs had their backs to the door.

A man was in one of the chairs. I presumed it was Earl. I gulped down a surge of anxiety. Most people would greet a guest who had just entered their home. This was not a stellar beginning, but then I had not expected one.

I READ WHAT YOU WROTE

I took a step further into the room, feeling something under my foot. Looking down, it was a fast food wrapper. I shook it off. I thought I should probably pick it up, but I wasn't going to do that. Jake had told me too many stories of diseases, bacteria, and even needles lurking under seemingly harmless objects. The condition of the beige carpet supported my decision. It was worn from what I assumed was a lot of foot traffic and there were brown stains along the edges of every piece of furniture.

I moved around the chairs to face the occupant.

Carol waved one hand in Earl's direction and said, "Emily, this is my husband Earl."

"It's Amelia," Earl said.

"Oh, I am sorry," Carol's hands rose up to cover her mouth.

"No problem, Carol, people make that mistake all the time." Turning to Earl, I stuck out my hand. "Hi, Earl. It's nice to meet you."

He remained seated and shook my hand. "Hello," he said.

My immediate thought was that Earl looked worse than my patient Carol. He weighed at least 300 pounds. His round face was framed by two day stubble and a few wispy strands of hair on the top of his head. I could see his swollen ankles extending from his worn sweatpants. They were discolored, most likely from cellulitis. Both his pants and shirt had stains on them. If someone had asked me who the patient was by appearances alone, I would have guessed Earl not Carol.

"I am here to help Carol and see if there's anything you need. I will be her hospice nurse." I continued, "My job is to make sure Carol is as comfortable as possible, and I am excited to be here to help."

Earl grunted and returned his attention to the television.

I wondered if I sounded too over the top.

"I am so grateful you are here." Carol smiled.

I returned her smile. "Oh good," I said. "I am happy to be here, too. Here, go ahead and have a seat. I have some things I'd like to discuss with you."

Carol sat on the couch, waiting.

I wondered where I would set my notebook. Besides the stacks of books and papers on the floor and the empty fast-food bags around Earl's chair, there were also at least a half dozen diet coke cans on the coffee table. I gingerly moved some of the cans out of the way. The surface was sticky but I set the notebook down anyway, making a mental note to dig the antibacterial wipes out of the trunk before I went back to the office.

I sat next to Carol on the couch, my thoughts whirling over the protocols I had been taught for new patients. I wanted to start with an ice breaker. "How long have you lived in Florida?"

"Oh, I've lived here–" Carol said.

"I think it's best to stick to business," Earl said.

My eyebrows rose. "Okay." I had no idea what else to say. I would leave it at that, awkward as it was.

"Oh don't mind my Earl," Carol said, fidgeting with her hands. "He sounds gruff, but once he gets to know you, he's a sweetheart."

I smiled. "Let's talk about some of your medical history then. How does that sound?"

"Good," Carol said.

We talked for almost thirty minutes about her history. Between Carol's lapses in memory and some storytelling, it took much longer than normal. Most of the information had already been documented by Diane, but when Carol asked Earl to fill in the gaps his version differed from the official one in the file. I had a feeling he was hiding something, adding to my anxiety about how well I would be able to help Carol. Her memory also concerned me. Early dementia was written down as one of Carol's ailments. I wondered if it had progressed. Her other diagnoses–cancer and congestive heart failure–could exacerbate her dementia. I would have to keep an eye on that.

When I got back to the office, I sat at my cubicle and finished writing my notes from my first solo day.

A noise caught my attention. I looked up to see that Diane had appeared at the top of my cubicle, leaning on it the same way she had that morning. "So, you made it through your first day. How did it go?"

"It went well, everyone was so nice. Luckily, nothing came up that I didn't know how to handle. I am just completing my notes now."

"How was your new patient, Carol?"

"She is very sweet. She seemed pretty good to me. We went through her pain medicine schedule and she appeared to be genuinely glad I was there. Her husband was another story. He looked in worse shape to me than she did."

"Yes, Dr. Houser said the same thing. How was he? Was he considerate to you?" Diane asked.

"Well, he didn't say much. He mostly sat in his chair while I examined Carol. When we went over her medication, I showed him the chart I had prepared for him so he could write down when he gave her medication and he seemed to be okay with it. I am concerned about her memory, though. She couldn't answer some of my questions about her health. He answered for her much of the time. The biggest thing right now is that their house is dirty and smelly. It's ripe for infections and disease if you ask me. I'd like to see them get a housekeeper and a CNA to help Carol with her daily activities."

Diane nodded. "Sounds good. We can recommend that. Just keep me up to date with your visits with her. I want to make sure we are keeping close tabs on her medication. We need to make sure it is being administered correctly. And congratulations on getting through your first day. You are going to be great at this, Amelia, I just know it."

"Thank you so much, Diane. That means a lot to me."

CHAPTER 4

AMELIA

The next week, I arrived at Carol's home with a mental list of things I wanted to talk to them about, the first being a housekeeper. As I reached the door only to see it swing open.

A tall middle-aged woman stepped out and smiled. "Hi, I am Mary. Are you the hospice nurse? I heard you were coming."

Her words tumbled out in that way people have when they're hiding something. I pushed the thought aside, chastising myself for being judgmental. "Yes, I'm Amelia."

"Oh, it's good to meet you. Carol told me you were coming. I think you'll be a big help. They need it. I help out Carol and Earl, too, but it's too much for me by myself." Mary's right hand fluttered to her throat. "I do housekeeping and run errands for them."

"Oh, that is wonderful. Nice to meet you."

A sense of relief washed over me, but it was short-lived. I noticed Mary didn't have any cleaning products with her and wasn't actually dressed appropriately for cleaning. She had on a white blouse, a pair of khaki shorts, flip flops and her hair was loose around her shoulders. She sure didn't look like she had just been cleaning a house. "Is this your first day? There's quite a bit to do to get things organized and sanitary."

"Oh no, I've been working for them for a year now. I do the best I can. You should have seen it before."

My relief turned to dismay. "Oh. I see."

With a tight smile, Mary left without another word.

I was certain I had offended her, but given the state of the house and her claim to be a housekeeper, I didn't care if she had her feelings hurt. I wondered how much Mary was charging them for her so-called housekeeping. With a rising sense of indignation, I knocked on the door.

"Come in," Carol called from inside.

I opened the door, peeking inside. "Hello, it is me, Amelia." They were sitting in their respective chairs. As I walked into their living room, I was hit with the strong scent of urine. I blinked as my eyes stung from the acidic odor. A quick look around revealed that nothing had been picked up from the last time I was there. The same fast food wrapper that had been stuck to my foot languished behind Earl's chair. If anything, it was worse. Earl's food wrappers were piled higher on the tv tray next to him. The growing number of diet coke cans on the coffee table had been joined by a few empty bowls with orange-colored residue.

"I just met Mary out in front," I said.

Carol beamed. "Isn't she wonderful? She is so nice. She helps us so much."

I could barely contain myself from saying, 'really, with what??' Instead, I said, "Oh good. What does she do for you in particular?"

Earl cast a sour look my way. "She's helpful. That's all you need to know."

I READ WHAT YOU WROTE

"Oh Earl," Carol protested, "don't be testy." She turned to me. "She is very helpful to Earl. She runs his bath, does the laundry, and tidies up the bathroom. She sometimes does the dishes."

I glanced toward the kitchen, noting the filth on the stove and the pile of dirty dishes in the sink.

Carol followed my gaze. "Of course, today she was much too busy to clean the kitchen."

I nodded and smiled. I decided to let it go. I would note the condition of the home and the work of the so-called housekeeper in my report and talk to Diane. I sat on the couch, turning toward Carol. I was happy to see that Carol looked clean and well-groomed. Her hair was in a cute little blond bob with a little gray coming in at the roots. Her nails were polished in a pretty pink color and her robe looked freshly clean. "How are you feeling today, Carol?"

"I am pretty good today."

"You seem like you are. I am so glad to hear that."

Earl moved forward in his chair, grunting, his arms shaking as he strained to lift his heavy frame. "Since you're here, I think I will go down and check the mail."

"Alright. Is there anything you need to share with me before you go?"

"No. She is the same. Goodbye, sweetheart," he said to Carol. He lumbered to the door. It looked as though each step took all the strength he had.

The door clicked shut. I was glad he was gone. I wanted to speak with Carol in a more relaxed environment. As I readied my materials to check Carol's vitals, I asked, "How is Earl doing?

17

He seems like he is struggling to walk."

She responded, "Oh, not good. I'm so worried about him. He has prostate cancer and diabetes and he has trouble with his legs. I worry about him."

"Prostate cancer?"

Carol nodded. "Yes, that's right."

I wrote Carol's vitals in my notebook. Everything looked about the same. "Do you think it might be a good idea to get some additional help here for you both? He doesn't look like he can get around let alone cook your meals or pick up the house."

"Oh, he does a good job. I warm up his food for him when I can so he doesn't have to walk around too much."

"Carol, you need to be careful walking around. There are many things that you could trip on in here," I said. I watched her face to gauge her response. I was concerned about being pushy, but I couldn't let this go.

"We have Mary for that. She is so sweet."

I had to bite my tongue. Clearly, Mary did not do a good job. Carol's situation was much worse than my other patients, and I wasn't sure how to proceed. I switched gears. "So how is your appetite?"

"I really don't get hungry anymore like I used to, but I eat," she responded.

"Can you give me an example of what you would typically eat, say for breakfast? What did you have today?"

"I had some orange sherbet."

Ah, the orange-colored residue in the bowls on the coffee table.

"That is a yummy dessert, but did you have anything

nutritious?"

"I really wasn't hungry, but sometimes I just eat what sounds good to me, and today it was orange sherbet."

"I understand, sometimes we need some comfort food. I would suggest trying to make sure you are eating something more substantial, not only to keep your energy up, but also to help the medications do their job."

"Okay, I'll try."

I smiled. "Do you feel tired during the day or do you feel like you have plenty of energy?"

Carol waved her hands in an 'I don't know' gesture. "I think I'm doing fine."

I nodded. I wondered how much of her cheery 'fineness' was that she didn't remember whether she was tired or not. Chances were slim she would remember the things I'd said to her, but we would see how it went. "Well, that's all for today, Carol, unless there's something else you can think of."

"Oh okay." She seemed disappointed.

"Are you sure you don't need anything else?"

Carol shook her head.

I stood to go. Carol stood, too, and tottered over to me.

Out of nowhere, she gave me a big hug. "Thank you so much for coming, dear."

I had received hugs from my other patients and their families, but this hug was different. It was so warm and tender. A lump formed in my throat. "Of course," I managed.

CHAPTER 5

MARIE

I was finishing up braiding Emily's hair when Elizabeth ran into the bathroom.

"I can't find my shoe!!"

"Both your shoes are by the front door."

"Noooo! Not those shoes! My Dorothy shoes!"

I caught Emily's eye in the mirror. Emily rolled her eyes. I held back a smirk. Glancing back at Elizabeth, I saw my 6-going-on-30-year-old standing with one hand on her hip, waiting for my response.

"I don't know, Elizabeth. We do this every day. I can't imagine what happened to your shoe." I had no more than finished saying this when I caught a mischievous expression on Emily's face. "Or maybe I do know. Emily, care to assist your sister?"

"Sure, I can help." Emily hopped down from the chair and both girls went to look for the shoe.

Elizabeth loved *The Wizard of Oz*, and we had bought her red sparkle shoes to go with her Dorothy costume for Halloween. She put away her costume, but she wouldn't go anywhere without the shoes.

It seemed that big sister Emily was getting a kick out of tormenting her…just a bit. I smiled. I could remember plenty of times my five siblings and I had done the same to each other. In fact, if things were too peaceful for more than an hour, one of us would poke or prod another just to spice things up.

Sure enough, just a couple minutes later Emily emerged from their bedroom, shoe in hand. "I found it, Mom!" Emily smiled as the triumphant heroine.

"Yay! My shoe, my shoe, my shoe!" Elizabeth chanted.

"It's a miracle." The look I gave Emily was intended to say, 'I know what really happened.'

Emily's triumphant smile faded at the corners.

"Okay," I said, "go get your coats and meet me at the door. It's time to go!"

I headed to the kitchen to put their lunches in their backpacks. Within a few minutes, we were at the door to walk to the bus. The girls skipped along the sidewalk giggling while I was pushing little Jack in the stroller. This was one of my favorite times of the day. I loved my little girls and their zest for life.

On my walk home I started to think about my day ahead. I needed to get Jack ready for daycare and then I was going to see mom. I loved spending time with her, but it had been a whole challenge since her dementia had worsened and Earl had weaseled his way into her life. I decided to give her a quick call to see what I might be up against today.

"Hello?"

My stomach lurched at the sound of Mom's voice. It was so much older, more fragile, than it had ever been. She had always been the strong one in our lives. She was our rock. But now... things were different. I wondered if I would ever get used to it.

I tried to sound cheery. "Hi, Mom. How are you today?"

"Marie! Hi, sweetheart! I am feeling pretty good."

"That's wonderful! Are you up for a visit today?"

"Of course! I love to see you anytime. You know that."

The relief that flowed through me was unexpectedly intense. "Great! I am almost ready to walk out the door. The kids are in school and John can pick them up after so I have the whole day free."

"Oh, that's wonderful!"

"Yes! In fact, Ann wants to come, too. She's taking a half day so she will head up about noon. I'll even pick up your favorite chicken and biscuits on my way. I can't wait to see you."

"Yum, that sounds good. I can't wait either. And make sure to get honey for the biscuits."

"Will do, Mom. See you soon!"

I hung up the phone and grabbed my purse off of the kitchen counter. It was still messy from breakfast and my floors could use a good sweeping, but I knew if I started to pick up, I would be there all day.

Kissing John goodbye, I went into the garage to leave.

Trying to get through the morning traffic was always tricky, especially on the turnpike, but the hour and a half drive was worth it to see my mom. I had done it so often, I could almost drive there blindfolded, so I turned on the radio and drove.

The phone rang, so I turned down the volume on the radio and answered, "Hello?"

"Hi, honey. It's me."

"Mom, what's up? I left about 15 minutes ago, so I should be there in a little over an hour."

"Marie, I don't feel up to visitors today. I am in a little

discomfort, so I am just going to lay low."

"But Mom, just a few minutes ago you were telling me you were feeling good. What happened?"

"Um, well I don't feel well so, please don't come," Mom said with a shaky voice.

"But Mom, I am already on my way there. I can take care of you." The anger rose in me. I knew the real reason for this.

"No, really Marie, don't come. I'm okay, I just need to rest today."

"But Mom–"

"Marie, please, don't come. I'll call you tomorrow." She hung up.

Unbelievable, I thought. I didn't know why I was surprised. It happened every time. I would be all set to go see her and then she would call and cancel. I thought, 'I should just go up there anyway.' I was seething, and worst of all I felt helpless.

I pulled into a parking lot to figure out my next move. First, I called Ann.

"Hey girl, guess what?"

"What," Ann said. She sounded annoyed. I was willing to bet that she already knew what I was going to say by the tone of my voice.

"She canceled!"

"You mean he canceled!" I could hear her almost spit the word 'he.'

"Yep. She called me back about 15 minutes after I had just talked with her and said not to come. She said she wasn't feeling well even though 15 minutes before she said she felt fine."

"He made her call and cancel, like always," Ann lamented.

"I was debating on going up there anyway. What do you think?"

"It's up to you. I wouldn't, I am so sick and tired of this. Why don't you just come over here. I'll be done with work in a couple hours, and we can go have lunch. And I think it's time we have another family call to discuss a game plan."

"Okay, I am going to run a couple errands to get something done today and will see you at your house at noon."

Ann was right. We all needed to talk and try to figure out how we can make sure at least one of us was setting eyes on Mom consistently. It was so hard after Dad died, especially that first year. All six of us kids took turns spending time with her, trying to help her through it while working through our own grief. We were hoping that in time she would begin to feel better and maybe start traveling with her sister. Unfortunately, she had some heart issues that put her in and out of the hospital over the first four years after Dad died.

Just when we thought Mom was coming out of her health issues, things got worse instead of better–in a direction none of us expected. It was my son Jack's second birthday and all of my Florida family was over for his party. We were all there, except Mom.

"Marie, have you heard from Mom? I would have expected her here by now," Ann asked.

"I called her two hours ago and she said she was just leaving. She should have been here about 30 minutes ago."

"Well maybe she stopped along the way to pick up something. I will call her on her cell phone."

Ann called her and put it on speaker. "Hey Mom, where are

you? Are you almost here?"

"I am not sure where I am, Ann. I think maybe I missed the exit off the expressway,"

I whispered. "She sounds scared."

Ann nodded. "Are you still on the expressway?"

"No, I got off an exit, but I am not sure where I am."

"Okay, tell me if you can see a street sign." I could see Ann working to stay calm.

"One is coming up. It says Magnolia Street."

"I have no idea where that is. Do you see a gas station or a store or something that you can stop in to see where you are?"

"Sure, I see a gas station coming up on my right. I'll pull in and find out and call you right back."

About 15 minutes later, Mom still had not called Ann back. Ann called her again. "Mom, are you okay? Where are you?"

"The man said I am in Lakeland. I am not sure how I got here."

"Are you still at the gas station?"

"Yes, he's trying to explain to me how to get to you."

"Put him on the phone."

"Okay."

After a few minutes of discussion, we knew where Mom was and how to get her to us. But she was 45 minutes away. I left to take care of the guests and food for the party, and Ann stayed on the phone with Mom the whole 45 minutes it took as she drove to my house.

A week later my brother Scott and I accompanied Mom to the neurologist suggested to us by her doctor. After several tests, she was diagnosed with the beginning stages of dementia and was given exercises she could do to help with her memory. Other than that, the doctor didn't offer too much more assistance as he felt it was too early to prescribe any medication.

As the months went by we continued to notice changes in her short-term memory and followed up with the neurologist at the one-year mark. This time the tests showed an increase in dementia and the doctor said she had the mentality of an 8th grader. We had hoped it would not progress so quickly, but all of this was beyond our control.

Shortly thereafter, we found out that Earl had made himself her knight in shining armor. Earl, of all people.

"What a snake," I said to myself.

With the day in shambles and my heart hurting, I left the parking lot. Lunch with Ann would be a bright spot in all of this.

I thought of the hundreds of times Mom told us when Ann and I were fighting, "You'll be so glad to have each other when you're older."

I could never have realized how true that would be.

CHAPTER 6

A M E L I A

The good mood I was in from Carol's visit vanished the moment I walked through my front door. I had to push away JJ's dump truck to even take a step inside. That was only the beginning of the trail of toys that extended through the family room floor and into the kitchen. Breakfast dishes were still on the table. Olivia's hair was in knots where her ponytail had loosened. Both of their faces were covered in some kind of red substance that I imagined was sticky and sweet.

"Jake, what is going on? This place is a mess, and the kids are filthy."

Jake opened the front door that I had just closed. "I had a very busy day. When I picked up the kids from daycare, they were so wound up I took them to the park to run around. I lost track of time, and now I need to leave for work, or I am going to be late!"

"Did they have dinner?"

Jake huffed and stared at me in that hard way I knew to be a warning to back off. "No, I didn't have time."

I wasn't about to be intimidated by that look, not with this mess that he had left me with. But I held back, gathering my patience. "I get that, but you can't expect me to work all day and then get home and do everything. I take the kids to school, and you have all day to sleep. Then you get to play with the kids while I do all the work. The least you can do is pick up the house and have dinner done. That was our agreement when I took this job!"

"We'll talk about this later. I have to leave." He walked out the door with not as much as a goodbye.

I blinked back the tears of rejection and helplessness that had welled up in my eyes. I stared at the mess in front of me. The kids ran into another room, screaming at each other. At that moment, I couldn't have cared less. I reached down to pick up a toy, throwing it into the toy hamper. I was too tired to make them help me. I would just get it done, let them duke out whatever disagreement they were having, and heat up some chicken nuggets and mac and cheese. It was the best I could do.

It seemed like every day it was the same thing. Jake didn't do anything and I had to handle everything. I was so tired when I got home. I was pouring myself into all my patients, and it was a tough job.

I loved my kids and would love to just be able to play with them in the evenings before bedtime, but that was impossible. I had to make dinner, clean up, give them a bath and put them to bed. I couldn't even remember the last time I cleaned the bathrooms or washed the floors. Something needed to change. I couldn't live like this anymore.

I got the kids in the tub and let them play, forcing a smile as they giggled and splashed. I wanted to enjoy this moment. Someday I would look back when the kids were too old to laugh with their mom and wish I could have one more day. I just couldn't muster the energy.

    I knew it would be hard when I started to work, but I was more exhausted than I thought I would be. I was only 26 years old. My friends were still out having fun, going to parties, and here I was. Jake was no help. He was probably thinking the same thing. I loved my family, and I couldn't imagine life without them, but I wondered how I had gotten here. My life was so different just 5 years ago. My mind fluttered back to when we had met:

    "So, it's your 21st birthday. Let me buy you a drink."

    I turned to see a cute boy my age with a crooked smile. I was sure that grin got him a lot of attention from the girls. He had longer dark hair, and brown eyes. Definitely not what I typically liked, but there was something about him, something intense and mesmerizing. Still, I was skeptical. I had never lacked male attention, but I had found that the guys in college only wanted a little fun, no relationship. None of the ones I had met were even worth it. I had no reason to believe this guy would be any different. I said, "No, I'm good."

    "Okay, well, you can't just sit here. It's your birthday. Let's dance."

    I did like the music that was playing. My friends had brought me to a local Irish pub, Gallagher's, to celebrate. Gallagher's always had a fun crowd. It was small and usually packed with college kids looking to let off steam from daily classes. We always had a great time here. There had been no lack of people buying me shots for my birthday, and I was starting to get a good buzz. I figured, what the heck. I got up to dance with him.

    He said, "Hi, I am Jake, and you are so pretty, what is your name?"

"Amelia." I offered a tight smile, wondering if maybe I made a mistake letting his good looks convince me to dance.

"That is such a beautiful name."

"Thanks." I struggled to think of something else to say. The effects of the alcohol pulsing through my system caused me to be selectively mute, but it also made me not care too much. The song was loud and had a fast beat so talking was unnecessary. I noticed he moved smoothly and in rhythm. Most guys were awkward dancers, but not this guy.

"Do you like this song?" he asked.

Again with that crooked little smile, I thought.

"Yeah." I began to relax and enjoyed the dance.

When the song ended, neither of us moved to leave the dance floor. Song after song, we continued to dance. I found myself staring more and more into his beautiful brown eyes.

My friends kept checking on me, thinking I probably wanted an excuse to ditch this guy, but I had no desire to be rescued.

A slow song came on. It was my favorite old Journey song. Jake had brought me into an embrace. That was usually my cue to find the nearest exit, but instead I found myself melting into his arms. We moved to the music, our hands touching. Another slow song began, and he drew me closer. As the next song ended, a fast metal song came on.

Jake shrugged. "Metal's not easy to dance to."

I nodded. "Yeah, it's not my thing."

We reluctantly broke apart. The trance had been broken. Immediately I felt completely sober, and he motioned me to a table. I sat down, beginning to feel nervous. I wasn't sure why.

Was this guy like all the others?

Again, he surprised me. He began asking me questions: where did I go to school, what was I studying, where did I grow up, do I have siblings? We talked for two hours. By the end of it, my friends had left and the bar was announcing last call. It was 2 am. It felt like I'd just gotten there.

"So, can I give you a ride home?"

Here it is, I thought. He had just bided his time and now he is coming in strong.

"No, I am just going to take a cab."

Surprisingly, he didn't push me to change my mind. He walked me outside and waited until my cab arrived. "It was so nice spending your birthday with you. Thank you for the dances."

"Thank you, I had fun." *When the cab arrived, he opened the door for me and I stepped awkwardly into the cab, clearly expecting him to have tried to kiss me before I did. I began to panic; did he not like me after all? I realized with an agonizing groan that we had only talked about me. Did I talk too much about myself, I hadn't even asked about him, I didn't even know if he was in school or even knew his last name.*

Just as he began to shut the door, he asked, "Would it be okay to get your number?"

"Yeah, sure." *I smiled in relief and gave him my number.*

A huge splash of water doused me, bringing me back to the present. Olivia started to cry. "JJ, be careful. You got soap in her eyes." I pulled Oliva from the water first and dried her off, wiping the water from her eyes.

JJ stopped splashing and picked up some bubbles, putting them in his mouth.

31

"Don't eat the bubbles. You know better than that."

After getting them both dry and in pjs, I settled them into Olivia's bed together, and I opened their favorite story. They weren't ready to sleep, but that was okay by me. I loved this time as much as they did. They always asked me to read book after book. After the third story, JJ moved to his bed and I tucked them both in.

When I got to bed that night alone as Jake was at work, I tried to remember how I had felt with Jake years ago. I didn't realize it at the time, but that night of my birthday I had fallen in love with him:

"So nice meeting you, I hope we can see each other again soon."

It was Friday, almost a full week after we had met, when I received that simple text. I was heading to my final class of the week. The rest of my walk to class had an extra pep in my step. That whole week, I hadn't been able to stop thinking about him. I had been so disappointed he hadn't contacted me right away. Now, finally, he had reached out.

My joy turned to panic. How should I respond? I wondered. I didn't want to sound too happy to hear from him, too desperate. He had waited all week to text me, and honestly I was kind of mad at him for waiting so long. Plus, there was always the possibility that he was just looking for a hookup for the weekend. I decided to wait until the next morning to reply, figuring I was going to give him a taste of his own medicine. When I woke up the next morning, I felt an urgency to reach out to him. I texted, "Nice meeting you too. Yes, it would be nice to see you again."

Within seconds I got a text back: "Would you like to go for coffee on Sunday?"

I was thrilled. I tried to hold back my excitement, but if I was honest with myself, it wasn't working.

On Sunday, I awoke with a start. The thought of seeing him again made my stomach do flips. I practically flew out of bed. What was I going to wear? I didn't want to appear too eager. I selected a casual black skirt and white top, pairing it with tan sandals.

I had only been to the coffee shop he chose a few times, because it was a bit out of the way of my apartment. It was in the center of town. I parked nearby, taking special care not to forget anything since my emotions were whirling. I caught sight of him as I approached the coffee shop. I imagined he would shake my hand, so I casually rubbed the sweat onto my skirt.

He must have already spotted me, because he had a big smile on his face when we made eye contact. Immediately my heart melted. He was even cuter than I had remembered in his olive colored quarter-zip sweater and faded blue jeans.

We arrived in front of the cafe at the same time.

Jake gave me a quick little hug. "You look really pretty. Thanks for meeting me."

"Of course." I gulped. It was all I could muster. My heart was beating really fast from his quick but warm embrace.

We got our coffees and headed outside to a small wrought iron table. We began talking. This time I consciously asked him lots of questions to learn more about him.

"So tell me about where you grew up and about your family," I said, trying to act casual.

"It's nothing exciting. I grew up in Orlando and I have two

older sisters. My sisters are both married and one of them has two kids. You should see my nephews. They are crazy but so fun to play with. My family all still lives in the Orlando area, which is nice because I get to see them a lot."

I nodded, making mental notes about him as he spoke. "What brought you here to Tallahassee? Do you go to school here?"

He shrugged one shoulder. It was a gesture I would come to know well. "I used to go to FSU, but I decided I wanted to be a firefighter so I quit college and am currently at the fire academy."

Ignoring the buzzes of our respective phones, we continued our conversation. It was amazing to me how easy it was to talk with him. My nerves were vanishing along with the coffee in my cup. We talked about family, friends, and school and surprisingly there was never an awkward silence.

Jake looked at his phone and said, "Can you believe it? It's 2 pm."

Surprised, I looked at my phone to confirm the time. "Oh, I have to go, I was supposed to meet my friends by now." I had told my friends I would meet them at two o'clock to tell them about my date. I really didn't want to leave, but I didn't want to blow off my friends either.

He said, "Sorry, I didn't mean to keep you for so long, but I really had a nice time today."

"Me too." I tried not to sound as disappointed as I was that our date was over.

He walked me to my car. It was an old faded blue Ford with strategically placed dents that were present when I took possession of the car.

I turned to him. "Well, this is me, don't judge a girl by her old hand-me-down car from her dad".

"I won't. You should see mine," he said, laughing. Just then he put his hand on my arm, "Really Amelia, I had a nice time today, and hope we can get together again soon."

"I would really like that," I said with an honest smile.

"Would it be okay if I kiss you goodbye?" His face moved slowly closer to mine.

"Um, yes." No one had ever asked permission to kiss me before. He leaned down, and his lips touched mine. His lips were amazing, soft and warm with a slight scent of coffee. It was all I could do not to grab him and kiss him again as he slowly backed away with that crooked grin.

"Thank you," I whispered. Mortified, I thought that was the dumbest thing I could have said.

Before I could worry further, he chuckled and said, "I was going to thank you."

We both laughed.

"Have a great time with your friends," he said as he waved goodbye.

I stood unmoving, watching him walk down the street, almost in a trance.

I laid in bed remembering those first few dates with Jake. My heart and body ached for his touch. It seemed like a lifetime since we were in that new and wondrous stage of our relationship where every moment was exciting because of our love for each other.

CHAPTER 7

A M E L I A

The smell of urine slapped me in my face once again as soon as I walked in the door at Carol's house. It was noon. I was supposed to eat lunch after this visit, but I wondered now if I would have the stomach for it. I was earlier than previous visits, because Tom had passed away the day before. Once again the place was filthy, the piles on the floor growing larger. Food wrappers littered almost every bit of counter space in the kitchen and on Earl's TV tray. Earl was sitting in the same chair. He looked more unkempt than usual. There were what looked like ketchup stains on his shirt, and he had some sort of sheet over his legs that was also stained. The closer I got to him, the stronger the urine smell was. I was sure he must have urinated on himself, probably because he couldn't get up from the chair easily.

"Good afternoon, Earl. How are you today?"

"I am just fine, Amelia," he mumbled through a mouthful of food. He seemed to have cracker crumbs on his face. "Can you grab me a Diet Coke from the fridge?"

"Um, sure." I was shocked, disgusted, and irritated. I wanted to say, get up and get your own coke, you lazy man, but I knew I couldn't. Now that he was getting used to me, he had no problem bossing me around. I could only imagine how he treated Carol.

I READ WHAT YOU WROTE

It wasn't that he was rude in how he asked. It was the fact that he had the audacity to expect me to wait on him, without as much as a please or thank you. It seemed the more I got to know this man, the more I didn't like him.

I reached for the fridge, gingerly grasping the sticky handle. Gross, I thought. This was just par for the course today. It seemed like all my patients had been particularly cranky this whole week. I felt like whatever I tried, nothing made any of them happy. My only saving grace was that today was my chance to see Carol, and here I was dealing with Earl.

I handed him his Coke. "Where's Carol?" I went to my purse, pulling a wipe out to clean my hands. One wasn't enough. I grabbed another.

He said, "She's in the bedroom. Go ahead and go in there. I am going to go out and get some lunch for myself."

I could feel my blood pressure rising. "Should I ask Carol what she would like so you can get something for her, too?"

"No, she doesn't like burgers, and that is what I am going to get."

I wanted to shout, 'then go get something she likes.' I swallowed my comment. I was determined to stay within my boundaries. Still, I would make sure she had some food. I made a mental note to make her something to eat before I left.

I walked back to the bedroom, dodging a line of grocery bags filled with clothes along the edge. How could she walk in this without falling? My goal was to persuade them to allow me to have other folks from hospice come in and help with cleaning and meal prep. I would have to convince them that Mary wasn't cutting it. The trouble was I was afraid to push too much, especially because Earl already didn't want me there.

I had asked Diane after my last visit for advice about how best to approach Earl and Carol about utilizing our other services. She told me that all I could do is make suggestions and that unless Carol was in danger, I couldn't make them do anything. I wondered now if these tripping hazards constituted a serious enough danger to force their hand. Hopefully, it would not come to that.

I walked to the bedroom door and knocked.

"Come in!"

Hearing Carol's voice helped me relax a bit. I entered, surprised by what I saw. When Earl had told me she was in her room, I had assumed she was lying in her bed. Instead, Carol was sitting at her desk, dressed in a blue flowered blouse and black slacks. Her hair was combed and she even had a bit of make-up on, though her face looked a little thinner to me. She stood and gave me a big hug. Her warmth and tenderness was exactly what I needed today and I enjoyed every second of her hug.

"It's nice to see you, Carol."

"Oh, it's nice to see you, too."

I looked around Carol's room. It was a large room. The first thing I noticed were the matching cream-colored bed, desk, and dresser with little blue flowers around the edges. The color and pattern reminded me of the ceramic dishes my family had when I was young. "Your room is so pretty," I said. A tall lamp hung over a tan, well used reading chair. Next to the chair was a small table with a vase and a frame containing a picture of Carol and Earl. The desk was loaded down with books and papers and more picture frames, so much so that Carol barely had a place to write.

There were pictures of several people, and I wondered if these were her children. "Let's sit on the bed for a moment, okay?" Her bed was four-postered with a teal comforter on it and loads of pillows, both regular and decorative. I set the notebook down and gestured for Carol to sit next to me on the other side.

"Okay." Carol dutifully sat beside me.

I got out my supplies to check her vitals.

"Did I ever tell you that I grew up in Michigan?" she asked excitedly.

"No, you didn't."

"Yes, we were very poor, though. Much different than today. Would you believe we didn't even have indoor plumbing until I was about 11? Our first house was divided by hanging sheets, not actual walls, which offered absolutely no privacy, even for my parents. We used an outhouse, which was not fun, especially in the cold Michigan winters. I used to be so frightened when I had to go out at night to use the–facilities–" she glanced at me. "I'm so sorry to speak of things so indelicate."

"No problem. I'm a nurse, remember?"

Carol nodded. "Oh, of course. You don't mind. Anyhow, I didn't like that one bit, because there were lots of creatures, including skunks, raccoons, rats and even snakes. One time, I remember it was quite late and I had to go to the bathroom before bed so I quickly ran out in my pjs and bare feet. After I completed my business, I started walking quickly back to the house and all of the sudden I stepped on a slimy snake. I screamed so loudly and ran so fast the rest of the way to the house. It took me a long time before I could settle myself down enough to go to sleep. I can still feel that snake squishing under my foot whenever I think about it." As she shivered slightly.

I shivered with her. "Oh my gosh, I would have freaked out. I hate snakes."

"It was terrible. Besides the bathroom situation, we had to go to the well several times a day to bring in buckets of water for cooking and bathing for the family. And of course, being the oldest, that job usually fell on me." Carol peered at me seriously. "You know, we are very lucky today."

I caught her eye and smiled. "You know, you're right. I don't always remember that. I think I take it for granted."

Carol nodded. "Most people do."

I completed my tasks and routine questions. While I was making my notes, Carol asked, "Amelia, if you have a couple of minutes, I would like to show you something."

I was intrigued. "Sure, I have a few minutes."

"Up there on the bookshelf, do you see those green binders?" She pointed to the wall by the window. "Would you grab the first one on the left and bring it to me?"

Looking in the direction she pointed, I saw seven or eight green binders in between several other books. I rose from the bed and walked to the bookcase, taking down the binder she had requested. "The Bitter with the Better: Volume One" had been written on the cover with a thick black marker. I handed it to her.

She opened the book like a little girl opening a present on Christmas morning. She asked, "Did you know I liked to write?" She turned to me, her face widening in a smile and her eyes brightening.

I smiled back. "No, I didn't."

"Well, I do. I've written a couple short stories and some

poetry."

"Wow, I didn't know that. How wonderful. Have you published anything?"

"I've had a couple of articles published in the local paper, but I haven't had my short stories or poetry published unfortunately. I am, however, going to get these published." She tapped the green binder.

"How exciting. What are they?"

"This binder and all of the others on my bookshelf contain my life story that I have been writing for the last several years. I am going to get my memoirs published!" Carol was beaming.

"How amazing, Carol!" Her joy was infectious.

"Would you like to hear one of my stories?"

"I would love to," I exclaimed.

"Let me pick a good one." Carol flipped through the pages. "Oh, here's one!" She began to read: "In every family, somebody has to be the firstborn. Sometimes being a firstborn is not necessarily the best spot in the family lineup. At least that's what I thought as a child. My parents were still struggling to make ends meet toward the end of the Great Depression when I was born five years after their marriage. I came into this world on May 22, 1936, in a southern Michigan town called Jackson after President Andrew Jackson. The city also claims to be the birthplace of the Republican Party. Without the benefit of a christening, I was named Carol Jean. I was a pudgy baby who learned early how to suck through a straw. My mother says she and Dad took great delight in watching my frenzied attempts to draw chocolate malted milk into my mouth. My first recollection, though, is a vague one of a birthday party, perhaps my fifth. Along with this happy memory is a rather frightening image of my father bellowing in a loud voice, something he often did. With blue eyes and short, straight blond hair, I was a shy, introverted and sensitive child. I sucked my thumb but only the left one.

"To me, Dad was a herculean presence and I viewed him as an ominous figure from whom I should steer clear most of the time. He had a handsome face, but his clear blue eyes seemed to shoot out sparks whenever he became angry. Dad's disposition could change in an instant and his voice would roar like the rumble of an active volcano. More often than not, when Dad raised his voice I sought out a favorite corner in the dining room. There I would stand on the warm air register and suck my thumb. Sometimes I got spanked for what seemed like no reason at all. Dad's hand looked as big and strong as a bear's paw. Once he spanked me twice. The second time was for crying. I once heard Dad say, "If you're gonna spank a kid, spank him, don't just hit him." "Hitting kids just makes them mean." Fortunately, Dad's ill temper was counterbalanced by a mellow, sentimental streak. But this only confused and disarmed me.

"Mother, almost a head shorter than Dad, was a pretty, soft-spoken woman with a gentle spirit. Dad often called Mother "Ma," preferring that to her given name or any term of endearment. She kept her brown hair neatly bobbed and curled, making occasional visits to a beauty shop where she willingly suffered being tethered by locks of her hair to a machine. The machine gave her a permanent, but the curls weren't any more "permanent" than they are today. Mother shunned the use of most cosmetics, save the occasional use of lipstick and perhaps some

I READ WHAT YOU WROTE

powder. In those days she wore house dresses only. Women who worked in factories wore slacks.

"In stark contrast to Dad, Mother never raised her voice or cursed. She was a devoted wife, wholly dedicated to meeting Dad's needs and whims. If Dad commanded, "Ma, take off my shoes," she immediately obliged him without hesitation or complaint. Mother gently tended to the needs of her children as well. Although few hugs or kisses were traded between mother and child and never between father and child, I always felt emotionally secure and loved."

At that point Carol closed the binder and said, "These books are full of stories about what it was like to grow up in a different time. It was a time of hardship for many people, much different than it is now. We were raised to work hard, mind our manners, and take responsibility for our actions. That is why I want these published. I want the younger generations to know what it was like back then. It was a hard time, but it built character."

I nodded. "I can see the value of that."

"What about your family? What was it like for you growing up, Amelia?"

"Oh, I had a much easier life as far as creature comforts than you," I said with a light laugh. "I was raised not too far from here and lived in a pretty nice home and had some really nice friends. My dad raised me because my mother died when I was nine."

"Oh, Amelia, I am so sorry. Was she ill?"

"No, she died in a car accident on the way back from shopping during a bad rainstorm." A lump always rose in my throat when I mentioned that night. I usually didn't talk about

43

it, but I wanted to tell Carol. "It was around Christmas and my mom went out to pick up some last minute gifts after dinner. I begged her to let me come shopping, but she said no. She had some "special surprises" she wanted to pick up so I couldn't join her. I fell asleep early and was woken by a bunch of people talking in the other room. Blue lights were flashing through my window and it scared me. I crept out of my room to peek at the unfamiliar voices I heard coming from the living room. There was my father slumped in a chair with his face in his hands. I could tell he was crying and I saw a man with his hand on my dad's shoulder. I was frozen. I knew something really bad had happened, but I was too afraid to go over to him to find out. One of the officers had noticed me and alerted my dad to my presence. He quickly came over to me and knelt down and told me my mother had gone to Heaven. I had nightmares for months about that night."

"My goodness sweetheart, I am so sorry." She rested her hand on mine.

"Thank you. It was very hard for a long time, and there have been some times in my life that I really wished I had my mother around." Taking a deep breath, I continued, "But my dad did a really good job taking care of me and as I have gotten older. As I became a parent myself, I have really realized how wonderful of a father he had been for me after my mom died."

"He sounds like a wonderful man, and he has raised a beautiful woman. He should be proud."

I usually did not show my emotions, but I found myself choked up by those simple words from Carol. "Thank you, Carol, I think he is really wonderful, too."

"Do you have any siblings?" she asked.

"Nope, just me and my dad. And his mom, my grandma. She moved here from Boston when I was in high school after she was diagnosed with cancer. She couldn't drive herself to her doctor's appointments and found it hard to do pretty much anything for herself, so she moved in with us. Though I was really busy with school and cheerleading, I still found myself spending a lot of time with her. We would sit and talk for hours. She would tell me a lot of stories about her childhood and about my dad when he was a kid. I really enjoyed that time with her. It was difficult at times–feeding her, helping her bathe and cleaning up after her as her sickness progressed. But I wouldn't trade it for the world." I stopped, not wanting to say too much and upset her with talk about the end of life. Meeting her eyes, I could tell she was not bothered at all. In fact, I saw so much love there. I sighed. "It's what inspired me to become a nurse and work with hospice."

Carol said, "Amelia, that is wonderful. God has us go through things in life for a greater purpose, and yours is to care for others. God bless you."

I swallowed the lump in my throat that rose up again. "No one has ever said that to me, and I guess you are right. I guess if I had never experienced that time with my grandmother, I never would have met you. Well, I better get going, I have some things I have to do to finish up my day. It was so nice hearing your story and spending time with you." I patted her hands. "I am going to the kitchen and make a couple of eggs for you and some toast. How does that sound?"

"Oh honey, you don't have to do that. Earl will bring me back something."

"He told me that he was going to get burgers and that you don't like them."

"Oh," Carol said. "He's probably right."

"Let me make something for you. It will make me so happy to do so."

"If you insist. Thank you, sweetie."

I went to the kitchen to make some eggs. Dishes were piled up in the sink, but I was able to locate a small frying pan. I got some eggs from the refrigerator and some milk, smelling it to make sure it was good, and proceeded to make her eggs and toast. Working around the mess, it was all I could do to not clean up the kitchen as well. Diane had warned me to not insert myself in areas that were not my responsibility, so as much as it pained me, I left the mess. At least I had the satisfaction of getting Carol a good meal, and I could justify cleaning up after my preparation.

After Carol had finished eating and I had tidied up, I gathered my notebook and supplies. "I will see you next week and as you know, if you need anything before then, please don't hesitate to call me."

Carol stood up and gave me a strong hug. "It was so nice to have you here today. Thanks for appeasing an old lady by listening to my stories. I am so glad you went into nursing, Amelia."

"I love your stories, Carol. Thank you for sharing them with me. I hope to hear many more."

I walked to the car, feeling a warmth in my heart I hadn't felt in a long time. Unbidden, the thought arose, 'if my mother was alive, I bet I would have felt this same feeling.' I began to

I READ WHAT YOU WROTE

cry. Most days when the thought of my mother crept into my head, I brushed the thought away. It was an unconscious coping mechanism, I guessed. But today I let myself feel the loss. I was surprised how much I still missed her and how much I needed her. It would be so amazing to be able to just go over any time and talk with her, to share my children and Jake with her. I sat in the car, allowing the tears to run their course.

Jake was in the kitchen fixing the kids dinner when I got home. He frowned when he saw me. "What's wrong? Did something happen at work?"

He was always one to spot any changes in me or the kids. As a firefighter, it was like a sixth sense. I was sure my eyes were puffy from crying. Sometimes, his attention to what was out of place drove me nuts, but today I was grateful for it. "No, I was just thinking about my mom."

"Your mom?" he asked. "What made you think of your mom? I've barely heard you speak of her since I have met you."

I shrugged, setting my work gear down on the kitchen table. "I was telling Carol about her and it just brought up all of the old feelings, and I don't know, it just made me cry."

"Why are you talking with Carol about your mother, Amelia? You know you shouldn't be getting personal with your patients. I hardly ever hear you mention anything about them except Carol. I'm afraid you're getting too close to her and when she dies it will be hard for you. Besides, isn't it against the rules to get too close to patients?"

"I'm not getting too close. I am just taking care of her," I said a bit too defensively. Deep down, I knew he was probably right,

47

but I couldn't help it. There was a connection between Carol and me that I could not–would not–deny.

CHAPTER 8

AMELIA

The weeks were flying by. Carol was getting worse. The days when she looked pale and tired were increasing. Whether she was dressed seemed to be my clue to the state of her health. The days I showed up and she was in her nightgown, I knew she was struggling.

Today she was dressed. She stood and greeted me with a warm smile.

"Hi, Carol. You are looking wonderful. How are you today?"

"I am in pretty good shape for the shape I am in," she replied.

I had to laugh. She had gotten into the habit of saying that to me every time she was feeling decent. I looked around and the smile left me. Even though she looked pretty good, her house was still a mess. And of course there was that urine smell.

I turned to face the source of the smell. "Hi, Earl." I tried to put a smile on my face. "How are you today?" As frustrated with him as I was, I had to keep in mind that he was not a fan of me being here looking after Carol. I wanted to make sure I was doing what I could for Carol, so I tried to build some sort of rapport with him.

"I'm good. Since you are here, I think I'll go get the mail and pick up some food."

"Before you leave, I wanted to mention to you both that we have many additional services through hospice available to you. We can get you some help with food prep, cleaning and even someone to give Carol a haircut if she needs it."

Carol nodded. "Oh, that sounds nice."

I smiled. "I can certainly help facilitate some of that for you if you would like." Every week, I made the same offer, and every week Carol said 'yes' and Earl said 'no.' I expected nothing different this time, but I was not going to give up.

"Thanks, but we have someone that helps us. No need for you to worry about it," Earl said curtly. He got up slowly and staggered out the door. He had even more trouble getting out of his chair and walking to the door than he did last time. My eyes went to his vacant chair. I could see a large stain on the seat. I was both disgusted and concerned. How often had he urinated there when he couldn't get up to go to the bathroom?

As frustrated as I was, I had to turn my attention to the job at hand, and that was looking after Carol. Her temperature, blood pressure, oxygen levels, and even her breathing sounded pretty good today.

"How would you rate your pain on the scale of 1 to 10, Carol?"

"Well, uh…" Carol looked confused.

I had told her how the pain scale worked many times, and I was hoping she would remember. I stepped in so she did not feel embarrassed. "On a scale of 1 to 10 where 1 is no pain at all and 10 is the worst pain you've ever felt."

"Oh, well, I guess a three."

"That's good. So the medicine is working."

I READ WHAT YOU WROTE

"Yes, I think it is."

I glanced at the empty medicine cup beside her chair. "Is Earl setting up your medicine for you?"

"No, I take care of it."

I wondered how often she forgot to set out her medicine for the day, and how often that was the real problem on her difficult days. I checked her pill bottle. To my surprise, instead of too many there were too few. "How many pills are you taking, Carol?"

"Three, just like the doctor said."

I was alarmed. "Two, Carol. Just two. And only twice a day."

"Oh my." Carol's hands fluttered to her neck.

"I'll bring you a pill case next time so it's easier to keep track. In fact, I'll drop it by tomorrow morning."

"That would be nice. I don't want to take too much medicine."

I nodded. "I don't want you to either." I placed a weight scale on the floor next to the landing. "It's time to weigh you for the month, Carol."

Carol dutifully walked to the scale and took a shaky step up. I held her hand to steady her while her other hand reached for the doorknob. "Okay, when you're steady, let go and let's see what it says."

The scale read 105 pounds. My heart sank. She was down five pounds from last month.

"What did you eat today, Carol?"

"I had some cereal and some toast. It tasted so good."

"Good for you. Eating will really help with your strength and it will help the medication make you feel better. Otherwise the medicine can make you sick to your stomach."

51

"Is that why I feel sick sometimes?"

"Sometimes."

I completed the typical questions and wrote my notes when Carol emerged from her bedroom with one of her notebooks. It had become our custom to take care of all of her health business and then she would share a new story with me.

She chose a notebook and began to read: "To me, the biggest attraction in the neighborhood was the red brick two-story building called Fire Station Number 4, just half a block south of our house. Neighborhood children were never allowed inside the station, but we youngsters were permitted to roller skate on the smooth blacktop expanse in front of it. I loved the clackety clack of my roller skate wheels on the sidewalk changing suddenly to a smooth hum as I zoomed onto the blacktop.

"Like my mother before me, I could hardly wait to go to school. On this, as on other special occasions like Easter, Mother dressed us in new clothes from the skin out and coiffed our hair in braided pigtails or Shirley Temple curls. In the fall of 1941, Mother and Marilyn walked with me five blocks to my first kindergarten class at Bennett School. On the way, I skipped along the sidewalk through areas where ankle-deep leaves crackled and crunched beneath my shiny new black shoes, singing a popular tune of the day entitled, "Don't Fence Me In." Once inside the schoolroom, my excitement lessened, and I began to feel a little anxious. Being led into a room of 30 children all my size was somewhat intimidating, but Mrs. Eistedt, the kindergarten teacher, quickly dispelled my fears as she reached out for my hand. "So nice to meet you, Carol," she said, cupping her palm over the handshake. I waved a tentative goodbye to Mother and

I READ WHAT YOU WROTE

Marilyn. The teacher showed me where to put the small rug that each kindergartner was required to have for naptime.

"Soon the teacher explained to the class that we would be learning how to print our names. She would help each child individually while the rest of the class would draw or look at picture books. I got as far as the "R" in my name. Blushing, I told the teacher I needed to use the bathroom and she decided to take the whole class to the restrooms. Like baby ducks we followed our teacher down the stairway to the basement. As I entered a cubicle in the girls' bathroom, I noticed that the toilet seat was up. I reached to pull it down, but it was hard to get hold of and wouldn't yield. Finally, I managed to ease myself onto the seat, still holding it down. Afterward, I carefully slid off the seat, still trying to hold onto it, but the seat sprang up and the toilet flushed in one violent action. I was terrified and wanted to run for home, but painfully holding back tears, I forced myself back into line behind the teacher. The fright kept replaying itself in my mind, but I was too embarrassed to mention it to anyone.

"Though I liked Mrs. Eistedt, the next day I balked at going to school. I dreaded having to use the terrible toilet again. The idea of it firmly squashed any pleasure about going to school, but Mother wouldn't hear of it. She took me gently but firmly by the hand and led me off to school for the second day. This time, though, there would be no singing or skipping. Instead, with my head bent low in submission, I kicked at the dratted leaves.

"The routine would be the same as yesterday's with printing and coloring. I tried hard to concentrate on writing my name but couldn't stop thinking about "the toilet," fearing I might have to go there again. The more I entertained the thought, the more

53

I began to feel the urge. I thought to myself, "I'm gonna hold it until I get home."

Earl walked into the house and the door slammed behind him, interrupting Carol's reading. "You still here?" he said rudely.

I held myself back from narrowing my eyes in anger. The truth was that his comment cut me to the quick, but I had to maintain my professionalism. He was holding a big bag of food and the largest soda cup I had ever seen. He waddled over to his chair as the soda sloshed and dripped from the cup, spilling onto his shirt. He was breathing hard and sweating profusely due to the walk from his car to the house. He sat down so hard that I was shocked the chair didn't collapse under his weight.

"Amelia, can you get me some napkins from the kitchen? That stupid woman at the shop didn't put any in the bag."

In disbelief that again this man was treating me like his servant, my blood pressure rose. I did, however, get up and started walking to the kitchen to get them.

"Amelia, I will get them. You don't have to," Carol said. "Earl, it isn't her job to wait on us."

"That is what we're paying her for."

I walked back with the napkins, tempted to throw them at him. He was a rude revolting slob. It was all I could do to hold my tongue. I wanted to say, 'you aren't paying me. Your insurance is, you arrogant jerk!'

"Are we paying her?" Carol asked.

"No, you're not. But your insurance covers my services just like when you go to the doctor's office." I was so glad she had asked, because it gave me the chance to say what I had been holding back. I glanced at Earl out of the corner of my eye,

I READ WHAT YOU WROTE

waiting for the satisfaction of his reaction, but he was noisily smacking his gums over his hamburger, ketchup oozing from the corner of his mouth.

"I only have a little more. Do you want to hear the rest?" Carol asked.

"Of course," I said, grateful for the distraction from the disgusting spectacle beside me.

"Do you mind, Earl?"

"Of course not, sweetheart. Anything for you."

Carol beamed.

It took every ounce of willpower I had not to roll my eyes. He said such sweet things to her, but he never lifted a finger for anything she really needed.

She continued reading:

"About midmorning, the kindergartners followed the teacher to the bathrooms once again. But this time I just walked into the bathroom and made a deliberate "U" turn. Then I sent a spiteful glance at the bathroom stalls and came right back out again, in no way relieved mentally or physically.

"After school let out, I began walking the few blocks by myself to the Northwest Avenue crossing in front of Fire Station Number 4. The walking wasn't too difficult and even though the urge to use the bathroom was getting stronger, I felt my willpower equal to the challenge. Unfortunately, I had to wait for a couple cars to pass before I could cross the street safely. Then, just across the street, I noticed several firemen sitting out in front of the Fire Station. They were casually seated; some of them leaning back on two legs of their spindle-backed chairs.

"Another car was coming. I would have to continue to "hold

it," waiting anxiously on the corner. Standing was clearly more difficult than walking had been. I crossed my legs, then jumped up and down, still waiting for more cars to pass by. Had the firemen noticed my dire dance of urgency? No matter, all of a sudden, my bladder rebelled and I felt its warm contents run in a steady stream down both legs. I was mortified! When the traffic finally cleared, I began taking baby steps across the street, bending only at the knees, and holding my thighs tightly together. With mock bravado I continued my walk of shame past the firemen, who I hoped hadn't seen my soggy shoes and socks.

"As soon as I made it past the blacktop, I ran the rest of the way home, bursting into the house and into tears at the same time.

"What on ear…?" exclaimed Mother.

"I sobbed out my sorry story and then Mother calmly took charge. She bathed me, fed me and then put me down for a nap. That was the first day in my young life in which I discovered exactly how grateful I was for my mother's comforting affection.

"Later, Mother explained to me, "You will have to use the girls' bathroom at school. If other little girls can, you can, too."

It took several more battles of playing tug-of-war with the toilet seat before conquering my fear of it. I never got used to it. I hated it, but I had to use it."

She closed the book and smiled.

I said, "Oh Carol, that is wonderful. I felt like I was right there with you."

"Thank you," she said, as proudly as a young schoolgirl

presenting her artwork to her mom. Her smile softened to an expression I hadn't seen on anyone's face in a long time. "I hope it doesn't make you sad for me to talk about having my mother with me. I'm sorry if that was insensitive. I should've read a different one." Her words tumbled out on top of one another.

"Not at all, I love it. I've heard and seen other people's stories and seen them with their moms all my life. I'm used to it." I offered a tight smile. What I said was only partially true. I was used to it, but it did usually make me sad. I noted with a sense of curiosity that it did not make me sad at all now, when I was with Carol.

The following week, traffic was heavier than usual on my way to Carol's house. It gave me time to think. These days, that was never a good thing. Inevitably, my mind returned to what was happening at home. Every day was the same. It made my blood boil.

Jake and I barely spoke except for me to nag and him to brush me off. That was followed by me doing everything to keep the family and the home running. Last night was no exception. My mind replayed the interaction, as if that would help it turn out better.

"Jake, did you get a chance to pay the utility bills and the mortgage today?"

"Oh, no sorry, I forgot."

I could feel my eyes narrow. His tone told me that he was not sorry at all. "You can't just forget things like that. You're not making dinner for the kids, so I have to do that. You're not picking up the house, so I'm doing that, too. I'm literally doing everything to keep this house running, and I have accepted that you're only going to do a couple of things. But you didn't even do those things! I can't do everything and double check that you do the things you say you are going to do."

He didn't respond.

I waited a full ten seconds, counting in my head.

Nothing.

That was it. "I can't depend on you for anything!" I screamed.

"Geez, you're always so crabby when you get home. What happened to the girl I married?" He sighed, turning toward the door. "See ya, I gotta go."

A second later he was gone.

He hadn't even looked at me.

Crabby, yes I was crabby and if he helped me, maybe I wouldn't be. Believe me, I thought, I would love to be the girl he married, before I had everything piled on my shoulders.

Jake rarely kissed me goodbye when he left for work, and I had stopped caring. I had also stopped asking how work was or how his day was with the kids. I would come home, drop my keys and purse at the table next to the front door and kick off my shoes on my way to the kitchen to begin dinner. Did I even say hello? I don't think so. He would get ready for work. The only thing that he would even bother saying was on his way out the door if there was something important that happened at daycare or if he needed me to pick something up at the store.

I was fuming. I needed to clear my head and move on with my day. There was a lot of paperwork to do this afternoon after the visit with a new patient, not to mention all the updates on my established patients.

Traffic cleared enough for me to make my turn. I was only a few minutes from Carol's house. That fact alone lifted my spirits. I just hoped it was a good day for her and that Earl was on his best behavior. That would be a home run.

When I knocked on her door, I heard her cheery hello, and I smiled. Yep, she was having a good day. I walked in to find Carol looked pretty in a pink top with matching colored-lace at the collar. She smiled and, as always, moved to stand up. I said, as I did each time, "No, no. Don't get up. I'll come to you." She obeyed. I sat beside her. We went through the typical routine of her check-up.

Suddenly she reached out and took my hand in hers. "Amelia dear, I am always telling you about my childhood, and I never ask you about your family, so tell me about your little family."

My heart lifted with her simple loving question. In the back of my mind, I knew I wasn't supposed to get personally involved. I could hear Jake's warning ringing in my ears. I pushed those thoughts away. "Sure. I'm married to a man named Jake. We have been married about five years and I have two small children, Jake Junior who we call JJ who is four, and a two-year-old girl named Olivia."

"Oh, perfect, you have one of each. What does Jake do for a living?"

"He is a firefighter here in Lake County," I said. Even now, in the midst of our struggles, I was proud of him.

"Oh, I just love firefighters. I sure hope I can meet him someday, as well as your kids."

"I would really like that," I said. "What about you? Do you have children?"

"I have 6 marvelous children so I know how busy you must be."

I was astonished. "Wow, six kids! How did you do that? I can barely handle two."

"Well, you just do what you must do. I didn't work outside the home after I had two children and didn't go back to work until my youngest was in school. It was crazy at times, but I wouldn't change a thing. I really enjoyed my babies." She paused for a moment, gazing unseeing at the carpet.

I held myself back, waiting for her to speak further. I imagined she was reliving some of those special times in her life. It occurred to me that someday I would be the same, recalling beautiful moments from this time in my life. They would be long gone. The kids would be grown, so no more giggling and laughing and blowing bubbles in the bath. No more screaming fights. Knowing me, I would miss those, too. And what about Jake and me? The bottom fell out of my stomach. I pushed the thought away.

She continued. "You just have to learn patience but also understand that the time will go really quickly so enjoy it while they are young. Before you know it, they will be off doing their own thing."

I nodded. "I was just thinking about that. Everybody tells me it won't seem like long before I'm your age, looking back at those times when the kids were young, and missing them."

Carol squeezed my hand. "Oh yes, honey. Time goes so fast. I always tell young parents to make sure they are focusing on each other and their marriage. Your marriage has to come first. It's easy to lose sight of that in all the confusion of the everyday, particularly with young children. But don't forget." Carol caught my gaze, her face a mixture of warmth and concern. "Be sure to make each other happy, because as long as the two of you are happy, your kids will be happy. The years are going to fly by, and when they leave home, you only have each other so you want to make sure your relationship is strong. If you don't…well, bad things happen."

I could barely breathe. Bad things. I loved Jake. I knew he loved me. Our family had started with our love. But now… "It's hard, Miss Carol."

"Oh honey." She drew me in for a big hug. Her thin arms were strong as they hugged my neck. It was everything I could do to hold back the tears.

That night I arrived home to the usual mess, but I gulped down the rush of frustration and tried to look past it. I turned my focus to Jake and the kids. I hadn't noticed before, but the kids were all laughing with Jake as they were wrestling on the floor. As I thought about it, that was usually what was going on when I came home. I had been so fixated on the mess that I never really noticed what they were doing when I got home.

The sound of Jake's laugh warmed my heart.

Jake looked at me and his face changed. I could tell he was ready for me to start griping at him.

He jumped up. "I gotta go."

I began picking up toys from the floor.

Jake returned from the bedroom with his work bag and grabbed his coat. The kids screamed for their goodbye kisses and hugs, and he obliged. He walked past me towards the door and mumbled a quick, barely audible goodbye.

I was overcome with emotion. Carol's words rang in my ears. This isn't what I wanted.

I didn't want him to leave without a proper goodbye.

I heard the door open behind me.

I ran to the door, swinging my arms around him. I kissed him, and for the first time in a long time I felt his lips on mine. I felt the love I had for him, as a man and as a father. As my best friend. "Have a great night at work."

Jake was a little taken aback. I couldn't blame him. To his credit, he smiled and said, "Yeah. You too. Oh, I did pay the electric bill."

"Oh great!" I said. "That really helps."

"Yeah." He didn't leave right away.

It felt a little awkward between us. We'd been at each other's throats for months. I smiled, wanting to ease the tension even more.

"Time to go," he said.

"Yeah, I know."

He walked to his car. I didn't close the door right away. As he reached the driver's side, he glanced up. He gave me a little wave.

I waved back.

Behind me Olivia began shrieking. I closed the door and sought out the source of the problem. No doubt JJ was needling his sister again, just for sport. I laughed. It was never a dull moment with those two.

That night I realized I was happy at home for the first time in a very long time. I spent extra time reading to the children. I ran out of time before bed, so I left dishes in the sink, and it didn't even bother me. Carol was right. Time was flying by, and my kids were growing up fast. I needed to make sure to enjoy them, and Jake too.

Carol answered the door wearing a pretty pink top and cute white slacks. She had her hair combed and even a little lipstick on.

That was the good news. The bad news was that her cheeks were sunken in more and the clothes were baggier than ever. I knew she was losing weight. I knew there was nothing that could be done about it.

I swallowed hard. Experience told me it wouldn't be long. I wished I had met her years before under different circumstances. I wish she had been my mother. I shook my head against the thought. She was my patient. I had to remain objective. At least, as far as I could.

While I couldn't change her rapid decline, I could arrange my days so that I could spend as much time with her as possible while still taking the best care of my other patients.

I entered and looked to Earl's chair, expecting to see the familiar bump of the top of his head. It wasn't there. "Is Earl home?" I asked.

Carol shook her head. "Oh no, he left to get himself some lunch."

I couldn't help but wonder how he actually was able to get up and go somewhere. His weight was increasingly out of control and his ankles were as big as tree trunks with purple and red rings around them. His skin had become scaly skin, indicating to me that he was in the beginning stages of cellulitis. I mentioned every time I visited that extra help was available to them, but he always waved me off. I was all set to push the issue. I knew if I could get the social worker to come back in for a visit, she would certainly recommend medical care for him. Part of our hospice care set up was an initial visit with a social worker, but I was going to make sure to have a social worker come back out for a visit. I didn't care if he wanted it or not. Carol deserved the best care and the state of this man's health let alone the state of this house was a real detriment to my loving patient.

I had told Diane my plan.

I could still hear Diane's comment ringing in my ears. "Carol won't be here long enough for it to be an issue."

I was speechless. My initial thought, 'how could she be so heartless?' was quickly replaced with confusion. "What?" I said in a weak voice.

Diane sighed. "Look, I know where your heart is, and you're right. But the thing is, hospice is a business of honesty and perspective. Without both, we would lose our objectivity, and that is what our patients really need from us. They need us to be that voice of stability and truth. I realize it seems heartless, but it isn't."

My eyes shifted to my lap. It was as if she read my mind.

Diane continued, "Being honest, especially with ourselves, is helpful. Really, it is. It's the only way to be a truly great hospice nurse. And sometimes, taking action, like calling the social worker, can do more harm than good when the family is resistant."

I accepted her answer though it didn't sit well with me. I thought about my growing attachment to Carol. Was that making me less effective, less helpful?

So today, in the face of the smell of urine, mold, and decay, I held my tongue. Carol looked happy, clean, and comfortable. That was my purpose here.

In any case, I was glad Earl wasn't home. "Anything new this week?" I said cheerfully.

Carol took her usual spot in her chair. "My cousin was in town and he stopped by for a visit earlier today."

I sat beside her and took her vitals. "Oh, how nice. Where does he live?"

"He lives in Tampa. And he was in Orlando for a couple of days and came by here to say hello. I haven't seen him in a few years, so it was so nice to see him."

"How nice for you. It is so wonderful to see family and you look so pretty today."

"That is what he said," she said with a little giggle. "I was afraid he would think I looked terrible and old." She laughed again.

"You are beautiful and you certainly don't look old."

"Oh honey, yes I do."

"Well, I hope I look as good as you when I'm your age. How has your appetite been?"

"Good. At least I think so. Maybe you won't. I know how you want me to eat. But today I did anyway. My cousin brought me some broccoli cheddar soup and a bagel. It was yummy." She licked her lips like a little kid.

I laughed. "Wonderful! I think your cousin should visit more often."

"I would like that, too, but he's very busy. Everyone is so

65

busy these days."

I nodded. "We do have a fast-paced way of life." I put away my supplies. "I have a little extra time today. Would you like to read a little from your books?"

She clapped her hands. "I was hoping you would say that. Why don't you grab that same book we were reading last time you were here."

I went into her bedroom and grabbed the first binder to the left on the shelf, bringing it to her. I sat as close to her as I could on the end of the couch and leaned forward.

She opened the binder and flipped through the pages. "Where were we?" She flipped through a few more. "Ah, here!" She began to read aloud: "Even in the best of times, Dad had a nasty temper, and his own special brand of sardonic humor. One night at the dinner table, he asked me to get a glass of water for him. Always eager to garner his approval, even in such a small thing as this, I quickly jumped to obey him. Carefully holding the water glass, I successfully returned to the dining room through the kitchen's swinging door and carefully set the glass down beside Dad's plate. There was no "thank you" and I went to my place at the table and began eating my salad. With the second bite I flushed, my mouth burned, and I began to cry with remnants of the salad falling back onto the plate. When Dad began laughing uproariously, I glanced in his direction. It was then that I noticed a jar of hot peppers in front of him. I cried all the harder, knowing that he had cut up at least one of them into my salad. No one else at the table was laughing. Suddenly Dad stopped too and ordered me to leave the table if I couldn't behave. Feeling utterly rejected and subjugated I made my way

I READ WHAT YOU WROTE

upstairs to my room without supper.

"Another night we were joined at dinner by an aunt and uncle. The grownups were visiting between mouthfuls. Dad enjoyed teasing people and sent a typical quip to my uncle. Everyone laughed, including me; but my aunt imitated my laugh in a loud raucous tone. My face turned red with embarrassment, and I wanted to disappear. From then on, I would be careful how I laughed and, in whose company, if I ever dared laugh again.

"Surprisingly, Dad came to my rescue. "Would you like some ice cream, Carol?" he asked.

"Was I breathing? Dad went into the kitchen and pretty soon came back with a flat slice of vanilla ice cream on a little plate. I scooped a big helping into my mouth. The unexpected, greasy taste of the white oleomargarine made me wince, and everyone laughed as I spat out the rest of it. My throat ached in pain, as I fought back tears, but I sat there until I was excused. Once more Dad had succeeded in humiliating me for no good reason other than to appease his weird sense of humor."

As Carol finished reading the story, I wasn't sure what to say. I tried to hide the sense of sadness for her and anger towards her father.

It surprised me to see that she had a small smile on her face. Had she really gotten past the negative feelings of pain that her dad had caused her at the time?

Carol spoke, her voice more strained than usual. "That was Dad. He liked to use me as the butt of his jokes many times, but that is okay." She quickly changed the subject. "Did I ever tell you that I used to work at my dad's sawmill?"

"No. Wow, what did you do there?"

"I actually helped him saw big trees. Believe me, back then there were no safeguards in place. I am surprised I have all of my fingers. You know, I was only 14 when I started working there. Let me read you this next part. You'll really think this is something: "With the responsibility of an additional family member to support, Dad had some tough decisions to make. My youngest brother David's birth seemed to serve as the means which motivated Dad to move the sawmill to another stand of timber. He found a fairly large wooded acreage on the Sandstone Road, near Jackson. I, for one, was glad to see the sawmill moved away from its present location, thereby freeing me from the likelihood that I would be called to work any time of day or night. The sawmill's relocation didn't mean that our financial situation had improved or for that matter that life would become any easier. But it was more bearable with David's presence.

"Even with the move, I had regular hours at the mill. Marilyn and I both continued to be Dad's full-time and only employees. Many mornings Dad awakened us abruptly by lifting the end of our bed about two feet off the floor, and then let it drop. That may have seemed insensitive, even a bit cruel, but I preferred to think it reflected his exuberance over David's birth, manifesting itself in strange ways. Whatever the rationale, the desired results were accomplished. We were awakened!

"Mother sent the three of us off to the woods every day with sandwiches and a gallon jug of iced tea. We worked hard in almost all kinds of weather, and encountered every type of creepy crawler, nettle, and stickweed on the face of the earth. (We called them stick-tights," because they stuck tenaciously to our clothing.) Although blue jeans were not a craze then, they

I READ WHAT YOU WROTE

were appropriate garb for farmers and lumberjacks alike. When there was a spare minute or so and we had the time to notice, the woods could become a three-dimensional pastoral painting. Patches of deep orange tiger lilies and purple violets accentuated the deep browns and greens of the trees.

"Dad managed to salvage the heavy, two-man chainsaw from his original equipment sell-off. He worked the business end of the chainsaw, holding both handles, while Marilyn and I together held tightly to the single steel handle at the other end. First, a horizontal cut was made into the base of a tree, then, with an ax, Dad made a notch above the cut. After the notch was completed, we carried the saw to the opposite side of the tree. Another horizontal cut was made into the tree, just above the cut on the first side. If all went according to plan, the tree would fall forward on the notched side. Sometimes one or two heavy steel wedges needed to be driven into the cut on the backside, to keep it from pinching the saw. The wedges were driven horizontally into the last cut, using a large heavy mallet, which Dad called a "maul." Felling a tree was only the start of the lumbering operation, but it was the easiest part for us.

"Ultimately, Dad had to sell the chainsaw and we were forced to use the far less efficient crosscut saw. Cutting was more difficult then, for it took much longer to cut down trees and saw them into logs. Since we were so young, pulling the saw through the tree or log, when it was our turn to pull it, and at just the right arc, was next to impossible. Dad's frustration would set off his temper; he'd accused us of "laying on the saw." If we had no choice in being Dad's lumberjacks, neither did he have a choice. The work had to be done, no matter how difficult and frustrating for us.

"After several trees were cut down, Dad trimmed the smaller branches from the trees with an ax. Though we could then take a break, we'd have to "stay put" or pour some tea for Dad, whose shirt was usually wringing wet with sweat by that time. Using a two-by-two with markings in eight-, ten-, and twelve-foot lengths, he marked with an ax each felled tree at various intervals to indicate the length of log needed. As we started sawing through a felled tree, the saw usually became pinched and a wedge or two would have to be driven into the cut in order to free the saw. Marilyn, though only eleven, learned how to swing the maul, at least some of the time, while Dad and I continued to saw through the log.

"I once overheard Dad tell someone, "Marilyn's the best little lumberjack I ever had!" I felt hurt from being excluded from Dad's praise. Most of the time I could forgive him for his unkindness and bad temper, but it was difficult to forgive him for complimenting Marilyn while ignoring me. In addition to all the other various feelings I felt toward Dad, I now had one more to add to the dizzying mix.

"Soon after selling the horses, Dad bought a red 1947 Farmall F-20 tractor with lugs on its huge steel wheels. After a few logs were cut, large tongs were attached to one end of a log, and it was pulled by tractor up onto a homemade log boat, something like a giant sled. The boat, loaded with logs, was then pulled up to the sawmill's runway.

"I was taught how to start up the F-20 and drive it. First, the gas and spark levers underneath the steering wheel had to be set evenly, then I would hop off the tractor and go around to the front of it. Dad taught me how to push in the crank and turn it with both hands in a right-hand circular motion until the motor started. After a few difficult turns of the crank, the motor started up and idled at a high speed until the spark and gas levers were readjusted. The speed of the tractor itself was determined by the gas lever in conjunction with the gear–usually low or first gear. Pushing down the clutch pedal required a full body stretch while gripping the solid metal steering wheel. With my right hand grasping the wheel, I was able to shift the tractor into gear with the other hand. Then as I slowly eased up on the clutch, the tractor would begin to move.

"Once the log boat was pulled up to the runway, cant hooks were used to roll the logs onto the rollway. The moveable metal arm at the end of the pole had a sharp spike and caught firmly onto a log. Many times, the logs were uneven in circumference from the wider base end to the top end. In those instances, the logs often rolled out of control off the runway. Productivity suffered repeatedly because of such mishaps. Often I felt sorry for Dad, but I didn't know how to express that sympathy, other than to jump when he said "jump." On the other hand, Marilyn always seemed to be emotionally detached from his moods.

"Next it would be time to saw the logs into lumber. Dad cut the first four slabs and the log became almost square using a cant hook to turn the log for each cut. He then adjusted the width of the next cut with a lever on the carriage, then guided the carriage past the saw after each cut. The first few pieces of lumber had stripes of bark on the edges. He stripped these away by stacking a few boards on the carriage, adjusting the width, and sending the wood through the saw again. My job, working opposite him, was to pull the slabs of lumber away from the saw. Marylin worked right behind me, rolling the materials down a couple sets of rollers and pushing the mill's products off at predesignated intervals.

"Dad seemed to enjoy this part of lumber production the most. Sometimes I noticed a fair-sized grin on his usually somber face, as he stood there pulling on the carriage lever. I longed to know the reason for his smile and worked all the harder, hoping the smile would somehow freeze on his face. About once a week, when Dad determined that enough lumber was sawed (usually two thousand board feet), Marilyn and I helped him load it onto the truck one board at a time. With chains and chain binders, he neatly completed the loading. We watched as he secured the load, which was to be delivered to a lumber company in Lansing."

Carol closed the binder and beamed. "Can you imagine that? I was a lumberjack!"

I laughed. "You were amazing!" My expression became more somber, and I took her hand. Softly, I said, "You are amazing, Carol."

"Oh, you," Carol said, patting my hand.

On my way home, I marveled at how different life had been for Carol. Her expectations of people and life as a whole were so much lower than mine. They had been set by the experiences she was sharing with me.

CHAPTER 9

AMELIA

Earl answered the door at my next visit.

My heart sank. This did not bode well for Carol's condition.

The moment he saw it was me, he turned away and lumbered to his chair.

"Hello, Earl. How is Carol today?" I knew the answer but I asked anyway.

"Not too well. She's in bed. You can go in and see her."

I walked in and found her asleep. I didn't want to disturb her. I knew I would have to, but maybe if I waited for a little bit, she would wake up on her own. I sat down in the chair next to her bed, noticing a green binder on the nightstand. I picked it up and began to read silently.

"Hi, Amelia," Carol said weakly.

I looked up from the story. "Hello sleepyhead. How are you today?" With her bloodshot eyes and the gray tinge to her face, I knew the answer to the question. Today was definitely not a good day.

"A little tired. I see you have my stories. Before I went to sleep, I was reading an excerpt about my father. Dad was a very big, strong man and had quite the temper. I did love him though and I think he loved me too, as much as he was able to. People have tough lives, but you must take the best from things and learn, grow, and change; not to repeat the mistakes of past generations. It is because of that premise that I came up with the title for my memoirs."

"What is the title again?"

"The Bitter with the Better," she said with a proud smile.

I smiled. That is what I loved about Carol. She gave me bits of advice about life, things that I knew my mother would have told me if she was still alive today. I thought about Carol and her remarks on my drive home. Her life was difficult. So was mine, but in a different way. I began to think about the beginning of Jake and my time together:

We started dating and spent as much time as possible together. We went to restaurants, saw concerts, hiked, and hung out at the beach, which was our favorite thing to do. I was falling hard for Jake, and he for me. By the time graduation came, we were practically living together. My father had met Jake several times but was very leery of our relationship. He wanted me to focus on my finals and of course prep for nursing school. If I had majored in nursing from the start instead of biology, I would have been done, but as it was I needed to attend nursing school before I could start my career.

A week after graduation Jake and I went to our favorite beach for a picnic. I was pregnant. I had known for about a week. In fact, it was the day of graduation that I had found out. On the day that I was supposed to be happy, with a bright future in my grasp, all my plans had gone up in smoke with one little pink line. I didn't tell anyone, not even Jake. I loved him so much. I wanted a future with him. I knew he wanted kids someday, but this wasn't the plan at all.

Today I was going to tell him. I had planned a picnic at our favorite park under 'our' tree, hoping it would calm my nerves and create a good memory. I brought fresh pineapple slices, strawberries, grapes, cheese, crackers, little ham sandwiches, and some brownies from our favorite bakery. The basket had been filled to the brim.

Now the basket was empty. I couldn't stall any longer. My heart pounded in my chest.

"This is all delicious, babe. Thanks so much for lunch," he said as he stuffed another brownie in his mouth.

I smiled weakly. He had devoured everything so quickly, I don't think he had noticed that I hadn't touched a bite. Nothing seemed very appetizing these days. Besides, my stomach was in knots.

It was time to tell him, but I was so afraid he would walk away and leave me pregnant and alone. I would lose the love of my life, my future, and be a single mom struggling to make ends meet.

I brushed the thought away. I couldn't think about that right now. "Jake, I have to tell you something." My voice shook.

"What's up, beautiful?," he said, leaning over to kiss my check.

I wanted his warm tender kiss on my check to remain forever. It might be the last time. But I knew I had to tell him. "Jake, I'm pregnant." I breathed in deeply, mustering the courage to continue, "and I am not saying you have to take any responsibility, but I am keeping it and I love you and I already love this baby, and...." The words had spilled out all at once, but suddenly they stopped. I could no longer speak, because I couldn't breathe.

He sat still for a minute, looking at me. I couldn't tell what he was thinking. Maybe he was in shock. I unconsciously clenched the pretty red and white checkered tablecloth I had laid on the ground to use as our picnic blanket. My hands gripped it so tightly, they began to hurt as I waited for him to say something.

"Wow, pregnant," he said.

I wasn't sure if that was a question or a comment. I certainly couldn't tell if he was mad or happy. I wanted to tell him to process it all, but the words wouldn't come. I nodded my head, desperately trying not to cry.

Then, it was as if a light switched on. His face completely changed into exuberance. He jumped up, reaching out to stand me up with him, and hugged me. "Wow, I can't believe it! We are going to have a baby! I am going to be a dad."

I had never seen him so excited. "Yes."

He kissed me again. "Are you feeling okay?" He pulled away and looked down at my stomach.

"Yes. A bit nauseous but okay."

"When are you due?"

"The doctor said the end of December."

"I am so excited!" He hugged me again. "We need to make plans!"

I began to cry. The tears flowed down my face. I sobbed into his chest.

"Are you okay? What's wrong? Are you not happy?"

I looked into Jake's concerned eyes. I nodded. "I'm really

happy. I–" The sobs overtook me again and I couldn't speak. I buried my face in his shirt.

"You don't seem happy."

"I guess it's the stress of knowing this and not knowing how you'd react. I–"

I looked up at Jake again. Jake looked confused and concerned. Really, he looked absolutely baffled. Suddenly it all seemed very funny. Here I was, telling him I was happy while sobbing my eyes out. I started to laugh.

Jake accepted this change in mood without question. "That's better," he said. "Here, you should probably sit down." He lowered me to the blanket. "They say women can be very tired in early pregnancy. You need to take it easy." He started pacing back and forth. "This is great! This is everything I've ever wanted–you, a baby, and then more!"

"But this isn't what we were planning. It's okay if this is freaking you out. It is freaking me out." I was relieved he wasn't upset, but I couldn't quite believe he was really happy.

"Amelia, you know I love you, you know I want to have kids. We talked about that."

"Yes, I know, but this isn't how we planned it." And then I tentatively said, "We aren't even married, but don't think I expect–"

He interrupted me. "Amelia, I want to marry you! I just haven't asked because I didn't want you to think it was too soon. I would have married you the first week I met you. I knew you were the one I wanted to spend the rest of my life with!"

"Me too, Jake, but I am supposed to go to nursing school. I mean, we have no money and..." Tears ran down my face again.

I couldn't control them. I was excited and scared all at the same time.

Jake flopped beside me, taking my hands in his. "Oh, babe, don't cry. I know you might be scared, but I will take care of you and our little boy." He gently, reverently, touched my stomach.

"Little boy? How do you know it's a boy?"

"I just know it." He shrugged. "We will be happy and it will all work out. You'll see!" Again, he hugged me.

We spent the next couple of hours talking about how we could work out our future. We laid out a great plan. Jake had already accepted a job to work at the Lake County Fire Department. He had already finished his firefighter training, obtained his EMT certificate, and spent the last several months working at the local fire station. He would work in Lake County when he received his certificate but work locally so he could be near me. I would waitress at the restaurant I used to work at during the summers while I was in college. I could go to nursing school and work at the restaurant part-time. I had also received a scholarship which would help with tuition at least. We would find a small apartment we could afford that wasn't too far from Jake's new station.

When the baby came, I would take a small break from school. The school counselor told me I could return to classes on a part-time basis until I graduated.

We still had to tell my dad. When we told him later that week, he was so mad he stormed out of my apartment before we could even tell him how we had it all worked out. I cried hard that night, but knowing Jake was there for me I felt like we could make it.

I waited for my dad to reach out, but he never did. Jake and I married a month later without him. There was no big fancy wedding like I had always dreamed of when I was a little girl. We were married by a Justice of the Peace with his parents and sisters as witnesses. We had dinner afterwards with his parents, but his sisters had to get back to their families that evening.

I guess a mid-week wedding wasn't that special to them. It didn't bother me too much. I was just so happy to be married to the man I love. Jake didn't seem affected either by the lack of fan-fair. We just focused on each other.

Nursing school began a couple weeks later.

Luckily, I didn't have the morning sickness like some people had. Just a little nausea, a little tiredness, and more tears. Overall, I counted myself lucky. I managed good grades and worked very hard, saving every penny I could. Jake picked up extra shifts late into the evenings to help with our finances which seemed to work well enough. As school expenses grew along with my belly, the time came for me to stop school. I was excited about the baby. Jake and I were as in love as ever.

Jake Junior came into the world late one night. I fell in love the moment I saw the beautiful little face of my precious little boy. Though it was a tough first few months with late night feedings, colic, and missing Jake while he worked constantly, I was happy. My only regret was that Jake had to work so much, because he didn't get to spend much time with his new little family.

CHAPTER 10

AMELIA

On the way to see Carol for her weekly visit, I could not get the image of her emaciated frame out of my mind. While some decline was to be expected, the rate at which Carol was losing weight was too great to be explained by her condition. The fact was she was not getting proper care.

The only one who could change this was Earl. Carol could not–she was at a stage in her dementia that she did not remember to eat. Last week's conversation ran through my mind:

"What did you eat for breakfast, Carol?"

"Oatmeal," Carol answered proudly.

"Oh really? Great!" I glanced at the stack of dishes on the kitchen counter. There was no sign of any bowls or pots for oatmeal. The only dishes were pots from Earl's lunch of spaghetti and fast food bags. "Where is the bowl you ate from?" I asked.

Carol looked in the direction of the kitchen. She furrowed her brow. "Well…come to think of it, I don't think I did have oatmeal. What did I have?"

"Are you sure you ate?"

I READ WHAT YOU WROTE

The look of confusion on Carol's face made me sad.

It still did. I sighed as I parked in front of their house. I had made the mistake of parking in the driveway one time. Earl had been nearly running when I got to the door. He had obviously worked hard to be as fast as possible. "Get that car out of my driveway."

"Oh, I'm sorry. Is it blocking you in?"

"No. I just don't want it there."

He had stomped away, huffing and puffing from the exertion of hurrying to confront me.

Carol had spent nearly five minutes making excuses for him that day.

I apologized, sorry most of all that it had put her in an awkward situation.

Today I was in for another confrontation with Earl.

I entered Carol's house, ready to be firm with him. I had to take action to protect her.

After greeting them both, I sat facing Earl. It was something I never did.

From a flick of his eye, I knew he saw me but he made a point of not turning to look at me.

"Earl, my biggest concern right now for Carol is her eating. She has lost much more weight than she should have, and at this point she is very vulnerable to disease, infection, or heart failure because she's so thin. Along with writing down when she is given her pain medication, can you please also write down what she is eating throughout the day? By doing this, I will get a good sense of her calorie intake and nutrition so we can make adjustments."

81

"She doesn't eat much because she's never hungry."

The cavalier way he brushed me off made my blood boil. I wanted to snap at him, when did he become an expert on nursing? I held my tongue. Instead, I addressed the real problem. "With dementia, the patient often forgets that they are hungry. It is crucial that she gets–."

He scowled at me and barked, "She doesn't have dementia."

I didn't know how to respond to that. Last week she wasn't doing well, according to Earl, but this week she was just fine. Not to mention the doctor's diagnosis. "Okay," I said. My mind whirled, returning to my training on how to cope with patients and families who were resistant. Asking questions was one of the best tactics. I took a deep breath. "So Earl, is it normal for people to repeat themselves or ask the same questions over and over within a short span of time?"

Earl looked away and did not answer.

"Also, how long can a person live without eating?"

"She eats."

I was done tiptoeing around him. I spoke directly. "Do you think she eats enough?" I waited for his response, but he said nothing.

"That was a question, Earl. Because if she doesn't eat enough, isn't it important to encourage her to eat?"

Carol's pleasant voice filled the air. "Earl, I'm sure Amelia means well."

I had been so engrossed in my tête-à-tête with Earl I had forgotten she was in the room. From the way Earl jerked to look at her, I think he had too.

"Of course, dear," he said.

I held back a deep sigh and waited, hoping Carol would deliver the knockout punch in her sweet way.

Carol smiled. "I have noticed that my clothes are much too big. I thought maybe they were someone else's clothes. Maybe I do need to eat more."

Earl nodded. "Okay, if you say so. You just need to tell me when you're hungry."

That was my cue. "Earl, she can't do that. She can't remember to tell you, and her condition means she doesn't know she's hungry." I pulled out the whiteboard, marker and eraser from my bag. "Let's start a new system. Whenever Carol eats, write what she has eaten on the chart. Then you can both see it, and I can too when I visit. This chart will be for the whole week: breakfast, lunch and dinner. What do you say?"

"Oh that sounds fun," Carol said.

Earl shrugged. "Okay. I'll do it. Anything for my sweetheart."

Carol twittered like a little girl. "See how sweet he is to me?"

I disagreed, but I did not want to make that obvious. "He is, Carol. And thank you, Earl. It's magnetic so I'll place it on the fridge." I went to the fridge. It was covered with food particles. Spying the can of antibacterial wipes I had brought last week, I took one out and wiped down the front before attaching it. "There ya go. All set."

"That's great," Carol said. "Ooo, I feel a little faint. Maybe I should go lay down." She tried to stand and staggered, grasping the edge of the chair.

I rushed to her side.

She waved me away.

I took a step back but still close enough to help. "Oh, I'm

alright. I just need to get my legs under me." She shook her legs a few times and then took a step. "Here, you better watch out. Once I get going I can't stop so clear the way!"

I stepped back even more, letting her walk on her own, even though it terrified me to watch her totter down the hall, holding onto the wall.

Before I left the room, I turned once more to Earl. "Keep in mind that her pain medication will work much better if she has something on her stomach. Do you make her food when you make some for yourself?"

"I don't cook. We have meals delivered a couple times a week or I'll go out and pick up some food. I ask her but she never wants anything."

He clearly could not care less about her getting fed, no matter what he said to Carol. With as much restraint as possible, I said, "Earl, I can't express enough how critical it is that she is getting food on a regular basis. My suggestion is to maybe have food delivered more frequently and just choose meals for her. And when you go out to get yourself food," emphasizing the word 'yourself,', "why don't you pick up something for her that you think she might like, even if she says she doesn't want anything. I have seen that many patients will eat something if it is given to them, even if they say they aren't hungry."

Earl grunted. I was going to take that as agreement. After all, he had let me put the nutrition calendar on the fridge. Time would tell if he would write on it.

I left, entering Carol's bedroom. It was becoming one of my favorite places, a safe place from the world where Carol and I could share our thoughts, our troubles, and our hearts.

She was already lying down, her eyes closed, her face haggard. I could see she was exhausted. I quietly conducted my exam and asked her the usual questions.

I stood up to leave. I wanted to read with her, but I could see how tired she was.

"Stay and read to me," Carol said in a small voice.

I sat down. "Of course. I'd love to."

I opened the latest of her green books and read aloud:

"As a teenager, I was unhappy with my self-image. Though I was quite aware of my physicality, random thoughts often meandered through the streets of my brain when I wasn't at school or work. I felt lonely and insecure, but no one seemed to notice. I simply did what I thought was expected by my parents, teachers, and employer. If I had had the slightest inkling there was turmoil going on in my mind, I might have sought advice from Mother or from a clergyman (although we had no religious affiliation). But how could I verbalize what I didn't understand? Who was Carol Jean? Subconsciously, I struggled to answer that important question by spreading my wings. Unfortunately, those efforts would fly off in all the wrong directions.

"Searching for a crumb of independence, I decided to skip school one day. Everyone else seemed to be doing it. As I walked out of the house that morning, I wavered, "Should I, or shouldn't I?" Failure to think things through and consider the consequences led to my departure off the conventional path.

"Feeling uncomfortable in my isolation, I walked slowly down the street, away from school. Halfway downtown, I was beginning to have second thoughts. I was experiencing a mental tug-of-war between the angel and the devil in me. One voice said, "There's no turning back now. Besides, you're already late for school!" Another voice asked, "Why, all of a sudden, do you want to rebel against all the values you've been taught? And, for what possible reason?" Ultimately, the devil won out, and I found myself at the door of the Mayfair Grill."

Carol chuckled softly.

I looked up.

She shook her head, her chuckle turning to a smile.

It seemed to me she was lost in her memories. I kept reading. "Only a few people were there, I seated myself at a small table, then a waitress materialized and politely asked, "May I help you?" "I'd like some coffee, please," I responded meekly, afraid she might question why I wasn't in school. But fortunately, she poured the coffee without comment, and I lit a cigarette. Though I wasn't consciously aware of it, I had probably taken up smoking (another harmful path), out of the same feeling of loneliness and insecurity.

"The hands of the restaurant clock didn't seem to be moving though I glanced at it several times over the coffee cup. The waitress poured more coffee. I thanked her and had another smoke. Gradually I realized that coffee or smoking would help kill time, but I still had no concrete plan for the day.

"The stores downtown weren't open, so I chose to window shop, moseying from store to store. By the time I reached Jacobson's, barely an hour-and-a-half had elapsed. For a time I stood there pining over the "cool" saddle oxfords in "Jake's" window, but they were still too expensive, especially since I was now buying most of my own clothing. Continuing down Michigan Avenue, I reached the Elaine Shop, an exclusive

I READ WHAT YOU WROTE

women's clothing store, where everything was high-fashioned and high-priced. It was barely nine-thirty and there were still six hours left until time for work. At the stoplight, I crossed the avenue toward the theaters, but they wouldn't be open until afternoon. A movie would not be part of the school-skipping adventure.

"With guilt-laced boredom, I asked myself, "Why didn't I go to school? Why did everybody seem to think it was such a great lark to skip school?" I felt stupid, just plain stupid! Aimlessly, I continued walking up the other side of the street, past Gilbert's Restaurant, owned by Jackson's famous candy maker, and reached Muir's Drug Store, directly across the street from where I worked. Briefly, I considered returning to school for afternoon classes, but quickly ruled that out. I had no wish to confess my errant behavior to Mother nor ask her to write an excuse for my absence.

"I passed by the city bus comfort station, the Hayes Hotel and Duchenne's Portrait Studio. Nearing the library, I decided to go there. Upon entering it, I felt relieved of some guilt by rationalizing though it wasn't school; at least it was educational. Besides, I could lose myself among the books, and time would pass more quickly. Oblivious to everything else, including lunch, I spent the rest of the day engrossed in the literary world. I felt relieved when it was time for work and vowed never to skip school again.

"The next morning, I forged an excuse, signing Mother's name. I experienced a twinge of nerves as I handed the note to the homeroom teacher, but after a few classes I felt more at ease in my deceit–that is, until the afternoon's History class. With a deep furrow in his dark brow, Mr. Kiley called me up to this desk. He said that the forgery had been discovered, my parents would be notified, and I would have to spend two weeks in after-school detention. He summed up the verdict by saying I'd be getting a red "E" for the marking period, the worst possible grade a student could receive. And this sentence wasn't quite all of it. I would have to explain why my hours at work needed to be reduced and the smaller paycheck would be the final penalty of the not-so-worth-it day of skipping school.

"I wasn't upset with Mr. Kiley. In fact, I had respected him since he urged us to get our priorities straight while we were young, namely God, family, and education. Standing in front of this esteemed teacher, my face flushed. I struggled to keep from crying. Then fear crept in and swiftly replaced the shame I felt. How would my parents and employer react? Facing them with my truancy was the most difficult thing I'd ever had to do. Equally humiliating was the time spent in after-school detention, even if I wasn't the only one "doing time." To my surprise, my parents never reprimanded me. Perhaps they understood their daughter was close to making out in the punishment department.

"I skipped school once and–" Glancing up, I saw that Carol had fallen asleep. I decided to skip to the last few pages of that book and open the next:

One Friday night, Marilyn told me she had a date with the cutest guy whom she had met at a high school dance. The doorbell rang, and I was surprised to greet Thomas Patterson. He was in my Spanish class and sat behind me in Study Hall. Marilyn hadn't remembered his name, and if it hadn't been for

I READ WHAT YOU WROTE

Thomas's initiative, I might have had to re-introduce them.

I too had begun to date a nice boy, also a classmate from Springport. We had renewed acquaintances one Saturday night at a town hall square dance. As an only child, he was required to do much of the farm work, since his father worked in a factory. As a result, our dating was limited to two or three times a month.

We enjoyed each other's company and bonded in teenage complaints about our mutual unhappiness. After we had dated for a while, Ben found a job in Jackson and bought a green '47 Chevrolet. Sometimes I made sack lunches for him and washed his car. None of our parents discouraged our dating although Dad didn't like the way he nervously jingled the change in his pockets. And before long we became each other's first love.

On Springport's senior prom night we gave in to our youthful passion with absolutely no sex education whatsoever.

"Amelia," Earl called from the other room. "Is everything okay?"

I was so engrossed with the story I almost dropped the book when he called my name. I hadn't realized that it was getting late, and it was way past the time for me to leave.

"Um, yes, just finishing my notes. I will be out in a second." I did not want to stop reading. 'I'm right at the good part,' I thought. In a split second, I put the book in my bag. I had to finish reading the story and couldn't wait until my next visit, especially knowing Carol may never have me read that story. A twinge of guilt rose in me, but I pushed it down. I knew it was wrong, but it was an impulse.

Just as I was debating whether I would take it out of my

bag, I heard Carol's sweet voice. "Oh Amelia, did I fall asleep?"

Now it was too late. I could not take it out without being discovered. "Um yes, but it's okay. We're done. I need to leave anyway. Please take care of yourself and I will see you next week. I really enjoyed seeing you today." I got up and exited before she could ask me about the book we were reading. I began to sweat as I hastened my way to the door, giving Earl a quick and cheery goodbye as well. I winced. It was much cheerier than usual. My dad would have known right away that something was up. I glanced at Earl as I opened the door. Much to my relief, he seemed oblivious.

I sat in my car, trying to catch my breath. I wondered what in the world got into me. Why would I take that book? That wasn't like me. "Okay, just relax," I said to myself. "I'll bring it back next week." Despite my promise to myself, anxiety and shame overtook me.

I took a deep breath and drove home.

CHAPTER 11

AMELIA

Breathing a sigh of relief, I walked into my room. Dinner was done and cleaned up and the kids were asleep in their beds. The rest of the house might be messy, but my room was my sanctuary. Dad had given us his old bedroom furniture when we moved into this house. It was a dated mahogany bedroom set with a four-poster bed, dresser and nightstand. It reminded me of something that would be in a castle with the clawfoot legs and little brass hardware. He said that my mother had picked it out when they were first married. He loved it because he loved her, but truth be told it was too ornate for him. Jake didn't mind. He knew it was special because it was my mother's.

The centerpiece of it all was the fluffiest white comforter I had ever seen. I had to have it, and I still counted it as one of my best purchases. I crawled under it, allowing it to envelope me in its softness. As the coup de grace to my cozy retreat, I pulled the throw blanket up to my neck. I bought it my first year of college. It was a bit worn, but it was still a pretty shade of lilac. I had spent many nights curled up with it while studying. My view at the end of the bed completed the ambience: a beautiful shag rug that matched the throw closely with a circular pattern of white and a dark purple. It wasn't a practical choice with dirty little feet that ran over it from time to time, but it felt right.

I was tired, but I was anxious to read more from Carol's journal. I opened the binder up to the part I had been reading before I had been interrupted by Earl:

Afterward, I felt terribly ashamed, I could barely speak all the way home from the dance. Ben was needless to say happy and didn't even notice how quiet I had become. When he said goodbye to me, he gave me a quick kiss and that was it.

When I arrived home from the dance mother was up sitting at the kitchen table having her favorite, popcorn and milk. "How was your night Carol? Did you have a good time?" It was all I could do not to cry, Could she tell that I had had sex? Did I look as disheveled as I felt? I quickly said, "Yes, it was fun but I am really tired. I am going to head to bed. Good night, Mother." I couldn't even give her a kiss goodnight like I normally would have. I just didn't want her to smell Ben on me, if that was the case.

I couldn't sleep all night thinking about what we had done. It wasn't special. In fact it wasn't pleasant at all. But at that point I thought it was what was expected in a way. Marilyn was sleeping in the bed next to me and had gone on and on before she slept about what a great time she and Thomas had that night. I wondered, did she have sex too that night? As much as she liked to talk, I assumed she would have told me if she had. Out of pure exhaustion, I finally fell asleep.

The next morning, I woke up with complete dread. Marilyn was getting dressed and humming some song I couldn't quite identify.

I READ WHAT YOU WROTE

When she saw I was awake, she started bouncing up and down, talking a mile a minute. *"Carol, wasn't that a great dance? Thomas is so cute, and he is such a good dancer. I noticed you and Ben didn't dance much. Does he not like to dance?"*

"Yes, he does, he is a wonderful dancer." I was surprised at myself. Why was I defending him when right now I was not too happy about the smug way I felt he had treated me on the way home? Clearly, I had made a huge mistake and was very concerned about what his expectations would be on our next date. I had decided then and there, I would not do that again, not until we were married.

For the first time, I was so glad I had to help Dad around the farm. I didn't want to think anymore of the night before. I think I probably worked harder than I ever had before. In fact my dad even said 'good job' to me at the end of the day. That was the greatest praise I had ever received from the man. That night I slept well. I didn't even think about Ben.

The next morning, Ben was at the front door as soon as I had cleared the breakfast dishes.

"Carol, Ben is here to see you," Mother yelled from the front door.

I immediately broke out into a cold sweat. I couldn't face him. What was I going to say? I slowly walked to the door.

"Hi," he said with a huge smile. *"How are you?"*

"Good." It was all I could muster.

"So, want to go for a ride? I thought we could go into Jackson and get some ice cream."

I turned to my mother, begging her with my eyes for her to say that I had to help around the house, or help Dad or something, *anything to get me out of going with Ben.*

She obviously couldn't read my mind, and quickly said, "Oh, how nice. I hope you two kids have a nice day." That was it. No lifeline from her.

"Okay, I will get my sweater," I said, defeated. I walked very slowly to my room, trying to figure out how I was going to face him. What we would talk about and how I was going to tell him I was not going to have sex with him again?

To my relief we ended up having a great day. We walked around the town and saw some friends and then a group of them joined us for ice cream. We went to my favorite place, Loud and Jackson Ice Cream Parlor and I had my favorite treat, a root beer float. They served amazing ice cream treats. It was such a great place for young people to hang out. Ben took me home and gave me a nice kiss goodbye with no further expectations, which was a great relief to me. I was surprised he didn't want to talk about what we did two nights before. Maybe he felt the same way as I did. Maybe he thought it was wrong too and wouldn't want to do it again until we were married.

Because Ben and I didn't have any classes together, and I had to go to work immediately after classes, I didn't see much of him during the week. The following weekend he had to help his father do some of the plantings so we didn't spend time together that weekend. By the middle of the following week, Marilyn was extremely cranky. She was complaining about having cramps due to her monthlies, and she used that as an excuse for not helping clear away the dinner dishes. She was always like that when her monthlies came. It dawned on me, I should be getting mine soon, but hadn't had any of the

I READ WHAT YOU WROTE

typical premenstrual signs like cramps or tender breasts. Oh, my goodness, could I have gotten pregnant? What would I do then? I was suddenly frightened. We had not used any protection. It wasn't like it was easy to come by in those days. I knew Ben had never had sex before and we clearly weren't educated on how to prevent pregnancy. For the next few days, I became sicker and sicker to my stomach. Was it just nerves or was I getting morning sickness? I remember that my mother always seemed like she was sick when she was pregnant with my little brothers.

A couple of days later my period came. Although I wasn't feeling too well, I was extremely relieved. I was not pregnant. I was so relieved to have avoided that disaster, but I still struggled with the guilt of having sex. Though my parents weren't really religious, I knew it was wrong with God and society to have put myself in that situation. Good girls didn't let boys do that to them before marriage, and the only way I could feel at least a little better about it was if Ben and I were to get married.

That evening Ben and I went out to dinner in Jackson. I wanted to share the feelings I was having and was very nervous to do so. I needed to make Ben understand my thoughts, but I was afraid he would think I was crazy and run away from our relationship. We walked hand in hand down the streets passing by the little store fronts. Like pulling off a band-aide, I blurted out, "Ben, we need to get married." That was it, short and sweet.

"Are you pregnant?" There was sheer terror in his voice.

"No, but we need to anyway," I said halfway pleading.

Still not convinced, he said, "Are you sure you aren't pregnant?"

"Yes, I am sure, but it wasn't right what we did on prom

night, and I think we should get married before we ever do that again."

He didn't say anything for a little while and then miraculously he said, "Okay."

His casual answer surprised me. It could have been a response to a question as simple as, 'want to go grab something to eat?' I was all ready to give him all the reasons it was important to me that we marry, but I didn't have to. I was not sure if it was because he felt like I did, or if it was simply because he had a rough home life and wanted to move on. Whatever the reason, I was glad he agreed. "Okay, we can after graduation."

I stopped walking and turned to Ben and hugged him. "Oh thank you for understanding. We will have such a wonderful life together."

I turned the page. It was the last one. I was so disappointed. I was shaken by the similarities between Carol and Ben's relationship and Jake's and mine. We both needed to marry sooner than was planned.

I wondered if there were further similarities that I would uncover in her other stories. I wanted to find out what had happened to their marriage. Obviously they were no longer married since Carol was now married to Earl. What happened to end their marriage?

A deep fear burned in me. Would Jake and I have the same fate? I knew we had a lot of issues and were not as happy as I thought we should be at this stage of our life. There was so much tension between us. We had lost that crazy romantic feeling we had before…before having kids, crazy jobs, everything. Did that mean we wouldn't last like Ben and Carol?

My mind raced. It was a long time before I fell asleep.

I was on a ship, being thrown up and down, up and down, I felt like I was going to go overboard. I awoke with a start and opened my eyes.

I was greeted by the sight of JJ jumping up and down on my bed.

I giggled. "JJ, please stop. I am going to fall out of bed."

"Sorry, Mommy." JJ threw himself onto me, hugging me tight. Then his head popped up. "It's time to get up! We don't have school today so we can play ALL DAY!!! Get up! Daddy is home."

As if on cue, Jake walked into the room.

JJ started jumping up and down on the bed again.

"Daddy, Daddy, come jump on the bed with me."

Jake laughed and jumped on the bed, once again, almost making me fall out.

"Jake!" His name came out as half yelling and half laughing.

JJ leaped from the bed and dashed down the hall. "Come on! Let's goooo!"

Jake and I laughed. Our eyes locked. It felt good to laugh with him.

Memories of Carol's story returned to my mind. My face fell. Whatever had happened to them, I didn't want that for Jake and me. "Hey Jake, let's go out to dinner together tonight, just the two of us. What do you think?"

"Without the kids? How?"

"Maybe I can get my father to come over. He loves being

with the kids. I know he hasn't spent much time with them alone, but I think he could handle it. JJ is such a big help with his little sister and Olivia is really an easy baby. I'll go call my father if that's okay with you…" My voice trailed off.

"Sure. If you can get him to come over, that would be great"

My heart lifted a bit. Did I catch a little enthusiasm in his voice?

Excited by the prospect of having alone time with Jake, I started planning our date in my head. The first thing I had to do was get a hold of my father to see if he would babysit. By the grace of God, he was free and agreed to watch the kids. Though I was a bit anxious about letting him watch the kids alone, the anticipation of spending an evening with Jake outweighed my fears.

I started getting ready an hour before our date. Jake was in the living room playing with the kids, so I had time to spend doing my hair, my makeup and choosing an outfit. After trying on ten different combinations of outfits, I settled on a cute mini-skirt that Jake had liked a few years ago and a blue top that I hadn't worn in a long time. I liked the blouse because it matched my eyes. I evaluated my reflection in the full length mirror. I wondered if the skirt was out of date. I decided to wear it. It still fit decently so I pushed the negative thoughts out of my mind. Jake wouldn't know what was in style anyway.

Going into the bathroom, I brushed out my ponytail. I hadn't realized how long my hair had gotten. I'd been wearing it in a ponytail for years. It was much easier to just throw it up because the kids seemed to pull it whenever I was holding them. But tonight was special. I pulled out the curling iron. Jake always loved my long hair. I hoped he would notice.

As I finished getting ready, I started to get nervous. Would we have anything to talk about, besides the children? We hadn't been alone together, really, for a long time. I hoped it wouldn't be awkward.

I walked down the hall, taking a deep breath to calm myself.

Jake was lying on his side on the floor, his long muscular form extending the length of the couch. My heart leaped, as it did any time I took the time to really look at my husband.

It didn't escape my notice that I had just spent an hour getting ready while he looked sexy without lifting a finger.

Jake looked up. He scrambled to sit up. "Wow, you look great!"

All of my fears were immediately put to rest. He hadn't reacted like that to me in a very long time. It felt great.

Hearing a knock at the door, I headed to the door. It was my father.

Within a few minutes, Jake and I were in the car together and on our way to dinner–alone. We decided to go to a new trendy little place that offered good food and had a mixology bar. It was a bit crowded but we didn't have to wait too long for a table.

"Jake, we have to figure out what we want to eat. The waitress has come by 4 times to get our order," I said, laughing.

"I know." He had a chuckle in his voice, too. "We just aren't used to being able to hold a full conversation without our kids interrupting."

We finally ordered: a salad with grilled chicken for me and a gourmet burger for Jake. We had a couple drinks and were able to enjoy our kid-free dinner.

After we ate we ordered another round of drinks and listened to the live music, chatting the whole time.

We arrived home at midnight. We crept into the house.

Jake whispered, "Why do I feel like we just broke curfew?"

I snorted in laughter.

"Shhhh," Jake said. "Everyone is asleep, including your dad. You're going to wake up the kids."

"Stop making me laugh," I whispered back.

Dad had fallen asleep on the couch. His head was crooked to one side. He would have a terrible neck ache in the morning if he did not lie down.

Gently we woke him up and suggested he stay the night in our room. Though I yearned for a night of lovemaking with Jake, we instead slept on the couches in our living room. As I laid on the small couch listening to the gentle snores of Jake, I played back the evening in my mind. It was such a lovely evening. I thought back to Carol's statement that the key to a happy family was a strong relationship between the married couple, and that meant making time together a priority. After this evening, I knew she was right.

Arriving at Carol's house a few days later, I found her lying in bed, but she seemed in good spirits. With the binder burning a hole in my bag, I wasn't sure how I could put it back on the shelf and find the one that would continue the story I had been reading. I just had to find out what happened between her and Ben. How was I going to be able to do it with Carol in bed in her room, which housed the journals? I asked Carol, "How are you

I READ WHAT YOU WROTE

feeling, have you had something to eat today?"

"No, I am not really hungry. My stomach is a little upset. I also have some pain in my side."

"Carol, when was the last time you had your pain medicine?"

"I don't remember." She yelled to Earl in the living room. "Earl, when did I have my pain medicine last?"

"Um, I think it was about 30 minutes ago."

I decided to step out into the living room and talk with Earl, who of course didn't get up from his chair. "Earl, are you keeping track of when you are giving Carol her pain medication? "

"Yes, it is right here, I gave it to her about three hours ago."

Again, I was shocked by the boldness of Earl's lies and manipulation. "That's not what you just told Carol."

Earl stared at the television.

'Okay,' I thought, 'I see how this game is played.' I took a deep breath to steady myself. I did not want to react to his tactics and give him a reason to keep me away from Carol, but I couldn't let this go. Carol was hurting. I needed to focus on the medical issue at hand. I thought of Diane's comments earlier: 'patients, including their families, need your honesty as well as your compassion, and sometimes you need to be firm.'

I chose a caring but firm tone for what I needed to say next. "You need to make sure you are tracking her medication and her pain level. There is no reason she should be as uncomfortable as she is right now. If you can keep track of the amount of medicine and how often, while keeping track of her pain level, then I can report to the doctor any issues in case he wants to adjust the doses." I paused, moderating my tone further to soften the strong words I needed to say next. "The key is we don't want her to get behind the pain. If you can't give her the meds on time, we'll have to discuss other options for her care. I will have to recommend that she be placed in a facility so a nurse can administer her meds. There are laws that protect patients."

Earl continued to stare at the television, but a slight twitch at the corner of his mouth told me that he heard me and that he was at least a little bit scared. I was happy to see that. I was also glad to see that my assertion of authority was accepted. Diane was right: I had to present the truth in a compassionate but strong way to do my job right. I continued. "Also, have you been writing down what she has been eating throughout the day like we talked about last week?"

"No. Was I supposed to?" His tone was somehow simultaneously one of condescension and feigned innocence. He knew full well he was supposed to.

"Yes, please record it on the whiteboard I put on the fridge." I spoke as sweetly as possible through my gritted teeth.

I went back to the bedroom to examine Carol. Her blood pressure and pulse were a little high, but nothing to be too concerned about. Earl came in then and gave her a pain pill, but it would take a while to kick in. 'Earl better do what I told him and track her pain levels, medication, and food intake,' I thought. I was fuming, just as much as if Carol were my mother. I pondered that for a moment, in the silence of Carol's room where only her soft breath and mine filled the air. I would never have this experience with my mom–caring for her, sharing stories, hearing her wisdom. It was true that I was getting too close, I knew it. I would be devastated when Carol passed. But I was determined I would not lose my objectivity. I was certain I could manage this. As for the binders, well…

"Amelia, tell me how are your children doing? And how about that handsome husband of yours?"

Carol's questions jerked me from my reverie. I told Carol about Jake's and my date the week before. I chattered happily. She wanted all the details. "So we ended up having my dad sleep in our bed and we slept on the two couches in the living room."

"Oh how sweet," Carol said. "It was an almost perfect date."

"Almost perfect?!"

She winked.

"Oh, Carol Schultz, I'm surprised at you."

She shrugged with feigned innocence. "I don't know why. I have six children."

I laughed. "Was Earl a good dad?"

"Oh no. Earl wasn't my husband then. Bud. My husband Bud passed away a few years ago from advanced lung cancer. It came on so fast. We were together 45 years. My children really helped me through that rough period. I had some very serious heart problems during that time."

My eyes widened. "I'm sorry."

She sighed. "I think it was my broken heart from losing Bud. I still have my children and beautiful grandchildren. But I don't get to see them very often."

"Why not?"

"Oh, it just doesn't work out."

I was surprised. Her response was cryptic, especially given her usual openness. I decided to let it pass and change the subject. "How did you manage six kids, all so close in age? I'm exhausted with just two kids. I couldn't even imagine three times that."

"Oh, it was hard at times, but it was almost as if they had built-in friends. They would keep each other entertained when they were little. It was hard though because I wasn't working for many of those years and Bud worked two jobs so he was never home. And when he was home, he was usually drinking." A cloud of sadness washed over her face.

"That must have been hard."

Carol was quiet. It seemed she was lost in a memory somewhere.

Bud. I wondered if Bud would show up in the binders. I imagined he would.

We did not read from the binders on this visit. Carol was not strong enough. I did manage to get a scrambled egg and toast into her, and by the time I left she said her pain was better.

I said my goodbyes. As I walked to the car, the binder thumped against my hip as if to say, 'hey, I'm still here.' I had tried several times to slip it out and back on the shelf, but Carol was very alert and didn't want to get up. I couldn't return it… or get the next one. I felt incredibly guilty walking around with it in my bag, but I also couldn't imagine putting it back and not taking another one to read.

Somehow, someway, Carol's stories filled a hole deep inside me. I didn't know what else to do but to follow my heart. I was sure that if I asked Carol she would say yes to me borrowing the binders.

I could not wait to switch out the binders. Especially now, knowing there was a "Bud."

CHAPTER 12

MARIE

The kids were in bed, John was on a business trip, and all I wanted to do was curl up in my mom's lap and tell her everything. But that couldn't happen. It may never be again.

That thought brought a lump to my throat. I swallowed it down and picked up Mom's manuscript. As I thumbed through to the last page I had read, I was so proud of her. She was such a good writer. She had always wanted to publish her life's story. Instead, it was collected in a set of green binders. She had given copies to me and my siblings and kept the originals. I loved reading from them, especially now that I didn't get to see Mom very often. To me it was a glimpse into the lives of two of the people I loved most in the world.

I found the page where I had left off. I had already read them all at least three times–except one. That one I had only read once. This one was my favorite. It was about when Mom met Dad:

Whenever a call came in on IBM's switchboard for the Service Bureau, I transferred it to their office manager, Mr. Howland. If he wasn't at his desk, I would have to page him; otherwise I rarely looked in his direction. One day, even though the switchboard was busy, I noticed that a visitor had entered the building and walked toward the Service Bureau. A short time after that, the visitor and Mr. Howland came to my desk. "Yes?" I said, confirming the guest's presence. Mr. Howland gestured toward the taller man and stated with emphasis, "This is Mr. Howland, and I'm Bud!" He continued, "My father is the controller at Walker Manufacturing Company in Jackson."

I must have said something in acknowledgement, but I remember only that they went back to the Service Bureau area. In a befuddled blush, I turned back toward the switchboard.

A few days later, near closing time, Bud came to see me again. "Would you consider staying after work and helping me with a speech for school?" he asked. He went on to explain that he was attending Michigan State University part-time. "Okay," I found myself answering. Bud, though less than six feet tall, had a calm self-assured presence about him that people respected. I noticed that he was fairly handsome and wore his hair in a crew cut. He looked most business-like in his suit with an impeccable knot in his stylish narrow tie. Though his demeanor and his speech impressed me, I felt nothing more.

A week or so later, while I was having breakfast, Bud came into the restaurant and asked, "Do you mind if I sit with you?" I didn't and he slid into the booth, seating himself across from me. He proceeded to do most of the talking, mostly about himself. He was born on July 31, 1934, just as the Angelus was ringing, and was named by his paternal grandmother.

Though we both had grown up in Jackson, Michigan, it's doubtful that our paths would have crossed since Bud was a grade school student at Queen of the Miraculous Medal

I READ WHAT YOU WROTE

Catholic School on the opposite side of town. In his eighth-grade graduation picture, he was seated in the front row on the far left and looked like Beaver Cleaver. Right after Bud's graduation from Queen's, Walker transferred his father to Racine, Wisconsin. Bud and his older brother didn't want to move and begged their grandmother to house them, but their parents insisted on keeping the family intact. Bud graduated from St. Catherine's High School in Racine, having been a class officer two years in a row. His dad arranged a summer job for him at Walker's and one day he asked Bud if he planned to always carry a lunchbox to work. He explained that if he wanted to make money, he would need to get his degree.

Bud made a strong first impression and I found him charming, even fascinating. He told stories with enthusiasm and had a way of describing things that made the commonplace amusing and interesting. He laughed at himself; without taking himself too seriously, he exuded a love of life. His personality was nearly the opposite of mine.

On our first date we went to see the movie 'Pal Joey' starring his favorite singer, Frank Sinatra. Though I let him hold my hand, his was uncomfortably sweaty. Afterward, we went to an out-of-the-way bar where he taught me how to play bumper pool. Following that we sat at a small table and he ordered a beer for himself and a coke for me. I looked forward to weekend evenings with him, usually spent at a bar. We spent many months together with the same routine, and I loved it. After one of our dates, he took me to my apartment and wanted to stay the night because the Noren's were out of town. I was definitely not ready for a physical relationship and had been putting him off for a while. I *felt it was time to be honest with him, so I sat him down and told him about my teenage marriage and divorce. He didn't say much and stayed for a short time and then left. He didn't seem mad, or to my fear disgusted, but I was sure that would be the end of our relationship. To my amazement, he called me the next weekend and asked me to go to the movies with him.*

Bud and I had been dating for six months or so, when one night he said he wanted to take me to a movie in Jackson. "What's the name of the movie?" Though his response was vague, I didn't pursue the matter. We drove to Jackson, but Bud didn't turn off Michigan Avenue where the theaters were. Instead he drove on through town. After several miles, and since he had been so fuzzy about the movie, I asked, "Where are we going?"

He responded confidently, "To Angola to get married."

"Oh, no we're not!" At the time, a couple could go to Angola in Indiana and be married right away. But Bud ignored my protest and kept driving. "Please take me home!" I begged. A serious discussion ensued, and he reluctantly gave in, made a U-turn and drove back to Lansing in a deep, conspicuous silence. I had never seen him so infuriated. Though I was greatly attracted to Bud and his many wonderful qualities, marriage was furthest from my mind. Why couldn't we be satisfied with the status quo? For a few weeks after that Bud maintained a low profile and didn't approach me for a date.

Perhaps I should have refused when he asked me out again, but I didn't. We sometimes dated during the week, but we spent many weekends with our respective parents. Bud would drop me off at the farm on the way to visit his parents, then early Monday morning, the trip would be reversed and the two of us would

I READ WHAT YOU WROTE

ride to work together. Mother liked Bud and often treated him to a breakfast of pancakes and sausage. Afterward we shared our weekend experiences on the way to work. This seemed to work well enough, for a while.

Without my knowing it, Bud had dropped out of college, apparently in order to intensify his pursuit of me. For the time being, all of his spare time and energy seemed to be focused on me, and I reveled in every single minute of it. On the other hand, I began to feel smothered by his attentiveness. I was somewhat apprehensive. I tried to put my feelings into words one day: "I think we're spending far too much time together," I told him. "In fact, don't bother to pick me up next weekend. I'll drive to my parent's house by myself."

Bud was not to be rebuffed so easily. He came to my apartment the following Friday evening anyway. When I arrived from work, he was already there, leaning against his car with his arms and legs crossed. He followed me into the apartment and watched as I packed some things for the weekend, all the while begging me to ride with him. I left the apartment, put my belongings into my car and slid into the driver's seat. Bud tried to stop me by putting his hands on the car door. "This is ridiculous!" he exclaimed, with uncharacteristic anger. "We're both going in the same direction!" Without a word, I sped out of the driveway, literally leaving him in the dust.

In his dogged determination, Bud must have reacted quickly because he arrived at my parents' house well ahead of me. Perhaps not even bothering to knock, Bud burst into the house and without a single pleasantry, confronted Mother with, "Mrs. Allan, what's the matter with your daughter?" She was shocked by Bud's effrontery and not waiting for a response to his rhetorical question, he passionately exclaimed, "I love your daughter and I'm going to marry her!" With that, he whirled around and left with as much fervor as when he had entered. Meanwhile, I had driven in leisurely fashion to my parents' farm, even stopping for donuts on the way. Driving along at a moderate speed, I felt reasonably confident I had discouraged Bud's possessive behavior. Still, I felt uncomfortable thinking about how I had been the cause of his distress. He was becoming much too serious; I would miss him, but I would have to end our relationship.

I looked forward to seeing Mother, but when I entered the house, I was taken aback to see her so upset. With a stern look and serious voice, she said, "Carol, sit down. We need to talk." She explained that she was disconcerted by Bud's fury, unlike the person who had enjoyed her Monday morning pancakes. Then regaining her composure, she told me if I didn't love him, I must tell him right away. She said, "It's not fair of you to string him along." Now I was the one in shock. Bud never once said he loved me. I assured Mother I would tell him.

After that incident Bud avoided me, which was a good thing because I was reluctant to hurt his feelings. Several weeks passed without seeing one another, except at work. During that time I began to miss his companionship, and after a while I found myself hoping he would ask me out again. At the same time, I wondered whether I could handle it if he did. However, my resolve to keep my distance from him weakened, and when he did ask me out I accepted, promising myself to keep emotionally detached. When I couldn't, it came as a shock; that's when I realized that my *feelings for him ran much deeper than I thought. We began to date anew with greater intensity, by showing physical affection for one another.*

Up until that time, Bud had not revealed himself as the romantic type. His rare attempts at romance were as tentative as a man on a tightrope. After a date one night, we sat parked in the driveway of my apartment. With a shaky hand, he gave me a small brown paper bag and asked me to open it. Inside I found a small box. As I cautiously began to open it, he blurted out, "I love you!" Then in a serious voice full of anticipation, he asked me to marry him. Joyfully and in tears, I answered, "Oh, yes!" Then he placed the modest diamond engagement ring on my finger and we embraced.

Bud had been steadfast in his pursuit of marriage. It was as though he was on a mission to marry me, do or die! I knew we loved each other, but permission to be married in the church was denied. Somehow, I managed to convince myself that we might receive the church's blessing after the fact. Although the inability to be married by a priest didn't discourage my desire to become a Catholic, it may have dampened Bud's faith somewhat. Nevertheless, no one, not even the Catholic Church, could deny Bud what he wanted.

I put the manuscript back in my nightstand. That was Dad all right.

Tears welled up in my eyes. I missed them both so much.

Somehow it was easier to cope with Dad being gone than with Mom's situation. Dad was gone from this earth, but Mom had been taken away by a man we should have been able to trust.

CHAPTER 13

A M E L I A

On my next visit with Carol, I was greeted by a stack of bowls with dried orange colored residue beside her recliner. Anger arose in me as I imagined all the simple things Carol needed that the lazy, selfish man beside her would not do.

As if he knew I was thinking about him, he coughed. It sounded croupy. I made a mental note to use more hand sanitizer during this visit.

As if the state of the house wasn't bad enough, Carol was up and in her chair but she looked unkempt. Her pretty pink robe now had stains on it, her hair wasn't combed, and had a slight body odor. One thing at a time, I told myself. Before I began my examination, I moved the bowls to the kitchen. "So has Mary been coming to help out with any cleaning?"

Carol spoke up. "Oh yes. She's so good to us."

I wanted to ask when she had been there, but I knew Carol would not have a good answer to that with her short term memory issues. Since Earl had not chimed in, I decided to let it go.

I set the bowls down on the filthy counter, glancing at the fridge door to see if Earl had been writing in her food and meds. To my surprise, there were a few entries. It seemed that my firm but calm threat about calling elder services made an impact after all. 'So Earl responds to authority after all,' I thought. Good to know. "Well done, Earl, filling in the calendar with Carol's meds and meals. I will be sure my supervisor knows there has been progress."

"Yeah, I've been doing it," Earl said.

I returned to Carol, congratulating myself for implying that a higher authority than me was at play here. I checked her vitals. The smell exuding from her was almost as pungent as Earl's chair. It made me so sad to see that. I knew Carol was a proud and lovely woman and would never have wanted this.

Trying to sound as casual as possible, I said, "Carol, when you are not feeling very well, I know it can be hard to bathe properly. I can have an aide come and not only help with bathing but also do some light housework like doing your personal laundry and changing your sheets and the like. We want to make sure you are comfortable and clean, which will always make you feel better."

"Well, Mary helps with the laundry and things, so I think we are okay," she replied.

"I know you have her coming, and that is wonderful. She's only one person. She can't do it all. She can focus on taking care of Earl's things and the main housework, but an aide can focus just on you, Carol. How about I have one come over with me on my next visit and you can meet her, and she can tell you all of the options available to you, would that be okay?"

"Sure, that would be fine, I guess."

I listened for Earl to object. He did not. A small win, I thought. I couldn't control how much Mary did for them, and

I certainly could not help, nor did I want to with Earl's mess, but at least I could help make sure Carol was clean and comfortable.

After I asked Carol our routine questions, Earl said, "I'm going to go check the mail."

This had become his ritual when I was there, and I was glad of it.

He grunted as he struggled to move his body forward to the edge of the chair. Pushing up with both arms, he found his way to a standing position and lumbered to the door. It was painful to watch, but I couldn't look away. It was like being at a horror variety show.

After he left, Carol said, "Why don't you grab another green book and read it to me?"

This was my chance to put the other book back and get the sequel, and my heart began to beat faster. Unfortunately, Carol was watching me so I couldn't reach into my bag and take out the other one to put it back. My hand was shaking as I went into the bedroom and grabbed a couple of books. I thumbed through them, trying to identify the one that would continue the story of Ben and Carol. It was hard to read quickly enough to identify the one that I wanted. Afraid of taking too much time, I selected one and hoped that it was the right one. I came back to the living room, sat down, and began to read the first page. "The day was warm and sunny, and everyone was excited. Graduation day was here."

Carol interrupted. "No, let's look at another book."

My heart fell. This was it; I knew it was the one I wanted. But clearly Carol didn't want me to read it today.

I stood up and walked back to the shelf. I placed this edition

I READ WHAT YOU WROTE

on the top of the stack and grabbed another one. I returned to the chair and opened the book, reading to Carol about her new job at IBM. She was writing about her interview and about starting the new job. The story was interesting but not what I wanted to know about, not yet anyways. I read for about 15 minutes, but I knew I really needed to leave. "I think I better stop there. I have two new patients this week. If I don't leave soon, I'm afraid I'm going to fall behind for the rest of the day. But before I go, is there anything else you need?"

"Oh that's okay. Yes, before you leave, can you help me to the bathroom? I feel a little weak today."

"Of course." I helped her up and walked her to the bathroom adjoining her bedroom. It was the sweetest thing, walking beside her and guiding her. I felt a tenderness toward her that I had only ever felt toward my children. I helped her reach the toilet.

"I can take it from here," she said.

"Okay." I moved to the door. "I'll be right outside. Tell me when you're finished, and I'll help get you back to your chair."

As soon as she shut the door I went back to my bag. I quickly took out the green book and put it on the shelf. When I went to grab the one that I wanted, I managed to knock down a couple of the binders. Praying Carol didn't hear, I replaced the other binders on the shelf and slipped the one I wanted into my bag. In the few seconds it took to make the exchange, my hands were shaking and my heart was pounding. Like a kid taking cookies out of the cookie jar, I strained my ears, listening for Carol to ask what I was doing. I heard the weak voice of Carol. My heart leaped into my throat..

"I am done. Amelia, can you help me?"

Relief flooded through me. I quickly walked over to the bathroom door and opened it. I helped Carol walk back to her chair, put a blanket over her, turned up her TV, said good-bye. As I walked to the car, the thump thump thump of the green book against my hip was both exciting and comforting.

I hoped against hope that she had not noticed how nervous I was.

CHAPTER 14

MARIE

I was looking at some pictures I had just developed and saw some from a past holiday season. I was not sure which year. Maybe three years ago? We used to have so much fun being together as a family. All of us kids and all of the nieces and nephews played games, ate, and just enjoyed being together. But that all changed. There was a missing face in all of the pictures: Mom.

Thanksgiving had always been a huge celebration time for the family. Mom used to say besides Christmas, it was her favorite holiday. She had always made such beautiful dinners and us kids were so excited to have her down at Ann's for dinner.

I called Mom. "Hi, Mom. How are you today?" I held my breath. I was never sure what she was going to sound like when I called her. Sometimes she sounded good and other times she sounded horrible.

"Oh I am good, Marie, how are you?"

I was relieved. Today seemed to be a good day. "Good, I am so excited for tomorrow. I just finished making the pies."

"What's going on tomorrow?"

My heart sank. "It's Thanksgiving, Mom. Remember? I

told you I would be up in the morning to pick you up and bring you down for dinner. Everyone will be here and we can't wait to see you. Ann says that she knows her turkey won't be as good as yours always was but it should be good."

"Oh, I am sure it will be wonderful, but I can't come." She said it matter of factly with no emotion.

"What do you mean? Are you not feeling well?"

"No, I just can't leave Earl here during a holiday. I am going to stay here."

"But Mom, we always spend Thanksgiving together. We haven't seen you in so long. You don't have to stay long," I begged. "Just come for a quick dinner, I will make sure to bring you home early."

"No, Marie, I can't. It wouldn't be right."

I knew by now I shouldn't push her. I was so disappointed. She had been making excuses all the time lately to not see us, but to miss one of her favorite holidays with her kids was unbelievable. I was certain it would be all we talked about tomorrow. We were so worried.

I flipped through the stack of photos. Christmas was the same–everyone was there except Mom. I could see the tension in our smiles. It was like we had pasted them onto our faces so that we didn't make each other even sadder than we already were.

We had argued a little about the root cause of her pulling away. Was it her dementia or was she consciously making this decision?

I had replayed our conversation a million times. I found myself doing it again now.

"I can't believe Mom is choosing him over us," Scott spat. He plopped down on the couch next to me.

"She isn't...well, she is but if she was in her right mind, she wouldn't be," Therese retorted.

"Oh, come on. She knows. She just wants to be with him, and she won't listen to what any of us are saying."

I understood where Scott was coming from and how heartbreaking it was to think that of one's own mother. I had felt that way when this all started, but I knew now it wasn't her. It was the dementia. "Listen guys, I am not sure if it is the dementia or if she is making her choice, or maybe a little of both. My question is what are we going to do about it?"

Ann said, "William said he would be happy to go up there and make it look like an accident." She said it with a half-hearted laugh.

We knew Ann was just kidding, but it went to show how frustrated we all were.

Ever the big sister trying to keep us in line, Therese said, "Let's just keep doing what we are doing and take turns getting up there to keep our eyes on her the best we can."

We all agreed. It was a helpless, sad situation. We were all struggling with the fact that the mother we had known and loved was slipping through our fingers.

It wasn't as if we wanted to deny Mom happiness. We knew she was a beautiful woman. If she had found someone who made her happy, we were all for it. We struggled with Earl though. We knew he was manipulating her; taking advantage of her because she had money and a –things he had lost years ago by squandering his wife's money and then our grandmother's. And

Mom was letting him do it, even believing in him, because of her dementia.

After the new year, the four of us children who lived somewhat locally decided to make an unannounced visit together to see Mom. This time, thankfully, Earl wasn't there when we first arrived. We were able to enjoy a nice visit with Mom. She seemed truly happy to have us there. She seemed like her old self, asking questions about what was happening in our lives and the happenings of her grandkids. We were so excited to spend this precious time alone with Mom.

Unfortunately, about an hour into our visit Earl arrived at the house. We looked at each other, crestfallen. Our time alone with Mom was at an end. Earl was truly shocked to see all of us kids there with her.

No pleasantries were exchanged with him. We basically ignored him.

When we were about to leave, Earl said, "Hey Carol, did you talk with the kids about the trust?"

Scott immediately jumped in. "What about the trust?"

"I don't remember. What was I going to ask them?" Carol faltered.

Earl flopped down in Dad's chair. "Carol, remember we went to visit the financial planner and you wanted to take some money out, but he said he couldn't without Scott's approval since he is currently the Executor to the Trust."

Uh oh, here we go, I thought. I watched my siblings' faces for their reactions.

"Mom," Scott questioned, "what do you need? I can help you in any way."

I READ WHAT YOU WROTE

"Oh, we wanted to get something. Earl, what was it again?" Mom sounded so confused.

"You wanted to get the gutters cleaned and windows washed," Earl piped up.

"Mom, you have money in your savings account for things like that. I can write you the check from the account or you can too."

Earl's temper rose, "Remember Carol, there is no money in the account."

Scott, not holding back, said, "What do you mean there is no money in that account? You had thousands in there last time I looked. Let me see your checkbook."

Carol got up and searched for the checkbook. After a few scattered minutes, she found it and gave it to Scott. He opened the book and saw that it was from a completely different bank.

"Mom, where is the bank account book from the joint account we are on together?"

"Earl, where is that?" she asked, starting to get upset.

"Remember, you closed that account and moved your money to this account," Earl said shortly.

"Why would you do that, Mom?"

Confused and shaken, she said, "I don't know."

At this point, I looked at Scott, silently pleading for him to keep his cool. I didn't need to because he always had amazing patience with her. Scott walked over and knelt down in front of Mom and held her hands. "Mom, we set that up so I could help write your bills and things since you were having trouble paying bills."

Earl spat out, "I help her now. It is much easier for her."

"No offense Earl," Scott with complete restraint, "but you are not family. I am here to help her. That is how my dad set it up."

"What is done is done," Earl provoked. "Now about the trust. We need that money."

"Earl, I will help Mom. Mom, do you still want my help with this?"

Earl answered before she could, "Yes, Scott that is what she wants, right Carol?"

"Right," was all Mom said, never looking up.

"But Mom, the trust is in place to help with any healthcare needs you might have. Especially if your condition gets worse. That is what you told us you wanted."

"Oh, you are right, Scott. Let's keep it the way it is."

Relieved, Scott offered, "Mom, I can call and get someone in to do the gutters, painting, and whatever else you need."

My sisters and I wanted to jump in and add our comments, but we knew Scott was the one that had been set up to handle all of the money issues. He was acting very calm and professionally, so we let him handle it. Mom seemed very relieved that it was settled and asked if we could all sit down and have the dessert we brought. Earl never spoke with us again that day. He just opened up a magazine and stayed in the chair.

A week and a half later Scott received a certified letter from a lawyer, ordering him to sign the trust back over to Carol. Scott called a meeting with all of the kids on the phone. "Okay guys, this is what I received today. Unless you object, I am washing my hands of Mom's finances. I am not about to get into a pissing match with that man."

I said, "But Scott, I was with you when we sat with the lawyer a couple years ago to get this all set up. It is what Mom and Dad wanted. We can't let him control all of her finances. They are not even married. He will take everything."

"Marie, I understand, but he has his claws in her. I am not interested in fighting him."

It was devastating. We had lost our mom to this man. We had all agreed that the money didn't matter except for what she might need later for her care.

Scott went through the process over the next few days to relinquish his control. He was told it would take a couple weeks for it to all process. Though he felt like he was letting his father down, he felt he had no choice.

No more than two days later he received another certified letter. This time, the letter indicated that if he did not make the changes required by "Carol," he would be sued for elder abuse. This threw poor Scott. He was so appalled by the actions; how could his mother sue him? He quickly sent a certified letter to his mother, stating that the paperwork had already been put into place and that the change would be taking effect in the next week or so.

Scott talked to me soon after that. He was so upset, he didn't know if he could face her again. He loved her so much, but he couldn't believe what she was doing. Again, the internal struggle for Scott, as well as us other kids, was our mom's decision-making ability. We weren't sure if she was truly feeling this way or if the dementia was causing this complete betrayal. The mother we knew who always had such a strong relationship with her children; the mother who always enjoyed multiple weekly phone calls and visits from her children, had just abandoned us. Or so we felt.

CHAPTER 15

AMELIA

When I got home that evening, I realized right away that chaos had ensued in my absence. Olivia had gotten sick on the way home from school, throwing up in Jake's truck.

'Crap, not now,' I thought. The week was already crazy with work. The two new patients required a ton of new patient paperwork and extended visits. I felt bad for Olivia, but I was also feeling bad for myself. I had no time or energy for a sick child. And of course, more than likely JJ would get whatever this was, too.

Jake was stomping around the house trying to get ready for work, talking to himself about how impossible it all was, while checking on Olivia every five seconds. He was a mess.

It never ceased to amaze me that he rescued people for a living, but if one of his own kids was sick, or if I was sick, he could hardly keep it together.

At 10:30 that night, I finally got Olivia to sleep. I was hoping she was done getting sick. JJ was crazier than ever tonight. When he finally slowed down, he was so clingy. He wanted all of my attention when I was caring for Olivia, and I desperately tried to keep him away from her.

With an exhaustive evening and both kids finally down for

the night, I took a long hot shower and crawled into bed. Though I was physically exhausted, sleep didn't come. I dozed off for a short while and then woke up and checked on the kids. Thank God, they were both still asleep. Laying my hand on Olivia's forehead, I was happy to discover she didn't feel warm. Getting back into bed, a little after midnight, I was now totally wide awake. I decided to pull out the new green binder. I began to read from the beginning:

The day was warm and sunny, and everyone was excited. Graduation day was here! I looked at myself in the mirror and smiled broadly. Looking at the pretty young lady in the mirror's reflection, I saw a young woman whose life was just about to change. Soon I was going to be a married woman and would be looking for a job and hopefully beginning a family of my own. I knew I wanted several children but wanted to have a little time with Ben first.

Ben and I had decided that the day after graduation we were going to go into the city to see if we could find a place to rent. I was also going to begin the job search right away because Ben and I wanted to make sure we had all our plans figured out before we told our parents we were going to get married.

When I came out of my room, I saw my parents in the kitchen and they were chatting away and seemed so happy. When I walked in to join them, my father gave me a rare hug and he told me how proud he was of me graduating from school. This was a moment I would never forget because he was a man of few words and usually not very pleasant words at that. He was a very big and intimidating man and always quick to criticize. I didn't want that moment to end, and felt a pang of regret knowing that in just a few short days he would probably be very unhappy with me when I shared our plans with him.

Graduation was amazing and after I received my diploma, I hugged what seemed like everyone in my class and several of my teachers. Many of my teachers and faculty members were very kind to me during high school, probably because I made good grades and never got into trouble, except that one skip day that I had lived to regret. So many people asked me about my future plans but I was so sad I couldn't share my exciting future with anyone until we talked to my parents. I again felt the pang of guilt as Ben and his parents came over to shake hands with my parents and congratulate me.

As planned, the next day we went apartment hunting. We were so excited about finding our future home.

Ben asked, "Do you want to go grab some breakfast at Smith's Cafe before we start looking at apartments?"

"No, I am too excited to eat. Let's look first and then eat, if that is okay with you," I replied.

The anticipation of my new life was overwhelming, and I envisioned decorating the place and entertaining family and friends in our new home. Unfortunately, after viewing apartment after apartment, we realized everything was way more expensive than we thought. By the end of the day I was completely deflated. Ben already had a job lined up at the factory which would only pay the cost of rent and nothing else. Apparently, I would need to find a decent paying job as quickly as possible if this was going to work out. We just had to make this work out. This was my dream.

Finding a job was harder than I had thought as well, but

luckily after a few weeks I found a job as a receptionist in a doctor's office. The doctor was very nice. As it turned out, his wife had been one of my teachers in high school and she vouched for me, telling him how hard I worked at my studies and so he hired me.

With everything finally set up, it was now time to tell my parents. Ben had already told his parents, and they were fine with it. In fact, they didn't seem to care one way or another. I knew, however, it would be way different with my parents. Though my parents liked Ben well enough, I was afraid my father would flat out refuse the idea and that would be that. On Sunday evening after our family dinner, feeling nervous but happy to see that my father seemed to be in a good mood, Ben came over and we sat my parents down to tell them. Ben explained that we were in love and proceeded to tell them about all our plans. After Ben was done explaining everything, there was dead silence. It seemed like 30 minutes, though it truly was only a minute or two. Mother didn't say a word. As usual she sat and waited for her husband to speak first.

Dad stood up, said "Do what you want, but don't look to us for support, for anything," and then walked off.

Tears began streaming down my face. Why was I surprised? What did I think he would do? Congratulate us, give me a hug and his blessings?

Mother remained seated opposite us and said, "Don't worry, he will come around."

That was it. A week later, Ben and I were married.

I closed the book, shocked at the raw emotion in her words. Until now, it had never occurred to me that the elderly people I cared for had been young, truly young, thinking and feeling all the same things I had.

I looked at the clock. It was now past 1 am, and I needed to get some sleep. Sleep continued to elude me as I contemplated Carol's story. What happened to the marriage with Ben? Marriages back then didn't end unless it was something really serious. Maybe he had died in an accident, I thought. Really that was the best case scenario. I knew from talks with my grandmother that divorce was a horrible social stigma in Carol's day.

I hated to think that Carol's innocent dreams for life would end tragically in one way or another. She seemed so happy, but young and foolish too. I couldn't help but see the comparison between Carol's life and my own.

Was I also foolish by getting married so young?

Why had their marriage not lasted?

CHAPTER 16

AMELIA

The next evening, I tucked the little ones in bed. Thankfully it looked like JJ didn't get what his sister had. Olivia seemed way better, and Jake had told me that she slept most of the day which allowed him to sleep as well. He was wide awake, but I was exhausted.

Since Jake was staying up to watch some sort of sporting event, I decided to go to bed and read. I pulled out Carol's binder to read some more and hopefully get some insights into what happened to their marriage.

Jake came into the room and laid down with me. "What are you reading so intently?"

I slammed the book shut. I hadn't heard him come in, and I was embarrassed that I was reading a book that I took from a patient. Still, I had to be honest with him. "It is a book of stories written by one of my patients."

Jake didn't seem that interested and turned on the TV to continue watching the game.

About a half an hour later, he turned to me. "Are you still reading it? What is so interesting?"

"It's about Carol. She wrote about her life. You remember

me talking about her."

"Oh yeah, the one you're getting too close to."

"The one I'm getting close to. Not too close."

Jake made a face.

"I'm handling it just fine."

"So what's so interesting about her life?"

"Well, she got married right out of high school. She wrote about that and how it was because she had sex with this boy on prom night and felt that she and her boyfriend Ben had to get married."

"Ah, so she got pregnant," he surmised.

"No, actually she didn't. She just felt so guilty that they had sex before marriage, she thought the only way to make it right was to get married."

"That's dumb, everyone has sex before marriage."

"Not necessarily. This was the '50s, and people had morals back then," I said with a small chuckle. "But the thing is, they didn't stay married. She had her kids with another guy–Bud. And that's really unusual for back then. So I don't know what happened."

"Why in the world would she share a book about her personal life with you, her nurse? That is so weird."

I did not respond.

He gave me his famous side eye, as if to say, "Well?"

I knew I had to tell him or he would pester me forever. Besides, it would be good to share with him about it and my reasons. "She actually didn't give it to me. You see, she has several binders of her writings about her life. She shares different stories about her childhood with me from time to time when I visit her." I was watching his face for a reaction, but he now wore that famous first responder frozen expression so I could not tell what he was thinking. I rambled on, as if I was in an interrogation room, confessing. "And this one is about her first husband. I wanted to see what actually happened so I took it last time I was there so I could read the whole story." 'There, I said it,' I thought. I braced myself for his response.

"What? That's just wrong. Boy, I hope she doesn't catch you stealing her things. You could get fired! Amelia, seriously, you are getting too close to this woman."

"It's okay," I said, trying to act casual, "She wouldn't mind. She likes sharing her stories with me."

"You're way too close."

"I can handle it."

"Okay, I believe you."

"Thank you." I cuddled up next to Jake and started kissing his neck. Looking up at his face, I thought, I love him, and though we struggled from time to time, I knew we were pretty strong. I just didn't want the same fate as Carol and Ben, whatever that was.

Wanting to feel close to him and feeling scared about losing him, I initiated sex with Jake. He seemed surprised. It usually wasn't me doing that.

Afterward, I couldn't sleep. I laid there for a few minutes listening to Jake snore contentedly. I decided to open the book and continue to read:

I was so happy, my dreams were coming true. Ben was very sweet to me, my job was going well, and I had just prepared an amazing dinner from a new recipe. I hoped Ben would be so happy with me when he got home.

"Something sure smells amazing," Ben said while taking in a big whiff as he walked in the door. He then grabbed me and gave me a big kiss. "I have some exciting news. I signed up for the Marines today with Thomas!"

I sat there stunned and wondering if I had actually heard him correctly.

He continued "I leave for boot camp in less than 2 weeks!"
I couldn't speak.

He continued "I will be in North Carolina for 6 weeks and then, who knows?"

"What? I have a job here and so do you!"
" I know but I quit today."

"What!" I screamed, completely flabbergasted. "But I don't know if I want to go to North Carolina. My family and your family are here."

"Don't worry. You will stay here while I am at boot camp, then we will figure it out."

I couldn't move, the proverbial rug had just been ripped out from under me.

I closed the binder, shaken by Carol's writing. I would kill Jake if he did that to me! How could he do that to her, without even talking with her first. I was afraid to read any more. Was that why their marriage ended?

I thought of Carol often over the next few days, imagining how disappointed she must have felt after hearing that Ben joined the Marines without discussing it with her first. She had sounded so excited in the story about her new life with him and then in a flash it changed. I knew this happened many years ago and she had moved on, but I still felt like I wanted to give her a big hug when I saw her that week at her appointment.

To my relief, Carol was having a good day. While I was giving her an exam, I asked her about Bud and their kids. I desperately wanted to hear about the happiness in Carol's life especially after reading about her sadness about Ben. Plus, she only casually mentioned Bud before, so I was really interested in learning about him.

"Holidays were my favorite, especially when we lived in Indiana. My husband Bud had a big family and it seemed like whenever there was a major holiday, or even a 3-day weekend, some family members or another would show up. I wasn't sure at the time if they told Bud beforehand, but many times they showed up unannounced." Carol's face almost looked younger as she continued. "Thanksgiving was my favorite. I made the best turkey around. Well, at least that is what everyone told me."

She wrapped her arms around herself, almost as if she was cozying up with a soft blanket. "We used to play cards with his aunts, and his sisters, and their husbands. We would sit around our cramped little family room and tell stories and laugh. Many times Earl would bring out his guitar and Jane would sing along with the rest of us. Jane's kids and our kids always enjoyed playing together and sometimes they would join in singing as well. I sure miss those times."

At the sound of the name Earl, I had a moment of shock. Earl, certainly not the lump of a man currently sitting out in the living room. 'Weird,' I thought. 'It couldn't be the same guy.' But Earl wasn't a name I had heard many times in my life. I

I READ WHAT YOU WROTE

quickly brushed that thought away and continued to listen to Carol. She was explaining that she was so proud to create a real home for her immediate and extended family. She prided herself in a clean organized home, behaved children, and most importantly a family dinner.

I asked her, "Carol, how did you keep a clean house with six kids?"

She responded, "I had the kids help, too. Every Saturday morning, we all chipped in. The kids can learn responsibility by having chores. It also teaches them the importance of a clean home. You know, your little son can help now. He is four, right?"

"Yes, he is."

"Make a game of it and the children won't look at it as work. I also would put record albums on our stereo, and we would listen to music while we cleaned, and we danced. The kids would have fun too." Carol continued, "I would also have the kids help by setting the table and cleaning up after dinner. They also helped by serving when we had guests. I am so proud of my children. They all keep nice homes today; my sons can even cook for their families."

"Carol, do you get to see your kids a lot? Do they come to visit much?"

With a bit of sadness in her eyes and voice, she said, "Well, they are busy with their jobs and their own families, and whenever they want to come it isn't a good time. But they visit when they can and it works out."

The alarm on my phone went off. I had to leave and get back to the office for a meeting.

"I have to get going."

"Oh, so soon?"

"I'm sorry. I have a meeting." I hated to leave Carol on what seemed like a sad note, but I needed to get going. "Carol, you must be so proud of the family that you have built. I wish I had a mother like you," I said. I couldn't help it. For the first time, I gave Carol a hug.

She hugged me back. "Oh, sweetie. You don't know how much this means to me. I miss my kids so much. You are doing what I call a big small thing."

I pulled away and looked in her eyes. There were tears there. I smiled. "What's a big small thing?"

"She wiped away the tears. "It's a small thing that you do that has a big impact on someone. You coming here, loving on an old lady like me, it's a big small thing."

CHAPTER 17

AMELIA

Carol's words were resonating in my head on the way home. No one had ever talked to me about such things: how to take pride in one's home and find joy in being there for family.

When I walked in the door that evening, Jake was running out the door to work as usual. "Hey," I said.

He stopped with his hand on the doorknob. "Yeah?"

"Do you want to invite your parents over for dinner this l\ weekend?"

Jake said, "Really? We never have them over. I didn't think you really liked them."

"I do. I just think maybe I need to get to know them better."

His parents loved the idea. We made plans for Saturday night at our house. When I got home from work on Friday, I began to get ready for our dinner guests who would be arriving in 24 short hours. I had to think of a dinner I could cook easily but would taste good and that everyone would eat. I didn't want any battles at the dinner table with the kids, so our cuisine options were limited. I decided on spaghetti.

'First things first,' I thought. 'I have to get the house

cleaned.'

JJ and Olivia were playing with their building blocks. "Okay, JJ, we need to get our house ready for grandma and grandpa. Let's do this together." I thought about Carol doing this with six kids. Certainly, I could do it with two. I put on the radio and found a fun station. "JJ, can you be my special helper?"

"Yeah!!!" He jumped up.

"First, let me see your muscles."

JJ flexed his arm.

I gently squeezed. "Wow, you are a strong boy! You are perfect to be my special assistant."

"Me too, me too," cried Olivia.

I picked her up and felt her muscle that she was trying so hard to flex like her big brother.

"Me strong too mommy?"

"Yes, sweetheart, you are strong too," I said, hugging her.

I started with the guest bathroom. It was dirtier than I thought, but I had JJ help me by wiping down everything after I did. He was so funny. Olivia followed behind, dancing to the music and playing with anything and everything I moved to clean underneath. As she picked up an open bottle of shampoo and started shaking it, I said, "Hey Olivia, how about if you hand me things to put back that I ask for."

"Yeah, yeah, yeah!"

I grabbed the bottle of shampoo before she emptied it onto the floor in her enthusiasm. "Okay, but only the things I ask for. So not the shampoo yet."

"K." She clapped her hands.

"Hand me that orange bottle."

I READ WHAT YOU WROTE

Olivia handed me the orange bottle. "Orange," she said.

"Right! You know your colors."

"Everybody knows their colors," said a jealous JJ.

"Maybe," I said. "But not everybody knows how to clean with me as my special helper."

"M-hm," JJ said. "That's right."

Surprisingly, I got through dusting, sweeping, and mopping the floors in a pretty short time. By the time the kids were ready to go to bed, we were all exhausted, but I was happy and impressed with myself and my kids. It had been so much better to clean with them as a fun game instead of chasing them around and breaking up their arguments.

As I kissed JJ good night, he said, "Mommy, can I be your special helper tomorrow?"

"Yes, my sweet boy. You did a great job."

On Saturday morning, I laid in bed longer than usual. I was still there when Jake got home from work. The first thing he said was "Babe, the house looks and smells so good. What did you do?"

As if on cue, JJ came running in, "Daddy, did you see the house? I cleaned it all with mommy!"

"Me too, me too!" Olivia said, jumping up and down.

"Didn't we mommy?!" exclaimed JJ.

"Yes, you did, you guys helped me with everything."

Jake gave me a funny look and then scooped up both kids in his arms, throwing them on the bed. They all laid on the bed with me while getting smothered with kisses from their daddy. I wanted to stay in that bed with my little family all day. They were happy and healthy, and I realized how truly blessed I was.

'This is what I need to focus on,' I thought.

As the day progressed, the butterflies in my stomach seemed to multiply. It was spaghetti which I had made hundreds of times before. I didn't really know why I was so nervous. I just really wanted dinner to be perfect and Jake to be proud of me. Dinner was about done, and the house was still somewhat clean.

Jake came into the house from his second trip to the store, fetching yet another item I had forgotten to pick up yesterday on my grocery trip. "I got the parmesan and this too." He held a beautiful bouquet of flowers. Truth be told, they were a little wilty, but to me they were the most beautiful flowers. I couldn't remember the last time he bought me some.

"Oh Jake, they are beautiful."

"Not as beautiful as you are," he said. He grabbed me and gave me the biggest kiss. I wanted to melt. I loved him so much. "Babe, thanks for doing this," he said and then left the kitchen.

I quickly looked through all the cupboards. I didn't have a vase to put the flowers in, and I couldn't send Jake back to the store yet again. Besides, his parents would be here any minute. I found a jar that wasn't pretty nor quite tall enough, but it would have to do. I set the precious bouquet of yellow and pink tulips in the middle of our kitchen table. A few flowers bent over the side of the makeshift vase. I tried to position the greenery around the flowers to keep them in place as much as possible.

A knock on the door a short while later made me gasp. A quick panic came over me. 'Why in the world was I doing this?' I thought. I shook it off and went to the door to greet them.

The evening went well. Everyone seemed to enjoy dinner

and the kids talked with their grandparents almost the whole evening. After I finished putting away the leftovers and cleaned the kitchen, I went into the living room. The kids were asleep on the floor. JJ even had his Star Wars guy in his hand. He must have fallen asleep mid-play.

Jake smiled at me, grabbed my hand, and pulled me down onto his lap. He gave me a long, sweet kiss. "Let's get these kids off to sleep and I will take you to bed."

After another warm kiss, I got up. "I will take her if you can get JJ."

The kids didn't even move. They were so exhausted by their grandparents' visit. We crawled into bed and slowly began to explore one another. For the first time in a long time, Jake was completely focused on me. He told me to relax and enjoy myself. He was so tender and slow I couldn't even breathe. It was like it used to be, with loving kisses and a tender touch.

After we made love, Jake held me and asked, "Why did you decide after all of this time to have my parents over for dinner? I know they really enjoyed it."

"You know, I just thought it would be important for the kids to spend more time with them. We should do it again."

"Yes, we should. My mother even asked if they could come again soon when she hugged me goodbye. Babe, they really enjoyed themselves and so did the kids." He gently rubbed the side of my face.

I was so happy the dinner went so well and that Jake was pleased with their visit. I especially loved the passionate evening we shared after the kids went to bed. It was as if we were the only two people in the world, with no concerns about the kids, jobs and finances.

After a few more minutes, Jake fell fast asleep, but I was wide awake. For once, I was happy I couldn't sleep. I was so grateful for the little bits of advice that Carol had given me and without that I wouldn't have had such a great weekend with my family and the nice dinner with Jake's parents.

I decided to pick up and read more of Carol's writings. I wanted to find out what happened after Ben's big announcement of joining the military:

After the devastating announcement from Ben that he had joined the Marines, I couldn't even breathe. I couldn't believe the short months of marital bliss was coming to an end, I was so devastated, I didn't sleep that night. All I could do was think about all of my unanswered questions. My biggest concern was where I would live. I didn't have enough money to support the bills on my salary alone. Where would Ben end up? Would I like it or hate the new town he would be taking us to? I know I would miss him terribly; would he miss me? The next day I decided to confront Ben with all of my questions.

The next morning after we both had a cup of coffee, I tentatively started asking him all of the questions that had been running through my mind all night.

"My job is decent, but If I am going to make something of my life, I need to do this."

My biggest concern was where I was going to live but he had thought of that himself and made the decision, again without asking me.

"I have already spoken with my dad, and he said you can live with him and my mom."

I READ WHAT YOU WROTE

"What? I can't live with them! Your mom is mean and besides, their farm is another 20 minutes away from my job." I was yelling, and I jumped out of my seat.

"Carol, don't be so selfish. I am doing this for both of us."

"For us, for us, I don't want this. I like our life as it is, I love our home, don't you?" I was shaking. I wasn't being selfish. He was.

Clearly done with my list of questions, he simply stated, "I am going to my parents. You need to calm down and when you do, you will see that I have made the best decision for us. You shouldn't be overreacting like this." And with that, he walked out of the apartment, slamming the door behind him.

I sat there stunned. All I kept hearing was that HE made the best decision for us. Like I don't have a say in what is best for us. Isn't marriage a partnership where we make these big decisions together? And then for him to tell me that I was overreacting! I couldn't hold it in any longer, I just sat down and cried, hot angry tears.

After pacing the floor, ranting and raving and crying to myself, I decided to drive the 45 minutes west to visit my family. My mother gave me a big warm hug when I walked through the door. While enveloped in my mother's sweet embrace, I completely broke down.

"Mom, Ben is leaving!"

"What do you mean leaving?" Marilyn exclaimed from behind mother. I hadn't even seen that she was there. So, I sat down hard on the kitchen chair and told them everything that happened, and all that Ben had said to me.

Marilyn said, "Oh Carol, relax. He is going with Thomas.

Can't you see he is doing this for you? Don't be so dramatic," she said with so much condemnation.

"For me? But I don't want this! And because he is leaving. I can't afford our apartment, so he arranged for me to live with his parents, without even asking me! I don't like them, and I hate their home!"

"Calm down, Carol," said Marilyn, "Just live there until I graduate and then we can get a place together."

I couldn't even comprehend that now. All I could focus on was that the life I knew was changing, and not for the better. I knew it.

Just then, Thomas came through the door. Marilyn forgot about me and ran to greet him. Mother reached across the table and grabbed my hand, "It will be okay; everything will work out."

My mother, always the calming force, gave me a small smile, "You are strong, Carol, you will be fine."

Thomas came to the table and said hello to us. I always liked Thomas, ever since we met when we were freshmen in high school. He started telling us all about the impending boot camp and about all of the benefits the Marines had to offer.

"Carol is being dramatic, Thomas. She doesn't want Ben to go."

I wanted to smack my sister for saying that, especially in such a snotty tone. What did she know? She wasn't married yet, though they talked about getting married after she graduated. She hadn't built a home or had a job. She didn't have to worry about living with a crazy mother-in-law.

Feeling empty and frustrated, I got up. "I have to go, love

you Mother."

As I walked to the door to leave, Thomas came up to me and gave me a hug. "Carol, I know this seems hard right now, but you will see, it will all be for the best. Ben will see you after boot camp and then he will probably get stationed somewhere really great. Surely it has to be better than here."

The next few days were a blur. We moved my things into Ben's parent's home. All of the lovely home decorations were put into sad little boxes. My dishes, glasses and utensils were all packed away, not to be used for God knew how long. I unpacked my clothes in the small corner bedroom in what was going to be my little prison until Ben got stationed in his new city. I put our soft sheets with little flowers on the musty mattress and tried to make it as much of my own as I could. Ben and I spent our last few days together in that room.

As the days grew closer to his departure, he was getting more excited and I was becoming more miserable. Marilyn and I drove to the bus together with Thomas and Ben. Marilyn was crying when they left, but I felt more hurt and anger than sadness that I didn't even shed a tear. I wanted to show Marilyn I wasn't dramatic but as it turned out Marilyn sure was. Instead of going back to Ben's parent's home, I instead went to my parents.'

It was Sunday and I knew Mother would be making Sunday dinner. As I walked through the front door, I was overcome by the delicious smells of a home cooked meal made by the loving hands of my dear mother. She greeted me with a loving embrace as usual. "You are just in time to set the table before dinner."

I placed the old dinner wear on the table and it instantly made me feel at home. It certainly wasn't fancy. The silverware was worn and every other plate had a small chip or little imperfection on it. But to me, it was as special as the finest China.

"Will you go call Dad for dinner? He is out in the field," she asked.

Dad was so proud of their little farm. They had about 90 acres where he mainly grew field corn. There were a few cows, one horse and a dozen pigs. Dad loved being on the farm. It was something he always wanted and just in the last few years was able to obtain it. Ben's parents had more than three times what Dad had, but to him it was the grandest of all farms. I found him over by the pigs, tossing them morsels.

"Hey Dad, how are the pigs today?"

"What are you doing here?"

"Just here for dinner. I moved into Ben's parents' place."

"I heard." Dad pointed to a huge sow. See Little Betsy there? She is about to deliver. I am expecting a good farrow."

"That is really good, Dad. Mother says it is time for you to come in for dinner."

"Okay, I will be in as soon as I wash up." I didn't know if it was the years of outside plumbing, but he always washed up outside instead of using his bathroom to clean up.

We sat down to a meal of meatloaf, potatoes, green beans, and rolls. I thought it was nearly the best meal I had ever had. While washing dishes after dinner with Mother, she said to me, "You know Dad and I would let you stay here."

"Thank you Mother, but that would mean almost an hour and a half commute to and from work every day. I guess I must stay at the Smith farm." I placed the dish in my hand on the counter a little too forcefully.

"Careful, honey."

"Sorry." I was more careful with the next one. "Mother, I just don't like them. Betty is just so mean and strange, and George just gives me the creeps."

Mother, in her soft sweet way, said, "They are just very country. They love Ben, and they will take good care of you. Remember, it is just for a short period of time. Just help them where you can."

After I helped Mother clean up from dinner and had a cup of coffee with a slice of pie, I left to make my way to my new home. As I pulled Ben's old beat-up car into the long gravel drive, I saw Betty sitting on the front porch. A quick feeling of dread washed over me. I walked up the steps and said hello. Of course, all Betty did was grunt and hold her rifle tighter. She had always had it with her. I wondered if she slept with it.

I had become used to seeing Betty's faithful companion at her side, but the first time I was so frightened. I was expecting to be staring down the barrel of that old rusty gun at any moment. I asked Ben about it right away. "Ben, why does your mom have a gun?"

"Oh, she keeps it close by for protection."

I wanted to ask from what? Ben didn't say, and I didn't ask.

As I walked in, I saw George sitting in his chair listening to the radio. He didn't say hi or ask how his son was at his departure. I was surprised that they were not present when Ben *left on the bus, but I was glad for it.*

I had just reached the landing to the upstairs when George said, "While you are staying here, I expect you to help out around here. Oh, and no coming home late. You mustn't disturb us."

"Yes, sir." I said in a weak shaky voice. I proceeded up to my prison room.

I managed not to cry all day, but as I closed the squeaky bedroom door, the tears flowed. I knew I was stuck and would have to somehow make the best of it. As the weeks went by, I tried to get into some sort of a routine. I woke up early every day and prepared breakfast, cleaned the dishes and then rushed around to get ready for work. Dinner time was the same most nights. I arrived home in time to help Betty make the meals, and of course I always had to clean everything up myself. Most of my weekends I stayed at my parents house once I completed the ever-growing list of chores that Betty and George assigned to me.

One night after a rough day of work, I came home to complete chaos. I heard screams coming from Betty inside the home as I got close to the front door. With apprehension, I entered the house and saw that Betty had her trusty friend pointed directly at George. I stood there frozen for fear Betty would turn and shoot me.

"Betty, put the gun down," George yelled.

My sudden appearance must have struck Betty, because as soon as she saw me, she did as her husband said and gave him the rifle.

"You will only get this back when you behave," he said

condescendingly.
  Betty went running to her room.
  "Carol, make me something to eat, now!"
  Afraid to say or do anything else, I complied.

  That next Saturday morning as I was getting my stuff together to go visit my family, George told me that he needed help in the barn immediately. I hadn't seen Betty since Tuesday evening when I came home to find her holding the gun on George. Apparently, she had just stayed in her room all week. Though I wanted to leave, I was too afraid to upset George, so I followed him. I was dressed nicely for my visit to my parents' house, not dressed to go into that dirty barn, but I went anyway.

  I followed George to the barn, dodging mud puddles that had formed from the heavy rain we had the night before. The day was already getting warm and sticky even though it was just past 9am. I figured the ground would dry out by noon at this rate. I had to swat a couple of big horse flies away as I walked towards the big red barn, anxious to get done with whatever chore he had in mind for me.

  George started mumbling something about the importance of taking care of animals or something as we walked into the barn. I couldn't really hear him because he was a good 10 steps ahead of me and the cows were mooing loudly next to the barn.

  "They need to not only be fed, but need to be cared for," he was saying as he took a brush and began brushing one of the large sheep that was in the barn. "You see Carol, they respond to nurturing, you must show the animal that you care for them, that you will take care of them."

I became increasingly uncomfortable as he was stroking the animal, thinking it seemed almost erotic. "Animals are like people. They need attention. They need the comfort of touch." He then turned to me and asked, "Do you take care of my son that way? Do you rub him to show him how much you care?"

I wanted to run but my feet wouldn't move. I was literally frozen in the spot where I stood. I thought, 'did he actually just ask me something that appalling?'

He continued to stroke the animal, very slowly. Before I could blink, he pulled down his filthy trousers and invaded the animal.

I didn't know if I would throw up or faint, but now my legs didn't fail me. I ran, ran as fast as I could out of the barn, into the house, grabbed my keys, and then to my car and drove off. About a mile down the road, I pulled over to the side because I couldn't trust myself to drive any further. I was shaking so badly; I couldn't even hold the steering wheel. What kind of man was he? Is this why Betty held a rifle all of the time? Did I see him actually do that? After a few very deep breaths, I calmed down enough to finish the drive to my parents' house. In my haste, I had left my overnight bag back at the farm, but I knew I could never go back there.

CHAPTER 18

A M E L I A

I slammed the book shut and looked up. "Oh my God."

Jake awoke at the sound of alarm in my voice. "What?!"

"No, everything's fine, Jake. Go back to sleep."

Jake looked drowsily at me then down at the book. "Oh, you're invading Carol's privacy again."

I gave him a withering glare. "Would you stop? You're never going to believe this. You know how I told you about Carol being married to Ben but then she had her kids with Bud?"

Jake flopped back down on his back. "I'm waiting with bated breath."

"Well, I don't know everything that happened yet, but I just read the part where Carol had to go live with Ben's parents and his father just invited Carol into the barn and then he, uh, violated a sheep right in front of her."

Jake rose onto his elbow. "What? What kind of people are these patients of yours?"

"It's not Carol! It was this father-in-law."

"I thought that was just stories that people told. You know, "Such-and-such a place, where men are men and sheep are scared.""

"Apparently it really happens."

Jake laid back down. "People are so disgusting."

I smirked. "So why have we dedicated our whole lives to helping them?"

"Because not all of them are disgusting."

Within a few minutes, Jake was back to sleep. It was now three o'clock in the morning, but I didn't care. I couldn't stop now:

At my parents, I tried really hard to act normal. I could never tell them what happened. In fact, I didn't even think those words could pass my lips. With borrowed clothes from Marilyn, that night I laid in my bed in my old bedroom and tried to figure out what to do. The walls had family photos sprinkled throughout the room and I felt safe laying on my old bed with the softest bed sheets. I couldn't go back to Ben's parents house, but I didn't know what to tell him. Certainly, he didn't know that his father did that! I would just have to deal with the long commute; it was far better than spending one more night in that nut house.

After very little sleep that night I woke to a thought. Could I leave Betty there alone with that crazy man? Maybe he had just lost his mind and that is why Betty had held a gun on him. Had he tried to hurt her? Ben would definitely want me to make sure his mother was okay. With my stomach in knots, I made the decision that I had to go back, at least to make sure she was safe. Though it scared me to even think about going back there, I just knew I had to. I also needed my clothes and things because I would need them for work.

When I walked into the Smith Family house, I was hit with the smell of some sort of burnt food. Betty was in the kitchen

I READ WHAT YOU WROTE

attempting to make dinner as if all was fine. George was in his chair listening to the radio as usual. I went to the kitchen and helped Betty.

"Hi, Betty. Is everything okay?" I asked tentatively.

"Yes, I just burnt the rolls," she said defensively. "Get the table set. The food will be done in just a few minutes."

"Oh, okay, um, I am not really hungry though. I ate at my parents house."

"Well, we need to eat so set the table!" she hissed.

I quickly grabbed two plates, knives, forks and napkins and quickly placed them on the table at their seats.

"All done," I said. "I will come out from my room in a little while to help clean up."

Betty grunted in acknowledgement and I walked quickly past George, trying to be invisible.

"How are your parents?" he asked, sweet as pie, as if our last interaction in the barn never happened.

"They are fine, thank you." I rapidly escaped the living room.

I hardly slept at all that whole week as I awaited the day that Ben would return.

Finally, the day I had been waiting for was here. Ben was due today from bootcamp. I climbed out of bed with a skip in my step. I was so excited to see him. I still wasn't sure if I was going to tell him what occurred with his father. I wanted to enjoy the time with my husband. That was my priority and besides, would he even believe me?

I was there at the bus terminal, anxiously awaiting the love of my life. Marilyn was there too in a beautiful dress. Her hair was perfect. I suddenly felt self-conscious. Should I have worn my best dress too? And when did she get that dress? I wondered. I knew she wasn't working, so I figured our parents must have given her the money for it. The same old jealous feelings came over me. I never got nice dresses like that from Mother and Dad. I always had to work for anything I wanted.

Before I could think any more about it the bus pulled up. There he was, dressed in uniform, his hair short and clean cut. Boy, was he handsome. All of my worries drained from me as I ran up and hugged and kissed my Marine.

I was anxious to get somewhere to be alone with my husband, but he insisted on going home to his parent's house. After several hours of boot camp stories, it was time for his parents to go to bed, which left us finally alone. That night was magical. Our love making took me away from that musty home and nasty people. Ben said he missed me so much and told me over and over how happy he was to see me. I was never so relieved. He was home and soon we could leave this place and begin our life together again.

"When do you find out where you will be stationed?" I spoke with excitement in my voice.

"I will be told by the end of the week. I sure hope it is in Memphis. Most people get stationed there."

"Is that where Thomas will go too?"

"No. He is going into another specialty so probably not." I was disappointed. I envisioned Thomas and Ben being together so Marilyn and I could get housing right next to one other.

That Friday, when I returned home from work, Ben came up to me, lifted me off the ground and swung me around.

"Carol, I just got word, I am going to Memphis, I got stationed where I wanted. I leave next weekend!" he exclaimed, practically jumping up and down like a child.

I returned his hug earnestly. I was so happy for him, but I was even more excited to be leaving this miserable house. In my typical fashion, I began to pepper him with questions: "Do we get an apartment or a small house? I wonder if I can get a job on base?"

Ben said, "Wait, you aren't coming with me, at least not right away. I will go first and get set up. You stay here and keep your job, so we have enough money coming in."

Feeling like I got punched in the gut, I blurted out, "What do you mean I stay here? I can't stay here!"

"Of course, you can. You keep helping my parents. You will join me soon enough."

"When?" I pleaded.

"I don't know, maybe a couple of months."

"A couple months! Why?" At this point I was yelling.

"I told you, I need to get settled. You stay here and we will be together soon enough."

At that point I wanted to grab Betty's gun. *Are you kidding me?* I thought. *How could I possibly stay with these maniacs for a couple more months, let alone one more day. After the other night and all his talk about missing me, why wouldn't he want me with him now?* As mad as I was, I knew there was no changing his mind. Trying to control my tears, I resigned to the thought that maybe he would get down there and realize how much he missed me and would send for me sooner. I hoped so with all my heart.

With as much strength as I could muster, I tried to enjoy my short few days with him. His parents seemed to be different people when he was around. His mom cooked and never asked me for help even though I did, and she didn't even hold the gun most of the time. George kept his distance and mainly tried to spend time in the field with Ben when we were there. I tried to keep us away from their home as much as possible: going to the show, taking walks in the park and visiting with Marilyn and Thomas. Though when they were with us all Thomas and Bed did was talk about the Marines. Thomas had been assigned to the Carolinas and he too was going without Marilyn for a short time until her graduation, and then they would be getting married. I thought maybe they all do that. Maybe the Marine Corp wanted them to get established before sending for their families. I slowly got resigned to the fact that maybe it wasn't that Ben didn't want me there. Maybe it was just the way it had to be.

The days flew by and soon it was time for him to leave. This goodbye, I couldn't hold back the tears of sadness for him leaving or more like fear of living with his family alone and for who knew how long. As if a light switch went off, returning to the farm, I was met with Betty sitting on the porch holding her gun and yelling to whom or what, I didn't know. I cautiously climbed the steps of the porch, trying so hard to be invisible. Betty didn't even seem to notice me. Closing the door behind me, I came face to face with George.

He said, "Get the dishes done, get the washing done and clean up this place. Betty isn't feeling well, and you have to start pulling your weight around here if you want to still live here!"

I went to work right away cleaning the house, not saying a word. I figured if I stayed busy inside the home, I could avoid George because he spent most of his time outside.

Days turned into weeks of my new schedule. After work I would cook, clean, and go to my room, sometimes writing to Ben. The letters from him were weekly, as well and they were short and basically said the same thing. He was enjoying his time and getting to know and become friends with a couple of the guys there. Training was hard but he said he was getting better and better with the work. He enjoyed his time off playing pool with the guys and exploring Tennessee. Not once in his letters did he answer my persistent question of when I could come and join him. He also never said when he would come to Michigan on any day off.

Marilyn was in her final year of high school and Thomas would come home to see her as often as he could. He officially proposed to her and they began their wedding preparations, even though it would be several months before she graduated. She was so excited planning their wedding. Marilyn was happier than I had ever seen her. She was glowing.

"Guess what? I am leaving right after we get married to join Thomas in North Carolina."

"But I thought we were going to get a place together in town?"

"Are you kidding me? I am going to be married and Thomas wants me with him."

My heart sank for what felt like the hundredth time over the last several months.

That was it. I was going to have to demand Ben have me come down now. I couldn't be here any longer. That night I wrote to Ben and told him I would be coming next month come hell or high water. I couldn't get the letter to the post office fast enough. Finally, a week later Ben's letter arrived. He said he missed me and wanted nothing more than for me to be with him, but they would be going on a training exercise in a week and wasn't sure when he would be back. He promised me that as soon as he did, we would make plans for me to come down. Though disappointed, I was relieved by his words that he wanted me there and we would be making plans soon.

About a month later with still no plans made, I was making dinner with Betty and George came crashing through the door.

"Carol, come out to the barn. I need your help...now!"

I was still dressed in my nice work clothes and told him, "I have to change. I am not dressed properly to help you in the barn."

"Out here now!"

I swore under my breath, if my clothes got ruined, he would pay for them. I quickly put on my old boots as Betty headed for her bedroom. I went to the barn to see what help he needed.

"What do you need?" I said as I carefully walked into the dark, smelly barn.

"Up here in the hay loft. I need your help. Hurry," demanded George.

I clenched the green binder. "No, no, no!" I whispered. I glanced over at Jake, hoping I had been quiet enough not to wake him.

I READ WHAT YOU WROTE

I couldn't keep silent. I couldn't believe she was following George up there! I thought about all the horror movies I'd seen. And then I realized that Carol, at that time, had never seen any such thing. She was completely innocent.

I returned to the book:

I reluctantly climbed the rickety old ladder. He was over in the far end. I couldn't really see him as the overhead single light was not on and it had gotten dark outside. Wanting to get this over with and away from him as soon as possible, I climbed through the small piles of hay, trying not to lose my footing.

As I got closer to him, I saw that his pants were off. Just as I turned to run, he grabbed me by my hair and literally pulled me back. I fell hard right on the back of my head; I saw stars and lost my breath. I tried to scream but because I couldn't breathe no sound came out. In a split second he was on top of me, his hand covering my mouth. I struggled as hard as I could, I started trying to kick him, but he had my legs pinned down by his fat sweaty legs. I was overwhelmed with the smell of sweat, alcohol, and cow manure. I thought I would vomit. I had one arm free because one of his hands was holding my other arm down and his other was covering my mouth. I tried to reach for the shovel that was laying on the ground somewhat near me, but it was too far from my reach.

Opening my mouth, I was able to bite his hand which caused him to lean back, giving me a moment to catch my breath and try to twist my body to get away. Suddenly I felt his hand slap me hard across the face. I fell back, my head and ears ringing. I screamed but was again muffled by his now bleeding hand. The taste of his blood was sickening.

"Stop it. It will be far worse if you fight me, you know you want this. My son is not here, and he doesn't want you. He left you for me."

That hurt more than the slap. Was this true? I brushed that thought aside. No, he wrote to me and told me he wanted me to come. I could feel the arousal of George. He was relentless as he seemed to be even stronger now, holding me down while pulling up my skirt and tearing away my panties. He pried my legs apart with his and entered me with such force I felt I would split in two. He was saying something to me, but I couldn't hear him. Why was this happening? With every thrust my mind detached further and further from my body. Finally, I felt his weight leave me. I was covered in sweat...and him.

In a weak state, I turned my head and threw up. I slowly got up. I wanted to kill him, I wanted to grab the shovel and strike him but I couldn't, all my strength was gone. There was no fight left in me.

He appeared behind me, dressed, and he grabbed me by the hair again and spat, "If you say a word of this, Betty will shoot you."

I didn't say a word and he let go of my hair. My legs were shaking so badly. As I tried to get up, my arms gave out and I fell. After a few moments I tried to get up again. This time I was successful in standing, but I almost fell walking across the loft tripping over the straw piles and going down the ladder. Suddenly afraid of Betty, I tried to straighten what was left of my good clothes and my hair. I stumbled into the house. Betty was nowhere to be found, and I had no idea where George had gone. Going directly to my room, I grabbed as much of my *clothes and things and put them into my suitcase and any bag I could find. Trying to get as much of my stuff as I could carry, I grabbed my keys and left.*

Luckily I didn't see either of them as I left and drove out of the gravel driveway for the last time. I knew one thing for sure, not even Ben could get me to come near this place again.

I must have been in shock because the next thing I knew I was driving up my parents' driveway. I had no idea or recollection of the drive. I sat there for a few minutes trying to come up with a good reason for coming mid-week to their home and in such disarray. I knew I couldn't tell Dad. He would kill George, and what would that mean for Mother and Dad? Deciding not to lug in all of my stuff right away, for fear I would be asked too many questions, I just grabbed my purse and my keys.

Mother was sitting at the kitchen table having a cup of decaf coffee. "Mother, I came to talk, where is Dad?"

"He went to bed early. He was really tired. Why are you here so late? Is everything alright? You look like you have gone through a tornado! What happened?"

At the sight of her, I tried to hold back the tears, "No Mother, everything is not alright. I need to get to Tennessee to Ben. I can't be at his parent's house for one more minute!"

Mother knew this wasn't just a wave of missing Ben. She knew something had to have happened, but she didn't push me to talk, she knew I would in my own time. "What can I do?" she simply asked.

"I need your help. Can I stay here for a couple nights?"

"Of course, this will always be your home," Mother said

tenderly.

"Thank you."

"Honey, what's wrong? You're scaring me."

"I will fill you in, but right now I just need a shower and to go to bed."

The next morning, I woke up disoriented, not knowing where I was. All of the horrendous memories of the night before came flooding back to me suddenly. I slowly got up and went to the bathroom. I was so sore that I could barely walk. Looking in the mirror, I saw a red, slightly bruised cheek. Mother must have seen this last night. Maybe that was why she didn't push me to talk further.

"Well hello, Carol," Dad said as I walked out of my room. "Your mother said you were here. What happened to your face?"

"Hi, Dad. I ran into a door. I am okay. I just wanted to visit."

"Well, be more careful next time. Your work is not going to want you around looking like that." He walked out the back door to the field.

I had forgotten all about work. I would need to leave right away. I was already going to be late. I decided to call off sick, for the first time ever. I didn't feel guilty though. I was sick–sick of my life and my situation. I went to the kitchen and sat down at the table with my mother and a hot cup of coffee.

"Mother, something really bad happened last night." I began to tell Mother about everything that had been happening at Ben's parents house for the last several months. I had to speak between sobs. I told her all the details of the night before.

"Oh my God, Carol, why didn't you come here sooner?" Mother was visibly shaken.

I READ WHAT YOU WROTE

"Don't tell Dad. I am afraid of what he will do." Seeing how scared I was, Mother promised she wouldn't tell Dad and we began to plan how we would get me down to Ben in Tennessee.

I quit my job a couple of days later and collected my last paycheck. With Mother's help, I purchased a bus ticket for Tennessee. I stood with my mother at the bus station, hugging her so tightly, trying to gain as much strength from her as I could.

Though she was never one to give advice, Mother said, "Carol, you are a special person. Don't ever let anyone hurt you. Stay strong and remember, you are loved."

With tears in my eyes, I got on the bus and turned to wave goodbye to her. I had never really seen Mother cry before and was surprised and sad at the sight of my weeping mother on the platform. Though it was a warm spring day, I sat down on the bus seat and was shivering. I felt chilled to the bone. I rummaged in the bag at my feet to find my sweater, pulled it on and hugged myself tightly. I couldn't stop shaking. I knew I should be excited because I would finally be seeing Ben, but oddly enough that wasn't the case. Maybe I was afraid that he would not be happy to see me, maybe mad in fact, because I was coming without warning. Most likely because I didn't know how he would react when I told him what his father did to me. There was a part of me that was afraid he wouldn't believe me. That thought made me shake even more.

Having very little sleep over the last several days, I was able to doze off for a short while about halfway through the trip. I was awoken by the squeaky brakes of the bus stopping at a station. The driver announced a short break, giving the driver and passengers a chance to use the facilities and stretch their legs. I slowly got up, my legs aching from the cramped seat, and left to go to the gas station where an attached café beckoned. I hadn't realized how hungry I was. I hadn't eaten that entire day. Early that morning at my parents' house, I was so anxious about packing and getting things together, I never ate breakfast. I also hadn't opened the little sack of provisions Mother graciously packed for me.

Upon entering the little cafe, I was overwhelmed with the tantalizing smell of fried food, and my mouth began to water. Though I was cautious about spending any of my savings, I purchased a small sandwich and devoured it. Soon I began to feel better. I retreated to the bus after using the facilities and settled back in my seat. I desperately needed more sleep, so I tried to push thoughts of my impending meeting with Ben away. With a full belly, I was able to fall asleep again.

Again I awoke to the loud squeaking of the brakes. I opened my eyes just as the driver stated that we had arrived in Memphis. It had been three hours though it seemed like five minutes. I departed the bus carrying my small bag and waited for the driver to unload my worldly possessions, or at least the only ones I could carry in one medium-sized suitcase.

Never having been in the state of Tennessee, let alone this city, I was frightened about finding my way to Ben's apartment. I had the address, and it was on base for goodness sake, so in my head I knew that any local should know where it was. I used the pocket money Mother gave me for a cab and the driver said it wasn't too far. I tried to sit back and relax though every muscle in my body was tense. I hadn't quite worked through how or when I would tell Ben about what happened, but I had to have an

I READ WHAT YOU WROTE

explanation for my unannounced arrival. The driver pulled up to the base where we were stopped by the guard. He asked who I was and what my business was there. I didn't even think that I would have a problem getting on base. I quickly explained that I was there to see my husband. I provided my license, and he waved us through.

By the time the cab pulled up in front of his apartment building my stomach was in huge knots. I got out of the cab and looked up at the Grove Apartment complex, my new home. The stone facade of the building was definitely dated and I could see that many of the doors had paint peeling off of them and were in need of repair. The so-called flower beds between the sidewalk and the building were mostly dirt but had a few half-dead plants sprinkled about. I didn't care though. To me it was my sanctuary; it was the place I could be with my husband.

I walked up to apartment number 218 while holding my breath and knocked on the faded blue door. There was no answer. I tentatively knocked again. He must be out, I realized. It was just about 6pm so I figured he was either still at work or had come home and gone back out with his friends for dinner or something. I realized that I might have to wait for hours, so I sat down on the ground next to my bags and leaned against the rough beige stucco wall.

The butterflies in my stomach had pretty much settled down after waiting for about 45 minutes on the cold hard concrete. I was getting hungry so I took a few bites from the uneaten bags of snacks Mother packed. About 15 minutes later I heard footsteps coming up the stairs. 'Could this be him?' I wondered as my stomach lurched and threatened to reject the food I had just eaten.

As I stood up, I saw him coming up the stairs. My heart was in my throat. As soon as he saw me, he ran up to hug me. To my relief, he truly seemed happy to see me, I was so relieved.

"What are you doing here?" His face was beaming with a huge smile.

"I just had to see you, I have missed you so much," I professed urgently.

"I just got back yesterday. Why didn't you tell me you were coming?"

Not knowing exactly what to say, I just said again, "I missed you, I had to see you." He picked up my bag and brought me inside. I couldn't take my eyes off him. He was so handsome. He was wearing a uniform, not the one he had on when he left me at the station in Michigan. This one was all a light khaki with short sleeves which allowed me to see his larger biceps pulling at the hem. He looked bigger and yet smaller at the same time. Gone was the stomach that I never thought was full, but now was trim and accentuated by the belt on his pants. He clearly had gotten in great shape, trimmed down yet larger in his chest and arms. As much as I hated that he had joined the Marines, it sure looked like it was good for him. In all of the time I had known him, I never had seen him look so good, so happy.

"I told you I would send for you. I just got back yesterday. We would have made plans. Are you okay? You look...tired." He seemed a bit concerned.

I immediately felt self-conscious. I must look like a mess from the long trip. Fear crept into me, and I wondered if he could see *deeper inside me. Could he see what I had gone through?*

"Are you cold? Can I get you some coffee or a drink?"

"Coffee would be wonderful. If it is okay, I would like to freshen up. It has been a long trip," I desperately looked around for the bathroom.

Noticing my search, he said, "The bathroom is down the hall on the right. I will make you coffee and you can get cleaned up and we'll go out. I am supposed to meet the guys for a beer and a sandwich. I would love you to come and meet the gang." He was clearly excited.

Though it was the last thing in the world I wanted to do, I didn't want to disappoint him so I would go. I walked down the hall and opened the door to a small bathroom. The room was dimly lit and painted all white. Originally it had been gray, I was sure, but it had faded with time. There was a pedestal sink that contained scratches and a rusty ring around the drain. The floor consisted of a very worn light blue tile with many cracks and chips and globs of grout around the toilet from obvious repairs. The mirror over the sink was hung a little crooked.

Its reflection looked even worse. I frowned at myself, turning my head this way and that to see if the bruise showed. It didn't. I took a few deep breaths, washed my face, reapplied my make up and brushed my hair. I began to feel like I looked a little better, on the outside at least, and changed into a pair of light tan pants with a pink sweater. This would have to do. Taking a few more breaths, I emerged from the bathroom.

He smiled at me and came over and kissed me softly, putting some of my fears to rest.

We went to a local pub and I was introduced to several of his fellow Marines. They were all very nice to me. I was relieved to hear that apparently Ben talked about me all of the time. I could see the true bond there was among Ben and his friends as they laughed and joked with each other. Never having traveled to the South before, I sat and marveled at the slow, country twang in some of their voices. It sounded so different from the folks back home. I was enamored with the manners of these southern men. Every fifteen minutes or so a different marine would say, "Would you like another drink, ma'am?"

Feeling the exhaustion creeping up on me as the time wore on, I sat on my stool, sipping my beer. They were all so busy telling stories and laughing, I didn't have to talk too much which was a great relief to me.

The butterflies that seemed to have set up camp in my stomach started getting active again as we drove home. I knew he would want to have sex with me, and I didn't know if I could be intimate with him. The minute we walked into the door, he immediately grabbed and kissed me.

"It has been so long. I want to take you to bed now," he said with much urgency.

I smelt the beer on his breath which made me feel sick to my stomach. It was a reminder of his father. I wanted to be close to him, but how could I make love to him after all that has happened?

As we moved to the bed, I just closed my eyes tight, hoping it would go fast. I knew he was a little drunk, so maybe he wouldn't notice how uncomfortable I was. Luckily, he really didn't seem to notice; he was ready and there wasn't any way to stop him. Within seconds he was on top of me and was kissing me hard, and I couldn't keep the memory of his father out of my mind. I closed my eyes as tight as I could and grabbed the bed covers so hard, I was afraid I would break my hands. Fortunately, it was over very fast, and he noticed I had tears in my eyes.

"Did I hurt you?" he asked with true concern.

His tenderness made me want to cry harder.

"No, I am just so glad to see you." I tried to smile at him.

"Me too," he said, kissing me gently on the mouth. He promptly rolled over and fell asleep.

I laid next to him for a long time, unable to sleep. I couldn't shake the memories of the rape from my mind. I had lost all nerve to tell him what had happened. I wanted happiness and hadn't felt that in a long while. I couldn't ruin our time, not now.

To my relief, Ben was busy over the next several days. He got home late from work every night and was completely exhausted from the day so he was too tired for sex. We watched tv on his uncomfortable, well-worn couch. I didn't mind because we were together. We would then lay in bed together with his arms wrapped around me, never having to talk about anything too important. On a few occasions he would ask about his parents, and I would say they were fine and then I would change the subject by asking him about his day or his friends.

During the day I would busy myself around the apartment, cleaning things that I assumed he hadn't touched since he moved in. The entire place was in need of painting and the furniture provided in the furnished apartment was terribly worn. There were no pictures hanging on the walls and it was in desperate need of decorating. The kitchen was small and had bluish green painted cabinets that looked like the doors would fall off if they were shut a little too hard. There was barely any food in the refrigerator and cupboards and no cleaning products except one bottle of bleach. I began to compile a list of items I would need to pick up from the store.

The weather was nice so I decided to walk to the grocery store that was about a mile down the main road to get the items from my list. Everyone I came in contact with on my adventure was very friendly which made me feel more comfortable. I decided to take daily walks after cleaning or doing laundry in order to get fresh air. During my second week there while I was out walking, I picked up the local newspaper and sat on a bench. Looking at the help wanted pages, I began to review the job openings. I found a receptionist position available at one of the offices on base. That was exactly what I needed–a job to distract me and a little extra pocket money would be great too. When Ben got home that evening, I talked with him about the job, and he thought it was a great idea. The next day I dressed in my nicest business clothes and went job hunting.

That night I met Ben at the door and announced I was now employed. Feeling so happy with myself, I had stopped by the little store and purchased the ingredients I would need to make a home-cooked meal for Ben. We had been eating just sandwiches or soup practically every night since I had arrived, so tonight I wanted to make something special. I made meatloaf, mashed potatoes, green beans, and rolls with butter, the meal my mother always made. I had purchased an apple pie at the store for dessert along with a bottle of wine. I had found a light pink table cloth to place over the round formica kitchen table and even lit a candle.

I READ WHAT YOU WROTE

He seemed genuinely proud of me and was grateful for the home-cooked meal. That night we made love again, and again I struggled through it, hoping that the trauma would soon pass. Ben told me he had to go out again for another two weeks for training. Though I would miss him being there, I was secretly glad so I could avoid having sex with him. During those two weeks, I started my job and rather enjoyed it. The work was not too difficult, and I picked up the nuances of the position. I liked my boss and made friends with a couple co-workers while having lunch breaks with them.

A couple of weeks later, Ben woke me up by kissing me goodbye as he left for work. I got up and began getting ready for work myself. I had been very tired lately but attributed it to being so busy with my new full-time job. All of the sudden I broke out into a cold sweat and an extreme wave of nausea came over me. I had to run to the bathroom and throw up. Oh no, I thought, I can't be sick, I just started my new job and couldn't take any time off. Surprisingly though, after I washed my face, I felt better. Grateful, for the relief, I contributed my episode to my stomach not agreeing with the dinner I ate last night.

My head was laying on my folded arms across the toilet seat after another bout of throwing up. It was a few days later, so it couldn't have been what I ate. Doing a quick calculation in my head I realized my period was at least a month late. I was so busy that I hadn't realized that I had never gotten my period. Now the reality hit me like a ton of bricks. I could be pregnant! I was scared but was also late for work. With not too much time to be able to contemplate my potential pregnancy, I

171

got cleaned up and ready for work.

A couple of days later I was laying on the hard examination table at the doctor's office. There had been no denying it so I had asked one of my favorite colleagues for a recommendation for a doctor. The next thing I knew, I was being told that not only was I pregnant, but I was at least eight weeks along. Doing the math in my head, I started to panic. If I was that far along, it could be my father-in-law's baby, not Ben's. I began to hyperventilate right there in front of the doctor. He told me to put my head between my knees and take deep breaths. He chuckled and said that a lot of new mother's reacted this way and not to worry. I would be just fine. He had no idea the real reason I was alarmed. I didn't know what to do. I hadn't told Ben about what happened with his father. I just couldn't ruin the happiness we had over the last few weeks!

I managed to keep my nerves at bay that evening by telling Ben that I wasn't feeling well and went to bed early. I just couldn't face him, especially not knowing how to handle the situation. The next day was Saturday, and we were supposed to go out with his friends and some of their wives. This caused more of an immediate issue; I couldn't drink so I had to tell him, but how? After a sleepless night, I decided I would just have to tell him.

I sat Ben down. "I have something to tell you, but I'm not sure how to say it."

"Just tell me. What is wrong? I can tell by the look on your face it is something bad."

Taking a deep breath, "No, it isn't bad, well not necessarily, but..."

I READ WHAT YOU WROTE

"But what, just spit it out." Patience was not his strong suit, and I wasn't making it easy on him.

I blurted it out without thinking another second, "I'm pregnant."

He immediately jumped up from the couch and grabbed me and gave me a big hug. He didn't hesitate for a second. "Oh, my goodness, that is amazing! We are going to have a baby, a baby!" He peppered me with questions. "How are you feeling? Are you okay? When will the baby be here?"

"Um, well," I hesitated, I hadn't been prepared to answer that question, "Um, I think around the holidays."

"Oh, that is wonderful. Is it a boy or a girl?"

"I don't know," I stammered.

"Well, of course we don't know for sure, but what do you think? I hope it's a boy."

I hadn't even thought he would be happy about a child. I was all set to tell him about what happened, but how could I now?

He was so excited. "I know we don't have a lot of money, but we could get a bigger place, one with 2 bedrooms, one for the baby. You can still work through your pregnancy, and we can save as much money as possible before the baby is born; we will be okay." Convincing himself, more than me. "I am doing well here and due for a pay increase at the end of the year." The questions continued, "How far along are you, what did the doctor say?"

He was talking so fast I couldn't think. "Um, I think I am about 5 or 6 weeks." I wasn't sure why I lied. I was so anxious with all of his questions. I was so afraid. I couldn't count the weeks correctly.

"When is your doctor appointment? I want to go with you and make sure everything is alright."

My heart sank, but I quickly said, "I just went yesterday so I don't have to go again for another month or so. Everything is fine."

We decided not to tell our friends that night. I told him it was just too early. The next day, while he was out, I laid in bed not feeling well, trying to rationalize my lie. If he knew it was his father's he would be devastated. If the baby came out looking like his dad, no one would be the wiser. And anyways, what good could come from telling him. I also could tell him I wasn't feeling well to avoid sex, which was still difficult since the rape. The next couple of days went by and he was so happy, he couldn't talk about anything else. On the other hand, I was more and more upset. I really wanted a family with him, but not this way. I also worried that I wouldn't be able to love the baby growing inside me knowing it was most likely his father's.

I turned the page, only to find that it was the end. "Oh shoot!"

Jake grumbled in his sleep and turned over.

I winced. I certainly did not want to wake him up again. Glancing at the clock, I winced again. It was 4am. The kids would be up in three hours.

Sighing, I set the binder down and turned off the light.

CHAPTER 19

A M E L I A

I was so anxious to get to Carol's house, my final visit of the day. I had been thinking all week about what I had read from her binder. I couldn't believe she was pregnant with George's child, and I couldn't wait to find out what happened. I wracked my brain all day to try and figure out how I could get the next one so I could read more. I also couldn't wait to tell Carol about the nice family dinner we had with Jake's parents. I would never have thought to do it if it wasn't for sweet Carol's ideas.

Carol greeted me at the door, dressed in a pretty yellow top and white slacks. It was a good start, but her hair wasn't brushed and her pale face possessed no color from makeup. Still, it was an improvement from last week. It was good to see her up and about.

I so wanted to be able to be alone with her, but Earl was wedged in his chair and it didn't look like he was going to move. I had always felt like he was looking at me sideways whenever I was there. Today was no different. I ignored the feeling and said cheerily, "Hi, Earl." I waved then turned my focus to Carol. "How are you feeling? You look pretty today."

"I am doing okay. It is so nice to see you as always."

Her smiling eyes warmed my heart.

"Let me take a look at your vitals, okay?" I went about taking her blood pressure and other measurements when I was interrupted by the grunt from Earl in the chair to my left.

"Well, I am going to go check the mail," Earl mumbled. As if on cue, he tried to get up from his chair, falling backward as his thick arms gave out. I instinctively reached out to help him but he waved me away and pushed himself up again, this time successfully. Both Carol and I watched him wobble out the door.

"Well now," I said with a sigh of relief. "Is there anything you need Carol?"

"No, no, I'm fine. How is it going with you Amelia?"

"Good, and I actually have to thank you."

"For what?" She got excited and clapped her hands together.

"Well, you had mentioned to me that you had extended family over to your home all of the time and it got me thinking. I hadn't ever had Jake's family over for anything formal. I mean, they have come over from time to time in the past to see the kids, but I never actually invited them over for something special. So I decided to have them over for dinner this past weekend."

"That is wonderful! How did it go?"

"It was great! They really seemed to have a marvelous time, and you know what? So did the kids! What made me the happiest was that Jake was thrilled that I had suggested it. He was so grateful after they left."

"I am so happy for you," she said, beaming.

"I would never have thought about it had it not been for your advice. I love visiting you, Carol. You give me such good advice when I am here." I reached out and held her hands in mine. The

I READ WHAT YOU WROTE

warmth that overcame me took my breath away. She had the softest, most fragile hands, and it touched my heart.

She gave my hands a squeeze. "Ask my kids. I am always giving advice." She chuckled. "Whether they ask for it or not."

After we read together from the binder she had chosen last week, I said, "Well, I better get going soon. Oh, before I go I just want to take a quick glance at the list where Earl writes down your medication. Do you know where that is?"

She looked around quizzically and then finally, "Oh, yes, it is in my bedroom, by my bed, I think, or at least somewhere in there. I remember he had it earlier today when he gave me a pill before I took my nap." She began to get up, when I said, "I'll get it." I realized this was my chance to put the binder back and try and get the other one, if I could be stealthy enough. I tried to think quickly and not look shifty. I picked up my bag and said, "I will go in and take a look at it, but I will leave it in there so Earl will know where it is when he comes back. It should only take me a couple minutes, okay?"

To my relief she said, "Sure, go on in. I will just wait for you out here."

I walked in and looked around, finding the sheet of paper with her medicine log on the desk next to the bookshelf. 'Boy, was I lucky,' I thought. I grabbed the binder from my bag. Taking one binder at a time, I tried to flip through quickly to see which one I needed to read next. I felt like a covert spy, but honestly my intrigue was stronger than my fear over taking another binder. Finally, the third one I flipped through was the one I was looking for. I stuck it in my bag. I took a few seconds to review the medicine log and saw that he was keeping track pretty well.

I walked out, saying, "I found it and all looks good. I better get going if you don't need anything else." I felt hurried. I wanted to get the contraband out of the house as soon as possible.

"I am good." She stood and gave me a quick hug. "It's so good seeing you as always, Amelia."

I squeezed her frail shoulders and walked out the door, swallowing the lump in my throat.

That evening after the kids fell asleep, I curled up on the couch, put a blanket over me and began to read from the new binder:

One night I was awoken by extreme abdominal pain, pain I hadn't ever felt before, and I just knew something was wrong. I went to the bathroom thinking I was going to throw up, but instead I felt a huge gush coming down my legs. It was blood. I yelled for Ben. He rushed in and saw me on the floor. There was blood everywhere. I was sobbing uncontrollably and in horrible pain and he held me, crying himself. After a while he cleaned me up, gave me new pajamas and carried me back to bed. We both knew I must have lost the baby. I bled lightly the rest of the night, and the following morning he took me to the doctors. It was confirmed, I had lost the baby. Ben was devastated. I took the next 2 days off work to rest. As I laid in bed, I was a mess. I was so conflicted. On one hand I was so sad to lose the precious baby that was a part of me, but I secretly was relieved to not be carrying my father-in-law's baby. I didn't grow up in a religious family, but I knew it was wrong to be partially relieved by the loss of a life.

I READ WHAT YOU WROTE

Was God punishing me? Did he blame me for the rape somehow? The other huge fear I had was that I wouldn't be able to ever have Ben's baby, though the doctor said I should be able to in time. The more time I spent lying in bed, the worse I felt, and continued to cry all day long. By the time Ben came home, I was completely exhausted. He saw me crying and kept trying to soothe me, but the sadness was different for me. He had no idea of the inner turmoil I was feeling. For the next couple of weeks, I was in a fog. I went to work, came home, made dinner, and sat listening to Ben talk about his day without truly listening.

As the following weekend approached, he told me he had made plans for us to go out with friends on Friday night. "You have been moping around here for weeks, I understand why, but Carol, you need to work on getting over it. My commander's wife lost a baby at first, but now they have two perfect children. We will have others. You just need to move on." He wasn't being unfeeling. He was just really trying to help me, but he couldn't. He had no idea of the demons running around inside my head. I felt like I was in a deep dark hole and couldn't see a way out.

I begged him to go without me. As much as I needed comfort, I really just wanted to be left alone in my own misery. "I would really like to go but I am just so tired. Work was really busy this week and my head is killing me. You are right, I will be fine, and I know you have been very patient with me, and I appreciate it, I really do. Just go without me tonight," I pleaded. "I will bounce back, I promise."

"Okay, but seriously Carol, getting out will help you. Maybe tomorrow we can go out for a nice lunch or dinner, promise me?"

Realizing I had won, I said, "Okay, that would be nice."

When Ben got home that night he came to bed and began to kiss me. My back was turned to him, and he laid closely and rubbed my back and kissed my neck. He was getting aroused, I could feel it, but it made me sick. Without thinking of how he felt, I pushed him away and said, "I can't, I am not healed yet. The doctor said to wait a few weeks."

"It has been a few weeks. Come on Carol, I need you and you need me. It will make you feel better, too," he said.

"No, it won't. Stop it!" I blurted a little too harshly.

I felt him turn away then with a huge sigh. "Carol, you have to get over this."

Ben basically ignored me the next day, never once mentioning the idea he had of going out for lunch or dinner. Sunday was the exact same, he completely ignored me. Though I hated that I hurt him, I was grateful because instead of feeling better, I was actually feeling worse.

Sunday night Ben called to me, "Carol, you have a phone call."

"Hello?"

It was Marilyn, "Ben said you were having a rough time. What is going on?"

I tried to hold it together. Why was she calling? I hadn't heard the phone ring. Marilyn said that Ben had called her to see if she could help me feel better and get back to my normal self.

From the next door, Ben said, "Talk to your sister. I am running out to meet the guys."

When the door shut, I began telling Marilyn about the

pregnancy and the miscarriage. Marilyn sounded sad and worried for me.

"*Carol, how about I come down for a visit? I can take a day off of work and come for a long weekend. Does that sound good?*"

I wasn't sure I was up for a visit from her but at least it would be a buffer between me and Ben. The day was set. Marilyn would be down in a week.

As the days went by the distance between Ben and I became further and further apart. After a couple more failed attempts of intimacy, he seemed to just give up. He never went to bed when I did, and he began spending more and more evenings out with his buddies. It also seemed to me that he came home more and more drunk as the days went by. He also stopped eating at home, which was fine with me because the last thing I felt like doing was cooking. My appetite had vanished and I couldn't remember the last time I actually ate a full meal.

Marilyn arrived a week later. She was shocked by the looks of me. "You are too thin, and you look ragged!"

That was the first thing she said as she hugged me when she got off the bus. Leave it to Marilyn to know just what to say to make me feel even worse. After we got home, I showed her around our small little home that once gave me immense happiness, and now seemed dark and depressing. When Ben came home from work that evening, he and Marilyn couldn't stop talking to each other. I managed to throw together a chicken casserole, a salad, and rolls. I sat quietly in my seat barely eating while they chatted away about Thomas, the Marines, and happenings back in Michigan. It wasn't until Ben asked me about dessert that I was even acknowledged. I had forgotten about dessert, which was rare for me because sweets were my favorite. I managed to scrounge up some cookies and placed them on the table with a fresh pot of coffee. Luckily after dinner Marilyn said she was tired, so I set her up on the couch to sleep. Ben quickly suggested that she sleep in with me and he would take the couch, which Marilyn thought was the most gallant gesture. I knew the real reason was because Ben didn't want to sleep with me.

The next day Ben was off with his buddies. They were going to go fishing and then grab dinner and some drinks. He wanted to give Marilyn and me some time alone so that she could get me back to normal, I assumed.

The minute Ben left, Marilyn turned to me and said, "You look horrible, and you are acting like a zombie. I know you are sad you lost the baby, but you will have other children. It has been almost two months. You have to stop acting like this and pull yourself together. Your husband won't even want to touch you, let alone try for another kid when you are like this."

"You have no idea what it is like losing a child! You have no idea what I am going through," I said, biting back.

"Then tell me," she begged, "Ben said you don't talk to him, he said you don't even let him touch you."

I wanted to scream. How dare they talk behind my back! "Stop Marilyn, you have no idea what is going on!"

"You keep saying that, so why don't you tell me what I don't have any idea about and maybe I can help." This time there was true compassion in her voice. She walked over and put her arms around me.

I couldn't keep it together any longer. Tears streamed down my face. "I can't, I can't explain it to you. I know it is all my fault." *I cried and started to shake.*

"What do you mean, all your fault? Your fault for losing the baby? That is impossible!"

"No, no you don't get it. It is all my fault, and I can't handle anything," *I sobbed.*

"Tell me what is your fault."

Without even thinking of the ramifications, I started telling Marilyn everything. I told her about Ben's parents, his crazy mother with the shotgun and what I witnessed his dad doing to that poor animal in the barn. I then told her about the rape, coming down here and not telling Ben about why I was there and what had happened. Words were just flowing out of my mouth, I was talking so fast through the sobs, I couldn't even register the look on Marilyn's face, nor any words that came out of her mouth, if there were any. I told her how I found out how far along I was and that it was most likely George's baby, not Ben's. Explaining to her that I was going to tell Ben everything when I found out I was pregnant, but he was so excited, I just couldn't.

By the time I was done telling her, I put my head in my hands and sobbed even harder. Marilyn sat there, in shock, not sure what to say. After a long pause, she said, "Oh Carol, I am so sorry, I had no idea what you have been going through. You shouldn't have stayed with those crazy people! Do Mother and Dad know?"

"Mother does. She is the one who helped me get the bus ticket to come down here, but Dad doesn't. I was too afraid of what he would do if he found out."

Marilyn took my hands and gently said, "I am so sorry, I can't imagine how horrible this is for you. Honestly, though, I think you need to tell Ben. He has a right to know what his father did to you and it would help explain to him why you are acting like you are. He loves you. He will be shocked of course, but I bet he knows how crazy his dad is. Give him a chance to comfort you. It will be alright."

"How can I tell him? What if he doesn't believe me? What if he thinks I am to blame for the rape? You know how it is, the person that is raped is always looked down on by society, and somehow blamed for it happening. I don't even think I can actually say the words to him! He will hate me."

"Look Carol, I can see why that scares you, but he is your husband. He knows you would never do anything to provoke his father to do that to you. Give him a chance honey. He loves you." She hugged me so tight, and I tried to calm down and stop crying. "Okay, let's get you together. Come on, go take a shower and get some makeup on for goodness sake and let's go out tonight. And Carol, you need to tell him. He is your husband. You will find the right time and way."

As usual, I listened to Marilyn and took a shower and got dressed. I actually felt a little better. I think it helped just being able to actually share with another person these horrible secrets and feelings I had been keeping to myself all of this time. On one hand I was completely drained, but on another a little lighter by getting the weight of the secret somewhat off my shoulders. I got dressed and put on a little make-up. I looked considerably better. My clothes were quite loose on me, and my eyes looked a little sunken in and had small bags under them, but I still looked *better than I had over the last several weeks.*

By the time I came out of the bedroom, Ben was home and was talking with Marilyn. A quick rush of fear came over me when he turned and looked at me. Did Marilyn tell him?

Ben turned to look at me. He smiled. "Hi, you look better. Marilyn said we must take her out tonight and show her the town. I will be ready to go in a flash."

With that I let out the breath I didn't know I was holding.

I looked at Marilyn when Ben shut the bedroom door.

Marilyn said, "All will be okay. You will see."

Marilyn's quick visit was coming to an end, and we never spoke about what happened for the rest of the visit. Though I loved her so much, I was relieved to see her go and take my secret with her.

After coming home from taking Marilyn to the bus, Ben came into the bedroom with me when I went in to get ready for bed.

"I am so glad you enjoyed your visit with Marilyn. It looks like she helped get you back on track." He came up behind me and put his arm around me and started to kiss my neck.

"No, please don't, I can't yet." I begged.

"Great, I thought you were better, what a waste! I am going out." He practically spat the words as he walked out and slammed the door behind him.

The next week was more of the same. I wanted to be back to my old self, especially after Marilyn's visit, but just couldn't. I fell right back to where I was before. Ben came home one evening and said, "You need to get a couple of days off of work. We are heading home for a few days."

"What, to Michigan?" I was puzzled and shocked.

"Yes, I have some time off and I haven't seen my parents for a long time. We need to go visit them."

My heart sank. I could never go back to his parents' house, ever again.

"I can't. I don't think I can get time off, maybe in a few months." I tried to remain as calm as possible.

"No, we are going next week. They will let you off knowing I have a break. We are going and that is that."

I started to panic. What could I do? They let spouses have time off to coincide with the Marines. I didn't argue, I didn't say a word. I just had to figure out how I could get out of this.

A couple of days later when I got home from work, Ben was there packing for our trip. "I bought our bus tickets. We need this break and enjoy some fresh air on the farm."

Without even thinking, I blurted out, "I can't go!"

"Carol, we have been through this. We are going. You can even go see your parents. Seeing them may make you feel better."

"I can't!" I stomped my foot like a child.

"What do you mean you can't?" He turned to me, dumbfounded.

"Ben, I can't. I can't go back there," I choked as I sat down hard on the bed, defeated.

"To your parents' house, why?"

"No, to your parents," I said, my voice barely a whisper.

"Why on earth not?"

And just like that the tears I didn't think I had left started flowing. Without thinking, I told him everything. I started by telling him about the rape; how his father made me go out to the barn to help him and he blindsided me and forced himself on me. I told him about the animal, all of it. The words just came flowing out of my mouth and I couldn't stop them.

When I was done, he just sat there. His face was as red as a fire truck but he didn't say a word. He stood up and turned away for a moment, then he turned back and slapped me across the face. "You bitch! How could you do that? How could you do that to me?"

"I didn't do anything! I–"

He yelled back, "Didn't do anything, anything? How could you do that to me? And to my mother! You whore!"

"Ben, it wasn't my fault! He raped me!" I pleaded for him to believe me.

"You asked for it! I know it. My father would never do that. You lived in our house, ate our food and then seduced my father. How dare you, you slut!"

"But Ben, I didn't!"

"You did. I want you out. I want a divorce!" His face was all scrunched up and his eyes were black. To me he looked possessed and it really scared me.

I needed him to understand! "But Ben, no, it wasn't my fault, and the baby..."

He cut me off again, "The baby, Oh God, was it his?"

"I don't know, maybe, I don't know." I was sobbing at this point. I started to lose hope. I couldn't get through to him. He wouldn't listen.

"You have been sitting in this house mourning your bastard, how dare you! I tried to take care of you, and this whole time you have been deceiving me!" He walked out to the kitchen. I heard glass breaking. I was shaking but I went out to the kitchen. He was breaking glass after glass, dish after dish.

"Ben stop, if you would just listen to me."

"No, you get your stuff, and you leave. Go back to where you came from!" He threw a bus ticket at me. "You go, I will stay here. Get out!"

I got up from the chair. I was afraid my legs would collapse under me. I was shaking so hard as I went back to the room and grabbed my small suitcase. Once again, I was putting my personal belongings in the same bag to leave as my life was falling apart.

When would I ever be happy again? When could I unpack this bag for good? I went back out to the kitchen, he was gone. The ticket lay on the counter. What should I do? Should I stay and wait for him to cool down? Maybe he would come back and listen to me. I tried to hold on to hope.

I knew it wasn't true. I knew that wouldn't happen. He didn't even for a second believe me, let alone be willing to talk to me. And he struck me. He never, ever laid a hand on me and now he did, just like his father had. How dare he.

My mother's words came back to me—'don't let anyone mistreat you.'

I had to go, I just knew it was all over now, so I left with my bag and ticket.

I walked over two miles to the bus stop. Though my ticket was for another day and time, they allowed me to change my ticket for one leaving in a few hours. I sat in the station. I was completely numb. He didn't believe me. My life was over. With too much time on my hands waiting for the bus, I kept running different scenarios in my head. Why did I tell him? I should have tried better to get over the loss of the baby. I didn't have to let him know. I am sure his father would never have told him.

His father. That is why I had to tell him. I couldn't go back to that farm, to those people, as if nothing had happened.

As I was waiting, a small part of me began to hope he would walk through the bus station door. Every time I heard people talking or the door opening, I quickly turned my head in hopes of seeing my marine walking through the door. He never came. And really, I couldn't go back to him even if he did. Not after what he had done in his reaction.

I boarded the bus and went back to my parents in Michigan.

CHAPTER 20

AMELIA

I couldn't shake the heartache I felt for Carol. How horrific. It was Monday morning and time to get up, but I was not quite ready. I couldn't imagine going through what she did with Ben's dad and then to go down to be with Ben and have him treat her like that. It was deplorable. I wished I could see Ben myself so I could give him a good slap across the face!

I was more amazed than ever that Carol was as sweet and loving as she was after going through something so terrible as a young adult.

An hour or so later, I was headed to my car after dropping off my precious cargo at daycare when my phone rang. I looked at the number on my phone and didn't recognize it. For a split second I thought it could be a sales call and debated on not answering, but decided to answer it after all. "Hello?"

"This is Lynn, the dispatcher from Fire Station 19 from Leesburg. Is this Mrs. Bardon?"

Hesitating, I confirmed.

"I am calling to let you know Jake was injured in a building fire this morning. Jake has been taken by ambulance to St. Francis Hospital in Leesburg. You are listed as his wife and emergency contact."

I wasn't sure I heard correctly, so I asked, "A fire? Jake Bardon?"

"Yes," confirmed the dispatcher.

Shock washed over me. My mind turned numb. I managed to breathe out the words, "What happened? How is he? Where is he again?" I couldn't stop asking questions long enough to hear the answers.

"He was taken to St. Francis Hospital on 34th Ave in Leesburg. That is all I can tell you except that he is in stable condition."

'If he is stable, then he is alive, thank God,' I thought. I thanked the voice on the other end of the phone. I needed to get all the way across Leesburg as quickly as I could.

I looked at the dashboard clock. It read 8:50am. My mind was racing. I struggled to think of what I needed to do. I called work to let them know what happened to Jake and that I would need someone to cover my patient visits today and told my boss I would update her later today.

I knew it was going to take a good thirty minutes in morning traffic to get to St. Francis Hospital. As I began to drive to Leesburg, our last conversation played in my head. Jake had said there was not much happening at the station lately and they were cleaning out old storage closets just to have something to do. Now this.

Every minute seemed like an eternity and every car was like a roadblock. When I reached the ER of St. Francis, it was 9:27am. I rushed to the desk. "I am Jake Bardon's wife. He's the firefighter that was injured. Can you tell me where he is?"

The lady in the blue scrubs took me directly to a patient stall and pulled the curtain open. There was Jake.

As soon as I saw him, a wave of relief washed over me. He was alive and he was conscious, but there was pain in his face. I bent over to kiss him.

He smiled and then winced in pain.

"Oh my God, Jake. Are you all right? What happened?"

Jake was drowsy and his speech was a bit slurred, but he was able to tell me that Rodney and he were on the 2nd floor of a building. The floor had given way and they had both fallen. Rodney hit his head on the floor and died instantly. Tears welled up in Jake's eyes.

"Oh God, Jake…I'm so sorry!" I bent over to hug him, but I was afraid of hurting him so I kissed him on the forehead.

Tears streamed down his face. I wasn't sure how to comfort him. He had pain in his eyes I had never seen before.

After a few minutes of just holding his hand, my face pressed against his head, I asked about his injuries. He said, "My shoulder is dislocated, and they fixed that, but my hand hurts really bad. But I'll be fine." He smiled. It was the smile he always gave me when things were bad but he wanted to be brave for me.

I smiled back.

He gulped. "I am going to need surgery on it right away. The bones are broken and they need to set them as soon as possible. They also want to look at the nerves and something else, I can't remember. It was something that made it so the surgery needs to happen now if I'm ever going to feel my hand again, much less use it."

"You can't feel your hand?!"

I READ WHAT YOU WROTE

Jake shook his head. "Not really. I think the nurse said that they were just waiting on the surgeon to arrive at the hospital."

Before I could ask him for more details, the nurse walked in. Okay, the surgeon is here." She checked his monitors. Without looking at either of us, she said, "Someone from the OR will be down shortly to take you to surgery."

I was trying to wrap my head around what was happening. "How long is the surgery?"

The nurse glanced over. "A few hours, hopefully no more. It depends on the damage. Then a couple more hours in recovery."

A sob left my lips unbidden.

"Try not to worry," she said. "Our orthopedic surgeon Dr. Santiago is doing the procedure and he's the top in his field here in Florida. Why don't you go to the cafeteria and get a cup of coffee. You also might want to call a few loved ones, just to let them know."

My eyes widened. 'Of course!' I hadn't even thought of that. Before I could ask her anything more, she was gone and an orderly from the OR had arrived for Jake. I followed them up to the second-floor surgical area. We were taken to a pre-op waiting area where Jake was given more medication and other pre-op preparations. I watched as they prepped Jake for surgery. He looked so helpless, sad and weak.

"Mrs. Bardon, we are taking Jake to surgery now. There is a waiting area down the hall."

"How long is the surgery going to take?" As soon as the question was out of my mouth, I knew I had already asked, but I still waited for the answer. I wasn't ready for them to take him.

The surgical nurse explained that it usually takes about an

hour and a half or so, as long as there are no complications.

The anesthesiologist came in and sat in front of him, arranging his equipment. "Okay, here we go, Mr. Barton. Say goodbye to the missus."

"Goodbye, missus," Jake quipped.

I leaned over and kissed him on the forehead. "I love you," I said, choking back my tears.

He nodded. "It'll be fine. I'll see you when I wake up."

I didn't want to leave him, but I had no choice. Arms crossed and head down, I walked to the waiting room, my feet moving as if of their own volition. Scanning the room, I saw several orange chairs and two-seat couches, some occupied with other worried-looking folks. I really didn't want to sit in those uncomfortable chairs for over an hour so I decided to follow the nurse's advice and go to the cafeteria for some coffee and wait there.

I really hadn't eaten anything yet that morning but I wasn't really hungry either. This was going to be a very long day of waiting. There would be plenty of time to eat later.

I went through the line, got my coffee, and sat down by the window. Outside was nothing but air conditioning units and maintenance doors. Whoever had designed this hospital had not considered all of the people who would sit here, waiting for a future they could not predict. A nice garden or patio would have been a better choice.

I sighed. I would need to make arrangements for someone to pick the kids up from daycare and take care of them until I could get home. I decided to call my father. Picking up the phone, I listened to it ring several times until his voicemail came on. I couldn't imagine where he could be. It was 10:15 in the morning.

My father Joseph Carpenter, in his mid-60's and retired from Bell Telephone Company after 40 years, he was a widower and vowed he would never remarry. But that didn't mean he disavowed the company of a woman altogether. He was currently dating a widow named Angelica. Angelica was in her middle 60s, Italian, and still very beautiful. She had lost her husband three years previously and had been introduced to my father a few months ago by some mutual friends. I was happy for him because they seemed to enjoy each other's company.

But right now, imagining he was with her and not answering my call, I felt annoyed. Jake and I hadn't yet secured a babysitter for dates or emergencies for that matter, because we always figured he would be around. I had to figure out what to do about the kids. I thought of Jake's parents. It hit me. Did they even know about his accident? I quickly called my mother-in-law Helen.

She answered right away. "Amelia? Hi, sweetie. How are you?"

My heart sank. Of course they didn't know. I was his emergency contact. I felt terrible. I should have thought to contact them on my way over here, before he went into surgery. And surely they would want to be at the hospital, not taking care of the kids. "It's Jake. There has been an accident. He is okay," I added quickly. "He has a dislocated shoulder and they fixed that, but now he is in surgery for a broken hand. They told me the surgery shouldn't last too long."

There was a long silence.

"I guess they responded to a fire where the floor gave way on the second story." My voice wavered. "The worst thing is that his buddy Rodney died."

"Oh my God, that was the fire? I saw that on the news!"

In the background I could hear Jake's dad. "What's wrong, honey?"

Helen said, "Jake was in that fire where Rodney Statton died. And…our boy is in surgery."

"They said he'll be fine," I said hurriedly.

After I got off the phone with his mother, still needing someone to pick up the kids, I thought of Rose, my friend and neighbor. We had children the same age and we seemed to have a lot in common. Her husband Dan was a big, tall, intimidating man, a few years older than Jake. He was the opposite of Rose who was petite and thin but very athletic. I would see her running outside every morning. If she saw me, she would invite me along. I had every excuse possible: work, the kids, cleaning, whatever I could think of, to not put my body through the daunting task of running. Dan and Jake had known each other a little before they moved in next door to us. Dan had just started working as a firefighter for Lake County, but he and Jake were on different schedules. Since moving in, Dan and Jake had become good friends.

I gave her a call. "Rose, I need a favor."

"Sure, anything."

That was Rose, always willing to help no matter what.

"Can you pick up the kids from school today? Jake has been in an accident and is in the hospital."

"Oh my goodness! Is he okay? What happened?" She sounded panicked.

I READ WHAT YOU WROTE

I explained what was going on and that I had no idea how long I would be at the hospital.

Rose said, "Don't worry about the kids. I will bring them back to my house and I will feed them. They will think it is a play date because you both have to work late. Why don't you just plan on me keeping them overnight? I have clothes they can fit into and I will just keep them and we can figure out school and everything tomorrow. You just take care of yourself and keep me posted. Amelia, let me know if there is anything else I can do for you. Tell Jake we are praying for him."

"Thank you so much. I am so sorry to put this all on you."

"Forget about it. I love your kids. Just take it easy. All will be okay," she said.

She sounded far more confident than I felt.

By the time I got back to the waiting room, Jake's parents had just arrived. His mother was clearly distraught. I went up and hugged her and told her that hopefully it wouldn't be too much longer until we got news. Within minutes a rush of people came in: Jake's sergeant and at least a dozen firefighters. Their large forms seemed to fill the room from floor to ceiling.

Dan walked up to me. "What's the status?"

"We are waiting to hear," I said.

He hugged me. "Don't worry. He will be fine. He is a strong man."

I nodded, gulping back a sob. "Rose has the kids."

"I know."

"Thank you. Both of you. You've already got your hands full and–." The lump in my throat would not let me speak.

"No worries. Double the kids is double the fun."

I smiled despite the growing pang of anxiety in my gut.

Another hour passed. Still no word. Jake's sergeant sat next to me. "Jake's got this," he said.

Though I appreciated him saying that, it didn't dispel my fears. The more time that passed, the more anxious I got. I had figured I would have seen the doctor by now. After another 45 minutes or so, Dr. Santiago finally came out to see me.

Helen ran up to him, getting to him before I could. "How is he? Is he okay?"

I had to almost physically push my way up to hear what the doctor said.

Dr. Santiago waited for me to approach, and he made sure to address me and me alone. I appreciated that, even as I waited on pins and needles. He said, "He did very well in surgery. We made sure his shoulder was completely in line and set several bones in his hand and stitched him up. He will need to go to outpatient rehab to help with the mobility of his hand. He also has a couple of broken ribs which will cause him some discomfort for several weeks, but they should heal up nicely. He will be in a bit of pain for a while, so we will give him some pain medication, but he should be good as new after a few weeks. We do need to keep him here for a couple of days for observation because of his concussion and to make sure his hand doesn't get infected."

Before he could finish, Helen blurted, "Can I see him?!"

I felt a twinge of annoyance, but then I remembered what she had said to her husband: "Our boy is in surgery." Our boy. I imagined JJ as a grown man. I would feel the same as Helen. I decided to hang back and follow her lead.

Dr. Santiago said, "Yes, but only for a few minutes because

he is groggy and needs to be kept quiet for some time because of the head injury." He must have seen the look in my eyes because he looked at me and said, "Why don't you come in first? I am sure he would want to see you."

I told Helen that I would only be there for a couple of minutes and then I would come out to get her so she could come in. I followed the doctor into post-op.

The moment I saw Jake I wanted to scream. He was lying so still. He looked pale. Though I have seen many patients post-surgery in my clinical days, it still frightened me to see my Jake like that. I leaned over him and kissed his forehead.

Much to my relief, he opened his eyes.

I said, "Hi, love. The doctor said you did so well in surgery, and you will be good as new in no time."

He gave me a small smile and mouthed, "I love you" and closed his eyes again.

Trying to hold back the tears, I just smiled and said, "I will be here while you take a rest." I then asked the nurse if it would be okay for his parents to come in. She agreed if we kept our visit short. I walked back to the waiting room to get them.

When Helen walked in, she rushed over to her son and cried, "Oh, Jake!"

His eyes opened again and said, "Mom, I'm fine."

Her relief was visible. All three of us spent just a few minutes with him and then the nurse came in and said it was time to let him rest. I kissed him on the forehead again and told him I would be just outside but would come back in as soon as they would let me. Once in the waiting room, Ted asked if he should go get the kids.

"Oh, thanks but I have my friend getting them and keeping them at her house. They will be fine, but thank you." I gave him a small hug. It felt so nice to have built a little stronger relationship with his parents. I felt incredibly lucky. I thought about the dinner I had invited them to, and how that had helped us grow closer, making today easier. I was more grateful than ever for Carol's wisdom.

About 30 minutes later, the nurse came out and said Jake was asking for me. The three of us went in. Jake had gained a little more color and seemed more awake. "Hi, sweetheart. How are you feeling?"

"Like I fell through a floor," he said and gave us a slight grin. As quickly as his smile appeared, it was gone. "How is Rodney's family?" Tears came to his eyes.

"I don't know, honey, but I will find out. You just need to relax and let your body heal."

He closed his eyes again and the tears spilled down his face. "Are the kids okay?"

"Yes, they're fine. I asked Rose to get them. They are going to spend the night with her. I will stay with you."

He reached out his good hand to me and squeezed mine tight. After a little while, I excused myself so I could call Rose to check on the kids and to try and call my dad again.

I spoke with Rose and gave her an update. JJ wanted to speak with me, and he sounded really good. He was excited to be able to have his first sleepover with his friend. I then called my dad and finally got a hold of him. Turns out he had spent the day with Angelica, just as I had suspected. He offered to go to our house and get the kids a change of clothes and take them over to Rose's house. With a sigh of relief knowing the kids were being taken care of, I called my boss to give her an update and take tomorrow off work as well. When I walked back toward Jake's room, I saw that the firefighters had all left. It was just my in-laws in the waiting room.

"Jake is asleep," Helen said.

She was much calmer. I was happy to see that.

She continued, "How about we pick up the kids from Rose's in the morning and we will stay with them at your house so you can come and go from the hospital without worrying about them? You can spend as much time here as you want."

I hugged Helen harder than I had ever hugged her before. At that moment I was so grateful to have her.

When I finally arrived home from the hospital that day, I was spent. I hadn't eaten all day because I wanted to spend as much time with Jake as I could. His parents left later in the afternoon once they felt comfortable that Jake was out of danger. They were planning to come in the morning to get the kids so I didn't have to worry about them. I decided to make a quick bowl of soup and try to relax.

After I ate the soup and some stale bread I had in the pantry, I decided to take a quick shower and go to bed. I got into my pajamas and crawled into my comfortable bed and took some deep breaths. Though I was completely exhausted, I was still a little too wired from the day to sleep. I decided to take out the latest binder I had taken, pushing aside the guilt. I opened the binder and began to read:

After arriving home and explaining to Mother what

transpired, I tried to figure out what to do next. Here I was, back in Michigan, without my husband. I had lost a baby and had no job or a place to live. Mother hugged me after hearing everything that happened and told me it would be okay, in time. She said of course, I could stay with them as long as I needed to and not worry about anything else for now.

"Carol, you just need to take some time to rest. You have been through an incredibly hard ordeal, and you need to get your mental and physical strength back." She was stroking my head as I leaned on her shoulder. We were sitting next to each other on the sofa.

"Oh, Mother, I don't know how this all happened. My life has fallen apart because of that evil man, and I just don't know what to do." Though I was so lost, the tenderness of my mother's touch and support gave me comfort.

"Let's start by getting your room ready. The boys can go back to sleeping in the same room and I will get your old room ready for you. Just sit here and have some coffee and then we will make a nice dinner and then you can go to bed early and rest. Tomorrow will come and we will figure it all out."

I wasn't sure what my mother told my dad, but he never said a word to me about anything when he got in from the fields. He just gave me a quick hug, said hello and asked what was for dinner. The boys were talking nonstop all through dinner, never asking me why I was home or where Ben was, thank goodness. I had never been more grateful for a somewhat normal, loud dinner without ever having to say a word myself. I slept more soundly that night than I had in months. I woke up later than usual and was still groggy. But I was feeling much better than

I had the day before.

Three weeks later, I received a certified letter. Ben was petitioning for a divorce citing "unusual cruelty" and I was expected in court in a month's time to finalize. "Unusual cruelty." That truly summed up my short young marriage. The problem was he was claiming I was the instigator of the cruelty. What about him deciding to change the course of our planned marriage by running away to the Marines without my consent, or even my opinion? He didn't consult me about moving to Tennessee, let alone my opinion of being forced to live with his parents while he was away. I couldn't even think about the cruelty put upon me by living with those horrible people, and of course, what his father did to me. Talk about cruelty. Ben blamed me for the whole incident, not once thinking about how horrific it was for me.

Mother suggested I should just go and get it over with. There was no reason to fight it. My marriage was over.

I was very nervous on the day of court for the dissolution of marriage. I tried to pull myself together and dress very conservatively, yet pretty. As much as I tried, I couldn't cover the grief that was apparent on my face. I was also so nervous about seeing Ben again. Would he berate me again, but this time in front of my mother and the judge?

As it turned out, Ben didn't show up to court that day. I was glad of that. I just couldn't face him. I didn't want to ever see his anger and the look of hurt in his eyes. All I wanted to do was forget everything surrounding the marriage from my mind and from my life. There were no material possessions to be divided and no children, so I took the easiest way out possible and chose

203

not to contest the divorce.
Just shy of the age of twenty, I was a divorcee.

CHAPTER 21

MARIE

The closer I got to Mom's house, the more my stomach hurt. I hated that I dreaded driving to the place that I used to look forward to visiting. The streets were lined with adorable little homes with perfectly manicured lawns and little old ladies with hats kneeling on a mat planting flowers in their miniature gardens that line the front of their homes. The roads themselves were filled with golf carts driven by men who probably shouldn't have their drivers' licenses. I wondered if they even needed one to drive a golf cart. I dodged at least a half dozen of them as they weaved back and forth in front of my car, blissfully unaware that they had just had a near-death experience.

This was the place that Dad had chosen over sixteen years ago for him and my mom to retire. He was so excited to get out of the cold midwest and move to sunny Florida. He envisioned them golfing everyday and then relaxing in front of the TV cheering on the Chicago Cubs while drinking his beer. Mom had a similar vision, but she wanted to add travel to their list of retirement activities. Unfortunately, traveling was something that didn't happen for her. Dad found this little haven and his travel radius was cut to about 5 miles. Getting him to even come to my home or those of any of my siblings' houses was not easy. We only managed it a couple of times a year.

We would come up to their place instead and go golfing with them. Sometimes Dad would organize a big family bowling outing which we all enjoyed. Other days Mom would spend all day preparing a nice meal for us and then we would sit around and play cards and laugh. Now, when I would come up here for a visit, I wasn't sure what I was going to get when I arrived. All I knew for certain was that all happiness was devoid from the house.

Driving up to the house, I saw the once beautiful little yellow home in disarray. The grass was cut, but only because I knew the association fees that were paid that covered the cost of mowing. The plant and flower beds were overgrown with weeds that had choked the life out of the flowers Mom had lovingly planted. The side of the house had large greenish stains on the stucco, an inevitable result of a lack of power washing. And then there was my mom's car, covered in carcasses of love-bugs, another notorious Florida hazard, as well as a yellow dust from pollen that had accumulated from months of disuse.

Avoiding the spiderwebs as I walked up to the door, still trying to control my growing stomach ache. I knocked once and opened the door, grabbing the newspapers that were piled up on Mom's rocker. "Hi, Mom. It's Marie." I tentatively walked through the small foyer of the house.

"Marie! We are in the bedroom. Come in," Mom said in a cheery voice.

'That's a good start,' I thought. I walked in and saw a young woman, about my oldest daughter's age, taking Mom's blood pressure.

"Hi, Mom."

Mom asked, "What are you doing here? Did I know you were coming?"

She sounded surprised. I took a deep breath, determined not to show my frustration. "Yes Mom. Remember, I talked to you on the phone this morning before I left."

She waved a hand, dismissing her forgetfulness like she typically did. "Marie, this is Amelia. She is the nurse from hospice I told you about. Amelia, this is my youngest daughter, Marie." She was smiling.

It warmed my heart to hear her voice sound so happy. My stomach started to settle. "Hello, nice to meet you. I have heard a lot of great things about you from my mother." I shook Amelia's now free hand.

"Hello, nice to meet you too. I am so glad to meet one of Carol's children. I have heard so much about you, too."

Relieved to see such a nice person with a cheery disposition helping my mother was a huge relief. I knew it was the right decision to have them come in and take care of her. Though initially I was concerned when the pain doctor dropped her, I could see this was a much better situation. I knew that at least someone was looking after her weekly. I would have given anything if Mom would have agreed to move in with us or one of my siblings that offered, but she wouldn't.

"Well how are you doing today, Mom?"

"I am in good shape for the shape I'm in."

It was her typical response, and it always made me chuckle.

Amelia patted Mom's hand. "Well Carol, you are looking

pretty good today. All of your vital signs are in order. Do you feel your medication is keeping your pain at bay?"

"Yes, I think so. I am sleeping pretty well, too."

"That is wonderful," she continued. "And are you eating well too?"

"Yes, Earl takes such good care of me."

My heart sank, as it always did when she said that. I knew he did not take care of her, but she was so delusional and it upset me to know end.

Amelia offered a tight smile in response to Carol's comment. It seemed to me that Amelia knew the score with Earl.

Amelia stood up. "Well, I don't want to keep you from visiting with your daughter, so I am just going to go sit at the kitchen table and look at the medicine chart and nutrition calendar that Earl is supposed to fill out and then write some quick notes."

Turning to me she said, "It is so nice to meet you, Marie."

After she left the room, Mom and I made idle chit-chat for the next few minutes. She asked me about the kids and their school and of course we talked about my job.

Amelia peaked around the corner. "That's all for me, Carol. I'm going to go now."

Mom's smile faded at the corners. "Oh, okay."

I turned to Amelia. "Would it be okay if I walk you out?"

"Of course," she said, smiling.

"Mom, I am going to walk Amelia out and see if there is anything she thinks I can do to help. I will be back in a couple minutes."

We walked out the door, exchanging pleasantries along the way. By the time we got to the driveway, I turned to her and asked, "How is my mom doing, in your professional opinion?"

She seemed to hesitate a little. "She is doing pretty well."

I could tell she wanted to say more, but she didn't. I wasn't sure if it was because she wasn't sure how much she was allowed to tell me or something else. I pressed on. "Do you think she is being taken care of well? Specifically, getting food, pain medication on time, and stuff like that?"

"Well," Amelia said cautiously, "I, um, have made some suggestions about her nutrition, and um, offered options for them to help with some things. But your step-father doesn't seem…"

I couldn't let her finish. It felt like I got punched in the gut. My heart started pounding out of my chest. "Step-father. He is not my step-father." I fumed, my voice rising a bit more than I intended.

"Oh, I am sorry, I didn't mean…"

Again, I interrupted the poor girl. "No, no, it's fine. I am sorry, I guess technically he is, but I really, really don't like him." Disgust oozed out of my mouth. "I know I sound terribly mean, but you don't know the story. He is not a nice guy, to put it mildly. I lost my dad about 10 years ago and Earl has been taking advantage of Mom for the last couple of years. I don't trust him as far as I can throw him."

"I am so sorry. That must be so hard. And again, I apologize. I didn't mean to upset you."

I felt bad for reacting so strongly. "Really, no need to apologize. I should be the one to apologize for my outburst. I am just so worried about my mom and I know he doesn't take good care of her, but due to her, well let's say, limited mental capacity, she thinks he walks on water. But nevermind that. You were saying about my mom?"

"Well, I am concerned about two major things. One is I am not sure if she is eating very nutritiously. She tells me she isn't hungry when I ask her about eating, which is normal for people with cancer. The dementia makes it worse, because they don't remember when they've eaten. However, it is imperative that she eats well. And I see that... Earl," she nodded confirmation to me, "goes out to get food from time to time, which is where I believe he is now. However, he doesn't seem to bring her home anything. The only thing I see that she eats somewhat regularly is orange sherbet."

Laughing, I said, "Yes, that's Mom. She loves orange sherbet and anything sweet. Did you see her candy drawer in the refrigerator?"

Amelia shook her head.

I continued. "Yup, the meat drawer is full of candy. No meat," I said with a smile. "At one point they were getting meals delivered, but I can never get a clear answer from them when I enquire if that is still happening. Is it?"

Amelia shrugged. "I believe so. I asked that Earl increase the number of times they come. I can't get a straight answer about whether they have or, more importantly, whether she's been eating anything from them."

"Sounds about right. And the state of that house. And the smell. It's disgusting."

"There's nothing we can do about the smell."

"I know. Believe me, we already tried."

Amelia nodded. "What is the second concern?"

"Well, honestly, it is the clutter around the house. I am not judging," she was quick to say, "but I am afraid there is a potential for her to trip over the stacks of books and things on the floor. I have met their housekeeper, but I haven't really seen the house picked up."

"Oh, she doesn't do anything. I have complained to Mom several times about their so-called maid. My sisters and I have come here from time to time to do a thorough cleaning, but honestly, we can't stand having to pick up after Earl. We also have offered to get a different housekeeper, but we are always told no. If you would have known my mom before, you would be shocked at how she lives today. Before Earl, my mom kept her house spotless. Her drawers were so unbelievably organized and she really prided herself on a clean home. But since Earl, it is a mess. I know she doesn't feel well, so she has trouble keeping up with things, but he has just trashed the place. I will talk with my mom again and see if I can't push her to allow us to get another maid. Anyway, I have a favor, can I give you my phone number and would it be okay if I get yours? I would really appreciate it if you would reach out to me if you see anything you think I could do to help. And if it's okay, I would appreciate being able to call you if my family has any questions. I was here when the doctor from hospice did his initial visit, and he was nice and all but since you are the one taking care of her, I would really appreciate it if we could stay in touch."

"Of course." She dug through her purse and pulled out her business card.

"Thank you. Is it okay if I text you my information to the

cell number listed here?" I looked down at the numbers listed on her card.

Out of nowhere, Earl swung Mom's car into the driveway. He drove right into the middle, forcing me to jump aside to avoid getting hit. For a moment, I wondered if he was trying to run me over. 'Get a grip, Marie,' I told myself. I glanced at Amelia and saw what I thought was disgust briefly flit across her face. 'Interesting,' I thought.

We watched as he tried to maneuver his large body around to get his feet out of the car. He grunted as he used whatever strength he had to get himself out. When he finally accomplished that obviously difficult task, he bent over to grab his sack of food from the passenger side. When his enormous head came back out of the car, he looked at me and said, "Hello, Marie. Nice to see you." Each word dripped with sweet syrup. He always had to act like he was the nicest guy in front of people, but truth be told he was the epitome of that old saying, 'a wolf in sheep's clothing.'

"Hello," I said blandly. "I am just talking with the nurse here and then I will be inside to finish my visit with Mom."

He grunted and started shuffling towards the door as Amelia and I watched him take every slow painful step. When he finally made it through the door I turned to Amelia, "Look, I don't mean to sound...well...unprofessional, but I really don't trust him. He has completely taken advantage of our mother and has done everything in his power to cause a rift between us kids and her."

"I am sorry to hear that. I honestly wondered if he was well enough himself to take care of her." She continued, "I hope I don't sound unprofessional either, but I don't think he is happy

I am here and he doesn't seem to care about the suggestions I make to him about improving her situation."

My blood was fully boiling now. "Do you want to know the background on them?"

I could tell she sensed my need to talk as she nodded. "Well, here is the scoop. Earl is actually my uncle."

Amelia's jaw dropped.

"Not by blood," I added quickly. "He was married to my father's sister until he started hanging around my mother. My father's family were alcoholics, almost all of them, and Jane, my aunt, his wife, was one too. She had fallen and had to go to rehab a couple years ago. While she was in rehab, Earl would come over all of the time to talk with my mom. Unfortunately, after Jane got home, he continued to come over to Mom's house. My sisters and I were very concerned and cautioned her about it. She said that it was not what we were thinking and that she had absolutely no attraction to him. She just felt sorry for him and wanted to be a supportive ear."

"The problem was," I continued, "he had a long history of manipulation. Heck, he could never hold down a job for long and had never owned a home. He was able to convince people to give him things all of the time though. His family used to come by our house a lot when we were kids. And we loved to hang with our cousins, but my father and my aunt would drink all day then pass out. Earl and my mom were stuck putting us kids to bed and picking up the house after the day's activities. They would lament to each other their frustrations of being married to alcoholics."

I needed to take a breath. I was getting really worked up.

I slowed down my rant. "He used those conversations and frustrations that he shared with my mom to deceive her into believing he could do all of the things for her that my father couldn't or wouldn't. And unfortunately due to her dementia, she fell for it."

Amelia said, "People have different memory issues with dementia. For your mom, she can remember the smallest details from the past, but she can't remember whether she ate breakfast and her reasoning skills have begun to fail."

"She remembers everything that happened years ago. Everything," I said.

"I know. She has told me some stories. I was amazed at her memory," Amelia added.

"Exactly, but for her it is her short-term memory. She repeats things a lot and can't remember a conversation from just a few minutes ago."

Amelia nodded in agreement. "But even more concerning is the lack of decision-making ability.

"Yes. And that is why she fell for Earl's manipulation so easily."

"I can't imagine how hard this is for you," Amelia said.

I looked away. "One night, while he was at my mother's house, she had a heart episode and they called an ambulance. My sister and I went to the hospital to see my mother when we heard about it the next morning. When we walked into the ER, we saw Earl sitting there next to Jane in the waiting room. I hadn't seen her in so long. I was shocked at her condition." The memory of that night came flooding back as if it were happening right now. I was visibly shaking. "We had asked why she was there

I READ WHAT YOU WROTE

and apparently while Earl was at my mother's house, Jane had gotten up and was wandering the streets completely disoriented. Someone called an ambulance and they brought her there. She was so malnourished and ill, she had to stay in the hospital for weeks. And there was no reason for it except Earl didn't care."

"Wow, that is terrible."

"Yep. And you know what? The hospital called the Department of Children and Families because of her condition. They went to the house they were renting and saw it in complete disarray. Food was everywhere, it smelled horrible, and the worst part was the bed that Jane pretty much stayed in all the time was full of human waste! He left her lying in her own waste!"

"Oh my gosh, Marie."

"And that is just part of it," I continued. I couldn't stop now that I had a chance to get it off my chest to someone in charge of Mom's care. "They were about to pursue charges against him, and he actually divorced Jane while she was in the hospital. I guess he figured he could get out of trouble that way. And it worked. Plus, he had run out of money, and Jane's pension wasn't cutting it for him anymore. My poor cousin had to come down and get her mother and move her back up north. After the DCF visit, he was thrown out of the house they were renting. So he went to my mom to ask her if he could stay in her extra room until he could find something else. Needless to say, he never left. He got very used to living off of mom and dad's pensions and mom's social security. Without us knowing it, he talked her into marrying him." I spit the last two words. "We tried so many things to keep that from happening and we know she never would have agreed to it if it weren't for her reasoning problems."

Tears of frustration and grief welled up in my eyes. "I can't let my mom meet the same fate as Aunt Jane." A sob escaped, but I choked back the next one. I took a deep breath to steady myself. "The hardest part of all has been that we no longer have any control over her care. And Earl is clearly neglecting her. Luckily her primary care doctor knew most of us kids because we used to take turns taking her to the doctor so we could communicate with him, well until Earl had us taken off of HIPAA. She had a pain doctor prescribing her medication until he dropped her. I had told the hospice doctor about that. Did he let you know?"

"Yes, I was told," she replied. "I understand it was because she kept running out of her medication prior to being able to get her refills. Is that correct?"

"Yes," I said, exasperated. "She would run out of pills sometimes almost a week before she could get another refill. We weren't sure if he was giving her too much from time to time, or if he was taking some himself. We really didn't know. Thank goodness her primary care doctor suggested reaching out to you guys for palliative care. I don't know what we would have done otherwise."

"Well, I have provided him with a chart to fill out every time he gives her the medication. It gives me the day and time, and I review it every week I come."

"That's great. And he's following through?"

Amelia raised her eyebrows. "I think he fears authority."

"He should," I said.

"I told him if he didn't track her meds and her meals, I would have to recommend that she be placed in a facility. So far, he has done pretty well with it, but I will make sure to really monitor it.

Thanks for letting me know."

"Thank you so much, Amelia. My siblings and I are so frustrated. We have always been an incredibly close family, but Earl has just done everything he could do to come between us. Every time one of us calls her to say we are coming to visit she is so excited, and then, she will call us like ten or fifteen minutes later and tell us to not come, that she isn't up for a visit. We know it is because he tells her that it's not a good time. He does not want us around her. We have tried so many ways to get our mother to see what he is doing, but she gets so upset when we challenge the relationship. We have all decided that the most important thing is our mother's health, and we are going to do everything we can to help her."

"I promise I will do everything I can. I know I shouldn't say this, but she is my favorite." Amelia said. "She is so sweet and always gives me little pieces of advice."

Laughing, I said, "Yes, my mom is always giving advice."

"Please call me anytime you want with any questions. I am here to help."

"Thank you so much." I gave her a hug, I was relieved to have met her and grateful to have someone I believed I could trust looking after Mom.

After I said goodbye to Amelia, I took a deep breath and headed back into the house. I needed to calm myself down some before I went back in there. When I walked in, Earl was sitting in his chair, finishing up his lunch. I walked right past him and walked into Mom's room. Mom was reading a book.

"You know," Mom said, "I hardly know what I'm reading anymore."

"Don't worry about it, Mom. It's just one of those days." I tried to change the subject. "Amelia is very sweet, Mom, don't you think?"

"Oh yes, she is wonderful," she smiled.

We spoke for about thirty minutes longer and then I could tell Mom was getting tired. I kissed her goodbye and walked out of her room.

"Marie, I don't think your mother needs hospice here. I am taking care of her just fine and I don't like them coming into my house," he snarled.

"Earl, this is Mom's house," I reminded him trying to control my anger. "She needs them here. They are providing her pain medication!"

"Yes, but we can find another doctor. That little girl is trying to push all kinds of services on us. We don't have the money for all of it."

"That is what Mom's money is for, anything she needs. It's not your money. Dad worked his ass off his whole life trying to set Mom up so she could live comfortably for the rest of her life." My blood pressure was through the roof at this point. "You told us you were coming into this marriage with nothing and that you wouldn't take anything from Mom. I know she has plenty of money for her needs. Now you're saying there's not enough. Where is the money going, Earl?"

He said nothing.

"And this place is a total mess. Mom never lived like this before you came along. She has more than enough for housekeeping, food delivery and any care needed!" I was yelling at this point.

I READ WHAT YOU WROTE

"Marie, what is wrong?" Mom called from her bedroom.

Giving him a nasty look, I quickly went into Mom's room. "Nothing Mom, just trying to make sure you have everything you need." We had all learned that whenever we confronted Earl. It just upset Mom. I tried to act as nonchalant as possible.

"Honey, don't give Earl a hard time. He is taking such good care of me."

"I am not, Mom. I am just looking out for you." Bile rose in my throat. "I love you. I better leave so I can pick up the kids from school on time. See you soon. Love you so much!"

"I love you too sweetie, see you soon." And I bent down and kissed her cheek.

I headed straight out the door, right past Earl without saying another word. I stopped next door to see Aunt Marilyn. She had become our saving grace. We would pop by after every visit and vent our frustrations to her. Us kids called her house "Switzerland." It was a safe haven for us after our visits. We would usually sit and have coffee and complain about our mother's situation. Marilyn had known Earl even longer than we had and had never been a fan. At this point, she couldn't even look at him. She too felt the loss of Mom because they used to have coffee together almost every morning. With Earl there now, my mom never wanted to visit and never invited Marilyn over to see her. Her own sister! Just like us, Marliyn would come over unannounced from time to time just to make sure Mom was okay.

It broke my heart how things had turned out. Aunt Marilyn had been so excited to move next door to my mother about two years after my parents moved here. She, my uncle, and both my parents spent a lot of time together back then. My mom and her sister had always dreamed of living next door to each other and had been so happy since they moved in. Aunt Marilyn lost Uncle Thomas just a few short years after Dad died, and so the two sisters grew even closer while being a support for one another. Now, just like us, her relationship with Mom has been strained because of Earl.

"I can't even go over there anymore. It just makes me so mad to see him," she told me again for the millionth time.

I sipped my coffee, hoping it would calm my nerves.

CHAPTER 22

AMELIA

I walked into the house, absent-mindedly setting my keys on the kitchen table, my mind a blur. I was shocked to learn Earl's true identity. There was something about him that always gave me the creeps, but I could not have imagined how truly terrible he was. I felt so bad for the kids and Carol too, even though she said to me on many occasions how great Earl was to her. She always spoke very lovingly about him. I knew that was her lack of reasoning talking, but at the same time a part of me was glad she didn't realize how bad it was.

I opened the door.

"Mommy!!!" Olivia and JJ both ran into my arms. I hugged them as tight and as long as their little wiggling bodies would let me.

Jake came to me with his warm smile, his arm still bandaged up, evidence of what we had been through this past month.

I was so glad to have him home. Though it had only been

a few days, it seemed like he was recovering well physically and emotionally. He would have to keep his hand immobile for a couple of weeks and then he would begin therapy. His hand was swollen and all kinds of shades of blue and black. He would have to do physical therapy a couple days a week and based on what the doctor at the hospital said he should gain most of the mobility back after a few months. He had warned us that it might not completely heal, and Jake might not be able to do everything he had been with that hand prior to the accident. If that happened, Jake might never be able to be a firefighter again. That terrified me. Jake loved being a firefighter. Yet he seemed to not be too concerned and said he was looking forward to the six weeks he would be off on medical leave from work.

"You need to rest so you don't hurt your hand worse," I scolded.

He shrugged and smiled. It was that half-grin he always gave me when he was trying to get away with something. "It'll work out," he said. "You'll see. Besides, the six weeks off will be good. There's all kinds of projects I've been wanting to do around the house."

I shook my head. It still pained me to see him injured. Oh how I loved him, and our relationship was better than ever. I was so grateful for all of the lessons Carol had taught me over these last six months.

He gave me a strong hug. In his arms, smelling his aftershave and body wash, I said a quick prayer to God that we would be able to have a long, happy life together. I looked into his eyes. My nurse's vision kicked in. His eyes were dilated, evidence that he was still taking the pain meds. I pursed my lips. It had already been a few weeks. Did he really still need them? Maybe it was the cracked ribs, I thought. But I had gotten through a broken rib with just anti-inflammatory meds. I shook it off, telling myself that he was fine. Everyone experienced healing and pain differently.

"How was your day today?" Jake asked.

"Oh, it was good. But I have to tell you later about all of the crazy stuff I learned about Carol and her husband."

"Have you been doing more spying in her journals?"

"No," I said, fibbing. "I met one of her kids when I visited her today. You will not believe what I found out. Hey, how did it go with the social worker today, did you like her?"

"Yes, she was pretty cool."

"So what did she say?"

"You know, the basic stuff. She asked me a million questions."

I could feel my jaw tense. Getting him to talk was like pulling teeth. Because I know him so well, I knew if I bombarded him with question after question he wouldn't talk at all, or he'd just give me one-word answers. 'Guys are so frustrating like that,' I thought. As casually as possible I asked, "Do you feel better after talking with her?"

"I guess."

'One word answers, ugh.' I decided the best course of action was to change the subject. "How was school today for the kids?"

"Good. They are as crazy as ever. I think they should give the kids more outside time during school to get all of their energy out."

I nodded. "Hey, I have an idea. It's not too hot out this afternoon, why don't I make some sandwiches and we can take a make-shift picnic to the park? That way we don't have to cook and the kids can run around and wear themselves out. And, added bonus, we don't have to clean the kitchen." While all of that was true, I also hoped that if I got him out of the house in a relaxing environment maybe he would share more of his meeting with the social worker today.

The kids were so excited. We made them ride in the wagon so we could contain their energy until we got to the park.

As we strolled down our little street and the park came into view, I couldn't help but feel light-hearted and happy. "I love our park," I said.

"Yeah," Jake said.

The neighborhood park was just perfect for the young families who lived in the community. It had several play areas that were specific to kids of a certain age with lots of swings, slides, and merry-go-rounds. There were vast areas of lush green grass that always seemed to have a group of kids playing soccer and several groups of people sprinkled across the lawn having picnics or tossing a ball. Somehow the grass area was devoid of the piles of fiery red ant hills that were typically around in any patch of grass in Florida. The kids loved being there.

After we pushed the kids on the swings, they wanted to go up and down on the slide. It was like a silver bullet of fast enjoyment for them, and they wanted to climb up and slide down over and over. They giggled so much. It made Jake and I laugh.

Jake and I went back to our picnic spot while the kids ran around.

Jake flopped on the blanket. "I am exhausted. I don't know how they have so much energy!"

I kissed him on his cheek, his stubble rough against my lips. My heart was overflowing. I couldn't believe how much I was enjoying this spontaneous family time. Still, I was worried about Jake's recovery.

Treading lightly, I asked, "So it went okay with the social worker?"

"Yes, like I said."

Nothing more.

Wanting to get more details, I decided to push just a little. "So did she say anything to help or was it a waste of time?"

He was looking down at the half eaten makeshift meal. "I guess, I don't know. She said that I need to be going to physical therapy regularly, but honestly, she has no clue how painful it is. It's hard for me to do anything. I told her I would, but I really don't think I need it. I can do it myself."

Jake needed more PT. That is what the doctor had said, and I knew from nursing school the importance of doing specific exercises after an injury to gain mobility and strength. I didn't want to fight him on this and upset him and ruin the wonderful time we were having. It had only been a couple of weeks since the accident so maybe it was too hard for him this early.

"She's also pushing grief counseling. I told her I didn't need that; I know terrible things happen, and I can handle it."

"I know, but sometimes it can really help people deal with loss," I said lightly.

"I don't need that. Things happen. That's life."

Afraid to say anything more, I tried to keep the subject light by talking about the kids and school, but his mood had changed.

He stood. "Let's get the kids. It's time to take them home. Oh and hey, I need to run out to the pharmacy later."

Reluctantly I got up and started gathering the picnic remnants. I called for the kids. "Time to go guys, it's getting late."

JJ whined, "Oh Mom, can't we stay longer?"

Before I could answer Jake yelled, "We are going home now!"

After the kids were bathed and put to bed, I went to the couch where Jake was sitting and snuggled up next to him. We sat in silence for about 30 minutes. He seemed relaxed and even laughed a few times at the sitcom we were watching on TV.

We hadn't had any intimacy since before the accident. I began to give Jake soft kisses on his cheek. Though I wasn't receiving any response from him, I decided to explore his body with my hands carefully while continuing to kiss his cheek and neck. I reached down to unbutton his pants, but he stopped me with his good hand.

"Don't Amelia. I am tired, and I don't feel well. I am going to bed." He got up and walked to the bedroom.

I felt totally rejected. As much as I didn't want to cry, tears welled up in my eyes. After a few minutes I got myself together and went into the bedroom. The lights were off, and he was already in bed. I quietly brushed my teeth, put on pajamas, and crawled into bed beside him. He was facing the opposite way, so I put her arm around him and said, "I love you."

No response. Not thinking I could feel worse and knowing he couldn't possibly have been sleeping this quickly, I felt further rejected. I laid in bed for hours unable to sleep. Though physically being close to him, I had never felt further away.

After a sleepless night I was woken up by Olivia jumping up and down in front of my face at the side of the bed. "Up Mommy, up."

Not wanting to disturb Jake, I got out of bed and took Olivia into her room to get her dressed and ready for school. The kids were dressed and fed.

There was still no sign of Jake. It wasn't like him to not get up and at least kiss the kids goodbye before school. I went into the bedroom before we left. Jake appeared to be sleeping. I kissed him on the cheek and said "Goodbye, we are leaving."

Again, nothing from Jake.

'Was this all because I had asked about the social worker?' I wondered. 'What was going on?'

My heart was heavy. I dropped the kids off at school and headed to work. My desk had a huge pile of files that I had plopped on top of it yesterday after my visit with Carol's daughter Marie. I had to quickly do the mountain of paperwork before my boss noticed I hadn't completed it. I usually hated paperwork, but today I didn't mind. It kept my thoughts off of Jake.

After a rough day, I decided to pick up some fast food for dinner. I was sure Jake hadn't made anything and I had absolutely no energy to make anything nutritious. The couch looked like it held a pile of blankets on top of it as the kids and I walked past it on our way in the house. I wouldn't have known Jake was under all of that had I not seen a foot hanging out, dangling over the edge of the couch. Jake didn't even move as we loudly traipsed past him. The kids were so excited to have a special treat for dinner that they didn't even notice him.

The following week, as I walked out of Carol's home, I knew I needed to share my concerns about her living conditions with Diane again. I was so afraid she would trip over the growing piles that littered the floor. And what would she do then? I knew Earl wouldn't be able to help her up. He could barely get himself up out of that nasty chair. And then there was her eating.

"Are you the hospice nurse?"

I looked up just in time to see that I was about to run into an elderly woman. I was so entrenched in my thoughts, I hadn't even seen her come up. "Oh! Excuse me!"

"Oh, dear, I didn't mean to scare you."

Trying to regain my composure, I replied, "It's okay. No problem. Yes, I am." I smiled. "Do you know Carol?"

"I am Carol's sister, Marilyn."

"Oh! Wonderful to meet you! Carol has told me so much about you." I could see the resemblance, for sure. She had her same hair color and facial features, but she looked younger and more put together. I could tell she went to a salon to get her hair done, and she had perfectly applied her make-up. She was dressed in a cute light blue slacks outfit that accentuated the same striking blue eyes that Carol had. I imagined this was how Carol looked every day before she got sick.

"Yes, well, I hope it was all good," she said. She gave a little chuckle, but immediately her face became serious. "How is my sister doing?"

"Today she seemed pretty good," I said. I tried to sound confident, I could tell there was hesitation in my voice. I wondered if she heard it.

"I am so concerned about my sister." Without even a momentary pause, she added, "And I know that asshole isn't helping."

I wasn't sure how to respond. "I am concerned, too. I am doing everything I can to help her. In fact–"

She cut me off. "Help her! Well that would be a first!" She crossed her arms and scowled. "Everyone says they can help her, but nobody does. Do you know how many people told us they would help us with Carol, just to leave us in the lurch?"

I shook my head.

"Her kids and I are just so frustrated. Do you know the kids have talked to lawyers, doctors, and anyone else they thought of to keep her from marrying Earl? They knew that based on her dementia she was not in the right state of mind to make the correct decision for herself, but no one could do a thing."

I shook my head again, but didn't say a word.

"The lawyers told them that the only way to keep her from marrying him and allowing him to take control of her health and her money was to declare her incompetent. You know, it is next to impossible to get a judge to do that. They said that it would take months and months if not years of numerous independent doctors doing tests on her and even then, there was a very slim chance that a judge would ever make that declaration. They even called the Department of Children and Family Services on them because of how concerned they were because she kept running out of pain medicine and she was feeling so horrible, not to mention the state of her home. Do you want to know what happened when they came to check things out?"

"What did they say?"

Her voice continued to get louder as she continued. "They came and spent less than 20 minutes there. I know. I watched out my window." Marilyn pointed at her house. "According to her daughter, Marie, they asked Carol how she was doing, and she said just fine, and that Earl was taking such good care of her." She grunted. "So, case closed. They saw nothing wrong." Marilyn stared past me.

"I am so sorry," I said. "I have seen the effects of her dementia, but others might not. Since her dementia only affects her short-term memory and decision-making abilities, people can't always see what is going on if they only spend a short time with her."

"I know. I know. I am just so angry." Her anger turned to resignation, and as she continued I heard the remnants of a southern accent coming out. "I didn't mean to unload all of this on you. I don't know what to do. I love her so much. But no one can really help. And here I sit, next door to my only sister, my only sibling, watching her be abused by that–monster." She spit the last word. "He's a con artist and a manipulator. It should be illegal to abuse vulnerable people like that. But it isn't. It isn't. What kind of country do we live in, that such a thing can be legal?"

"I will do all I can to help her be as comfortable as possible. I promise you that." I desperately wanted her to understand the true commitment I had for Carol.

Marilyn's eyes met mine. "Sweetheart, I know you will. I can see it in your eyes. And I really do appreciate it. Please let me know if you see anything that I should know about. I am right next door." She turned and pointed to the tidy, little white house just to the left of Carol's. "Well, I will let you go. Thanks for talking with me. Mostly listening. And it was nice to meet you." She grabbed my hand and squeezed it with both hands.

"Nice meeting you," I said.

I watched Marilyn take the short path between the two houses. I wondered how many times she had walked those same steps in happier days.

A full minute, maybe two, after she had disappeared from sight, I realized I was still standing in the same spot. I went to my car, climbed behind the wheel, and put the key in the ignition, but I did not turn on the car. In my hospice training, I had been prepared for the patients' health to fail, for them to continue to decline, but I had not been prepared for this. Sure, the trainers had made comments about family issues, and I had noticed the haunted expressions on their faces when they mentioned it. I had never realized it would be this hard, that I would feel this helpless. I hated that Carol was with a user like Earl. He was so manipulative, and now to hear that he was taking advantage of her. If I was honest with myself, Marilyn was right. There wasn't much I could do either.

At least she was truly loved by her kids and her sister. Although they were just as powerless as I was to get real help for her, I vowed there and then that I wouldn't let them down. I would do everything I could.

CHAPTER 23

AMELIA

Once dinner was complete and the kids went into their room to play, I headed to my room. Even though I had laundry to do, I decided to pick up Carol's binder and read a little while the kids were entertaining themselves:

Sometimes I wondered whether I would ever be happy again. I missed Ben, no matter what had happened. I had heard that time would heal the wounds, but what about the scars? I went to the Michigan Employment Security Commission's office in Lansing. I completed the usual job application, and the interviewer scanned it. She exclaimed, 'I have just the job for you!' Then she added, 'Oh, I hope it isn't already taken!' Her enthusiasm stirred my curiosity. She placed a quick telephone call and sent me off to the International Business Machines' (IBMs) branch office. As soon as I stepped into the lobby, my heart pounded with excitement; I knew I wanted to work there. The receptionist paged the office manager who interviewed me right away. When he asked me to wait in his office while he talked to Mr. Bellow, the Branch Manager, I flushed in hopeful excitement.

My heart fluttered as Mr. Bellow cordially shook my hand and waved me toward a chair. He asked several questions and patiently listened to each response. He only interrupted once to ask, 'Are you always this effervescent?' Even though I was not exactly certain what the word meant, since he asked this with a smile, I quickly answered 'Oh yes.' I was hired right then and there as a switchboard receptionist and began training the following Monday. I had never felt so thrilled about anything before in my life and I was deeply grateful to be given an opportunity for a new start. This was no doubt the principal pivotal point in my life, especially from a social point of view. The people with whom I worked essentially broadened the scope of my overall knowledge.

Operating the switchboard was a delightful experience. I thoroughly enjoyed interacting with all the people with whom I came in contact. I learned how to answer customer service calls and dispatch repairmen called customer engineers to IBM's various customers in the area. Some customer engineers maintained and repaired data processing equipment while others serviced electric typewriters. The salesmen were rarely at their desks, so when a call came in for one of them, I often had to page him on a microphone. "Telephone for Mr. Campbell, I would announce cheerfully. If they weren't in the building, a handwritten message would be put in one of the horizontal slots on a revolving, three-foot metal tree on my desk. Each customer engineer and salesman had his own slot on the tree. Mr. Bellow's secretary Mimi and I became good friends. Sometimes I helped her with a letter or operated the Teletype, located in a cubby hole behind my desk. From the beginning, I felt very much at home in this new bustling environment and with the people who worked there. The only problem was that the long commute to work was getting more and more difficult.

One day when we were talking, I told Mimi I was looking for a place. One of the customer engineers, Charlie, came over to where we were sitting and said he had an apartment for rent. He asked what my salary was and then suggested a modest figure, wondering whether I could afford it. I jumped on the offer giving no thought to the location and whether I would have a way of traveling back and forth to work. That evening Charlie took me to his large, old, two-story brick house on the westside of Lansing and introduced me to his wife named Shirley. They lived in the second story; the first floor they said was for rent. The door to the apartment opened into a large living/bedroom area, perhaps twenty by twenty, with a set of tall windows on the left and far walls of the room. There was an open doorway on the right side of the room, leading to a bathroom and a small kitchen. It would be perfect for me.

After moving in, the next problem to be solved was the need for transportation. Charlie again came to my aid and helped me find a used car. Charlie was a topnotch negotiator and finding a car for me was pure sport for him. We'd go to one used car dealer, drive one of their cars to another dealer and ask the salesman how much it was worth. This was an exciting adventure, especially when it came to dickering for a price. Charlie found what he thought was just the right car and just the right deal, but before he let me sign the contract, he saw to it that rocker panels would be replaced and the car repainted. After the salesman finally agreed, Charlie insisted that the dealer take care of a few other incidentals, such as replacing the windshield wipers. *My first car was a royal blue 1951 Plymouth, which I named Bessie, perhaps after one of my grandpa's cows. Naming a car after a cow may seem ludicrous on the surface, but I was still clinging to the happy childhood memories spent with my grandparents.*

Next, I went shopping for car insurance. The auto insurance companies considered me to be transient, and therefore uninsurable. Charlie interceded on my behalf once more and persuaded the insurance agent to take a chance on me. I sold my wedding rings to Charlie for probably half what they were worth to insure the car, but I didn't care; I was just grateful he had taken the time and trouble to help this needy young woman.

Shirley, his considerate wife, offered to take me to church with them. They belonged to Holy Cross Catholic Church in Lansing, and I felt very comfortable being there on Sundays. Even though the Mass proper was said in Latin, small missals were provided allowing the service to be followed in English. Soon after that I began to take instructions from a kindly priest named Father Cyprian, who had come to America from Holland. He loved to play the church organ and played it beautifully. He taught catechism in a way that made sense. At last, I had found a religious home. It was a huge revelation to learn that Catholics didn't worship statues, as I had always thought. Instead, they provide a place to pray, somewhat as when Jewish people pray at the Western Wall in Jerusalem. Self-confidence and self-worth began to flourish in me. I now began to feel that I had a purpose in life and that I was finally on track.

The new goal in my life was to become and remain economically and emotionally self-sufficient. But that was only part of it. In studying the Baltimore Catechism, I discovered a more profound goal and purpose. There I found a credible answer to the question "Why am I here?" The answer seemed simple enough: "To know God, to love Him and to serve Him in this world and the next." However, it would require the greater part of a lifetime of study, perseverance, and prayer for me to try and put those beliefs into practice.

Dad and Mother never came to visit me at work or at my apartment. From my perspective, they didn't seem to care how I was living or what I was doing. Perhaps they were afraid that this was just a temporary fix and that I might want to move back in with them again. Or, more realistically, they simply did not have the time or the energy. In fact, they were busier now that Mother had taken a job at the IGA grocery store in Eaton Rapids. I decided not to stand on ceremony and visited them nearly every weekend. As for the apartment, the car, and the job, I don't remember that they ever asked about them.

Although I dated a few times, those relationships were merely social and strictly platonic, for I was content with my new life just the way it was. The only thing that marred it was the times I visited the farm. My brothers often took me aside and complained about Dad being hard on them. Though they were only eight and six at the time, Dad dumped some of his farming chores on them, and then ridiculed them for ineptitude. It was frustrating and heartbreaking. When I was there, Dad usually found some way to hassle me too, but it didn't hurt quite as much as before, since I began to realize that was only his opinion of me, not necessarily the real me. Subconsciously, I was beginning to put some of the puzzle pieces together. I once told Dad, 'If I knew what makes you tick, I would know what makes me tick.'

After a weekend with my parents, I looked forward to going back to work on Monday. The change in atmosphere from my parent's home to the bustling excitement at the IBM office was a matter of polar opposites. One morning Mr. Bellow stopped by my desk and asked, 'Como esta?' 'Muy bien,' I answered. ' Y usted?' He smiled that his greeting had been understood, and not long after I received a raise in pay.

About half a block down the street from IBM was a greasy-spoon type restaurant, where I sometimes ate breakfast or lunch. One day a friend and I were discussing marriage, since she hoped her boyfriend would soon propose. I shared my view on the subject by stating, "I'm not ever going to get married again unless he's tall, dark, handsome and rich!" Then I hastily added, "and goes to church every Sunday." This statement must have seemed a safe posture against making another mistake.

I read through more of Carol's early life with Bud as they married and coped with family expectations. But it was her first pregnancy with Bud that caught my attention:

It seems to be a common assumption that women give sex to get love, while men tend to give love to get sex. While that may be true, sex can also beget babies. Close to Christmastime, I discovered we'd be getting one. I was surprised, since missing a period was not uncommon, but headed to the doctor's because I had been through this before and was quite concerned. Would the outcome be as before? Would I be able to carry this baby full term? I still had the incredible fear that because of my conflicted feelings the last time, would God allow this pregnancy to come to fruition? The doctor came into the examination room and told me all was good and that I should be expecting a little bundle of joy in May. I sat in the kitchen waiting for Bud to walk through the door. I couldn't wait to tell him but also had a slight fear of his reaction. I hoped he would be excited too. We had talked about having a baby in the future but was this too soon for him?

He walked in the door and I immediately started to tear up. "What is wrong? Are you okay?," he asked with concern on his face.

"Bud, I have something to tell you. I am pregnant," I blurted out.

"Really, are you sure?"

I couldn't quite tell what he was thinking. "Yes, I went to the doctor, and he confirmed it."

"Oh, that is amazing!" A big smile warmed his face. "How are you feeling? Are you okay?"

"Yes, I am fine." Tears now flowed down my face. I was so happy and so relieved. I couldn't help remembering, though, the reaction Ben originally had and then how terribly wrong everything went. But this was different. Bud and I loved each other and there were no secrets being hidden. I was extremely nervous about the prospect of being a mother, but Bud's reaction made me so excited. I was concerned about how we would handle things financially, but Bud reassured me and said we would be just fine. That following weekend we visited Marilyn and Thomas and then later his parents. Everyone was thrilled!

As we prepared for our upcoming arrival, Bud's mother gave me a baby shower and we received most of the necessities we needed. In the meantime, Bud quit his job at the Service Bureau and began selling household garbage disposals. We spent evenings going over his sales pitches, and afterward we generally played Scrabble with Bud frequently trying to invent new words for the English language.

By the time I was six months pregnant, I had to quit my job at IBM with no medical benefits and no job security; that was company policy at the time. It was boring being at home alone all day, a lady in waiting...waiting for Bud to come home from work and waiting for the baby to come. There was little more to do than wash baby clothes and put them away. At first, Bud had not been able to feel the baby move, but now he could actually see it move and was concerned. "Doesn't that hurt?" When I reassured him that it didn't, we spent precious moments observing the calisthenics of our unborn baby.

Bud telephoned one afternoon and asked me to meet him at a downtown pub. I asked, "How shall I get there?" Since I had sold the Plymouth to Lisa, my replacement at IBM, we had only one car. "Just take a taxi and I'll meet you out in front." As we walked into the bar Bud said, "You'd better sit down. I have something to tell you." Immediately, my heart sank, sensing an unfamiliar seriousness in his tone. What terrible news might be forthcoming?

I inched my way backward into the booth, sitting the only way I could, sideways. Bud came right to the point, listing the day's accomplishments in order. First, he announced, "I quit my job today." Then, "I signed up for the GI Bill and enrolled at Michigan State University full-time. I put us on the waiting list for married housing and got a part-time job at MSU's Tabulating Department." He was clearly excited and pleased with himself. Then he added a contingency to his plan. "Of course, after the baby comes, you'll need to go back to work." He looked at me, waiting for some sort of a response, but mentally I was still on, "I quit my job today." All would go according to Bud's latest "game plan." He would always have a "game plan" for meeting his goals. Marilyn and Thomas joined us afterward and we celebrated the news by spending our last dollars going to a movie.

Two days before the move to MSU, Bud noticed that our neighbor's cat had fallen off the porch railing and was hanging by the neck on its leash. Bud had no particular fondness for animals; nevertheless, he ran out to save it. The neighbor's dog, tethered to the side of the house beside our walkway, clamped its teeth onto Bud's leg as he ran past it to save the cat. Though he hated hospitals, he reluctantly allowed me to take him to the emergency room. Just as the doctor began swabbing Bud's leg I fainted, but at the end of the day, the cat was saved, Bud's wound was treated, and I revived.

Early on the morning of May 6, 1959, I awoke with what seemed to be labor pains, judging from what the doctor had told me to expect. Bud, getting ready for school that morning, noticed my discomfort. "Shall I stay home today?" he asked. When I said, "Yes," he telephoned his class instructors and left word that he would be absent. After that, he became a bundle of nerves, and his ruddy face turned ash white. He kept pacing around the apartment asking, "What can I do?"

In an hour or so, we were on the way to the hospital. I could tell that Bud did not want to be in the labor room, but as his sweaty hand held mine, he tried his best to comfort me. He was probably glad to have missed the delivery room experience, since that was not permitted at the time. Later, he often told people, "I paid the nurse to check on Carol a lot." Perhaps nearer the truth, he may have deliberately asked a nurse to examine me so that he could leave the room, but his version was funnier.

By mid afternoon, our first baby was born, and Bud's face returned to its normal color. We agreed on the name Therese (Therese is my sister's middle name). After Bud held her for a few minutes, he was off to celebrate, as though he would ever need a reason to have a few beers. He once told a group of his friends, "I'd even drink to a train wreck."

Since there was no health insurance, the hospital demanded a down payment, "in good faith," before they would release Therese and me. If we couldn't pay, would they have housed us permanently? Bud offered to sell back to his folks the small TV set they had given us, asking only for the exact amount needed to release us from the hospital, even though we could certainly have used some extra cash.

Bud, an inveterate social butterfly, found many friends at MSU with whom he could indulge in sports and drink. He always seemed to need a retinue of friends who would laugh at his frequent, original one-liners. Somehow he instinctively knew that I wouldn't interfere with those friendships, but it sometimes became a vexation when he opted for social activities in lieu of his home life. Ironically, when he was at home, I often had to leave in order to buy groceries or do the laundry. I remember one night, after carrying the laundry downstairs, I went around the corner of the building and just sat down on the ground and cried. I had no idea why I was so upset; I simply needed a good cry. Just because the term "premenstrual syndrome" was *unheard of at the time did not mean it did not exist, along with other potentially devastating female maladies.*

After the lonely pity party, I pulled Therese's wagon to the nearby laundromat and came back with clean clothes and a bad headache. A sincere hug from Bud, without his expecting sex, might have helped a great deal, but who would have thought to ask for that in an era where husbands were the accepted family leaders in everything? On other occasions when Bud noticed me crying, he would ask, "What's wrong?" I would say, "Nothing." I didn't know what was wrong, much less how to verbalize those feelings.

Bud quickly learned how to juggle school, work and social commitments in order to allow time for family pursuits. That he was always exceptionally cheerful and good to us were his redeeming qualities. Therefore what right did I have to be upset when he chose to be absent from the family when he didn't need to be?

Bud preferred being at his parent's house, since the setting was more cheerful and they doted on our children. Besides, Bud had a beer-drinking buddy in his dad. On the other hand, my parents' home was unexciting. They were usually exhausted from stress and overwork. I asked Bud, "Why don't you like to go to my parent's house?" He said, "I feel out of place there," or "Your dad and I have nothing in common." Bud, strictly a city boy, nearly gagged when Dad took him down to the smelly barn to see such things as baby pigs. However, even though Bud's interests differed greatly from Dad's, they seemed to like and respect one another. One day, though, Bud nearly went too far. He told Dad, "Al, you ought to turn this farm into a golf course."

It is a wonder Dad, with his all-work-and-no-play ethics, chose to ignore the remark.

Bud made certain he stayed on target academically, in spite of his busy life. He changed his major from "general business," to "accounting" and reviewed his class schedule at the beginning of every term to make sure he was taking the right number of credits. Once he elected a class in Catholicism, calling it a "Mickey Mouse course" for an easy credit or two. That was the one class he nearly failed; he was often absent and chose not to purchase a study guide or a book for it.

The summer of our second daughter Ann's birth was a busy one. In his new position as an auditor with the Michigan State Highway Department, Bud was required to travel throughout the state during the week, which meant the girls and I had to go it alone days at a time. Then, Bud's youngest sister, Jane, wanting to leave home and be on her own, decided to rent an apartment. Bud's mother quickly squelched that idea and asked if Bud and I would house the teen for the summer. I just couldn't say "No."

Other than taking Bud's sister, Jane back and forth to work, the five-year-old Ford just sat in the parking lot and gradually self-destructed. First, the faux black leather-padded dash split wide open, revealing an ugly, yellowish, fluffy batting, which nearly obstructed the driver's view. Then one day I heard the muffler and tailpipe assembly clatter to the cement. Bud's dad consented to co-sign the note for our new car, a small four-door Chevrolet Corvair with bucket seats, the backs of which did not lock into place as they do now. In those pre-Ralph Nader days of 1962, cars also lacked seatbelts, but this one did come equipped with safety locks on the rear doors.

With graduation in sight, Bud began scheduling job interviews. On one particular trip, though the accounting position was no longer vacant, the interviewer asked if he wanted to test for an industrial engineering position, instead. Not about to pass up an opportunity for employment, Bud agreed to take the exam. The messenger of the test results told Bud, "I hope your car doesn't break down on the way home!"

Ann was just a baby when she developed an upper respiratory infection and the doctor gave her an injection. Bud had planned to drive to East Chicago, Indiana, the next morning for an interview with Inland Steel Company; but Ann was worse. We telephoned the doctor's office, and he came to our apartment and re-examined her. When Bud expressed concern about leaving us, the doctor reassured him that she would be all right, then he handed his home telephone number to me, "If there's any change in her condition, please call me." That night I put Ann into her crib beside my bed and listened for her every breath. All of a sudden, her breathing became alarmingly wheezy and shallow. I immediately called the doctor. His instructions went like this: "Do you have any whiskey in the house?" "Yes." Then he said, "Give a teaspoon to Ann with some juice and have a shot for yourself." That got us through the night.

The next morning there was a rattling sound in Ann's chest, and in the midst of eating baby cereal, she threw up a gross amount of mucus. I called the doctor again and he arrived at the apartment about the same time Bud came home. It was then that the doctor informed us that Ann had pneumonia. Bud was angry with him and reproached him, "Why didn't you tell us she had pneumonia!" The doctor said he felt confident I would watch her closely enough and that I would call him if her condition worsened. He also knew how important job interviews were to graduating students and he did not want Bud to cancel his interview. Then he added, "Besides, I would have had to scrape Carol off the ceiling." That he would!

In the four years we spent at MSU, Bud's parents visited us perhaps once a month and usually brought food. One Saturday, we found a babysitter and took them to an MSU football game against Notre Dame, which MSU won. After coming back to the apartment Bud and his dad, a Notre Dame alumnus, began to rehash the game. Bud's dad said it was a "referee's game all the way," citing a particular call which the men began to contest. In the midst of the argument, Bud excused himself, went around the corner to Ed Buddie's apartment, and invited him to arbitrate the discussion. The dispute ended abruptly when Bud's dad saw the huge hulk of a football player stoop through the doorway. After that, they discussed the rest of the game in an amicable fashion.

My parents weren't able to visit us very often while we lived in Spartan Village, but one morning just before graduation, I was surprised to see Dad at the door. Richard was with him. Dad had an especially big grin on his face. Pleased that he had made the effort to visit, I quickly offered to prepare breakfast. He declined, and then asked about Bud. I explained he would not be home until evening, but invited Dad in to wait for him. Dad could not hide his disappointment; and with tears in his eyes, he held out Bud's graduation gift---a hand-pull golf cart! Bud could not possibly conceive of the extraordinary place in Dad's heart from which this gift had come, let alone the tremendous effort he made in shopping for it. To me, Dad's gesture symbolized the genuine respect he had for Bud and his accomplishments. I was equally proud of Dad!

It had been an arduous four years; however, some of Bud's memories were apt to be quite different from mine. Nevertheless, we both looked forward to graduation day. He did not want to join in the exercises though, citing the fact that he was two or three years older than his classmates. His Mother was the one who finally convinced Bud to participate. I was never more proud of him than on that day, and jubilant that our financial struggles would soon be over. One of Bud's conditions for accepting a job was that a prospective employer would pay for the move.

Though I managed to give a small party for Bud, I felt badly that there wasn't enough money to buy him a gift; we couldn't even afford his 1962 class ring. Instead, I made a scrapbook for him, and pasted several bits and pieces of college memorabilia into it. There were MSU stickers, his student I.D cards, news clippings indicating intramural basketball standings, showing the points scored beside his name, student loan receipts, and football ticket stubs. The "MSU Memory Book" was prefaced with a letter in which I wrote, in part: "Your roles and responsibilities were as many as they were varied---husband, father, student and part-time breadwinner, to name a few. However, you managed to carry out all that had to be done, not only successfully, but cheerfully, in addition to maintaining above-average grades. May the rest of your life be less complicated and more enjoyable. May the world respect you, and may God love you most of all."

I closed the book for the night. I could see Bud's looming alcoholism on the horizon though I could see that she and Bud were in love and strong. Again, I felt sad for Carol. Yet I also admired her. More and more, I could see her incredible strength and steadiness through all that she experienced in life. 'I want to be that kind of woman,' I thought.

CHAPTER 24

A M E L I A

When I arrived home the next day, Jake was on the couch wearing the same clothes as the day before, clearly unbathed and unshaven. The sight of him in that state immediately angered me, especially because I was so worn out. I had started my day off behind on my paperwork, and I had a heavy patient load. But I still had to complete everything in time to get the kids from daycare since Jake couldn't, or should I say, wouldn't. He seemed very groggy and he had a dirty plate of a half-eaten sandwich and an open bag of chips on the coffee table. The kids ran up and gave him a hug which he barely returned.

Trying hard not to be angry and frustrated with him, I walked over and kissed him on the cheek and said, "How are you feeling today?"

He said "fine" without looking up from the television.

Not pressing him further I walked into the kitchen, stepping over shoes and toys on my way to make dinner. The kids were playing as usual, completely unfazed by the lump on the couch. When dinner was ready, I called them all in to eat.

Jake said, "Can you just bring me a plate in here? I don't feel like going to the table."

Reluctantly I complied, setting his food in front of him. No thank you or anything. He just continued to watch TV. Our evening activities proceeded, cleaning the kitchen, bathing the kids and getting them to bed–and still Jake never moved.

My 10 hour day had turned into a 15 hour day since I was doing all of the family work, too. After the kids were asleep and the laundry done, I came and sat down next to Jake on the couch.

The moment I sat down, he got up and said, "I am going to bed."

I was hurt and frustrated. I felt like he was pulling further and further away. I had to control myself, I was so tired and needed to relax. I knew I could very easily wallow in my sadness so I decided to turn on the TV and find some brainless sitcom just to clear my mind.

The next morning, it was the same routine from the day before. Jake slept while I made breakfast and got the kids ready for school. When I went into the bedroom to say goodbye, he opened his eyes and said, "Hey, I need more of my pain pills. Will you go by the drugstore and get my refill?"

I told him I would and that was all that was said between us.

The day repeated itself for the next several days until the weekend came. Jake seemed to move around very minimally and talked even less frequently. My kids were pretty resilient so they didn't seem to notice Jake had been closing up more and more. Saturday morning, I decided to push him a little. "So, I have some errands to do. Want to go with me and get out of the house for some fresh air?"

"No, I don't feel like it."

"Okay, but remember, Rose and Dan are expecting all of us for dinner tonight."

Jake said "You guys can go. I don't feel like socializing."

"But Dan has been looking forward to seeing you. It should be fun."

"No, I said I didn't feel like it," he said gruffly.

I tried not to lose my temper, so I took a deep breath and decided to go about my day, hoping he would change his mind and go when the time came.

I tried again at 5:30, just before it was time to go.

"Not tonight."

He had only been on the couch or in bed all week, and he hadn't had a shower for days, yet there he sat. I was flabbergasted.

I called Rose, "Hey girl, I don't think we can come tonight. Jake doesn't feel well."

Rose said "You and the kids come. I have dinner almost ready. You need a break, and Connor is really looking forward to seeing JJ and Olivia."

I hated to go there without Jake, but she was right. I didn't want to sit around all night fretting over him. "We'll be there in 20 minutes," I responded quickly before I changed my mind.

The kids grabbed their favorite toys and we walked over to Rose's house. It was so pretty, one of the prettiest homes on the block, and if truth be told, I would have bought this house if it was on the market when Jake and I looked for a house in this neighborhood. It was pale yellow with the sweetest white shutters. It had a wide front porch that covered the entire front of the house. Rose had decorated the porch with a set of adirondack chairs and little pots of flowers. The lawn was well-manicured. The shrubs were perfectly groomed. Beautiful pink, white and yellow marigolds were strategically placed in the flower beds. The beds themselves were lined with white and yellow daisies.

I had often asked Rose to help me do something with my flower beds, and of course she was willing to help, but I never made the time to actually do it. The ideas I had when we first moved in were of working on the yard and planting flowers beside Jake. Working on other little projects together that would make our house a home. Unfortunately, reality was quite different from my idyllic dreams. Another realization that we weren't really living our lives, we were just going through the day to day. And with the way Jake has been, it was only getting worse.

As I walked up to the porch, I promised myself that I would talk with Rose about scheduling some time next weekend to get our hands dirty and plant some flowers, or maybe even try to talk Jake into gardening with me. I needed to start making changes.

Dan answered the door. "Hey Amelia, come on in. What is up with Jake? Why didn't he come?"

As casually as possible, I said, "He wasn't feeling well. He's sorry to miss tonight, but thanks for having us over."

"Of course. I just opened a bottle of wine. Rose is in the kitchen. Come let me pour you a glass."

Rose and I caught up on the neighborhood gossip and talked about the kids and school and drank almost the whole bottle of wine in no time.

JJ burst into the room. "Connor wants me to spend the night, can I?"

Before I could respond, Rose said, "Great idea! Amelia, why don't both kids stay over. I will give you a bottle of wine to take home to Jake and you two can have some alone time."

"No, thanks, that is nice of you but not tonight." And then adding a little bit under my breath, "I don't think Jake wants alone time with me anyway." I wasn't sure if it was exhaustion, frustration, the effects of the wine, or maybe all three, but tears welled up in my eyes. Desperately, I tried to control them, especially in front of JJ.

JJ's shoulders slumped. "Aw Mom."

"Another time, honey. Just not tonight. We'll do it soon. I promise."

Being the best caring and astute friend I had, Rose ushered him out of the kitchen, and said, "Amelia, sit down. Tell me what is wrong."

Tears ran out of my eyes as freely as the cabernet had flowed that evening. I explained how dark Jake had become, and I even told her about my sad attempt at intimacy earlier in the week. "I thought having the social worker come would help him. Instead it seems to have made it worse. I can't even tell you the last time he said more than two words at a time to me, let alone showered."

Rose burst out laughing.

Initially shocked by Rose's response but then out of nowhere, I started to laugh as well. Then as quickly as the laughter began, it turned to crying again.

"Look," Rose said, "I am not trying to make light of your situation, and I am not laughing at you. I am just trying to picture Jake unshowered and lounging around. That just doesn't sound like him. He has been through a rough time, and this will pass. He just needs time to heal."

"I get it, but he is doing nothing to help himself. He won't go to physical therapy and the social worker suggested a grief group, but he won't even consider it. I just feel like something is really wrong."

"I'll ask Dan to go over and see him tomorrow after church. He'll help get him moving."

"No, that's okay, I am sure he will snap out of it." I certainly didn't want Dan to go over and talk to Jake. He would kill me if he knew I was telling Rose and Dan about our business.

The next morning, I made a big breakfast for the family, thinking maybe a nice breakfast would put Jake in a better mood. The kids were up playing quietly in the living room so I busied myself in the kitchen preparing breakfast, taking big sips of strong coffee as I went. I even decided to put on some music to brighten the mood.

Ever since Carol had suggested listening to music while I cleaned, it had become a habit whenever I did anything domestic. I was surprised at how much the kids enjoyed it. Once the music began to play, the kids seemed to get excited. They knew that it was time to do something and that their mom would dance with them.

One of my favorite songs came on, and I found myself singing along with the lyrics.

Like Pavlov's dog, in came the children. "Dance with us, Mommy!"

I twirled the kids around one at a time until they fell on the floor giggling. Oh, how much I loved seeing my kids laugh. At the same time, my heart was heavy. I glanced in the direction of the bedroom. I wished Jake was out here dancing with me and the kids, they would just love that. Instead, he was still in bed, no noise coming from the room. All morning, I had desperately hoped to hear the shower start running. I pushed the thought away. I didn't want to spoil the moment.

A slow song came on next, detering the kids from the excited dancing. They went back to the living room. The bacon had begun to sizzle on the stove and the kitchen started smelling really good. I was hungry now and was looking forward to a nice meal with my family.

As I finished up the pancakes, I noticed I still hadn't heard Jake stir. It was time to go wake him up before all of the food got cold.

Entering the bedroom, I could hear him snoring away, hidden under the covers.

"Jake, honey, it is time to wake up, breakfast is almost ready."
Nothing.
"Jake, sweetie, time to get up, I made a nice breakfast."
Nothing.

Swallowing my growing anger, I decided to move to the bed and leaned down to kiss him on the cheek.

"Jake, time to get up," I said in the sweetest voice.

"Geez, can't I even sleep in for once, I'm tired." he growled.

Anger surged within me. I felt like taking a pillow and hitting him over the head, but I took a deep breath instead. "I know you are tired, but it is a beautiful Sunday morning, and the kids are happy and the food is ready. Why don't you hop up and take a quick shower and have something good to eat. If you need a nap later, you can take it."

I stood still, waiting for a response.

He didn't move.

Neither did I.

With his eyes still closed he mumbled, "I will be out in a minute."

I was skeptical, but I accepted his response. I walked out of the room and went back to set the table. As I dished out the food to the kids, I decided to go back into the room as I hadn't heard anything more from Jake.

He was still in bed, exactly how I left him. Fully angry now, I slammed the bedroom door and went back to the kitchen. He was so infuriating. He seemed to want nothing to do with interacting with the kids or me. Trying to not cry in front of the kids, I sat down to make my own plate, but picking up my fork, I realized I couldn't eat. I had lost my appetite. Luckily, the kids didn't seem to be disturbed by the fact their father wasn't eating with them. Had this become the new normal for our family? Just me and the kids at meals and at the park and at everything?

After the kids ate, with my plate remaining untouched, I cleaned up the kitchen, this time to no music. I wasn't in the mood. Thinking to myself, I should have planned a quick breakfast and taken the kids to church. Knowing Jake wouldn't go, I had decided against it and instead made a big breakfast for him. Next time, I thought, I am going to go ahead with my own plans and not worry about him. The more I cleaned and thought about that, I began slamming cabinet doors and dishes out of frustration.

JJ padded into the kitchen.

I turned.

"Mom, are you okay? You are making a lot of noise."

Instant guilt merged with my anger. I hadn't realized how loud I was. "I am so sorry, JJ, I didn't mean to. Hey, do you want to go to the park this morning? It is so beautiful outside," trying to sound excited.

"Yes, yes!" He jumped up and down.

Olivia ran in behind her big brother. "Yay, yay!"

"Okay, let's go get dressed."

The kids ran off to their rooms and I went into my bedroom to get ready. Of course, Jake remained in the same place. I went into the bathroom and put on some comfortable clothes, shoes and socks and went out the door without a word from Jake.

That night I sat on the couch. Jake remained in bed.

The next morning I was running around getting ready for work. I grabbed a sweater from the closet, dropping three or four hangers in the process.

Jake got out of bed at the sound of my scuttling about. Without saying a word, he lumbered to the couch, turning on the TV.

It was a new day, so I decided I would start out trying to be sweet and loving to Jake. "The coffee is done. Do you want a cup?"

"No."

"How are you feeling?" Still trying to hold it together.

"Not great. I am in pain and the ibuprofen you gave me isn't working. Do you have something stronger you can give me?"

"No, that's all I have. Give it time. It'll kick in. I left the bottle on the counter. You can have more in three hours."

I was running late. I had overslept, and I had forgotten to put my clothes in the wash and now didn't have anything to wear. Of course, the kids weren't listening either. "Jake, can you help? I am trying to get to work, and JJ won't get dressed. I could really use your help."

"He needs to do these things for himself. JJ, get dressed now!" he yelled from the couch.

"Jake, go help him, please. And could you make sure Olivia has finished her breakfast?" Again, Jake yelled from the couch, "Olivia, finish your breakfast!"

I came out of the bedroom "Jake, really, can't you get up and help? I am late and I could use your help this morning. Do I have to do everything? Really, you just sit there and do nothing, and I am late!" All the sweetness in my voice was gone.

"Geez, I am in pain and all you do is nag me. I am not one of the kids."

'Interesting he would say that,' I thought. 'He sure was acting like one.'

A crash came from the kitchen and a scream from Olivia. "Jake, damn it, Olivia spilled her cereal all over herself. Please help me. She needs to be changed."

"Okay! Stop yelling at me. All you do is gripe at me."

"Well if you would help me, I wouldn't gripe so much. I am trying to do everything, and you do nothing but sit on your butt all day. You need to get to therapy so you can get better and start helping around here. I don't understand why you're still in so much pain. It doesn't make sense."

Jake went into the kitchen and grabbed Olivia by the arm and practically dragged her into the bedroom. By now she was wailing, "Daddy, you are hurting me!"

"Jake, stop! You are hurting her. I'll do it!" I pushed Jake aside and took Olivia into her room to change her clothes. "Seriously, Jake, you have to get a grip on yourself."

Jake stormed into the bedroom and slammed the door.

CHAPTER 25

A M E L I A

Seeing Jake in bed when I got home from work should have infuriated me, but it didn't. I was so mentally and physically exhausted that I think I was just numb. That changed in an instant to sadness when Olivia came bursting through our bedroom door. My children loved their dad and it upset me so much to see their need for his time and playfulness.

"Hi, Daddy!" Olivia jumped on the bed next to him.

Startled from his sleep he jerked but quickly tried to get a hold of himself.

"Hi, honey. How was school today?" Jake asked Olivia.

"Great, Daddy! Are you sick? It isn't bedtime. The sun is out."

My heart lurched. The kids had seemed oblivious to Jake's lack of attention, but maybe it was catching up to him. They missed him.

"No, honey. I just took a nap."

I walked up beside the bed and bent down to kiss his cheek. "How did physical therapy go today, was it hard?"

"Uh, fine, I guess. I am a little sore but good."

"Great. I brought home some chicken for dinner. I bet you are hungry after all of that hard work."

"I am not hungry. I grabbed something on my way home from PT."

"Oh, okay, I will eat with the kids, why don't you relax since you had a hard day, and Jake I am so proud of you for pushing through your PT, you are such an amazing man." I had true compassion for this man. I was so worried about him and still angry from what happened this morning, I tried to remind myself that he was still healing. And even more, he was grieving the loss of his friend. I needed to be more patient.

"I think I will just stay in bed and try to sleep if that is okay, I am really worn out."

"Of course, love you."

I was so concerned about him. It seemed odd to me that he was so exhausted from PT so much that he didn't even have the energy to shower, especially before going to PT.

That night I finally had a chance to read more of Carol's story:

On moving day, Therese stood on the balcony outside of our apartment, looking forlornly through the railing at the moving van. She watched as our few pieces of furniture were loaded onto it. Although we told her we were moving, I was so busy cleaning up after the movers that I did not spend as much time with her as I wanted. A photograph taken of her on that day clearly shows a sad, bewildered face.

The next day we left for Indiana and parts unknown, as they say. Nearing Gary, Indiana, on the Indiana Toll Road, the sunny sky gradually became overcast with soot and air pollution from the several steel mills dotting the southern end of Lake Michigan. As we became shrouded in soot, I asked Bud, "What kind of a

God-forsaken place are you bringing us to?" Bud, in his usual optimism, calmly stated, *"Don't worry; the air is much better south about ten miles, where we'll be living."* We rented a new basic, three bedroom house at 2701 26th Avenue in Griffith.

Bud loved his job as a management trainee and his starting salary at Inland was $517 a month before deductions. He managed to join a carpool, with three other men, who always waited patiently for him to emerge from the house. Bud hustled out the door like Dagwood Bumstead, with his tie flying in one hand and a sack lunch in the other. I often marveled at the staying power exhibited by his fellow carpool members, as they continued to wait for him, with the endurance of flagpole sitters. I sometimes wondered what happened when it was Bud's week to drive; I know the car ran out of gas at least once. It was amazing that people generally had such an uncanny respect for Bud that they accepted aspects in his behavior that they might not have tolerated in anyone else.

During the first few months in Indiana, Bud and I usually sat at the kitchen table on Friday nights after the girls were in bed. Those evenings were reminiscent of our dating days, except that he talked about his week at work. As always, I relished every crumb of his attention. He had a captivated audience even though some of the accounting and steel-making jargon was difficult to understand.

Bud made friends easily and one evening we were invited to join a group of husbands and wives for a night at the harness races. Since I had nothing suitable to wear, Bud agreed to stop at a discount store on the way there, where I found a simple dress and comfortable shoes. I changed clothes in the car. We had no problem finding his friends, and the men soon entered into discussions about the horses that were running that evening. Bud bet conservatively on nearly every race and broke even overall.

Most people can remember where they were on the day that President Kennedy was assassinated. On November 22, 1963, I was cleaning out the front seat of the Corvair in readiness for a trip to visit my sister Marilyn and her family in Oxford, Mississippi. When I reached to turn on the radio I heard, "President Kennedy has just been shot." I hurried into the house to telephone Bud at work, but he had already heard the shocking news. The next morning we left for Mississippi. The girls traveled well as usual, but I had contractions both on the way there and on coming home.

The birth of our third child proved to be the most difficult for Bud as well as myself. Labor began late one evening, and he took me to the hospital. He still abhorred hospitals to the extent he might have preferred a firing squad to long hours spent in a hospital labor room. Shortly after our arrival, the contractions slowed, and a perspiring Bud was visibly relieved when I assured him it was okay for him to leave. A nurse of robust physique and stern countenance examined me, using such force that my head bumped against the top of the bed, possibly shoving the baby out of position. Later on, she gave me a sleeping pill, but it had so little effect that I kept walking the hallways hoping for some activity. The bulldozer of a nurse noticed me and gruffly stated, "Well, if you're not asleep by now, you aren't gonna be!" "Such kind, tender words of encouragement, those!" I angrily mused. Labor refused to progress and I finally lay down to rest.

Later on, Bud returned to the hospital to find me ambling up

I READ WHAT YOU WROTE

and down the hall while someone examined my roommate. In a voice bursting with cheerful kindness, Bud said, "I expected a call from the hospital during the night. What's going on?" Close to tears, I wailed, "Nothing's going on and the doctor hasn't even been to see me!" When the nurse came out of the labor room, we went back there and I introduced my husband to the couple. In his typical jocund style, Bud told them that having a baby was a "piece of cake." The perspiration-soaked husband stared at him as though he had arrived from another planet. Within a couple of hours, someone wheeled his wife to the delivery room. I envied her.

Our third child, and first son, was born on Income Tax day, April 15, 1964 and we named him Scott. Bud was so excited about the birth of his first son that he could hardly wait to telephone everyone. The conversation with his mother was the most amusing, and though I only heard one side of it, it was easy to guess what she said on the other end of the line. Bud kept repeating, "It's a boy!" In surprise she must have questioned, "It's a boy?" They exchanged those happy phrases several times before they finally went on to discuss the rest of the baby's features.

When Bud brought us home from the hospital, it was as though Therese and Ann thought Scott was a present for them; in one sense, perhaps he was. After he was a few months old, I helped the girls to take their small brother to the downstairs playroom. They put him into their red leatherette armchair rocker, and then took turns feeding him play food. Scott obligingly pretended right along with them, by pursing his tiny lips and saying, "Mmmm!" Observing their playful interaction was enormously

263

pleasing; I loved being a stay-at-home mother.

That summer Bud spent a week's vacation in Michigan working for his Dad so he could earn money for a swing set for the children, and the following weekend his favorite aunt came to help him assemble it. The first order of business? Have a couple of beers while studying the instruction sheets. Nevertheless, neither of them had much of a talent for construction. It was amusing to watch as they reviewed the plans, and became wide-eyed as though staring at blueprints for an Eiffel Tower. It was nothing short of a miracle that by nightfall they managed to have the swing set with a glider stand on its own.

I found out I was pregnant again before Scott was even two years old. I couldn't believe our rapidly growing family was getting larger. We welcomed our third daughter in November 1966. She was a sweet pink girl who weighed eight pounds–my largest baby yet. The delivery was difficult, but at least I had a much better doctor. We named her Marie and she was such a happy baby.

In October of 1968 Bud received another promotion which came at a great time since we now had four children, our third daughter was two at the time and I was just about to give birth to our fifth child. He was made Reports Review Supervisor of cost and operations accounting, and by Thanksgiving, we moved into our new home. To us, this was a be-all end-all as houses go. This was the house in which our children would thrive and grow and have a great deal of fun along the way.

In order to bring in extra income, Bud found a job teaching accounting two nights a week at Purdue's Calumet Extension. One evening, after he left for school and the kids were tucked into bed, I proceeded to unpack more boxes from the move. As I opened a carton, a mouse scurried across the kitchen floor. I jumped up on a chair and stayed there until Bud came home. He laughed at my self-imposed confinement and wondered how a former lumberjack could be so afraid of a tiny mouse. He promised to set traps.

If the sixties were devoted to having children, then the seventies were dedicated to the immense challenge of meeting their many needs. Time flew by in those days, and before I knew it Therese and Ann were on Easter break from school. The kids and I had fun roller skating around our spacious basement. That is, until I fell squarely on my sit-down. The kids must have thought I did this on purpose, for they laughed and whizzed past me on their skates, not even stopping to help. At last I got to my feet, hung up the skates and afterward walked strangely for a couple of days.

After our fifth child Chip was born, Bud and I broached the subject of birth control, in spite of the Church's stance against it, but before we acted on my decision other than taking a self-imposed brother/sister vow, I suspected that we just might be expecting another child. For the first time in our marriage Bud accompanied me to the obstetrician's office. Dr. Polite wasn't absolutely certain I was pregnant and said he would give me an injection of some sort. If we were going to have another baby, neither of us would want an abortion; Bud and I were together on that. The doctor smiled and said something like 'You don't understand', If you aren't pregnant, this will help start your menses; otherwise it will strengthen the lining of the uterus and protect the baby.

We were both silent on the way home, but as soon as we walked through the front door, I motioned Bud to follow me into the living room for a private conversation. We sat down together on the sofa. We need to talk, I said, beginning to cry. Chip was still a baby and here we might be having another child. Through the tears, I blurted out, "Just how many children did you want, anyway?" Bud with his wry grin, calmly stated, two. Once again, his clever wit and endearing sense of humor saved the day and we hugged.

"Honey, did you iron my shirt yet? I am going to be late, and I need to get going." Bud questioned as he ran down the stairs.

"I will be done in a minute; can you warm up a bottle for Frankie while I finish?"

"Where do I get that? I don't know where you have that. Besides, he seems fine. He doesn't need a bottle."

"Forget it, I will get it, when I am done with your shirt."

Bud ran out the door, late as usual, to catch the vanpool that took him downtown for work every day. I was exhausted; I was always exhausted lately. Six small children and one busy husband that worked two jobs meant that he was never home, certainly never available to help me with the kids or the house. I got Frankie fed and down for his nap, little Chip, who recently learned to walk was not walking but running around the house. Running into everything in his way. The older kids were off at school, so I thought today was the day I was hoping to get a handle on all the housework.

Chip managed to wear himself out and was asleep in front of the TV and Frankie was still napping so I couldn't vacuum.

As much as I would have liked to rest myself, I instead took the opportunity to do some other cleaning. I had managed to clean the kitchen earlier and was working on the bathrooms. I went out into the kitchen for more cleaning supplies and found water all over the floor. Oh my gosh, what is going on? I noticed water was coming out from under the dishwasher. Great! Just great, it was broken. I immediately turned off the dishwasher and grabbed towels. Luckily the water stayed in the kitchen and didn't travel further, or the carpet would be ruined. In the midst of all this chaos, Frankie started crying and Chip woke up. I quickly grabbed a bottle and went up the stairs to get Frankie. Chip tried to follow me up and I forgot to close the baby gate and turned around at the top of the stairs just as Chip proceeded to fall down the couple stairs he managed to climb up, luckily, he was okay, but I now had two babies crying, and I felt like crying myself. My day pretty much was managing the little ones, and not finishing any of the chores I had hoped to accomplish. The older ones came home from school and my day got crazier. Snacks, homework, babies crying, trying to get some sort of dinner prepared, that was my chaotic routine every day. By the time I got all the kids to bed and Bud finally showed up, I was exhausted. He told me all about his day, never once asking how my day was. I felt like I was losing my mind. Luckily the next day I had my appointment with Dr. Conrad. I was out of my diet pills and needed more, at least they gave me my much needed energy lift.

When I picked up the little ones from the neighbor's house, I went home and fed the boys. They had a good time, and both were tired, so they went right down for a nap. That is good I thought, I can get some stuff done. Instead, I sat down on the couch and turned on the tv. I never get time to do this, I told myself. I will just sit here for a minute. Forty-five minutes later I was woken up by the sound of Frankie crying. Wow, I don't know how I fell asleep; I quickly ran upstairs to get the boys. The older kids were due home soon, so I tried to finish the bathrooms that weren't done the day before. A short time later all the older ones got home from school. The noise in the house went up about 20 decibels and it was giving me a headache. Bud called to see how my day was going and I told him I just needed a break, and he suggested going out to mow the lawn. "Carol, just go outside and mow the lawn, it will give you a nice break from the kids. Therese and Ann can watch the little ones for you. Not really thinking much about that, I decided to go ahead and do just that, anything to get out. After fighting to get the mower started, I began the arduous job of mowing our large lawn, bending down every few feet to pick up balls and other toys so as not to run over them. About halfway through mowing, I was physically exhausted. It was hot and I was sweating heavily. Why am I doing this? What an idiot I am to take his suggestion. I had to laugh, I was so gullible, and Bud was always one step ahead of me.

There was no denying Dad's excitement when he telephoned and asked us to come to Michigan and see the rig that Mobil Oil company had set up by the barn. Oil had been discovered on several neighborhood properties and Dad was eager to share in a financial piece of the action. When we arrived, Dad immediately took us to the shack where geologists were monitoring a panel of *instruments and introduced each of the men as though they were his dearest friends – which they might have been at the time. Next, he ushered us close to the oil rig to watch the drilling. Dad was completely captivated by this new activity and showed it off as though he was its principal owner. When Dad wasn't out with the oil men, he sat in his rocking chair, donned his hard hat with the Santa smiley face, and using binoculars stared rapturously through the picture window at the goings-on.*

A few weeks later, Dad telephoned to tell us that his only brother had died on the farm that had been homesteaded in 1836, a hundred years before I was born. He wanted me to come up for the auction and I brought Therese, then 13, with me. As soon as we walked through the door, Dad started in on me. "You don't know anything about an auction, so just be quiet and I'll do the bidding."

This time Dad went too far. "You've put me down for the last time!" I shouted at him. Then I began to cry, but that didn't stop the tirade. Not sure if it was my exhaustion, or if he finally broke the last straw but I said, "No." I screamed, "You've always belittled me and criticized me, but I'm not going to take it anymore!" Sobbing and barely stopping to breathe, I continued, "I've come up to visit you and Mother because I love you, but if this is the way you plan on treating me, I'll stay home where I belong!" I was still going strong, but shaking with anger, I reminded him of the many times Bud had willingly stayed home to care for one or more of the children so that I could come for a visit. "Yet you cut me down every time I walked through the door!" I exclaimed. By this time both Dad and Mother were crying too, but they didn't say a word.

Finally, Dad said something to the effect that he hadn't realized he had hurt me so often. My diatribe didn't last long, but it cleared the air; and afterward we settled into normal conversation. Thenceforward, Dad treated me with respect and never again belittled or insulted me. Why had it taken so long to stand up for myself?

In August of 1973, Mother telephoned with bad news. Dad was in the hospital; he'd had a stroke. I asked how he was doing, and Mother said she didn't know – he was unable to speak. I assured her that I would drive to Michigan the following morning. Afterward, I climbed to the top of the stairs, sat down on the top step, and cried. Bud's nephew Mark, who had been spending the summer with us, came up and put his arm around me. When I told Bud about Dad, he didn't or couldn't say a word.

The next day I packed a few clothes for Ann and me and drove directly to the Eaton Rapids hospital. I was shocked to see Dad, once huge and robust, now ashen, thin, and semi-conscious. Mother was sitting by the window when I came in, but we met in the middle of the room and as we hugged, I couldn't take my eyes off Dad. His breathing was shallow despite the oxygen tube in his nose and there was an IV connected to one of his arms. Though he couldn't talk or scarcely move it was easy to tell when he became restless. At those times, Mother went to his side to comfort him. He reached for the modest silver band on Mother's left hand, and feeling it, he would settle down again. That scenario played out several times during the next few days.

My brother's wife Debbie arranged to have her parents take care of Ann. If I had understood the seriousness of Dad's illness, I wouldn't have brought her with me. Mother was in shock and went mechanically back and forth from Dad's room to a nearby restaurant, always accompanied by one of us children. One night I drove to Mother and Dad's house in Onondaga, since there wasn't a decent motel for miles, but even then, sleep eluded me.

The family took turns staying with Dad, rarely leaving him alone. I can still remember how uncomfortable it was just sitting with him, yet when we left to get a bite to eat, we felt compelled to hurry back there. Once, when it was my turn to sit with Dad, I patted his dry lips with water and bathed his face with cool, moist cloths. Then, a thought occurred to me: Had Dad been baptized? Though my attempt may have been short of perfection, I prayed over him and gave him a conditional baptism.

Poor Marilyn, who was living in Oxford, Mississippi, tried to determine whether she should fly up to Michigan. I'm certain it was a difficult call for her, especially with the prospect of leaving a husband and five children behind. However, the doctor answered the question for her. He told Mother that if there were any relatives who needed to be informed of Dad's condition, she should accomplish that as soon as possible. Marilyn flew into Detroit on the next available flight and nearly fainted when she saw Dad. After two or three days without much sleep and stressing over my parents, it felt as though every fiber and fluid had drained out of me. I was in dire need of a restorative sanctuary, a peaceful haven where I could have a few hours of uninterrupted sleep.

When I told my younger brothers and sister that I planned to go home, they freaked out, and so did my mother. But there was 12-year-old Ann to consider, and the good people taking care of her. They all seemed to feel that I was the proverbial *rat deserting a sinking ship. But I had to go home, since I stood badly in need of the comforts that only Bud and our home could provide. My siblings told me I could leave on one condition: if Bud approved. Inside I was furious but amazed at my exterior calmness. I was determined to go home no matter what they or Bud said. I knew I would be needed after Dad's death, but I also knew that I couldn't cope with anything further without first receiving some sorely needed rest.*

My siblings were unrelenting and drove me to a coin telephone in downtown Eaton Rapids. With my siblings watching intently, I called Bud collect at work and explained the situation. He seemed to sense my dilemma, and said, "Whatever you think is best, Hon." At the sound of his voice, I felt tremendous relief and asked him to repeat the statement to my family. Though they seemed genuinely shocked that Bud didn't side with them, they stuck to our agreement. By the time we returned to the hospital, it was late afternoon. I said goodbye to Mother, trying to reassure her that I would return the next day, but I don't think she believed me. Soon afterward I collected Ann, and we began the three-and-a-half-hour trip to Indiana and home, sweet home.

By the time we reached Benton Harbor, I was having trouble staying awake, a problem I had never encountered before behind the wheel. The book, "God Is My Co-Pilot" came to mind and I prayed, "Please bring us home safely." That seemed to help and so I prayed for us the rest of the way home, and right into our driveway. Poor Ann; I was no help to her as I started up the stairway, stripping off my outer clothing on the way. Even too exhausted for a shower, I put on a nightgown and fell into bed, which awakened Bud. He asked, "Are you all right?" The only response I could muster was, "I'll tell you all about it in the morning."

The next thing I remember was an adrenaline rush when the telephone rang about 8:00 a.m. It was Mother who said that Dad had just died, but that Robert had been with him. The date was August 12, 1973; Dad was only 62. For some reason, Mother thought I was angry with her and my siblings. I tried to reassure her that I wasn't and that we would leave for Michigan as soon as possible to help with the funeral arrangements.

The next few days were a blur as we chose the casket, the flowers and helped with the obituary. Attending the wake was somewhat easier since friends and relatives kept us busy visiting. I could barely stand to look at Dad's remains lying in the open casket and right then I made a promise to myself: no open casket for me! I wouldn't want people filing past my dead body saying such things as "Doesn't she look so natural, so peaceful, etc.?" Never mind the unnecessary expense of it all. Henceforward, I would never be convinced that viewing a person's dead remains is germane to closure after a person's death.

The funeral was typically quiet and somber, and I don't remember a thing the minister said. I only knew that the only way I could endure the service without coming completely unglued was to recite the Our Father over and over. After the service at the Onondaga Cemetery, Mother gave permission to have some of the flowers sent to St. Peter's Catholic Church in Eaton Rapids. Bud and I went there to request Masses for Dad, which I doubt meant anything to my non-Catholic birth family, but was especially comforting to me, even though I still wasn't a Catholic.

Over the next couple of months, I frequently shed tears and thought about the sort of person Dad was. He had made a tremendous impact on my life, for good and for ill, which often caused my emotions to swing from high to low, but in my estimation, he was inherently a good man with a big heart. He possessed an endearing streak of sentimentality, and tears could be seen in his eyes at weddings and funerals, the only times he ever went to church. Eventually, I think I came to understand him as well as anyone, except for Mother, though he never seemed to understand himself. He lived moment-to-moment and reacted accordingly, but I loved him.

I am not a person customarily given to apparitions or visions of any sort, but about six months after Dad's death; I was abruptly awakened one night. It suddenly felt as though I was being rapidly propelled toward the double doors of a closet across from our bed. I was stopped short of a collision and suddenly saw a large glowing vision of Dad, dressed in the most lustrous, pure white robes. His face glowed and looked beautifully serene with a slight smile and his skin was as smooth as a baby's. Remarkably, the scar from the accident was gone! Though this image occurred more than thirty years ago, lasting only seconds, I remember it vividly. I've told only a select few about this experience and have had no other such visions since.

What is the definition of a marriage? The Bible says, "... the two shall become as one." Bud and I were "one," in that we lived in the same house and had children together; otherwise we pretty much functioned separately; Bud to his job and other activities, while I stayed home with the children, period. Like some other stay-at-home mothers, I began feeling like a virtual prisoner. Many times I resented the self-imposed confinement, especially due to an ingrained sense of responsibility that I could not deny. However, at the time, I had no thoughts about how to change anything.

After being a witness to some of Bud's verbal fictional flights of imagination, it tarnished at least some of the trust I had in him. It wasn't until I accidentally found a credit card and a bank statement in his name only, that I felt crushed at his deception. The items were found in a suit of his when I took it to the cleaners. Later, when I confronted him with the items and asked why he felt a need to deceive me, he had a ready answer, as usual. "Oh, everybody I know does that."

The first welcome benefit from that disappointing turn of events was the fact that Bud didn't drink for about three days. The second was that he agreed to participate in a Marriage Encounter weekend. Though an "encounter" weekend is designed to draw a couple emotionally closer together, which I deeply longed for in our marriage, it is not intended to solve marital problems. I knew that going in, however I hoped that in this venue Bud, who always seemed quite satisfied with the status quo, would somehow be able to share some of his feelings.

We checked into the motel on a Friday evening, and entered the conference room just in time to participate in the introductory meeting. A Catholic priest was the principal facilitator, with support from a previously "encountered" couple. Father was explaining the agenda and the format for the weekend, when all of a sudden I noticed Bud lift a small brown paper bag to his lips. In it was his standard "beverage of choice," Budweiser. I was surprised when Father politely admonished Bud, in front of everyone, to leave his paper bag in our room. He said, "It's out of place in our meetings." After that, Bud, in his own deep thoughts, began doodling in tight, heavy drawings.

After each meeting, couples were given one or more questions and a prescribed length of time in which to return to their room and write a letter to their spouse about a specific topic. Bud's note to me in answer to the question as to why he came was barely legible: "out of curiosity." He went on to criticize what he called a "canned presentation," and said, "I am very doubtful whether I can overcome the people presenting the subject." He ended the note by printing, "I love you." After the third meeting he settled down somewhat, and began sharing some of his thoughts in more legible handwriting, but he continued to doodle during the meetings. At one point he must have been hungry, for he drew a recognizable knife, fork and spoon.

The most beautiful, open and honest letter that he ever wrote to me was in answer to the question: "What are my reasons for wanting to go on living?" In it he was finally able to share some of his innermost thoughts and feelings in a way that he never had before, even waxing poetic, sometimes. Over the years I have read and re-read this cherished letter, and each time I appreciate the truly wonderful person he was underneath the protective alcoholic persona. I will be forever grateful for the setting and the intercessory prayers, which allowed him to put into words his life, his loves and his philosophies.

"Dear Carol:

Boy, this first question is a dilly. I can see why no one gets by the first question and really, the other questions are very good also. There are so many reasons why I want to go on living that to enumerate them all would [be] and is difficult.

I suppose I basically want to go on living because death is so final in respect to what I am aware of here on earth. But death could be a very happy reunion with God in heaven. Even with all the love one can have for Him and since His place is eternal, it will always be there, so I will have to ask Him to wait for now.

There is really almost too much to live for to put them [the reasons] in any sequence at all, so I will just take the thoughts as they come. Probably the most important reason is for myself. I have much to do in respect to every aspect of my existence. Or, maybe I am just curious as to what will happen. But that would suggest that I would just be sitting around waiting for things to happen instead of living and making things happen. Like going to a movie to see how it will happen, even when you know the good guys will win or the boy will get the girl. I think I would prefer to be an actor in the movie, but without a script to tell me how it ends. I don't mean that there isn't any script for life because there is, but it is more of a set of principles, guidelines, experience, wants or desires, goals [and] expectations that tend to be the script that one follows through life.

So, maybe I will never see all of the above to their conclusions. I sure want to give it a good shot. Then, there are times that maybe my goals, principles, etc. are not properly expressed or possibly not even thought of, but I know I have a "game plan."

Some of the expectations are very short-run, for example: looking forward to making love to you the next time or seeing Ann without her braces or having Scott ask to use my razor *or even getting a seven-letter word in a crossword puzzle that you could not think of and have it fit. Watching Marie get ever so more beautiful in her heart. Watching her goodness grow (provided we can keep her hair cut). Seeing you preparing a big holiday dinner and trying to emulate all of the enthusiasm you muster for the occasion. Or, waiting for our first game of bridge, as partners. Or, both of us watching Frankie receive his First Communion. Or, Scott at his Confirmation. To see if Therese is still alive or just broke. Wondering what bone Chip will break first in his next sporting effort, or even if he can survive.*

These are probably very short run, but there will always be the next short-run or to see them all happen over and over again. But I know as all the events happen---some small and some big, that I would like to see happen---I believe there are many more that I don't know about that I am looking forward to seeing and experiencing. Such as a first wedding of one of our children. Seeing you as a grandmother and have the experience of sleeping with a grandmother. (I bet it's the same as it was when you were my bride).

It is all of the new experiences that will happen to me or to those I love that I want to be there to share them. I know all of the experiences ahead will not be joyous ones. There will be hurts, sicknesses, deaths and many other unhappy events. But, there are so many good ones that all the bad is definitely worth the price. It's like putting up with a heavy rain that causes flooding. It also makes things grow and blossom. Or, it's like the parable we heard yesterday about the seeds. Some seeds were thrown in the path and were stepped on, others were eaten by the birds, but my seed, I know, hit the fertile ground. So, now I want to see those seeds sprout and spring forth from the ground and turn into beautiful plants or flowers that also have seeds of their own to fall [upon] the fertile ground, so they too, will sprout and grow. I guess knowing and being able to see this happen and knowing I have been able to provide the atmosphere of the fertile ground to all those around me that I love, then I don't think I will mind when harvest time comes.

I guess the feeling of anxiety and hope with fulfillment is the best feeling I have for wanting to go on living. It's like a drive---like a salmon swimming up the river to spawn---it's one hell of a challenge and fight to get up the river of life, knowing that at the end you must die. But, it's worth every struggle, fallback and effort to get there.

Everyone is up now milling around and I wanted to get to question number 2, "What are my reasons for wanting to go on living with you?" but I think we have to leave now. It would be like the salmon taking the first bend in the river and really not getting to the end without you.

Love, Bud

I know that if someone else read the letter, they probably would not think it was very touching or romantic, but it was Bud through and through, and I loved it.

Then, in his last letter of the weekend he reverted back to his usual protective self and wrote, "I believe the weekend opened a door for communications for us, but like any other door it will be opened sometimes and it is also frequently closed."

I don't know if the fears and feelings that Bud kept to himself were comparable to how other men in our era felt, I only know that Bud usually did a good job of suppressing anything that hinted of emotion or threatened his self-protective wall. That is why I will always treasure this one beautiful letter. It seemed that the only other times Bud allowed himself to express emotion was when he went nose to nose with the police or when watching his favorite sports animals: the Bears, the Bulls and the Cubs.

As we go our way through life, it seems inevitable that we're forced to encounter the bitter with the better. I believe that the manner in which we choose to cope with the difficult times can make all the difference in whether our character becomes stronger or weaker, since we rarely emerge unchanged from some of life's trials. My family and I were about to experience a true test of our collective courage.

The alarm went off on my phone. Darn, I thought. I had set it so I didn't stay up too late.

Much as I didn't want to, I had to stop for the night. Even though tomorrow was Saturday, I had to get some sleep with everything going on. I set aside the binder, turned off the light, and closed my eyes.

CHAPTER 26

AMELIA

It was a beautiful day, and I was able to talk Jake into helping me run some errands, including going to the home improvement store. I wanted to plant some flowers in the front yard and wanted his help grabbing some mulch. We dropped the kids off at Rose's house so they could play while we went shopping.

I received a call when we were pulling into the home improvement store. It was Earl.

"That was Carol's husband," I said to Jake. "She isn't doing too well today and he wants me to come check on her, she fell trying to get out of bed. Do you mind if we run by her house really quickly? She lives very close to here and I don't really want to take the time to run you home and then go. I could ask the on-call nurse to go, but since it is Carol, I would prefer to go myself, would that be okay?"

"Sure, it won't take long though, will it?" I could tell he wasn't thrilled with the idea.

As we pulled up to the house, I suggested, "Why don't you come in with me, I would love for you to meet Carol. She is my favorite as you know. She knows all about you and it might make her happy to meet you."

"Okay, but let's not be here too long, I am still sore from

all the work I did yesterday."

"We'll hurry," I promised as we walked in the door.

"Hi, Earl. What is going on?" I was surprised to see him answer the door. He usually either called for me to come in from his chair.

"Thanks for coming. Carol fell when she got up to go to the bathroom. I heard her fall and by the time I got into the room, she was trying to get herself back in bed. She asked if I would call you."

"I will go right in. Hey Earl, this is my husband Jake. Is it okay if he stays out here with you for a few minutes? We were out this way when I got your call and so we came right over."

Earl grunted a hello and nodded.

I walked into Carol's bedroom, "Hi, Carol. I heard you took a little fall. How are you feeling? Do you hurt anywhere?"

"Just my hip a little." I began to examine Carol, she seemed to be able to move her leg and hip without too much pain, so I figured she didn't do any major damage. Carol's blood pressure was elevated a little but nothing too serious. It was probably due to the anxiety of the fall.

"Thanks for coming Amelia, I panicked when I fell and that is why I asked Earl to call you." She sounded weak and was shaking a little.

"No problem, Carol, that is what I am here for, and it looks like you didn't do any damage, I am happy to say. I do have to report the fall, that is procedure, but glad you are okay. Are you up for a visitor? I brought Jake with me. We were shopping right near here when I got Earl's call, so I brought him."

"Of course, please. I would love that! Do I look okay?" Her

hands patting down her hair.

"Carol, you look beautiful as always," I assured her.

"Awe, that is what Bud used to say to me all the time. Sometimes I really miss him, Amelia."

"I am sure you do, Carol. It sounds like he was a very sweet man." I peeked my head out of Carol's bedroom door and asked Jake to come in.

"Carol, this is Jake, my husband."

Jake walked over to the side of the bed and reached for Carol's outstretched hand. "So nice to meet you, Carol. I have heard so much about you, Amelia just loves visiting you."

"Oh, she is such a dear, she makes me so happy every time she comes to visit. She reminds me of my children."

"When did you last eat?" I questioned.

"Oh, I ate something this morning."

"What did you have?" I had learned to ask specifics when it came to questions about eating. I know she forgets a lot, but I need to make sure she has some nutrition.

"Um, I am not sure, toast maybe."

"Carol, remember you need to make sure you are eating. How about pain, are you in any pain right now?"

"I have some discomfort I guess." Her hand automatically rubbed her side and stomach.

"I will ask Earl when you are due for your next dose."

Carol looked at Jake and said, "So Jake, I hear you are a firefighter."

"Yes, ma'am I am." He stood up a little taller with pride.

"God bless you; I love firefighters. They are amazing people to me."

"Oh, thank you, I do love my work."

"Amelia said you had an accident. How are you feeling?"

"I am getting better and will be going back to work in a couple of weeks, I am anxious to get back." I was so glad to hear that. Jake hadn't talked with me about his return to work. Everytime I brought up the subject he never wanted to discuss it.

"Just be safe and take your time recouping. You don't want to hurt yourself worse," Carol stated in the most mothering way.

"Yes ma'am."

"Amelia, your husband is so handsome and so sweet. I can now see why you talk so highly of him all of the time." I looked over at Jake and we smiled at each other. I could tell Jake liked her. In just a matter of a few minutes she seemed to have brought us closer, through her words, than we had been the last few weeks.

"Yes, I am very lucky. He is an amazing man. Carol, Earl said you are due now for pain meds. I am not technically supposed to give this directly to you, but I told Earl I would. He said he will record this dose on the spreadsheet." I reached for the bottle that was sitting on top of her dresser and put one into the small cup for her.

"Amelia, I still have to go to the bathroom. I never made it there, and now I really need to go. Can you help me? Urgency in her voice.

"Sure," I said as I put down the pill bottle.

Looking at Jake, I said, "I am just going to help her to the bathroom and then we should be all set to leave, Jake."

I got Carol all settled back in her bed, and I have asked Earl to get something nutritious for her to eat. At this stage of care, I am not supposed to give Carol her medication directly, but not wanting to interrupt Earl from getting Carol food, I go to her dresser to grab the pill I had set aside for her. The pill was not in the cup where I placed it just a few minutes ago and immediately looked down to see if it had fallen to the floor. As I do, Jake took a big step backwards and I instinctively looked up at him. His face was as white as a ghost and looked incredibly guilty. I immediately thought, did he just take that pill? He couldn't have, he would never do that, would he? I was shaken at the thought, but had to recover quickly and get another pill out for Carol.

After the goodbyes, Jake and I walked out to the car. I put my bag in the trunk and got in the passenger side, put on my seatbelt and didn't say a word. I knew I had taken out that pill and put it in the cup, but I couldn't believe he would take it! A million thoughts were running through my head. I was interrupted by Jake saying, "So, back to Home Depot?"

"Yes" was all I could muster.

We drove in silence. Should I confront him with my fears? It was such a terrible accusation, and I just couldn't bring myself to question him.

"She is a nice lady. I see why you like her so much." Jake said lightly.

"Yes, she is." I couldn't trust myself to say anything more.

In the store, our conversation was limited to functional things, necessary statements. "Jake, go grab six large bags of mulch in that cart over there, get the dark brown ones. Can you grab them one handed, or do you need my help?" I spoke through gritted teeth. I couldn't believe he would do such a thing, but the reality was undeniable. I knew I had to confront him, but I was so angry, I didn't trust myself to broach the subject in a way that would be constructive.

"I got it."

We drove home in silence, but at this point, alone in the car, I found myself getting angrier and angrier. We pulled into the driveway. I couldn't hold it in any longer. Before we got out of the car, I exploded. "How could you Jake? I could get fired. We could lose everything. You could go to jail, so could I, and what would happen to our kids?"

"I didn't," he responded, fully knowing what I was referring to.

"You didn't? You didn't? Don't try to deny it, Jake. You took that pill. I know you did. I'm the one who put it in the cup! How many did you take?"

"I just took the one." Jake shifted in his seat uncomfortably. "Geez. You're overreacting. And you don't know how hard it has been for me. I'm in pain. I need them, and the doctor won't give me any more!"

"That is because they're so addictive. You need to be able to manage the pain without those. How could you do that to me?"

"Calm down, you are totally overreacting. It was only one pill. She had a full bottle. She will never know."

"Oh, you noticed that, did you? You noticed the bottle was full? And you're in pain without them, even though you have no reason to be in pain any more." My heart sank further. My worst fear was coming to pass. Only an opioid addict would be in pain without the pills. That was how the addiction manifested itself: when the body had the chemicals in the system, it felt at peace but when the drugs were absent, the body sent pain signals to the brain.

"You don't know that. I do need them. You don't feel what I feel."

"Jake, it is illegal! She is dying. She needs them. How dare you?! Give me the pill Jake." I stretched out my hand.

"I threw it out already."

"You threw it out." I paused. "You're lying."

"When?"

"At the store."

"Seriously, you did. Even though you need it so bad, you threw it away. How can I believe you?"

"Yes. Come on Amelia, you know me. I can't believe you don't trust me. I am going next door to get the kids." He left, slamming the front door behind him.

I didn't speak with him the rest of that day. He tried to be helpful. He made dinner and fed the kids and even gave them a bath. I was not sure how he did that one-handed, but he did. He played with them and put them to bed. Suddenly, he was the model husband.

I was on my computer most of the rest of the day and didn't say a word to him. The next day was pretty much the same. As the week progressed, he seemed more and more disheveled and irritable. He stayed on the couch or in bed almost the whole week.

That night as I lay in bed, Jake sleeping beside me, my mind spun. He was addicted. I knew it. There was no denying it. Even his breathing sounded different. His body needed this detox. Maybe it would just take a few more days for him to get through it. He had no access to pain medication that I was aware of. Maybe he would just have a few rough days and then be able to move on. I pulled out Carol's binder, anticipating the joy I felt when I immersed myself in her story:

It took a long time for me to realize that Bud's gentleness didn't mean that he was any less of a man. On the contrary. He could be firm and persuasive, using his intellect and sense of humor instead of yelling and fit throwing, as Dad had done. I, on the other hand, unwittingly became a lot like Dad; it was as though that was the only way I could garner Bud's attention. I possessed little self-esteem or self-understanding. In fact, I even surprised myself one day when I lost my temper and sent a Revere Ware tea kettle crashing through the bottle-glass sidelight of our front door. After one of my temper fits, I felt strong remorse at first, then I usually cried. Poor Bud had no notion why I was behaving like a petulant child, and he often asked, "What can I do for you?" He must have been extremely frustrated without realizing that the attitude I had toward his drinking played a part in my erratic behavior, and neither did I have a grasp on my feelings in some situations.

The decision to take my psychiatrist's advice in getting educated about the disease of alcoholism was another important step toward improving my mental health. There is a lot to learn, both in what to do and what not to do regarding the alcoholic, and I continued making mistakes. I found that, just as with psychotherapy, the do's and don'ts are difficult to put into practice. The saying "knowledge is power" really makes sense in the day-to-day struggle of living with and loving an alcoholic. Perhaps the same holds true for those who have loved ones suffering from any addiction, even if it's only a craving for chocolate.

That first meeting at Al-Anon was a huge eye-opener because I quickly discovered that one cannot change the alcoholic, only oneself. It was somewhat comforting to hear others describe many of the same pitfalls and problems that I was encountering, and as a result I no longer felt so alone. On the other hand, our situation did not seem as bleak as some. If there was to be any success in coping with the effects of alcoholism in our marriage, it depended on getting my own act together. For starters, I would no longer walk the floor on those nights when Bud was gone. Maybe I wouldn't sleep well, if at all, but I learned to avoid this particular emotional roller coaster and began trusting in "a higher power." To get my thoughts together on Bud's problem I began to think back to the various times in our life that I felt Bud was out of control, not just a social drinker like I thought in the beginning but truly had a problem.

The first example of putting this new bit of wisdom into practice was the night someone called from the Highland Police Station. The angry voice on the other end of the line asked, "Mrs. Howland?" "Yes?" I responded, with an immediate adrenaline rush. "We have your husband here." "He's drunk and he ran a red light!" "We're going to keep him here all night." Perhaps the officer thought I was going to put up an argument. Instead, I said, "OK, thank you for calling," and hung up the receiver. For a short time, I felt enormously pleased with my new serenity. But within an hour, a policeman called back. Bud must have given them a rough time. "Mrs. Howland, we're going to release your husband if you can come and get him." "He's too drunk to drive *his car."* Now, the ball was clearly in my court, but we had only one car. In looking back, I probably should have told the officer to keep him. Instead, I found a neighbor to take me to the police station. As Bud and I turned to leave, an angry officer yelled after him, "Don't ever let yourself be caught back here again, or we'll throw the book at you!" I had the feeling that the Highland Police were only too happy to get rid of their prisoner.

The local hospital was giving a five-night seminar on alcoholism and I attended all five nights. The talks began with a description of the disease, yes; it was called a disease there, too. The presenter cited many reasons why a person turns to alcohol and drugs in the first place. He went on to explain that an alcoholic metabolizes alcohol differently from the rest of us. He said that in a normal person an internal alarm signals when we've had enough, and we stop drinking. On the other hand, when an alcoholic drank, the more he craves it, and usually drinks himself into oblivion. I learned that alcohol addiction isn't so much about self-control (as I had originally thought); rather, it has to do with a decision to drink in the first place. An alcoholic must choose not to take that first drink. Equally important, he/she needs to understand why they drink, and there are many reasons for that: a hereditary factor, lack of self-confidence, wanting to be the life of the party, stress at work or at home, grief over losing a loved one; the list is endless.

It had taken a complete mental breakdown and a competent psychiatrist to begin rebuilding my psyche, but the greatest good I could do henceforth for our marriage involved further maturation through prayer, attendance at Mass and Al-Anon. So far, the greatest "hello" in our marriage was when I discovered *that I had apparently misunderstood Bud all along. From the first time I met him, he had always been consistently even-tempered, kind and considerate. How sad it was to discover that I had mistakenly believed that "real men" must all be like my father. On the other hand, I don't know if Bud fully realized the damage that his alcoholism was doing to himself and to our marriage.*

I continued attending Al-Anon meetings and kept on referring to One Day at a Time in Al-Anon. Oh, how I wished I could share all this new wisdom and common sense with Bud, but I didn't exactly make a secret of it, either. In fact, when he asked where I was going one evening, I told him straight out. What could the poor man say, especially since he was always reluctant to share his thoughts or feelings?

There were the children to consider in all of this too, and I felt they should learn something about alcoholism beyond what they could observe at home. There are meetings about alcoholism for adult children of alcoholics, ACOA. Though I took two or three of our older children to a couple of meetings, the younger ones didn't really seem to grasp much at the time. But what I hoped would seep into their subconscious was that if they ever needed help of any sort, it would behoove them to seek it.

I often looked to Bud for emotional support but received precious little of it. When I became upset, it made him uncomfortable, so he often used his wit and wiles to pre-empt my unfriendly sad moods or avoided them altogether. It was a sadistic circle; Bud generally knew when he fell short of meeting my needs and dealt with it the only way he knew how; by drinking. My pride would not permit complaining to my mother or my sister. Neither did I have any close friends in whom I could confide. As a result, I sometimes resented being stuck at home, still clueless about the need to expand the confines of my world. On the surface, Bud seemed to be at least moderately sympathetic to my needs, to the extent it served his own need to be free to drink whenever and with whomever he pleased. It was a tenuous situation at best.

Now and then Bud failed to make it home at night after an outing with his friends, sometimes telling me where he was going and sometimes not. When he went to see belly dancers in Chicago, I heard about it later from someone else's wife. Still, no matter how much I worried on those occasions, I only prayed for Bud's safety, while crying and pacing the floor for hours at a time. After each such emotional roller coaster ride, I fell into bed, exhausted. In the morning Bud usually had a clever way of averting or dispelling my anger altogether. One of his favorite tactics cheerfully unfolded thusly: "Carol, you'll never guess who I ran into last night!" I would stare blankly, while he followed with something like, "I ran into so and so and he thinks you're so pretty," or maybe it would be "so nice" or "so smart." "Oh, really?" I would say, falling once again into the abyss of his clever manipulation. This type of ploy worked for him for longer than I care to admit.

One evening he announced he was going to a friend's house in Miller Beach (near Gary), to play poker. I protested, to no avail. On weekends Bud did pretty much whatever he wanted. Hours later, after the usual worrying and pacing, I finally fell asleep. The next thing I knew, dawn's first light was streaming on a well-lit Bud knocking on a front window. *Apparently, he had enough sense not to ring the doorbell and awaken the children. When I let him into the house, his first words were, "I wish I could say I was out with another woman." Adrenaline shot through me and quickly obliterated any remnants of sleep lingering in my foggy brain. He said he was on his way home from the poker party and felt sleepy, so he pulled over to the side of the road and went to sleep. Someone came along, woke him up, and robbed him, taking his wallet and even his wedding ring. Suddenly my anger vanished completely and melted into complete ingenuous sympathy. "Oh, what a relief! You could have been killed!" I exclaimed, hugging him. My theme song back then should have been, "What kind of fool am I?"*

A couple of weeks later, Bud said the police had found his wedding ring. With this improbable bit of news, I began to doubt Bud for the first time. Part of his story just didn't ring true, but I failed to ask the obvious questions. Was he really robbed? Was he out with another woman? Had the police picked him up? Instead, I internalized feelings of anger and betrayal throughout a one-way, ten-mile walk, ending about 10 miles from our home. Having trudged off the worst of my frustration, I called Bud from a gas station and asked him to come and get me.

Not long after that incident, Bud and his friend Jim, carried into the house a radio-stereo console housed in a modern mahogany cabinet. When I turned on the radio, Nat King Cole was singing my old favorite "Mona Lisa," and in a profusion of grateful tears, I hugged Bud tightly. All the feelings of anger and suspicion were suddenly cleansed from my thoughts. In retrospect, though I was easy in those days (easy for Bud to hoodwink), I wasn't cheap (it had cost him plenty to bail himself out of the doghouse).

Bud was not a workaholic in the customary sense. He took the view that if a person could not do his job in eight hours, he was mismanaging his time. On the other hand, he enjoyed spending time with his company cohorts after working hours and on Saturdays, usually at a local bar. When I protested, Bud told me, "Carol, you just don't know how much work gets accomplished after hours." No, I didn't.

As certain as the tides come and go, it was time for another one of Bud's Saturday golf outings. I begged him to stay home with us for once, but he ignored my plea, as usual. I always prayed that he would be rained out, but he never was. It infuriated me that he was so self-assured and happy in our marriage, while I often felt the opposite. That day I was so consumed with anger at feeling second best to his friends and his pleasure, that I took the kids to the department store and bought all six of them new outfits. Then I had the car filled with gas and packed a picnic lunch. I was resolved to take our children on a vacation, maybe even a permanent one, to my sister's home in Mississippi. I was so completely enraged I didn't even write a note.

The weather was beautiful, and the children loved to travel as much as I loved to drive. After a few hours, I found a peaceful, shady roadside table and let the children get out of the car and run around while I unpacked the lunch. They were creative and made games out of virtually everything, including their lunch, taking bites out of each other's sandwiches and racing to see who could finish first. My anger waned somewhat as I watched the children's amusing antics, but after we finished eating, I ushered them back into the car and continued southward.

It was late at night when we reached southern Indiana, and quite unexpectedly, I began feeling guilty about not having left a note for Bud. Then some of my earlier anger returned and I thought, "It will do him good to worry about us, for a change!" Next, I envisioned him pacing the floor full of anxiety, just as I had done on so many occasions. "He deserves to know what that feels like," I mused, with bits of hostility still clinging to my thoughts, like ivy to a wall. Surely, Bud would call the police and send them to look for us, or at the very least ask them to send out an "APB." All of a sudden, a combination of fear and guilt washed over me like a tsunami. After making sure the children were comfortable, I turned the car around and headed for home.

By the time we returned to our home town, I was a mental and physical wreck. Driving up the street, I fully expected to see a horde of police cars with lights frantically revolving and all the house lights aglow. Instead, the house was dark, and the street was quiet, without a single cop car in sight. I was, at the same time, disappointed, yet relieved. The children got out of the car, tagging sleepily after me, as I went into the house in search of the head of our family.

At first, I stood staring in disbelief at the loudly snoring hulk splayed out on the sofa. My first impulse was to put the kids and I back into the car, but sheer exhaustion prevented it. Then I thought about the ordeal I had put myself through by turning the car around and driving hundreds of miles to return to him. I became furious that I'd allowed my sense of decency to extend to a husband and father who, at present, couldn't have cared less about us. Why had I returned? Returned to what? A drunk! Unadulterated fury overcame me, and I wished I had a megaphone. Instead, I yelled my loudest directly into his ear, "Bud! We're home!" The hulk only groaned a bit and slightly repositioned himself. He could just keep right on snoring on the couch!

My thoughts quickly returned to the children and I ushered them off to bed. This was not the first, nor would it be the last time I cried myself to sleep. In the morning, I had to know, "Weren't you terribly worried about us?" Bud answered somewhat arrogantly, "I knew you had gone to visit your sister." I thought, "Not only am I being taken for granted, but now my behavior is also completely predictable!" This bit of self-introspection should have been a signal that something needed correcting in me and in our marriage. Instead, I became angry all over again and had a difficult time being civil to him for the next few days. However, I could never stay upset with him for very long; I loved him too much.

There was much to learn from Al-Anon and just as with psychotherapy, the tools were a challenge to remember and sometimes difficult to apply. Since Bud was aware of these meetings, that may have been a factor in his occasional attempts at sobriety; though he just couldn't seem to accomplish it on his own. I suspect he may have felt too proud to seek help. It was upsetting to learn that it is usually the mother or the spouse who plays the role of "enabler" that is the one who makes excuses for an alcoholic, bails them out of jail, and in general willingly usurps the responsibility which rightly belongs to the alcoholic. Al-Anon teaches that a "hands-off" approach, with "loving detachment," be taken, thus allowing the person to "hit bottom." This was an extremely difficult concept to grasp. How was I to "lovingly detach" from Bud and still show how much I loved him? It seemed impossible.

At least I wasn't making all the standard enable mistakes, such as trying to track him down when he wasn't home or nagging at him, although I occasionally gave him the silent treatment. I didn't even withhold sex, as some women did. Instead, I continued to attend meetings and read self-help books.

On one visit from Bud's parents, he and his Dad spent some time talking, probably about an emotionally safe and superficial subject such as sports. Then they said they were going to go out and bring home some fried chicken for dinner. An hour or so later, Bud's mother noticed the two had more than ample time to bring food home, and she wasn't shy about complaining. I judiciously withheld comment, but then she began pacing the floor. She worked herself into a tizzy and in a voice bursting with vehemence, she asked, "where can they be?" I answered, "I don't know." But she wouldn't let it go. "Well, where does Bud usually go for beer? Now, she was on my case, I calmly mentioned a couple of places, and she pounced on the information. "Okay, which one has a pool table?" That narrowed the possibilities, and I blurted out the name of the closest bar where they might be.

With that information, she now had a mission. The next thing I knew, she told the children, "Kids, get your coats and hats on! We're going to find your dad and your grandpa!"

I protested, suggesting that they should be home any minute. She glared at me. The children did as they were told, and we all piled into the car. Feeling extremely uncomfortable, I drove to the parking lot of the nearest tavern that had a pool table. I thought since his mother was the one so committed to finding Bud and dad, the children and I would wait in the car. But no, she instructed the children in a mock cheerful tone. "Come on kids, we're going in to see your dad and your grandpa." Of course, they dutifully followed her out of the car and into the bar.

Sure, enough there they were, one sipping a beer, the other poised over the pool table for a shot, a pool shot, that is. Their faces blanched when they saw all eight of us trooping into the bar, Bud's dad was the first to speak. He asked the question always foremost in an alcoholic's brain, "What would you kids like to drink? Bud's mother fairly levitated off the floor. "Nobody's going to drink anything. You two are going straight home and we'll pick up the chicken."

CHAPTER 27

AMELIA

Jake's detox symptoms did not pass as quickly as I had hoped. A week later, his mood and appearance was pretty much the same. Now it was Wednesday, and I pulled into the driveway, discouraged. I knew what faced me inside.

I opened the door, fully expecting the same mess, the same tension, the same chaos.

The first thing I saw was Jake in the kitchen, dressed, showered and shaved, and making dinner. Peeking into the living room, I saw that the house wasn't a total disaster. The worn blanket that I had become accustomed to seeing him under was gone from the couch.

Jake smiled. "Hi, sweetheart. Chicken and rice tonight, with a side of hidden broccoli." He whispered, "I found a way to slip it past the kids."

We enjoyed a pleasant evening with the kids and even made love that night, which was the first time since the accident. I was relieved. He had made it through his need for the pain pills and now he could completely recover. Though he wasn't going to PT or visiting the social worker, he was getting back to himself.

By the end of day on Friday, I had settled down and was

happy again. Jake would go back to work in a week. Everything was returning to normal. With a wry smile, I thought about how I had complained about that 'normal' state of my family so many times and wished it was better. Now all I wanted was to get it back.

I put my hand on the doorknob. Jake was slamming doors and cursing inside. The children were crying. My smile faded and my gut twisted into a knot. I was confused. What could have happened?

I entered quickly, going to the kids without acknowledging Jake.

Jake raged, "They're driving me insane! I can't take this anymore!"

I ushered the kids into the playroom and walked back to the kitchen. "What is wrong, Jake?"

"I just need to relax. I need something to relax. Why don't we have anything to drink in this house? Why can't a guy sit and enjoy a drink in his own home at the end of the week?" He rummaged through the cabinets.

"Jake, I don't understand."

"I just would love to have a drink and relax. This is ridiculous. Why don't you have at least a beer in this house?" A can of olives slipped out of his hands and broke on the counter, splashing juice and olives everywhere. "That's it. I am going out!" He passed me, pushing me out of the way, grabbed his keys and left.

I was dumbfounded. He had been doing so well. Like a flip of a switch, he was worse than ever. I was at a loss as to what to do.

I READ WHAT YOU WROTE

He came home an hour later, and he was better. Best of all, he didn't smell like alcohol. Maybe he just needed to clear his head.

He apologized for his outburst and then went to the couch to watch TV. I was so grateful he was home in one piece and much calmer, I just left him alone.

The rollercoaster of his moods continued. I wasn't sure when I would get home from work if he would be happy or miserable. Something was definitely going on. His erratic behavior was a huge concern, and I feared his addiction was worse than I thought. My biggest concern was where he was getting the pills. Based on all I knew of addiction, the mood swings were a big identifier. He must be getting something from somewhere or he wouldn't have the highs, but how and where I wondered.

I called him the next day from work right after a meeting to check on him. The night before he was crawling out of his skin, I could tell. I tried to talk with him, but he just shut me out. I could have pushed him and asked about his mood swings and my concern about an addiction, but I just couldn't. I was so afraid of how he would react. I was such a chicken.

There was still no answer an hour later. I began to have a horrible feeling and I just couldn't be at work with this fear inside of me. I decided to tell my boss I wasn't feeling well and needed to go home. My boss let me go without a hassle. I knew I had to go check on him.

Our home was just two houses in from the corner and as I was about to turn onto our street, I saw his truck pulling out of the driveway. I stayed at the stop sign to see which way he

301

was going and saw him head in the opposite direction. I had to follow him.

I tried to keep some distance between us because I didn't want him to see me following him. The longer we drove, the harder it was to stay behind him as the traffic became more congested. I had no clue where he was going, but I knew we were getting closer to an area that we typically avoided. We were about 20 minutes from home now and I was unfamiliar with these roads. Traffic also cleared up more so I really had to stay back so he wouldn't see me. He turned down a street that scared me, it was full of old, run down houses, some empty and the ones that appeared occupied were unpainted, and worn. Bushes, trees and grass were overgrown in every yard and there were broken down cars in driveways on cinder blocks. It gave me the chills just driving down the street. Why was he in this area? What was he doing? I was getting more and more frightened as we drove.

I saw him pull over and park on the side of the street. I had to quickly turn at the next block or I would have had to drive right past him. I drove around the block and came back around a few blocks further away. When I got back on the street, I could no longer see his car. He must have left. I pulled over and put the car in park, not sure what to do next. Before I could get my thoughts together, he drove right past me and parked where he was two blocks down. Did he see me? Was he going to get out of his car and walk to my car? I sat still, watching.

As the minutes passed, he never moved from his car. Maybe he was waiting for me to drive up to him? I debated what to do. I finally decided I would just drive up to his car and confront him and ask him what the hell he was doing in this neighborhood.

Then a thought ran through my head that chilled me to the bone. Was he here to see another woman? A cold sweat ran down my back. I had been so concerned about his addiction, I didn't even think of another woman. Could that be why he was so irritable? Fear surged through me. Maybe it wasn't an addiction. Maybe he was just unhappy with me and he didn't know how to tell me. I was in a full panic now.

Minutes passed and neither of us moved. What was I going to do? I decided, I just needed to ask him. I needed to find out what the hell was going on no matter what. I was just about to put my car in drive when all of the sudden several cars went flying by me and came to a screeching halt about 2 blocks past Jake. It was as if every cop car in the state descended upon this street. I was shaking, not sure what to do. Were they after Jake? Did he do something terribly wrong? I slumped down a little in my seat, shaking. What the hell was going on? Undercover cops and men in uniform were pouring out of the cars. Pow! pow! It was like a movie. Were those gunshots I just heard? What the hell? I was frozen and slumped in my seat. Men were yelling and I couldn't quite see what was going on since I was several blocks back from the commotion. I sat there for what seemed like an hour, though I am sure it was only minutes, just shaking and not knowing what to do. I tried to see if anyone was by Jake's car, but I couldn't see clearly since there were so many cars on the street.

And then suddenly I saw Jake's car move. He pulled into

the driveway of the house he was in front of and turned around. Then he drove right towards me again. I slumped further, not wanting him to see me and then he was out of sight from my rear view mirror. After a few moments I tried to catch my breath. I did the same maneuver and headed towards home. No chance of being able to catch up to him.

I am not sure how I was able to drive home. I couldn't stop shaking and had trouble maintaining normal breaths. By the time I got home, Jake's truck was in the driveway. I grabbed my purse and went into the house. I found him sitting on the couch with his head in his hands. He looked up at me the minute I walked in and his face was completely pale and sweat was visible on his face and shirt. He looked so horrible and I wanted to go give him a hug, so grateful he was okay and wasn't part of whatever it was that I had just witnessed. But my legs wouldn't move. I just looked at him.

"What the hell are you doing here?" he asked with a very shaky voice.

Not sure what to say and how to process what I just witnessed, I did not respond.

He put his head back in his hands.

I could see he was having trouble controlling his breathing.

Gaining a little control of myself, I finally said, "Jake, what the hell just happened back there?"

He looked at me, shocked. "What are you talking about?"

The whole way home, I had been trying to process what I had just witnessed. It was a drug bust, I was sure of it. Jake wasn't there to see another woman. He was there to get drugs. He obviously knew where to go so I assumed he had been there before. "How many times?" I asked.

"What?"

"How many times have you been there before?"

Jake turned away. "I have a problem. I can't seem to feel any better without some pain medication." He looked defeated. He looked nothing like my strong, handsome fireman husband. Tears welled up in his eyes.

Instead of feeling supportive and sympathetic, I was angrier than ever. He wanted me to tell him it was okay, that he needed the drugs and I understood.

Not in a million years was he going to get that reaction from me. I was seeing, right before my eyes, the well-documented manipulation and self-serving behavior of an addict.

I lost it. I had reached my breaking point. "So you went there to buy drugs? Did you just see what happened? You could have so easily been caught in all of that. You have no idea how lucky you are that they didn't bust you!"

"Stop, just stop! I really don't need this right now!"

"Really? Because I think you do! You could have totally screwed up your life and even worse, you could have screwed up the kids and my life too! What would have happened if you got caught? You would be in jail, that's what. You would have lost your job, we would have lost this house, I probably would have lost my job. What would have happened to our family, Jake?!"

Suddenly, he was on his feet, towering over me, pointing his shaking finger at me. "You gave me no choice Amelia! You could have helped me, you could have given me just a little something to help get me through this time. But no, you are more concerned about your precious patients than you are of me. I needed your help and you couldn't do it."

I stood my ground. "Oh this is my fault? I should have illegally given you my patient's medication to help you out."

He backed up a step and looked away.

He knew better, and I knew he knew. "C'mon Jake. You know the classic addict behaviors. And you're a textbook case right now."

"I am not some crazy addict. I'm not one of your patients that you can boss around! What I need is a supportive wife, not someone that is constantly nagging me!"

With that, Jake stomped to the bedroom, slammed and locked the door.

I was in shock. I sat for a long time, staring at nothing. I had no idea what to do. After what seemed like forever, I realized I needed help to handle all of this. Who could help? Who could I trust that Jake would listen to?

I picked up my phone and called Rose. Dan answered.

"Is Rose home?"

"No, she is out shopping. Are you okay?"

Though I was trying to keep it together, Dan could tell I was upset.

"No, no I am not. Dan, I don't know what to do." I started to cry.

"What is going on Amelia?"

"It's Jake, he is in bad shape. I don't know how to help him."

"What's wrong?"

I wasn't sure if I should tell him. If Dan told anyone at

work, Jake would be fired for sure. But I was helpless. At this point, I just wanted Jake to get better and keep him out of prison. His job was suddenly secondary to our survival. And I had no idea how to help Jake by myself. I had to take a chance and trust in the friendship between Jake and Dan.

"Dan, he tried to buy pills from a dealer. He is an addict." I paused. Dan remained silent. I continued. "He almost got caught. I don't know what to do." I filled him in on the events of the day. I didn't mention the fact that he had previously stolen a pill from Carol. I knew I could trust Dan, but I still didn't feel comfortable telling him about that incident.

Dan asked, "Where is he now?"

"He is in the bedroom. We had a huge fight. He's out of control."

"I'll be right over."

I walked out front to meet Dan. He took our front steps two at a time, hugging me close on the top step.

I fell apart all over again. "He is going to kill me for telling you about this. I just don't know what to do."

"Where are the kids?"

"Oh my gosh. I totally forgot about the kids. How could I forget about my own kids?!" I looked at my phone. "Oh no. It's almost time for me to pick them up."

"Why don't you go get them and maybe grab a bite to eat while you are out? I will call you when I get done talking with Jake."

"Okay." I was a complete wreck, but I had to pull it together for my little ones. They had been through enough with their dad these last few weeks. I needed to be strong, solid.

I picked up the kids. It took every ounce of energy in me to put a smile on my face and take them out for dinner at their favorite fast food restaurant. The kids were excited for this unexpected treat and gobbled up their chicken nuggets and french fries.

I couldn't eat a bite and looked at my phone every other minute to see if Dan had called. The more time that went by the more sick to my stomach I felt. I felt sure Jake was going to be so pissed at me, but I didn't know what else to do. We couldn't continue like this. Jake couldn't and neither could our family. Something had to be done. I just hoped I made the right decision by reaching out to Dan for help.

With still no word, the kids were getting fidgety so I offered to buy them an ice cream as well. Life was so simple for them. Just a little treat could make them happy, they had no idea that their family was currently crumbling.

Finally, Dan called.

"Why don't you bring the kids over. I will fill you in and then you can go talk to Jake. Rose and I will watch the kids."

"How is he?"

"Just come over and I will fill you in."

"Thanks, Dan." I was dying to know more, but I realized he was probably right. Talking in person and in the privacy of his home was better than having a potentially life-altering conversation in the middle of a fast food restaurant.

Rose was home when we got there and took the kids in to play with Connor. I sat in the kitchen with Dan. He told me everything that happened when he went into our house.

Dan knocked on Jake's bedroom door.

"Go away!" he yelled.

"Jake it's me," said Dan. "I am coming in." and he opened the door. Jake was sitting in a chair facing the window.

"C'mon man, what are you doing here?"

I tensed at the anger in his voice. "Listen Jake, Amelia told me some of what is going on, let me help."

"Get out of here, I can't believe she called you; she had no right telling you our business, get out of here."

Dan slowly walked over to Jake and leaned up against the ledge of the window. "Listen man, I get it, you are pissed at her for telling me, but she loves you and she doesn't know how to help."

"I don't need anyone's help. Leave, really, I don't want you here." He just stared out the window, he wouldn't look at Dan.

"Listen Jake, you have been through a lot. Most people can't do this alone; you need some help."

"I don't need anything, leave, seriously or I will throw you out." He stood up now and took a step closer to Dan.

"Ha ha, I have you by at least 30 pounds, I would like to see you try." Puffing up his chest. "Jake, did you really try and buy drugs from a dealer? Do you know how much trouble you could have gotten into?"

"I don't need you in my business." Jake then pushed both hands into Dan's chest. Dan just stood there, he didn't budge.

"Jake, you don't want to do that again Bud. I am here to help you."

"I said I don't need your help!" This time he curled his hand into a fist and held it back, ready to punch Dan. He then slumped back into his chair and put his head in his hands.

"Jake, listen to me man, you are heading down a serious path. You need to stop this shit and get some help. Pain pills can help you initially, but they are so addictive. You need serious help so you can get back to work and back to your family. Let me help you, I can take you in someplace that can help you through getting off the pills and help get you back in shape. It is now or never, Bud. You know what it's like when we get to a fire, we must get there fast and put everything into getting that fire out, if not, everything will be lost, everything.

After Dan finished telling me about his visit, I asked him. "How did he know about that place to get drugs? I can't imagine him ever in an area like that."

"I asked him, and he said he had heard about that area being a place for some big dealers. Apparently he went to a local bar a few weeks ago and got the address from the bartender. Amelia, he admitted that he had gotten some there before. Don't be mad, he is only human. I am going to take him later to a place I know of to help. He will admit himself for a few weeks. It will not only help him with withdrawal but will also get him talking to a counselor and get him going on PT again. He will be okay Amelia, I will help too. He just wants me to take him. He doesn't want to face you or the kids right now."

As hard as it was for me that he wouldn't want me, his wife, to help him, I tried to get past my own feelings. At least he was going to get some help. I hugged Dan and thanked him so much and stayed over at their house until Dan took Jake to the facility.

CHAPTER 28

MARIE

I stared at the phone. I needed to call Mom. Even though I longed to hear her voice and I wanted to know if she was okay. As okay as she could be, I dreaded it. It seemed like every time I called Mom lately, she would put me on speaker so Earl could hear the conversation. It really limited what I could say to Mom or what she would say to me.

There was no love lost between Earl and me. I had tried to stop him from marrying her a couple of times. We all did. To no avail.

My mind flitted back to the day I had had it out with Earl. I had taken the day off work so that I could drive up and go to a doctor's appointment with Mom.

"Hi, Mom," I said in a cheery voice as I walked into her house. I saw her sitting on her chair in the living room.

"Hi, sweetheart."

I smiled in spite of everything. Hearing her say those words and call me sweetheart, in the same way she had done all my life, was the most precious thing to me.

She held out her arms for a hug.

I leaned over her in her chair and gave her a tight squeeze. "How are you feeling?"

"Oh, I'm okay. I have some pain in my lower left side. I am not sure what is going on." She sounded confused and frustrated.

"Hmm, I don't know either."

"What are you doing here, honey?"

"Well Mom, I wanted to come up and see your pretty face. Also, you had mentioned on the phone the other day that you had a doctor's appointment today. I thought I would go with you."

"I had one this morning. Earl took me."

"Darn, I had thought you told me it was this afternoon. Well, what did the doctor say?"

"He said it was most likely my diverticulitis acting up again, so he gave me an antibiotic."

"Mom, maybe we need to go back to Shands and follow up with that doctor."

"No, I don't ever want to go there again. They don't know what's wrong."

I took a deep breath to remain calm. Having a discussion with her could be so frustrating. I knew it was the dementia, but somehow it didn't help. I steadied my voice. "Remember you have a small tumor on your pancreatic duct, maybe that has gotten bigger. We should really look to see what they think."

"No, Marie, I think my doctor is right. It is probably my diverticulitis."

Earl appeared in the doorway and scowled at me. "Your mom went to the doctor yesterday and was given an antibiotic. I got that filled today. She will begin to feel better soon."

"But she told me she went this morning, not yesterday."

Earl said, "Carol, remember we went yesterday, not earlier today."

"Oh, I guess I forgot," she said.

I was fuming. She couldn't even remember what day she went to the doctor. "Mom, why don't you come stay with me for a little while until you feel better? I promise I will take really good care of you. I know the kids would love to have you spend time with them. We all would."

"No, honey, I am more comfortable here. Besides, Earl is here and he is taking such good care of me."

Ugh, I cringed every time Mom said that. I wanted to yell, 'No mother, he is not!'

Earl stared at me in a way that said 'I win' and walked out of the room.

I pushed my anger aside as best I could. I wanted to enjoy my time with Mom no matter what was happening. I sat and talked with her about the kids, John, even what she was watching on TV.

After an hour, she leaned her head against the back of her chair. She looked pained. "I am getting tired. I think I would like to take a nap."

"Of course, Mom.

She stood up. I followed her into her bedroom. I sat and chatted for just a few more minutes and then gave her a kiss and said goodbye.

I didn't want to speak with Earl, but as I shut the door to her room, he was in front of me, filling the hallway. "Hey Marie, I wanted to let you know that your mother and I are going to get married soon. She has written a letter to all of you kids to explain that we are in love, and we want to spend the rest of our lives together."

I stared at him. I knew there was hate in my eyes. I knew I should not hate him, but in that moment I did. The worst part was, his face told me clear as day that he did not care one bit, because he knew he had won. He knew he was in control and there was nothing I could do.

I had known this was coming after speaking with Ann. She had already received the letter. But now I had to face it. Worse, I had to face him, gloating in front of me, blocking my only exit from the house.

"Excuse me, Earl. I need to get past you."

Earl moved out of the way.

As I was passing him, I could hear his heavy footsteps behind me.

"I will take really good care of her. We are in love."

I whipped around. "In love? With my mother? And you think she's in love with you? Earl, she has dementia. She is in no place to make that kind of decision."

"No, she doesn't. She does not have dementia!" he bellowed.

I consciously kept my voice calm. "Yes, Earl, she does."

"No, she doesn't. I have asked her doctor."

I stated, "According to her neurologist, she does, and over the last year and a half she has gotten worse."

Earl interrupted, "That is not true."

"Earl, I was with her. Twice. I heard what the neurologist said after her tests two years in a row! She has dementia and she doesn't have the capacity to make these kinds of decisions!"

I decided to go about it from another angle. "Do you think if your daughter came to you when she was in the eighth grade and said she wanted to get married, you would think she was smart enough to make that type of commitment?"

"What do you mean? Your mom is not an eighth grader," he spat.

"No, she is not, but that is what the doctor said her mentality is. That is wrong. Earl, you have to be able to see that!"

"Listen, I took her to the doctor, and he said she didn't have dementia. You just don't want to see your mother happy, that's all!"

"That is not true. I want her happy and more importantly, I want her safe and well cared for! Look, I get it. You have nothing. No place to live, no money, and now no wife. I am sure it is very attractive for you to see my mom and weasel your way into her life. But I am here to tell you, we won't let you get away with it. I know that you took all of Grandma's money, too. I was there when my dad had to tell his mother to stop giving you money every month because you were draining her dry. It made my dad so mad. Because of you, she ended up having to spend the last several years of her life in a horrible nursing home. Well, you aren't going to drain our mother dry. We are going to make sure she has enough money to live her life as comfortably as possible. She deserves that! Without you!"

His face was red.

I was just about to add to my comments when I heard my mom call me from her room. "Marie, what is going on?"

I poked my head into her room and said in a calm voice,

"Nothing Mom. We are just talking."

"Yelling is more like it," she said curtly. "Marie, be nice to Earl, he takes such good care of me. You need to be respectful," she reprimanded.

"I'm sorry Mom, I just don't understand why you need to get married. Just live together. You don't need to marry him."

"Marie, you know I can't do that. It isn't appropriate."

"Mom, I am sure at this stage of your life, God isn't going to judge you for living together. This way, we can make sure you have everything you need both healthcare and financial wise. Just think about it okay?" I went over and hugged and kissed her again. I didn't want to upset my mother, but I just couldn't let this man take advantage of her.

I walked out of her room, past the lumbering presence of Earl, straight through the house and outside. I couldn't argue with this man any longer.

It took every ounce of self-control not to slam the door. I stood on Mom's porch, shaking in anger. I couldn't drive in the state I was in. I decided to go next door and visit my Aunt Marilyn. I needed to talk it out with her and then calm down a bit before my long drive home.

A few days later I stood in front of the beautiful old church I had been attending for many years. My children had been baptized there. I sat in the same pew week after week with John and the kids. I needed to walk up those brick stairs and enter the big double doors if I was going to be on time. I had been so sure when I made this appointment that speaking with Father Dexter was a good idea, but now my legs wouldn't budge. Would he think my issue wasn't a big deal? Would he think that I sounded like a spoiled brat and think all I cared about was some sort of inheritance?

No, I told myself, this is the right thing to do. I needed to talk with someone, and he seemed to be a very smart, loving man all the years I have known him. I also needed my soul to be saved. That was the most important thing for me. I had had so much hate in my heart ever since Earl pushed his way into my mom's life. I was so angry with him, and if I was honest, angry with her, too. I had always been such a happy person. I hated conflict. I always wanted peace. Mom had seen it in me ever since I could remember. "Marie, you are a peacemaker," she would say. "Blessed are the peacemakers."

I didn't feel like one now. My heart and soul were dark, and it was killing me.

I pulled up my proverbial big girl panties and marched up the steps. I pulled the door open. The bright sunshine gave way to a dark candlelit area. It took my eyes a little while to adjust. I made my way past the memorial votives on the right side of the church vestibule to the church office. I told the receptionist I was there for my appointment with Father Dexter.

A few minutes later I was ushered into his small cramped office. He sat behind a desk loaded with books. As soon as he saw me, he got up and shook my hand. "Hello Marie, please sit down." He took his usual seat behind the desk and gestured to the chair across from him.

His warm smile put me at ease, but this was still hard. I sat down, staring at my hands. "Well Father, I am having a rough time with my mother and I could really use your guidance."

He got up and walked around the desk to sit in the chair beside me. "Please, go ahead. Tell me what is troubling you."

Between the tears and deep sobs, I explained everything that was going on with Mom and Earl and our family. As far as I knew, I didn't even take a breath or look to see his reaction. I just had to get it all out. I had to get it off my chest. When I finally finished, he took my hand and scooted up to the end of the chair, facing me.

"Do you know much about dementia?," he asked.

I shook my head.

"I do. Quite personally actually."

I glanced up.

His gaze had settled on a point in space behind me. "If she feels safe and loved by him, there really won't be anything you can do about it. There will be no changing her mind."

My mouth fell open in shock. I wanted to yell, 'What do you mean there is nothing I can do?!' Instead, I looked away and swallowed hard, keeping the rising heat of fear and anger to myself.

He said, "You need to just love her and support her as best as you can. Of course, you need to keep an eye on her and make sure she is safe, but other than that, there is nothing much you can do for her." He paused before continuing. "Here is my advice…"

Okay, finally. I couldn't wait to hear his pearls of wisdom. I turned my eyes back and caught his. I was ready.

"You and your siblings need to be there for one another. You need to support one another with no judgment, just love. It is imperative that you keep the relationships between you

I READ WHAT YOU WROTE

all strong."

That was it? That was all the advice he had? I searched his eyes for something else, some sign that more would follow, more about what we could do for Mom.

There was nothing more.

I felt let down, even betrayed. This didn't solve the issue with Mom.

I kept all these thoughts to myself. I smiled at him, thanked him, and left.

I sat in my car for a long time. Angry. Shocked. Staring at the church, I thought about the faith I had been taught and what was right and wrong.

What Earl was doing was wrong.

My poor little mother was an innocent victim.

Again.

And again.

All three of her husbands, in one way or another.

And I couldn't protect her.

Then it hit me.

Like a ton of bricks.

Father Dexter's words echoed in my mind: 'You and your siblings need to be there for one another. You need to support one another with no judgment, just love. It is imperative that you keep the relationships between you all strong.'

Those would have been the exact words my father would have said to me if he were alive today.

I just knew it.

He always loved our family bond, and he would want to make sure we preserved it.

I began to cry. Again. It was as if I could cry forever. My whole body shook with each wracking sob. I had lost my mom. Even though she was still alive, she was gone.

That's why I needed to stay close to my brothers and sisters.

We were all we had left.

I cried for my siblings.

I cried for my father.

After what seemed like forever, the sobs subsided. I glanced at the clock. Four o'clock. I needed to get home.

I drove away from the church, and I noticed my heart had lightened. I would do what my father would have wanted. I would make sure us kids kept our strong bond. I would do my best to keep the strongest relationship possible with my mother. I wouldn't focus on the hatred I had for Earl but on the love of my mother. I sent up a quick prayer to my father, thanking him for his words through the priest that day.

CHAPTER 29

AMELIA

"Good morning Carol, how are you doing today?" I asked, walking into Carol's living room. It was the same way I greeted her every time, but I cherished it. It had become an important part of our time together, just that simple greeting.

Today more than ever, I needed that simplicity and warmth. I was so drained from everything that happened with Jake. Working was keeping me busy, but my mind was just fixated on my family. I really wished I could just crawl up into a ball and stay in my bed all day. Even visiting Carol, my favorite part of the week, was hard for me.

"I am in good shape for the shape I'm in," replied Carol.

I smiled weakly. "It is so good to see you up in the chair, have you had breakfast today?"

"Yes, some orange sherbet."

I just shook my head. This woman needed some good nutrition, but I had no fight left in me. At least she was eating something.

Earl got up and said, "I am going to go get the mail. See you later Amelia. Bye sweetheart," he said to Carol.

He gave me the creeps and now that I knew the true story behind his and Carol's relationship, I could barely stand to look at him.

"So, Carol, let's take a look at you." I brought out my thermometer, blood pressure cuff, pulse oximeter, and stethoscope. Everything seemed to be pretty much in order and Carol's color looked good as well.

"How is your handsome husband doing?" she asked me.

"Oh, he is okay, thanks for asking," I said, trying to hide my feelings.

Carol immediately asked, "Amelia, what is wrong, I know you too well by now, something is bothering you, is he still feeling poorly?"

Apparently, the truth was written on my face. I didn't know why but I couldn't hide anything from her like I could with my other patients, or even my friends for that matter. Over the last five months, I felt like we had made such a huge connection. She had helped me with so many things with regard to my family, especially in raising my children and my marriage to Jake. It was as if God had put this woman in my life as a surrogate mother.

"Well, we had a rough weekend." I thought I could just leave it at that, but Carol pushed me further.

"What happened? Are you alright?" she asked.

Hesitating, trying to think if I should make something up to quickly end the subject. Looking into Carol's eyes, I just couldn't deny my feelings. "Jake is struggling with his pain and he um, well, he has become a little too dependent on his medication. He is actually in rehab now, but just for a short time." I spoke quickly like I was pulling off a band-aid.

"Amelia sweetheart, I'm so sorry. That can happen. It can

happen really easily. That is so good he is getting some help now."

"I hope he can beat it. He was really worrying me. It's like he isn't the same man I have been married to." Tears filled my eyes.

"Amelia, life is really hard sometimes. You go along in the status quo for a while and then bam something happens, and life becomes difficult. Sometimes it's so difficult you can't handle it. Sometimes you really need help to get through it, too, even if you're not the one with the problem. I had to learn that during some of my hard times."

I thought back on all the really tough things I had read in Carol's stories thinking I knew all of the tough times Carol was referring to.

Carol continued. "I had some really bad things happen and on top of all of that I had become addicted to diet pills. Well, that is what the doctor and I called them, but they were amphetamines. At first, I was given them by my doctor to help with my low energy and ever battle with weight, but in actuality, I became dependent on them, not even realizing it. And to top it off, just when it seemed life got difficult, the doctor stopped giving them to me. I had a horrible time. Be patient with Jake. He has been through a lot. He'll be okay. Just love him and support him, the more support you give him, the better. I had some support from Bud, but due to his drinking, he could only help so much."

"I had no idea Carol, I am so sorry. That had to have been so difficult for you."

CHAPTER 30

CAROL 1974

I cannot recall the day, the month, or even the year when I became dependent on a daily diet pill, but I do remember that the first order of business every morning was to take one with my coffee. At first, I did not feel at all guilty about taking them; I persuaded myself they helped to keep my mind and body in synchronization, and gave me the energy I felt I needed. There seemed to be no bad side effects, so without any knowledge to the contrary, I continued the habit. Doctors had no compunction about prescribing them for me, even when I was pregnant, and we were now expecting our third child.

Though Dad's death may have served as the catalyst, I think I was headed for a fall sooner or later. The blips in Bud's behavior due to his drinking were a constant vexation to me, despite his good nature. Then, the pressure of trying to be a good housewife and mother to six children was extremely taxing, yet it never occurred to me to pursue any interests outside the home. The daily diet pill seemed no longer to help very much, and even though I was afraid to take more than one per day; it didn't occur to me that they might be dangerous.

Everything about my life was suddenly beginning to overwhelm me. I felt mentally and physically out of synchronization. Ultimately, the last supporting stilt was about to be plucked from beneath me. The doctor who had been writing prescriptions for diet pills told me that the AMA recommended that doctors stop prescribing them. After being addicted to diet pills for nearly ten years, this news was overwhelming. My mind went to work right away. "There are other doctors," I reasoned, "and there is a plethora of other drugs out there." But, through the grace of God, my conscience wouldn't allow me to search for another doctor or another drug.

Okay then, I'd try to get along without diet pills. But I had serious doubts. It was a struggle just to get through an hour, let alone a whole day without an "upper!" Though the children didn't understand the change in their mother, they went about their duties, and Bud managed to conceal his frustration with me. The family needed motherly and wifely attention regardless of how I felt, and I buckled under the self-imposed pressure. Within a week or so, I suffered a complete physical and mental breakdown. I wasn't able to force myself to do anything, so I cocooned myself in our room and slept a great deal. Fortunately, Therese was old enough to handle things until Bud came home at night, but after a few days' struggle, Bud wisely took me to see our family physician, Dr. Conrad.

We were directed to an examining room, where I stumbled to a corner and slumped to the floor in a lethargic, introverted heap. The doctor came in with his usual cheerful greeting and glanced at each of us. We respected Dr. Conrad, who, in my opinion, was an extremely proficient diagnostician. He generally knew what tests to run and what medications to *prescribe. After the results of an EEG, he put me on Ritalin and asked me, "Would you consider seeing a psychiatrist?" "I'll do anything!" I responded in desperation. I had hit bottom, the cellar, the pits, call it what you will.*

Bud went with me to the first appointment with Dr. Murphy, a psychiatrist, who was a little on the heavy side and a pipe smoker. I don't know what I expected, but I thought his office was rather dark and drab. He talked in a quiet monotone and asked a few pertinent questions, such as "Why did you come here?" My desperate response was, "Why don't you just put me in Our Lady of Murphy Hospital and be done with it?" He smiled at the slip; I'd said "Murphy" instead of "Mercy." Then he laughed and said, something like "Sounds as though you just castrated me." I don't remember what else was said, but he and Bud did most of the talking and soon the scheduled hour was over. Another appointment was made for the following week, but I canceled it at the last minute. When I next saw Dr. Murphy, he quietly said, "If you cancel another appointment, I'll have to charge you." Our insurance would cover his fee, but not a cancellation. I had no wish to put a further strain on our budget, so I didn't cancel subsequent appointments.

Dr. Murphy's approach seemed to begin with where a patient was psychologically, instead of going back to the womb. His "down to earth" style seemed to help one sort out current thought processes. The first thing he told me to do was to explain to Bud and the children that my illness wasn't in any way their fault. That made perfect sense. Unfortunately, I got worse before I began to get better. At first, I felt so low that I couldn't bear to face anyone, not even the children. Dr. Murphy

I READ WHAT YOU WROTE

prescribed an antidepressant but warned that it might take a month before taking effect. That bit of news was discouraging. I wanted immediate help! Patience wasn't my strong suit.

No matter how sorry I felt for Bud and the children, I couldn't bring myself to do anything. I felt frozen in time. That period was sheer torment for all of us. Although Bud was kind to me, I rebuffed his thoughtful gestures. Every night after work he came to our room and asked, "Is there anything I can do for you?" For the first few days I'd answer his question with a curt "No!" I blamed him, at least in part, for this terrible breakdown. I was much nicer to the children when they came to visit, but it took sheer willpower to fabricate a smile.

I had never felt so disconnected or so "out of it" as I did then. Fleeting thoughts of suicide crossed my mind, but ultimately, I promised God that if He wouldn't give up on me, I wouldn't give up on Him. It was that simple. I came home from the next appointment and began another journal destined to be a catharsis of my discomfiting thoughts. Writing things down seemed to help "sort things out," as Dr. Murphy put it. I wrote angrily at first, the pen making deep marks in the notebook paper. Then, I'd feel a terrible wave of hopelessness and my scrawls became barely legible. For the first month or so, I refused to talk with anyone on the telephone, even to Mother and Marilyn. They didn't have to know that I was in such a miserable state.

On one visit to Dr. Murphy, I told him I didn't feel like talking. Completely unperturbed, he simply responded, "It's your nickel," and we just sat there in what was for me, an uncomfortable silence. Finally, I realized that he could out-sit me and I broke the self-conscious quiet. "Aren't you going to ask me anything?" I inquired. When he answered in the negative, I talked my head off, sometimes causing him to laugh. Or he'd challenge one of my opinionated statements by saying, "I don't know if that's true."

Over the next few months my weight escalated from 138 to 180 pounds. In retrospect, perhaps my subconscious was rebelling in the hope that Dr. Murphy would take pity on me and prescribe more diet pills. He made it clear that he would not write a prescription, and reminded me, "You're not Superwoman, you know." I rationalized to him that Bud's mother had been taking sleeping pills for the greater part of her life and she seemed okay. What was the difference? "I'm not her doctor," he suavely remarked. Dr. Murphy was a lot like Bud; they both had ready answers for everything!

Knowing deep down the kids and Bud needed me, I still locked myself in my room, not helping the family at all. The days turned into weeks and the weeks turned into months. The kids were all in school at this point and I wasn't even sure how they got there or for that matter how they even got themselves ready in the morning. My older daughters helped with everything, they would help get the little ones ready for school and even apparently came up with a system to help prepare lunches. I found out later that they would trade off making each other's lunches from week to week. The girls would prepare some sort of dinner and when Bud got home from work, he would clean the kitchen and make sure the kids got off to bed. He would help with homework when necessary, but I would learn much later that they pretty much managed their own work.

I READ WHAT YOU WROTE

Unfortunately, this confine was the most difficult on the older girls, as they were both in the middle of their difficult early teen years. When clothes or shoes were needed, they had to wait until the weekend until Bud could take them to the local department store. He wasn't much of a fashion man and quickly ran out of patience when the girls wanted to buy a specific in style pair of jeans or shirt. It was even more difficult when Ann needed to purchase her first bra. Poor girl had to go with her father to buy it. She was completely mortified, and so was Bud.

Once the anti-depressant kicked in that Dr. Murphy finally wrote, I felt better and was able to function again, but not to the extent that I would sweep sidewalks after mowing the lawn or wash and iron the kitchen curtains every week. I had to learn how to budget my energy and time. Bud gave me a St. Jude (Patron Saint of Desperate Cases) medal for my birthday that year and I sadly wondered, "Does he really think I'm a hopeless case?" With their baby-sitting money, Therese and Ann bought a Shirley Temple doll for my 40th birthday, which has been saved in its original box, along with their cheerful birthday card. How fortunate the mother who has such thoughtful children!

After making appreciable progress in recovering, my attention began turning toward others, including Dr. Murphy. One day I asked, "How did you happen to become a psychiatrist?" He said that he had had a medical practice at first but found that he was spending too much time with each patient, so he studied for a degree in psychiatry. I asked how he coped with hearing a constant barrage of problems, a difficult case or even problems of his own. He answered, "I consulted with another psychiatrist." Another time, when I walked into his waiting room, a couple of nuns happened to be sitting there. By now, not afraid to ask him anything, I asked why they were there. With a smile he gave me something to think about; "Nuns are human beings, too, aren't they?

Therapy went on for a couple of years and incredibly, it wasn't until one of the last visits that I mentioned Bud's drinking. Dr. Murphy strongly suggested that I get myself educated about the disease. Yes, that's what he called it, "a disease." I also mentioned the idea of getting a job. He said, "Maybe part-time, for starters," but I still tended to jump into things with both feet.

As anyone who's gone through psychotherapy can attest, it takes a while to put into practice what's been learned. The "real world" out there doesn't understand what you're going through, nor does it care, since wounds to one's psyche are not visible to the naked eye. They haven't a clue, unless they've been told, that you're a fledgling who's just hopped to the ground from the comfort of a psychological nest. I cannot understand why most people don't like to share the fact they've been through psychotherapy, since I believe it's one of the most courageous and loving things one can do for oneself and one's family. In short, I finally came to the realization that the only person I could really depend on in this life was me! Not that I wouldn't backslide sometimes, but then who doesn't? Dr. Murphy cautioned me, "Very often when one family member gets better another may get worse." That was scary news!

When I left Dr. Murphy's office for the last time, there

I READ WHAT YOU WROTE

may have been a few more stubborn birds still roosting on my antennae, but I had been given new tools which, if put into practice, could do nothing but help our whole family. The first thing on the agenda would be to take "Murph's" advice and get educated about alcoholism. I loved Bud deeply and certainly owed that much to him as well as to our children. Thus, I set about learning how to better cope with life's ups and downs with a certain amount of newfound self-confidence, equanimity, and optimism. Whatever resources and talents may have been given to me, I planned to make a sincere effort to please God by dedicating my energy and time to Him, and to improving my own individual, indelible mark in time. The bottom line: I now began to entertain loftier and more realistic goals for the rest of my life.

CHAPTER 31

AMELIA

I was so excited and nervous all at the same time, I practically skipped on my way over to Rose's house. And then probably knocked on the door with a little too much enthusiasm.

"Amelia! You look so pretty. Come in." She stood aside to let me pass.

"Thank you." I stepped into the entryway. "And I can't thank you enough for picking up the kids today after school. I am just not sure how long it will take to check Jake out of rehab."

"No problem, and hey, I will just bring them here and if you and Jake want to have alone time when you get home, wink, wink," she literally winked at me as she said that, "I will keep them here for dinner and some play time after. You can come get them right before their bedtime."

"Thanks, but I don't know about all of that, but thanks for the options." I gave her a quick hug.

"Jake is going to be so happy to see you."

"Thanks." I looked down, mindlessly smoothing out my little dress. "Rose, I am so nervous. I mean, I am excited to have him come home. I really missed him." I sighed. "But I am so afraid too. They said he was doing really well. He has been working really hard at physical therapy and the psychologist is pleased with his progress mentally. But..."

She smiled and nodded her head, encouraging me to continue.

"But...what happens if he backslides. I just couldn't go through that again."

I thought back to the day Dan had come over and convinced Jake to go to rehab. I was so grateful for his help. It had been one of the most difficult days of my life. I paced and cried while Rose consoled me. She kept assuring me that Jake would be fine. She said he probably didn't have an addiction, that he was just 'attached' to the painkillers. I didn't want to argue with her, but in my line of work, I had seen and learned about addiction and he clearly was at that point. Stealing a pill from Carol's house and then buying them on the street were clear and definite signs of addiction.

When Dan finally got home, four hours had passed. He sat me down and explained what went on when he was over with Jake. He told me, "Be patient with him, Amelia. He has been through a lot and he needs your understanding now. Don't push him about the rehab, he will go. I have already set it up. I will be taking him later today, by myself. Please give the man his dignity and let us handle it."

I nodded. "Of course." I was so grateful to him for his help, and so worried about Jake.

Though I was so happy to have him coming home, I was worried about him back sliding. He was due to go back to work at the beginning of next week, the physical therapy doctor said he needed a few more weeks of therapy before he would release him back to work. We were able to get his medical leave extended without work knowing about his time at the rehab facility. He was able to get more intense PT while he was being treated for his addiction. A lot of counseling was part of the program as well, which I hoped would help him manage his grief, and addiction.

Dan had been great, he visited him several times in rehab and he had also come by the house several times as well. Last night when he was over, he confirmed my hopes. He felt Jake was ready to move on with his life. He also promised me that he would look after him at work and would keep coming by the house whenever I wanted him to.

Rose put her arms around me and gave me a light squeeze. "Sounds like he is doing great and of God forbid, he starts making bad decisions, we are here for you and we will help. Dan has spent some time with him over the last few weeks, he isn't going to let him go back there, I am sure of it."

I walked into the stark-white room, which smelled of bleach and stale air, not sure how Jake was able to make this his home for the last couple of weeks. He was sitting in a chair, with his bag packed right next to him. I cautiously walked up to him, placed my hand on his shoulder and leaned down to give him a kiss. "Hi, hon. Are you ready to go?" I tried to sound as bright and cheery as I possibly could.

"Yes, they just gave me my release papers." He got up, grabbed his bag and started walking toward the door. I didn't say a word, not sure what to say.

"I just want to go, okay?"

"Okay."

One of the nurses yelled to Jake, "Bye. We will miss you Jake, but I never want to see you around here again, hear?"

Jake chuckled. "Yeah."

"Good luck," she said.

He turned with a warm smile and said, "Thanks, Jen."

When we got into the car, he buckled his seat belt. "I am so glad to be getting out of that place. I'm with Jen. I never want to go back there. I never want to be in that situation again."

I reached for Jake's hand and gave it a squeeze. "I am so proud of you. I know that it was rough for you."

"It was, but I hope that is the last time I am in a hospital, of any sort, for a long time."

I didn't want to push him, so I stayed quiet as he did the entire ride home. When we walked into the house, he walked to the bedroom. Though I wanted to follow him, I thought better of it and went to the kitchen to make some coffee. Minutes later he came out to the kitchen and hugged me from behind.

"I am sorry I put you through all of that. I...well...I don't know...I am just sorry."

I turned and we hugged for a while. "I made some coffee. Want a cup?"

"Sure, that would be great. What time do you have to go pick up the kids?"

"In a couple of hours. You can have some peace and quiet for a while." He took a couple sips of coffee and then put his arm around me again and whispered, "I love you, I am sorry."

"I am sorry too," I said, hugging him back.

He kissed me then, at first very light soft kisses and then

deeper, and then he was all over me.

"Want to head to the bedroom?" he said between kisses.

"Yes, oh yes, Jake, I have missed you so much." I couldn't remember lovemaking so wonderful with him as we just had. Tears came to my eyes as we laid together. I savored the gentle caresses of his hand on my arm.

CHAPTER 32

CAROL 1982

In the late 1960's, I began to observe with keen interest the beginnings of America's feminist movement. Younger women were on a mission to "find" themselves and urged all women to do likewise, even if undertaking this odyssey meant abdicating their traditional roles as housewives and mothers. Paralleling this movement, daycare centers began springing up throughout the country and working mothers packed off their children to them, while they went off in droves in pursuit of jobs that would afford them more material goods than a one-income household could provide. At the time, I remember questioning whether two incomes were really necessary, but I believe this exodus from home to the job market eventually created the necessity for it.

Some women sought higher education in order to pursue careers and equality with men in the workplace. This shift of values, it seemed to me, brought about more problems than it solved. Family life became disrupted with the ever-increasing incidence of divorce and the associated harm, especially to young children. It also generated an irreversible economic situation in America, which now tends to force both marital partners to work outside the home for basic necessities if not the more luxurious lifestyle wrought by conspicuous consumption.

When Bud and I went out socially, even to high school reunions, I noticed that women no longer gathered together to discuss children and home life; rather they tended to emphasize their jobs, cars and designer clothes. Homemakers were virtually excluded from these conversations, since they had nothing to contribute. In some instances, the responsibilities of wife and mother were actually derogated, as though they were the only skills of which they were capable. However, I continued to hold to the belief that my responsibilities as wife and mother were not only the most challenging and difficult, but perhaps the most rewarding. Yet after a time, even I began to envy the glamor of jobs in which those well-dressed women earned enough to indulge themselves in the latest fashions, luxury cars and new houses.

By the late 1970's, when the children were in school all day, I finally found some spare time, but I became bored and joined a bridge club. Their conversations, far from edifying, centered mostly on local gossip. This was not the way I wanted to spend my Time and so I decided to join the ranks of working women. Certainly, any money I earned could be invested in the children's education. Besides, I began to realize that there could be a whole new life in addition to the rearing of children.

Since I had been at home for nearly eighteen years, I was out of touch with the working world, so the thought of searching for a job was a wee bit intimidating. When I asked Bud what he thought about the plan he expressed no objection but left it up to me. He may even have welcomed my willingness to assume a share of the burden of supporting the family.

Before undertaking the job search, I needed to rent a typewriter so that I could hone my typing skills; and that might also help to bolster my confidence. My first interview with a local lawyer proved fruitless, but I didn't allow myself to become discouraged. Bud suggested that I apply for a job at Inland Steel Company's Harbor Works, since he knew the employee benefits and pay were good. I went for an interview, completed an application and passed the typing and written tests, but afterward the telephone didn't exactly ring off the hook. I began to think that at age 43, perhaps I might be considered too old to hire.

One day while I was sitting on the front porch, a family friend by the name of Cathy stopped by on her way home from work at Inland's Personnel Department to say she heard I was looking for a job. Her office was in the market for someone, and she had put in a good word for me. Shortly after that I was called in for another interview and in September of 1979, I was hired on a six-month probationary basis. Not only was 1979 a turning point in my life; it was a good year for Inland, as well since the number of its employees peaked at an all-Time high of 37,340 plus me. Since Bud had our only car and worked in Chicago, Cathy offered to let me ride to work with her.

I was given the lowest job on Inland's employment ladder, but that was okay with me for starters. By hand, it took at least two hours just to open the mail. The volume of medical, dental, and sickness and accident claims were astonishing. After the mail was opened, the claims had to be sorted by *payroll number and broken down into about five batches, all of which absorbed an entire day and generated some dandy paper cuts. One day, with arms loaded at least a foot high with claims, I tripped over an electrical cord shield and papers, like leaflets from a helicopter, went flying. Although I didn't fall, I was embarrassed beyond words as the girls working the front windows immediately came to help. Since they all knew who Bud was, this might have been the icebreaker in penetrating the nepotism attitude which some may have held against me.*

Our "customers" were other Inland employees, including hourly, salaried and ore boat fleet, together with Inland retirees. Three or four people had private offices around the perimeter of the main floor, and they processed all of the hourly sickness and accident claims. My new responsibilities began with learning Inland's various health care benefits, a mind-boggling task, since medical and dental benefits varied among hourly, salaried and retirees.

Once I learned some of the basic benefits, I was allowed to answer telephone inquiries and to work the front windows. in addition, claims had to be processed and approved for payment, based upon an employee's eligibility. The telephones in our office rang constantly with all manner of inquiries. One day a woman called from the emergency room of a local hospital. She complained that her husband wasn't being cared for well enough or fast enough and asked that if she had her husband transported to another hospital by ambulance, would that be covered. Time and Time again people amazed me with questions but that was my job, I needed to answer them in the best and most professional way possible.

I READ WHAT YOU WROTE

After the bad years of my depression, I continued to go to Al Anon, but not as often. We kind of got into somewhat of a routine, and time was going so fast. We had first communions, confirmations and the first high school graduations. I had decided it would be best for me to go back to work. I had missed doing something for myself and of course we could always use the money. I was able to get a job in the HR department of the same steel company Bud worked at. I quickly gained some new friends and more importantly self worth. Not that raising kids wasn't important, but these were accomplishments I could make that gave me accolades outside of the home. Bud transferred from the downtown Chicago office to the office in the harbor in Indiana. Now we could share rides to and from work and we would often stop by our favorite watering hole for a quick drink and sometimes dinner together. Though I didn't want to encourage his drinking, at least now we were together. He would always praise me in front of our friends at the bar and I found myself really enjoying all the attention from the friends we met.

The kids were busy with their sports and friends so this extra time with bud was very enjoyable. After finishing my religious education classes at our church, I was finally ready to become a catholic which would allow me to finally marry bud in the church. I was so looking forward to getting our marriage blessed by God. We had arranged a marriage renewal in the church and I so wanted to have the kids with us. Bud said no because at this point, the kids had never known that I had been married before and that we had to go through the steps of an annulment which would let us get married in the catholic church. Though I was so disappointed not to be able to share this special day with the kids, at least we were going to finally do it.

The kids knew we were getting our vows "renewed" but didn't understand the magnitude of this occasion. The girls helped me dress that day, I had gotten this pretty little pink dress and they helped by doing my hair and makeup. They even got me a garter for the occasion. Though they were happy for us, no one really questioned why they couldn't attend. I guess at this age, going out with their friends was more exciting. And I was actually glad, because I would have had a really hard Time telling them that they couldn't attend.

All through our marriage, I had continued to study Catholicism and the more I learned the stronger my faith became. I did not find Darwin's evolution or the "big bang" theory to be in conflict with those beliefs, because no matter how we came into being I believed that a higher power, whom I called God, was the creator of all things. How He accomplished all of it wasn't necessarily germane to those beliefs.

When I agreed to marry Bud by a Justice of the Peace, I naively believed that in time, the church would see it our way and allow us to receive the Sacrament of Matrimony after the fact. Otherwise, I wouldn't have married him, since by our marriage, Bud had to forfeit receiving Holy Communion. Once I began to understand the tenets of Catholicism, I yearned to become a Catholic, not only for Bud's and our children's sake, but my own as well. I wouldn't be a so-called Cafeteria Catholic," picking and choosing whatever rules suited me. Furthermore, the peripherals such as what people were wearing, the music, and even the church décor would not be central to my worship or beliefs. At the same time I had no illusions about the clergy, I understood that priests were human beings, subject of the same faults as anyone else, except when offering Mass, a most holy and prayerful rite, which is the same in Catholic churches the world over. Actually, "Catholic" in the religious sense means "universal."

As the children grew in their own faith, they often asked why I wasn't Catholic. All I could do was promise that I would continue to work on it. Now that I had more time, I actively pursued permission for Bud and me to have our marriage blessed in the church. Ironically, this issue seemed far more important to me that it did to Bud, but first things first. I needed to make the trip to Michigan to the Diocese in which my divorce was granted. One weekend when Bud's Aunt Pat came, we sat up one night and discussed the matter. She said she knew of a parish in Michigan, in the diocese where I needed to go, which was active in helping marriage situations such as ours, and she offered to make the trip with me.

A kind priest explained what was necessary in order to present my case to the marriage tribunal and warned that the process was often lengthy, with no guarantee of a favorable outcome. A great deal depended on the reason for the divorce and the results of questionnaires sent to others. After returning home, I immediately began tackling my part of the necessary paperwork, hoping that by the Time our 25th wedding anniversary rolled around in 1983, Bud and I could celebrate by repeating our vows at St. Thomas More Church. Bud seemed unenthusiastic, but I was thankful Aunt Pat was *solidly in my corner. She completely understood my desire to give back to Bud what he had sacrificed by marrying me. Admittedly, she had spent a great deal more Time listening to my thoughts than Bud had, but still, why was he so standoffish about the matter? After all, he had been an altar server and had even taught catechism in our home.*

Toward the end of the 1980's, Bud reached a point in his career where he said he'd "had enough." He complained about what he called "the new culture" at work and refused to accept a computer for his desk even though other managers were getting them. He was often absent from his office and began carrying breath mints to conceal the odor of his liquid lunches. Yet, it was obvious that Bud's tolerance to alcohol had increased even though he could usually conduct himself appropriately despite the drinking; at least to a point. People were drawn to his vibrant personality and admired his tremendous accomplishments. At the time, his knowledge of employee benefits was unmatched by any other person in the company. It's sad to recall that bud became increasingly unhappy with his job, at the same time, I couldn't have been happier with mine.

 Even when he decided to make a trip to Florida in search of a retirement location, it didn't occur to me just how serious he was about quitting, since he hadn't mentioned anything about a specific quit date. At the time, I wasn't eligible for a vacation, so he flew to Florida by himself, armed with ads for retirement communities clipped from AARP magazines. About mid-week he telephoned requesting money for a deposit on a lot in Orange Blossom Gardens (OGB), Florida, which sounded far more like a cemetery than a retirement community. I sent the money without further thought. After returning home, bud didn't seem particularly enthusiastic about his find, but gave me a thumbnail description of what he found and said that we only had two years in which to build a house there, if we were to keep our deposit. But since Bud was only 55, it didn't occur to me that he might be considering an early retirement.

Well before our retirement I finally began to "get it." Belittling, nagging and otherwise appealing to an alcoholic's sense of right and wrong never works. The alcoholic's behavior, good, bad, or somewhere in between, must be left strictly up to the alcoholic, no matter how difficult that may be. However, this does not mean that the spouse or others must bend to the alcoholic's wishes, or to suffer any sort of abuse, be it physical or otherwise, but have the courage to prayerfully manage one's own life. In other words, "Let go and let God, "according to "One Day at a Time."

In 1991, Inland Steel Company continued to downsize its salaried force and Bud, as Benefits Planner, was asked to put another retirement package together. This time, however, he would make it attractive for both of us. I don't recall the precise formula; Bud simply called it "two plus two."

Our daily ritual in getting ready for work was usually the same. But one morning in April of 1991, Bud changed the course of our lives. When he came downstairs, the first thing he asked was, "Would you type up my resignation?" I asked how soon he wanted it. "Now," he answered, showing no hint of emotion. Typically, Bud hadn't shared his thinking with me, so when he announced his decision to retire that day I was flabbergasted!

We briefly discussed retirement plans on the way to work. I loved my job and wasn't eager to leave it, even for Bud's sake. My superiors were equally shocked and said, "But we created that position for you!" I countered with the obvious, "You wouldn't expect me to keep on working and let my husband retire to Florida without me, would you?" After work that night we stopped for dinner and continued the retirement discussion we'd begun earlier that day. Under his new retirement plan for Inland, I would be eligible to participate on my 55th birthday, May 22, 1991 and would receive a small pension.

There was a glitch in Bud's private thinking, which didn't surface until two days later. He assumed we would keep our current house until I brought up the subject of how we would go about selling it. Since I had no wish to single-handedly take on the upkeep of two homes, I told him there would be no reason for me to retire if he didn't want to sell the house. Though he may have psychologically recoiled at this, he reluctantly agreed to sell it, which might have been his unspoken wish not to retire without me. I thought, 'poor Bud, if only he hadn't tried so many times to spare me by not sharing his thoughts and feelings throughout our marriage, we could have been so much closer and happier.' But as I often told the children through the years: "coulda, woulda, shoulda, doesn't count." As for our retirement, I wondered whether he would continue his self-destructive behavior and harbor private thoughts, even though we would finally have more time together. I would *have to wait and see.*

We were given several retirement parties and I enjoyed every one of them. But the best party of all was the one our children hosted at our house. Therese, who was living in New Jersey at the time, went to New York City in search of a special gift. She found a tiny crystal golf cart with two sets of gold clubs on the back, with a male driver and a female passenger with a pink heart.

What followed was a flurry of activity in preparing to sell what had been our happy home for over 20 years. Without Bud's help this project absorbed most of my time and energy for the entire summer. When it was all over, including a garage sale, we sold the house ourselves in less than two weeks. Bud sent me a bouquet of roses. He commonly sent flowers when he was happiest with me.

CHAPTER 33

A M E L I A

It was Friday and I was so happy my workday was almost over. It had been a very busy week. I couldn't wait to get home and spend some time with my family. Jake was doing much better since he had been back at work for a few weeks. He was also very diligent at going to his physical therapy, as well as meeting with the counselor twice a week for his grief and drug counseling. Though he felt he didn't need to go to that any longer, he had promised me he would continue for the next month or so. I was so proud of him; he was almost back to his old self and had begun spending time playing with the kids like he had before the accident. I knew he still had a way to go, but was so proud of him for working hard.

I stood up from my desk and grabbed my purse, and the phone rang. It was Earl. "Amelia, I need you to come over. Carol is not doing well. She seems to be moaning a lot and is having trouble speaking."

A lump formed in my throat. Was this the day? "I will be over in about 30 minutes." I called Jake at home and told him that I would be late, I had to go and check on Carol. Carol had been declining rapidly over the last few weeks and I knew she was reaching the end of her life.

I had lost several patients since I began working in hospice care and of course all the deaths were sad for me, but nothing bothered me as much as the thought of losing Carol. In these months I had come to love this woman and felt like she had been like a mother to me. Through the loving stories and advice she had provided me, I felt like I had been really growing as a mother, wife, daughter, and daughter-in-law.

When I arrived at Carol's home, I spoke with Earl, of course he never got up out of his chair. He told me that Carol had been sleeping most of the time and didn't drink much and of course was not eating anything, even her orange sherbet. I walked into Carol's room and saw her asleep. She looked so pale and was so thin, way worse than she was just a few days ago. I went to Carol and stroked her head and whispered quietly, "Carol, it's Amelia." It took a couple of tries and finally Carol opened her eyes, she gave me a weak smile, but didn't say anything. I checked the colostomy bag that had been inserted a few days ago and saw that it needed to be changed. I also looked at her feet and hands, her nail beds had that blue tinge in them that was one of the signs of near death. Tears welled up in my eyes, I couldn't help it, I really loved this woman and the feelings I had like when my grandmother was dying rushed back to me. I knew, I had to pull it together.

"Carol, can you tell me how you are feeling?"

Carol spoke very low, "Not well. I think this is it, Amelia. I am dying."

"I know, hon, but I am here, and I am going to make you as

comfortable as possible." I swallowed the tears that threatened to come. "Here, have a sip of water." I tried to prop Carol up to give her some water. Carol took a sip and started coughing, water flew out of her mouth. It was obvious she was having trouble swallowing, another sign that the end was near. I sat next to Carol and just rubbed her face, "I am here Carol, just rest." As I watched Carol sleep, sadness engulfed me. I still had the final binder in my bag. I had been looking for an opportunity to put it back at previous visits but none had presented itself. Now was the time, but I resisted. I knew I had to. I pulled it out of my bag and held it in my hands. Unlike the other times I had tried to quickly return the binder, I just couldn't bring myself to let it go. It was a way of holding on to her, physically. But I knew I had to. I stood up and walked over to the bookshelf. I carefully placed it back and ran my hand across all of the binders that had been my companion at one time or another. A tear ran down my face. I was still for a few minutes until Carol was asleep again, and then walked out of the room to talk with Earl.

"Earl, have you reached out to her children and her sister?"

"No," is all he said.

I pushed, "Earl, it is time for you to reach out to anyone you think needs to see her. It is very close now. They should be contacted."

"Okay," he said simply.

I wanted to yell at him, especially knowing all that Marie had told her about the strained relationship that he had caused with her family. I knew the kids would want to be there, I just knew it based on all I knew from Carol and of course Marilyn would want to know. "Earl, Marie asked me when she was here last that she would want to be contacted, please call her."

He said, "Fine, I will call her. How long does she have?"

"Not long, days at most, possibly hours. Please call her at least." I then instructed Earl once again the steps for providing the morphine and the anti-anxiety medicine that Carol was now taking. "Please make sure you are giving it to her on schedule, so she does not suffer."

Earl said he understood and was giving it to her as directed. I knew professionally I couldn't say or do more than that, but I felt I owed Carol at least that much. "I am going to go back in for a few more minutes."

I sat there and watched Carol sleep, groaning from time to time and instinctively she would run her hand along her stomach while she was sleeping. Poor Carol. She needed to be comfortable. I did not want her to suffer in the least. As I sat there, my eyes went over to the bookshelf that contained the books that I had read both with Carol and on my own. I found myself thinking about how the women's 81 years on this earth was mainly contained in those eight books. Those books that opened the door to the soul of this incredible woman. I thought about my own mother, oh how I wished my mother would have done the same thing. To have written down information on her life, the life that I didn't know, stuff about her young life and her life with my father. Was my mother happy? Did she have terrible things happen to her? The emptiness that I hadn't realized I had suppressed all of these years since my mother's passing, flooded back. I realized I didn't know much about my own mother. And I was sure my mother would have had many pieces of advice she would have wanted to share with her own daughter. I had never felt so alone; I sat there and cried. I cried for my mother just as much as I did for Carol.

When I finally walked out of Carol's room, I saw that Earl was on the phone, telling the person on the other end that it was time for them to come see Carol. He hung up and said, "Amelia, that was Marilyn. She is going to call Carol's children and I am sure they will come to see her."

"Thank you Earl. I know Carol would be happy to have her family near her at the end. Please call me if you need anything. I will come by tomorrow, but please call me if there are any changes."

As I got into my car, tears flowed again. I called Jake and told him I was on my way home. I couldn't wait to go home and hug my husband and children. At that point I promised myself that I would make sure I talked to my kids. I wanted to make sure I shared stories of my own life, about their grandfather, and about the grandmother they never knew. I wanted to make sure I gave them as much advice as possible to help them be good people and parents when they were grown, and for them to know about mine and Jake's story as well.

I visited Carol daily for the next couple days. I was happy to hear that Marie, her siblings and their Aunt Marilyn had come to visit.

The following Tuesday morning I received the call that Carol had passed. I was told she had passed in the middle of the night and the on-call nurse had gone and managed the protocol after a patient died. I hung up the phone and cried and Jake hugged me as I sobbed. He said "I know how important she was to you, and you know she cared for you."

I had decided to go to Carol's funeral. I didn't do that with any of the other patients that had died, not wanting to interfere with the family's time. I couldn't, however, not go. I had to say goodbye to Carol. I stood in the back of the family and friends gathered at the funeral. When all was over, I sought out Marie and gave her a hug. "I really loved your mother. She was such an amazing person. I feel blessed that I got to know her."

Marie said, "She really loved you, too, Amelia. She spoke so highly of you when I visited her, and I know how much care you provided her. Thank you." At that moment, Carol's sister Marilyn and a couple of ladies walked up to Marie. I didn't want to interfere in this family time so I touched Marie's arm to bid her goodbye. Marie stopped me and said, "I want you to meet my sisters , Mom's sister. This is Therese and Ann. This is Amelia, the hospice nurse that had been taking care of Mom."

"Oh, hello," they said in unison. Therese spoke, "Thank you so much for taking such good care of our mother. We know it was a tough situation, but our mother mentioned you whenever we spoke with her and she always said you were such a sweet person and how much she enjoyed spending time with you. We are forever grateful."

"Well, your mother was amazing. I felt an immediate connection to her. She shared so many stories of her life and you kids with me every time I visited. I will truly miss her."

I spent a few more minutes talking with them, they were so sweet, and I could see Carol in each of them. Especially her sister Marilyn. Her mannerisms were just like Carol's. It made me want to hug her. They also called over their brothers and I was introduced to them as well. I felt like I had known them because of all of the stories Carol had shared, it was almost as if they were family to me. When I left, I was so happy to have met them. They all seemed sweet and appreciative. I was so glad I went and was finally able to meet the family that I had come to know. It made me miss her so much. I noticed, though, that I didn't see Earl there. To say the least, I was surprised he was not in attendance at his wife's funeral. What a sad state.

CHAPTER 34

MARIE

I received a call from Earl the day after the funeral. He said that he had ordered some furniture and had someone scheduled next week to come and remove things he no longer wanted in the house and if anyone wanted anything, we would need to come get it in the next couple of days. Not shocked by his call, we all decided to drive up that day and go through Mom's things. She had always taken movies and pictures of us kids and we wanted to make sure we got those before he threw them out. There were also special items that we had each given our parents over the years, so we wanted to get those items as well.

When we arrived, we went right to work and filled boxes with whatever we thought we might want to keep. The place was a mess and there were stacks of papers and items all over the house. Earl gave us strict instructions on the areas of items we were not allowed to touch.

We came in like wrecking balls and went to work, not as much as a hello to the man that had robbed us of the precious last couple years of our mother's life. Though they were unhappy with his callous ways, at least we were given the opportunity to come get what we wanted.

Chip was going through the side table next to Mom's bed and said, "Hey look. There is an envelope here in Mom's handwriting with the name Amelia on it."

CHAPTER 35

AMELIA

The kids were so excited. It was Saturday, and we were all headed to the park. It was a beautiful day and so we had decided to do a family picnic at the park. Jake was busy getting the toys together and a blanket as I finished up packing the basket with all kinds of goodies for our picnic. The doorbell rang so I headed to answer the door. It was a delivery man from Fed Ex. "I have a package for Amelia?"

"That is me." I signed my name and accepted the box the man handed to me. It was heavy. I opened the box and pulled out a wrapped package with a note attached to the top.

Dear Amelia, we were going through Mother's things and we came across this. We wanted to make sure we got this to you and thanks again for all of the amazing care you had provided our dear Mother.

Scott

My hands were shaking as I opened the envelope with my name on it.

My Dear Amelia,
I am so grateful I got to know you over these months. I

have looked forward to your visits and enjoyed sharing my stories with you. I know my time here is coming to an end, but I wanted you to know that you have come to be like another daughter to me. I have seen you blossom in these short months that we have been together, and I am so proud of you, and I know your mother would be too.

I have asked that these binders be given to you. I know you have enjoyed the ones we read together and the ones you read on your own. Yes, I know you read what I wrote. In fact, I'm glad you found an interest in them. Hopefully you will continue to find some little pearls of wisdom as you finish reading them. The greatest legacy is when you can share what you have learned with others. My children know these stories so well and I am sure they would agree that it is important to share with you. Please do what you want with these stories, and I hope you can share them with others. Remember, you are special. You are a great mother and wife, please remember that.

Love,

Carol

"Who was at the door?" Jake asked as he came into the hallway.

"It was a delivery for me. Look, it is all of the binders of Carol's writings. She wrote me a note before she died, here look."

Jake read the note. "Wow, she knew you took and read them?"

"I guess so. I know I should feel bad, but she really wanted me to read and have them." Tears came to my eyes.

"What are you going to do with them?"

"I am not sure, but I think she wants her stories out there. She helped me so much over these months. She had such a hard life. So many things happened to her but through it all, yet she was still such a positive woman. Jake, she was like a mother to me," my voice cracked. "She gave me so much advice about being a better mother and wife. I hadn't really realized how much I needed a mother, how much I missed mine. I have realized that no matter how tough times get, you can persevere. You must work hard at building the life you want and that only you can control your happiness."

Jake came over and hugged me, tears were flowing from my eyes at this point. I was really going to miss Carol, but I wanted to make her proud of me. I was going to work hard on my marriage, and I was going to try and be the best mother I could be to JJ and Olivia. And maybe, just maybe, I could finish her story.

AFTERWARD

I hope you enjoyed my book and maybe even learned a few pearls of wisdom. My mother always gave my siblings and me advice throughout her life. Though I don't think I understood all of them until I became a married adult and had children. Now I am constantly leaning on her words and miss her so much. What I wouldn't give for another five minutes with her or my father.

My mother spent several years writing her memoirs that contained her sometimes-difficult life but when she developed dementia, she couldn't finish them. Several of her chapters were included in my book. I wanted to be able to share with you the writings she had always dreamed about publishing and to finish her story. Through this fiction story, you are able to get a glimpse into her life and hear some of the kind-hearted advice.

Every family goes through difficult times, but nothing really prepared me for my mother's dementia. It took the ever present, loving mother away from me and my siblings. We had to mourn the loss of her for a few years. And then mourn her all over again after her death. The inspiration for writing this was to hopefully bring awareness of dementia and what a thief it is to one's life. When I started this journey, I will say it helped a lot in the grieving process. I wasn't sure if I would ever finish it, but after five and a half years I did. I am hoping she would have been proud.

I have learned a lot about dementia, but still have more to learn. I really wanted to get across to those that have family members who suffer from this disease to know that you are not alone. The interesting, and quite challenging issue is that dementia affects everyone differently. Unfortunately, at the time we went through it with my mother we didn't have the knowledge, nor could we find the right resources to help. As my book suggests, sometimes people who have dementia struggle with their decision-making skills and because of this, get themselves in situations that they would not normally get into. We tried very hard to protect our mother from putting herself in such a situation, to no avail. My goal is to bring awareness of such situations in hopes that one day we can have resources in place to protect elderly people who may fall victim and rights for family members. I encourage anyone going through this with a family member to get educated. A great resource I have found is at www.dementiasociety.org The site is full of great information.

In hope to bring more information to light, please go to my website www.jillhales.com where I have included some blogs about dementia and the process of writing this book. In addition, you will have the opportunity to share your stories so we can continue this important conversation.

And finally, if you can, I would love you to go to Amazon leave a review of my book. Thank you for reading!

ABOUT THE AUTHOR

Jill Hales, author of *I Read What You Wrote* is a Chicagoland native who spent most of her 26 year career in advertising. She had always been inspired by her mother's love of writing, but it wasn't until her mother's passing that Jill discovered the same passion in herself. Jill is married to her husband John of over 35 years and enjoys spending time with her three adult children and her little dog Sparky. She loves to read, write, travel and play tennis.

Printed in the USA
CPSIA information can be obtained
at www.ICGtesting.com
LVHW011231130324
774240LV00013B/705

9 798988 788430